G

Courting Greta

Ramsey Hootman

G

Gallery Books

New York   London   Toronto   Sydney   New Delhi

G

Gallery Books
A Division of Simon & Schuster, Inc.
1230 Avenue of the Americas
New York, NY 10020

First Gallery Books trade paperback edition June 2013

GALLERY BOOKS and colophon are registered trademarks of Simon & Schuster, Inc.

For information about special discounts for bulk purchases, please contact Simon & Schuster Special Sales at 1-866-506-1949 or business@simonandschuster.com.

The Simon & Schuster Speakers Bureau can bring authors to your live event. For more information or to book an event, contact the Simon & Schuster Speakers Bureau at 1-866-248-3049 or visit our website at www.simonspeakers.com.

Designed by Davina Mock-Maniscalco

Manufactured in the United States of America

10   9   8   7   6   5   4   3   2   1

Library of Congress Cataloging-in-Publication Data is available.

ISBN 978-1-4767-1129-4
ISBN 978-1-4767-1130-0 (ebook)

for Kelson
who believed in me
when I did not

Courting Greta

1

SAMUEL WATCHED HIS BROTHER'S big hands walk over the steering wheel, turning the pickup into the campus parking lot. He should have driven himself. Nobody who saw his prematurely graying hair would mistake him for a teenager, even as small as he was, but being dropped off still felt juvenile. The stupid things he did to make his brother feel useful. Samuel shifted, adjusting his seat belt, and double-checked to make sure the bus schedule was in his pocket.

Chris glanced at him. "You okay?"

Sometimes it seemed like that was all anyone ever asked. Samuel leaned forward, peering through the windshield as the main building came into view. The high school was a single-story building branching off in several directions, barely salvaged from eyesore status by the redwoods towering around it. The hallways looked dark and empty from across the parking lot. "Where is everyone?"

Chris stepped on the clutch and checked his watch. "Maybe class is out?"

"Dammit." Samuel grabbed his brother's wrist, reading the analog upside down before thrusting the muscular arm away: 3:27. "My appointment's in three minutes!"

"Yeah? We're here, aren't we?"

"And what, I'm going to jog across campus and get there in the nick of time?" He twisted, reaching into the extended cab for his elbow crutches. The first one caught and he swore, jerking it free.

"Bro." Chris put one hand on Samuel's shoulder, quieting him, and used the other to free the second aluminum pole. "Relax. It'll be fine, okay? You'll do good."

"*Well*. And I doubt it." Briefly, Samuel wrestled with the temptation to shove his crutch into his brother's washboard abs; he mastered himself by redirecting the urge into the stubborn cab door. "How long has this stupid handle been broken?"

Chris reached over and shoved the door open.

Samuel closed his eyes. Chris was not a bad person. Yes, he possessed a small lump of lead in lieu of a brain, but he wasn't trying to be a douchebag. Samuel was just nervous. They weren't going to fire him for being a few minutes late. Still, as he swung his legs out of the cab and shouldered his backpack, he couldn't help muttering, "You always make me late."

Chris gave Samuel's arm a rough pat. "I know. Sorry."

Now he felt like a jerk. Probably because he was being one.

"You gonna be all right? Getting home and everything? I can stay another night if you want."

As if he hadn't been living on his own for a decade. "I'll be fine. You should get on the road." Samuel slipped his arms through the cuffs and planted both crutches on the ground before sliding out of the cab. "Thanks for coming up to help." Not that he'd asked.

"No problem. Keep in touch, huh?"

"Sure, sure." They always went through this routine before getting back to the business of ignoring each other. He cleared his throat. "Drive safely."

Chris's reply was interrupted by an eight-bit rendition of "Take Me Out to the Ball Game." "Must be Tammy." He dug through the garbage-littered dash and came up with a cell phone. "Oh, it's Dad. Here, you can say hi." He punched a button. "Hey, Dad. Sam and I are—"

Samuel slammed the door. Chris quirked an eyebrow, then shrugged and waved.

In spite of the time, Samuel forced himself to stand on the curb and watch as the battered Ranger pulled away. A gust of autumn wind hit him in the face, and the smell of freshly cut grass slid up his nostrils, sharp as a knife. He drew in a breath and let it out slowly.

When the truck disappeared around the end of the block, Samuel turned away from the curb and started toward the nearest doorway. He frowned, glanced over one shoulder, and realized where he was. "Shit." Chris had dropped him off in the wrong lot.

Then a bell shrilled, and eight hundred students came pouring out of fifty-odd rooms.

IT TOOK SAMUEL fifteen minutes to hike across campus and all of his upper-body strength to squeeze through the spring-loaded door of the portable office building, but it wasn't until he'd stepped into his own classroom that he wondered what the hell he had gotten himself into.

The secretary had been nice enough, reassuring him when he showed up breathless, perspiring, and twenty minutes late that "Vince" was still out with the track team. Though the petite brunette was college-age at best, she invited him to "take a seat, dear" and fetched him a paper cup of water from the cooler. Two decades past puberty and every woman on the planet still felt compelled to mother him.

Vince Irving had entered a couple of minutes later, along with a heavy whiff of cologne. He looked more like a football coach than a principal, barrel-chested and clean-shaven, with a windbreaker sporting the school logo over a crisply ironed shirt. "Mr. Cooke!" he'd said, too loudly, and shoved a hand forward.

Oh, look, a walking cliché. Samuel took the proffered hand briefly. "My pleasure, Mr. Irving." He grabbed his crutches and pushed himself to his feet. "Please, just Samuel."

"Sam. Vince."

No, not Sam. Samuel. He clamped his mouth shut on the correction. "Apparently I've got a ream of paperwork to fill out?"

Irving shrugged it aside. "Come see Joyce in the next week or two and she'll get you squared away. Thought you'd be more interested in your classroom, eh?"

A glance at the secretary confirmed she was Joyce. "Sounds good."

"Toss 'em." Irving held up a palm and Joyce pitched a ring of keys. "That's my girl. Back in a few." He shouldered the door open for Samuel.

Samuel shuffled down the ramp and squeezed to one side, making room for Irving to pass. "Why don't you go first?" They weren't going to fit side by side on the narrow sidewalk, and the grass bordering it was a muddy mess. It hadn't rained *that* much overnight; they were probably still dousing the area with sprinklers.

As the principal ambled toward the main building, he dug a bag of sunflower seeds out of a pocket and dumped a handful in his mouth. Samuel counted the shells that fell to the ground as he trailed behind.

Indoors, the halls were white-tiled and vacant, bearing enough similarity to hospital corridors to be disconcerting, save for the smell of stale sweat and rain. Irving fell back now that there was room, but he left the kind of wide, anxious gap between them that always made Samuel want to say, "Relax; I'm not going to break if you trip me."

"You know," Irving said, "we have full inclusion here."

Wow. "Fascinating." Obviously he was dying to hear about everyone else who happened to have some god-awful condition.

"Yessir." Irving missed the sarcasm completely. "Started in the early nineties." He had switched to spitting the shells into his hand, and he paused to shake the soggy handful into a big gray garbage can. "We're considered very progressive, even by California standards."

Was that why the nearest handicapped spot was half a mile from the office? Samuel needed to change the subject before he said something he couldn't take back. "So . . . she's your daughter, then?"

Irving's bushy white eyebrows went up. "Who?"

Crap. "Um, Joyce?"

He burst into laughter. "Joyce? My daughter?"

"I thought . . ." Samuel had assumed they were related, because otherwise—well, if Rashid, CEO of the software firm Samuel had worked for in L.A., ever addressed any of his female employees as "my girl," he'd have angry lawyers lined up around the block. Maybe Irving and Joyce had worked together a long time, although Joyce was pretty young. Maybe things were just different here.

Irving pulled a wallet out of his back pocket. "These," he announced, "are my girls."

Samuel offered the obligatory murmur of admiration and saw that Irving's family really was quite attractive. He had two cheerful blondes in their twenties, and although his wife was showing her age, she was a dignified, handsome woman. "Nice."

"My pride and joy. Ah, here's your room." Irving jammed the key into the lock, jiggled it, then grabbed the knob and threw his shoulder into lifting the door. "Damn keys have been copied so many times," he explained, stepping inside.

Four rows of outdated computer banks stretched from the front of the room to the back, paired so students sat facing left or right.

The right wall was composed entirely of windows, looking out over a concrete courtyard that had been painted by students. The only problem Samuel could see, initially, was the teacher's desk, positioned on the far side of the room. He didn't relish the thought of threading through the mess of chairs and naked cables, but he needed the lesson plans for tomorrow.

He made it to the back of the room without performing a face-plant in front of his new boss and found the promised binder centered neatly on the desk. It bore a sticky note with his name. He lifted the cover—and found a single piece of college-ruled paper. It said, in loopy red handwriting:

> *Keyboarding, Mon.–Thurs.: Students use typing prog. to*
>   *improve.*
> *Fri.: Print out stats and give awards (in desk).*
> *Programming: Students researching history of programming.*
>   *Presentations due next month.*

Underneath was a bell schedule and a roll sheet for each class.

"Mrs. Phelps said she'd leave her lesson plans," he said weakly. They'd spoken on the phone three times before he'd accepted the position, and she'd promised—*promised*—to leave everything he needed to run the class until Christmas.

Samuel opened the desk drawers one by one, but there were only a few overphotocopied awards with blanks for names and typing speed.

He looked at Irving, willing him to recall that Mrs. Phelps had left a box of supplies in the office. Irving shrugged. "You know how women get when they're pregnant."

"I don't, actually." Samuel looked out the window, biting the inside of his cheek. Was this some kind of sick joke? What the hell was he going to do? Phelps had said it was easy. Said his programming expertise more than compensated for his expired credential and almost total lack of classroom experience. Clearly the school board had agreed; they'd been thrilled to have someone with his "distinguished résumé." And he'd believed her. Them. The truth was, he had no clue what he was doing. He'd been depending on those lesson plans to carry him until he figured it out.

And in sixteen hours, he would be standing here in front of thirty-two kids who expected him to be in control.

Irving shifted. "You want some time to . . . ?"

"Nope. I'm done." Or screwed. One of those. Samuel flipped the binder shut and picked his way back around the edge of the room. He guessed from Irving's thoughtful frown that the man was wondering why anyone in his right mind would abandon a lucrative career in software design for a low-paying interim position at a public institution. Samuel was beginning to wonder that himself.

Then Irving said, "So what happened? Car accident or something?"

"Excuse me?"

He gestured to Samuel's lower half—the aluminum elbow crutches and the ankle braces outlined against his pants. "How'd you get hurt?"

Right. Because it simply wasn't possible to mind one's own fucking business. It didn't bother him much if it was a kid asking, or someone with an obvious mental impairment. But any thinking adult ought to understand this wasn't an appropriate topic for casual chitchat. Granted, Irving reminded him of Chris: about two hitters short of a lineup.

Still, this was his new boss, so he swallowed the sarcastic comeback and gritted his teeth. "Occult spinal dysraphism." See if Irving could remember that long enough to Google it. "It's a congenital birth defect. Disappointing, I know." That was half the story, but it was all Irving would get. Samuel stumped past him into the hall. Though he had half a mind to keep going, he had known this job wouldn't be easy. He wasn't about to throw in the towel over this dumbass. Or lesson plans.

Irving locked up and handed Samuel the key, which he took to mean that the orientation was over. Thank God. His thighs ached from the trek across campus, and all he wanted to do was spend the evening with the most surreal novel he could find in his to-be-read pile. Unfortunately, what he'd actually be doing tonight was poring over the Internet for lesson plans. At least the fiber-optic line had kicked in yesterday; dial-up would have turned this disaster into an emergency of epic proportions.

Irving rubbed his hands together. "How d'you like sports, Sam?" He grinned, revealing a row of broad white incisors so perfect they had to be dentures.

Samuel had a fleeting, irrational vision of his body stretched unconscious across the hall tiles, Irving bending over him, rubbing his hands furiously and yelling, "Clear!"

"Honestly? I make a lousy shortstop." Samuel shouldn't have said it, but he was tired and annoyed, and he really, *really* didn't like to be called Sam.

He expected Irving to go red and apologize, but the principal just looked puzzled. And then he guffawed. "No, no, I mean *watching.*" The laugh descended into a chuckle.

Samuel revised his opinion of Irving from "affable cliché" to "unbearable ass."

"I'm sure you've heard we're famous for our girls' basketball."

Samuel hadn't. Or he'd forgotten. "How could I not?" So long as it brought the conversation to an end.

"Great! We've got a home game in twenty minutes. I'll show you the gym."

"Um. Yeah. I'd love to, but my brother dropped me off on the way out of town and the last bus on my route comes at five." Actually six, but he was betting Irving didn't know that.

"The *bus*?" Irving gave him a look that said he might be a little daft. "You're in town, aren't you? I'll give you a lift." He reached out and gripped Samuel's shoulder with one big hand. "Come on, make your first day at Healdsburg High complete."

He shrugged out of Irving's grasp. "Like I said, I'd love to, but seeing as Mrs. Phelps failed to fulfill her obligations, I need the time to plan."

"Oh." Irving's face fell. "Sure, I understand. Gotta make your first day a good one, eh?" He flashed another big smile, but there was something forced in it. As if he was genuinely disappointed by Samuel's refusal.

Oh, God. He was going to regret saying this. "Some other time?"

Thankfully, an alternate date and time didn't pop out of Irving's mouth. "Sure," he said. "Another time. Take care, hm?"

Samuel nodded and busied himself tucking the key into a pocket, allowing Irving a head start. Now all he had to do was locate the bus stop and he'd be home free. He'd taken a good long look at the map, and now that he had a moment to think, he oriented himself easily. The stop should be out the doors behind him and across the parking lot. It was nice not to have his thoughts interrupted every two seconds.

Nice. To be alone.

Samuel closed his eyes. He was already retreating. Just like his father had said he would.

No.

Irving was annoying, but he wouldn't be the only person at the game. Basketball wasn't Samuel's cup of tea, but so what? At least it wasn't baseball. And how much time did he really need to plan for a subject he could deconstruct in his sleep?

Samuel opened his eyes. Irving hadn't quite reached the doors at the end of the empty hall. He could still fix this.

"Hey, Vince?"

Irving turned.

"Wait up."

THE GYM SMELLED like the hallways, only more so. Parents and older relatives filled the wooden bleachers on the far wall; younger kids shot hoops on the empty court. Standing in the doorway, Samuel flinched when a rogue basketball smacked the wall above his head.

Almost everyone lay on the spectrum between Caucasian pink and Latino brown, with a couple of Asians thrown in for good measure, and for a moment he imagined every eye upon him. Samuel, the one who never went out to lunch with the guys. Who never spoke about his personal life because he didn't have one. Who had refused so many happy-hour invitations his coworkers no longer bothered to ask. What was he doing *here,* at a basketball game?

It was all in his head, of course. Nobody knew him from Adam. If he was here, at the game, he would be the kind of guy who went to basketball games. Simple as that.

In front of him, Irving lifted his arms and stretched, exuding a kind of paternal aura over what was clearly his domain. He surveyed the gym and then glanced at Samuel. "My brother's in town—supposed to meet me here. I oughta hunt him down before the game starts. You want to come?"

"That's all right, I'll find a seat."

Irving patted Samuel's shoulder for—what, the third time now? "Enjoy the show!"

And then Samuel was alone.

He surveyed the stands. Senior citizens and sulky teens had already taken most of the bottom row, and he had no hope of getting any higher. A smaller set of seats, about five rows high, ran along the wall to the right of the door he had come through, interrupted in the center by the scorekeeper's podium. A few middle-aged men and women sat along the top row, backs against the wall. From the way they chatted, intermittent and casual, he guessed they were his soon-to-be coworkers. Samuel couldn't quite work up the guts to introduce himself, so he shuffled a third of the way down the court and sat in the vacant bottom row, tucking his backpack and crutches behind the bench.

A referee appeared and began shooing kids off the floor. Shoes squeaked and balls went flying.

Samuel checked his watch and wondered how long the game would take. He wished to God he'd brought his car.

"You can't sit here."

"What?" Samuel blinked and looked up. He was being addressed by a large, blocky woman with a clipboard. Her graying hair was cropped close, and she wore a man's polo shirt tucked into cotton shorts.

"You need to move. My team sits here."

"Oh. Oh, right, sorry." He slipped his backpack on and reached for the crutches. His legs didn't want to move, and he had to shove himself up. *Now* where was he going to sit?

"Hey."

He looked at the coach.

She gestured to the end of the row. "Just slide down. You won't bother anyone."

He felt a rush of gratitude. "Thanks."

She gave him a curt nod, then hiked up one leg of her shorts and stepped over two rows to the scorekeeper's podium. "Harry," she barked, "get my center's name wrong again, and I will shove that microphone down your throat."

Yikes.

Samuel had just gotten resettled when the locker room doors opened and the girls thundered out. The floor shook as the two teams jogged around the court and started shooting layups. They warmed up for five minutes, and then the game began.

Since basketball seemed to be a Big Deal in his new hometown, Samuel tried to pay attention. It wasn't bad, really. The contest was tense; the teams were well matched, both determined to win. He made it about fifteen minutes before his attention wandered. The people in the stands were much more interesting.

Mothers gripped knees and smiled with clenched jaws; fathers hollered at the refs. The local sportswriter was easy to identify, trying to scribble notes, cheer, and balance his enormous camera all at once. Samuel spent several minutes studying an unshaven man in the first row who was chanting what might have been antiquated cheerleader's rhymes. The aging alumnus wore a fifteen-year-old letterman jacket with pride.

Samuel tried not to stare at the coach, but it was hard to ignore someone just a few feet away, particularly someone so focused. She stood motionless for most of the game, clipboard clutched between her large hands. Her eyes never left the floor except to glance at the board, and every now and then she called out a girl's last name and a command, like "Morales! Out of the key!" She was not ignored. The contrast between her and the visiting team's coach, who paced and shouted and paced some more, was striking.

Irving reappeared at halftime, trailed by his own clone. Irving Two looked a little bulkier, a little older, and a little rougher around the edges, as if he did something physical for a living. Both towered over Samuel, who didn't bother to stand.

The original Irving gave his sibling's shoulder a friendly whack. "Butch, Sam. Sam, my brother. Oh, Butch, did I mention about Mrs.

Phelps? Some sort of high-risk pregnancy deal, she's out for the year. Sam here's taking over her keyboarding classes."

"And programming." Samuel's preference would have been programming only. "Nice to meet you."

"So," Irving prompted, "whaddaya think? About our girls?"

It felt like being asked to pass judgment on a child's crayon drawing. Samuel wasn't sure what he was supposed to see. "Well, they're tall." He glanced at the scoreboard. The home team was down by three points. "Looks like they have a chance."

Butch smirked. "If they lose, it won't be *her* fault." He nodded to the scorekeeper's podium, where the girls' coach was leaning over the table.

"Nguyen," she said loudly. "It's *Nguyen*. Why is this so difficult for you?"

The man shrugged and mumbled an excuse.

The coach grabbed the pencil out of his hand. "Look. I'm writing it out phonetically, right here so you can see it. W-I-N. Nguyen. Get it right." She snapped the pencil in half, slammed it on the podium, and stomped down to the floor. "Ladies," she called. "Huddle up."

"Wow," said Samuel. She had physical presence *and* an acid tongue.

Mistaking his admiration for shock, Irving laughed and turned his back on the coach. "She's an old battle-ax," he confided, "but the girls would be nothing without her. You ever have to deal with the woman, my advice is, don't argue."

Butch tucked his meaty hands into the front pocket of his sweatshirt. "Better not to deal with her at all," he muttered. "She'll rip you a new one."

"And Butch would know," Irving said.

Butch gave his brother a shove. "Shut up, Vince."

The coach cast a glance their way, almost as if she had heard. Her face darkened.

Samuel averted his eyes. "Uh, right." The Irving brothers engaged him in a little more obligatory chitchat and then departed as the third quarter began. "I'd still like that ride," he called, lest he be forgotten.

Irving tossed a wave over one shoulder.

The second half of the game was tooth-and-nail, and when the final buzzer sounded the home team was down by two points. The girls filed into the locker room, faces showing how much it hurt to come so close.

Samuel scanned the gym for Irving, but he couldn't spot the principal in the confusion of the emptying stands. He stayed put, figuring he'd have better luck waiting for Irving to find him.

Slowly the crowd dissipated. The players began to emerge from the locker room in twos and threes, sweaty, tired, and defeated. They hugged, slapped shoulders, and parted to return to the unconditional love of their families.

Then the gym was empty. Samuel worried Irving had forgotten him until he heard a telltale bark of laughter beyond the open doors. He glanced at his watch and sighed. Two hours and all he'd accomplished was meeting Irving's doppelgänger.

"Does this look like a hotel?"

Samuel looked up to find the coach coming out of the locker room, dragging a netted bag of basketballs. She turned to lock the door as Samuel levered himself to his feet.

"Um . . . Irving was supposed to drive me home." That sounded idiotic. What was he, twelve?

She looked him up and down. Not disdainfully—simply taking him in, sizing him up in a matter-of-fact way. Slight, sharp-featured, and prematurely graying. Oh, and crippled. Couldn't forget that. Samuel guessed he didn't make a very impressive show.

Well, so what? So he couldn't handle the sack of basketballs she hefted over one shoulder. He was neat, he was clean, and he was well shaven. That counted for something, didn't it? He hoped so, because he didn't have much else.

"You're Cooke?" It wasn't much of a question; she knew exactly who he was.

"Yep."

She lumbered past him with the slightly hip-centered gait of someone who'd had knee surgery—twice, he saw—throwing extra weight into her stride to compensate for the basketballs. "Irving family's big on talk," she said, not entirely in a friendly way. She didn't seem very friendly on the whole. "I'll take you."

He started after her, slowly. His knees were stiff from sitting so long. "Don't feel like you need to—"

"Don't start."

Samuel wondered what he'd done to offend her, then realized she probably wasn't irritated at him so much as the outcome of the game. He followed her across the court to a low-ceilinged entryway and waited as she unlocked the storeroom door and tossed the basketballs inside.

"Thanks," he said to her back. When she turned, he added, "Too bad about the game."

She frowned, and he worried she might be preparing to chew him out, or maybe snap him in half like a pencil. Then she shook her head. "We'll do better in the finals." She put a hand out, making the gesture a kind of rough apology. "I'm sure Vince has told you what he thinks of me, but I doubt he mentioned my name."

"Uh." Samuel wasn't often or easily embarrassed, but as her palm closed around his slender fingers, he knew confirmation of her guess was written on his face.

She laughed. "Don't worry, it's an even trade. Cassamajor. Everyone calls me Cass."

"Is your first name too horrible to mention?"

She laughed again. Samuel had a feeling that might be some kind of record for her. "Greta."

He smiled. "I like it. Greta Cassamajor. Entirely my pleasure."

She gave him a sideways look, as if trying to decide whether he was for real. Then she shrugged and started for the door, digging in her pocket. Outside, she pulled out a second set of keys and nodded toward the central parking lot. "That way."

"Right." Samuel left her to squint at the lock in the waning light, grateful for the head start over the cracked, uneven pavement.

"Irving!" he heard her call. "Cooke's with me!"

"What?" came the distracted reply. "Oh—give me one minute—"

"Forget it, Vince." The way she said his name sounded like "asshole."

A moment later the crunch of gravel signaled Greta's approach, and Samuel sensed she had to check herself to keep from passing him. She was the kind of woman who functioned on one speed: efficiency. Maybe he couldn't pace her physically, but he was betting Irving's intellectual lag was far more irritating.

Greta drove a Suburban. She unlocked the passenger side and let the door swing open. "Need help?" She reached into the seat and shoved a couple of binders out of his way.

"I've got it." He set about to make good on his words as she circled to the driver's side, but the vehicle was higher than it looked. Or he was more tired than he thought. When she slid in and slammed the door, he wavered dangerously between a crutch lodged against the gearbox and legs that simply would not hold his weight.

Greta stuck the key in the ignition, leaned over, and pulled him in by one arm.

Prior experience dictated there would now be an awkward silence, followed by the hasty initiation of a conversation totally unrelated to his disability. And yes, the car was quiet as she navigated out of the parking lot, but it wasn't the tense, uncomfortable silence he was used to. Greta wasn't embarrassed; she was genuinely indifferent.

Which wasn't exactly heartening, either.

"Right or left?" She was about to turn out of the lot.

Samuel looked both ways. "Uh . . ."

Greta gave him a withering look. "You don't know."

Samuel swallowed. He'd only known the woman a few minutes, but he was already quite certain he didn't want to end up on the short list with the brothers Irving. "Hey, I've only been in town a week." The excuse sounded lame even to him. "There's some supermarket down the street . . . Amsted, Almsbed?"

"Anstead's." She turned right. "What street?"

Samuel knew that one. "Four-forty-two North." He was rather proud of having discovered the little two-bedroom, slab-floor bungalow. Because of the lack of foundation, he didn't even need a ramp to get in. It didn't have a dishwasher, either, but he'd arranged for a part-time housekeeper to worry about that. All things considered, it was perfect—almost worth the arm and a leg it had cost to buy. Though Healdsburg didn't look like much, the tiny wine-country town was apparently a weekend haven for wealthy San Franciscans.

Greta knew her way around; she found the street without a single wrong turn and pulled up next to the curb when he said "here" as though she hadn't needed the verbal cue. She yanked the emergency brake and opened her door.

"I can—" She was already halfway around the car. Although getting down was much simpler than going up, Samuel let her manhandle him to the ground. He didn't thank her this time; she didn't seem to require affirmation.

"Well." He shrugged his sleeves down. "Would you like to come in for, um, a cup of coffee, or . . . something?" It seemed like a neighborly thing to offer.

Her eyebrows went up. "Coffee? This late? No."

"Oh." Probably for the best, given that his coffeemaker was in a box somewhere in his living room. "Right." There was silence. This time it was awkward. "So, have you been teaching here for long?"

"Yes."

He waited. She didn't elaborate. "I'm, um, not a teacher. I mean, I wasn't. I was programmer at this place in L.A. We made architectural design software for large-scale projects. Stadiums, skyscrapers—" Like she cared.

"So why are you here?"

Was that a question or a challenge? "I, well—" He wished he'd prepared an answer in advance. "There was this accident." Oh, genius. Use Irving's idiot assumption. Playing the tragic-accident card will win everyone's respect. "Uh, that's not why I'm—I mean, I wasn't hurt, but I kept thinking, if I had died, what had I ever done that was worthwhile?" Better. "So I came up with some innovative stuff, big deal. I get a footnote in Wikipedia. Meanwhile, my life is twelve-hour days and takeout on the way home. So I thought, you know, teaching."

The corner of her mouth twitched. Barely. Suddenly he felt very silly and naive.

"Stupid, right? But I did get my credential in college, and—there were supposed to be lesson plans. But there aren't, and I honestly have no idea what I'm doing, and . . ." And tomorrow was going to be a complete disaster. What did he expect her to do? He had gotten himself into this hole, and he would have to dig his way out. She didn't give a damn, she just wanted to drop him off and go home. "I . . . whatever. Thanks for the ride."

They looked at each other in the half-light.

This was the point when Samuel sort of expected her to leave. He cleared his throat and tried again. "I doubt we'll be seeing much of each other, so—"

"Not unless you have a problem with my players. Half of them are in your sixth period."

Samuel frowned. Why would that mean there would be . . . unless she wanted him to— "You need me to let them off for games?" Great, his first day—no, his minus-one day, and already he was being confronted with a major ethical dilemma. Standing on the sidewalk in front of his house at night in the almost rain.

"Don't be an idiot," she snapped. "I expect you to give them makeup work. Playing sports is a privilege, not an excuse."

Whew. "I agree." He hadn't imagined the basketball coach would share his opinion.

"Good." She started around her car. "Some advice for tomorrow and the rest of the year. Don't trust your students." She gave him a thin, joyless smile as she opened the driver's-side door. "Even the good ones don't see us as human. Good night, Mr. Cooke."

"Good night, uh—" Did she expect him to call her Ms. Cassamajor? The formality seemed right in her mouth but strange coming out of his. Just Cass seemed weird, too. In the end the problem solved itself: she got into her car and shut the door.

Samuel waved and started up the front walk, puzzling over her warning. Were the little buggers going to trip him in the halls? Steal his keys? Surely they weren't that low. Were they? Great, something new to worry about.

He didn't hurry getting his keys out, but when he stepped inside and turned to close the door, he wished he had. Greta's car was just pulling away.

At least she hadn't called him "dear."

2

AFTER FIVE HOURS OF sleep and a double espresso (obtained at a drive-through near the supermarket), Samuel was nervous. Really, really nervous. And not just because Greta's dour warning had kept him up half the night. In Architective's early days, he'd frequently been called upon to give presentations to potential clients—an event usually followed by furious upchucking. That particular duty had vanished from his job description the second time Rashid found him passed out on the bathroom floor. Though the visceral terror of those meetings had faded, the curious eyes of thirty teenagers playing over his body was bringing it all back.

He distracted himself by taking a quick mental survey of the class. Roughly half were guys wearing large white shirts and pants so big they could have housed three of him. He'd read online about Healdsburg's history as a farming community, so these had to be the sons of laborers and migrant workers, mostly. The other half were descendants of the Italians who had migrated here a century earlier, now the successful owners of the vineyards sprawling across every hill. The outliers were three blondes, one redhead, and an Asian kid in the back.

Gradually the muted chatter died. The clock showed two minutes past the hour, but Samuel hadn't heard a bell. "Um. Sorry, did the period begin?"

A nervous titter rippled through the room.

"I'll take that as a yes." Okay. He could do this. Samuel drew in a breath and began with the words he had rehearsed while trying to sleep the previous night. "Good morning. I understand that you've had a succession of subs since Mrs. Phelps left. Fortunately, that's over. I'll be with you until June."

Silence. They looked disappointed. Or indifferent.

He plowed on. "My name. Samuel Cooke, no relation to the singer." Blank stares. Apparently they had no more knowledge of the musician than his mother. "Mr. Cooke to you, I guess. Before I take roll, do we have any football players in the room?"

They did. Which was fortunate; his arms, locked at the elbows, had nearly reached their limit. A minute of uneasy jockeying and some assistance from a few other hands got the unwieldy teacher's desk from one end of the room to the other. "Could someone get the chair? And that binder? Thanks." He sat, gratified to find that the chair had casters, and tucked his crutches under the desk.

Now. Roll. He grabbed a pencil and started in the middle of the sheet. "Silvia Jimenez?" One of the girls in front raised her hand. He'd memorize the list later using a couple of mnemonic tricks; the real issue was pairing names with faces. Fortunately one of the online teaching guides he'd consulted had a solution. "Silvia, tell me something weird about yourself."

"Um . . . something weird?" Her stricken expression screamed, *Oh God, don't put me on the spot!*

Samuel hadn't expected this to be a big deal. "To help me remember you."

She chewed her lip. "I don't like pizza?"

He penciled "pizza" by her name. "Hope you're not planning on college. You'll starve to death."

The joke wasn't even funny, but everyone in the room laughed. It was like running a board meeting with a bunch of children. And they *were* children, he realized, all terrified of being singled out for ridicule. It was painful to watch: the girl in the corner, tracing her mouth with a finger to ensure her prostitute-pink lipstick was in place; the boy by the window ducking his head to pick a zit unobserved. Samuel tried meeting a pair of eyes. They flashed away. He tried several more with the same result.

His status—teacher, adult—automatically cloaked him with an aura of confidence. As far as these kids were concerned, he wasn't capable of anxiety or insecurity.

They don't see you as human, Greta had said. Maybe that was a good thing.

He picked another name. "Fernando Juarez."

"Yeah. I think this class sucks ass."

Samuel looked up and pinpointed the genius, a pint-sized kid in the back row. Fernando held his gaze. Interesting. "How original," Samuel said, loading his voice with sarcasm. He paused and then, perhaps childishly, wrote "sucks ass" after the boy's name. "Melinda Lopez?"

He took his time finishing roll, taking care to note each face and name, then opened his backpack and took out a ream of white printer paper. He grabbed half an inch off the top and held it out toward the redhead (Sadie, World of Warcraft addict). "Everyone take a piece. Fold it lengthwise"—he demonstrated, as the guide had suggested—"and put it over your hands as you type."

They groaned.

"Hey, hey." It wasn't hard to deduce that the class had spent the last few weeks fooling around and were reluctant to return to work. "Look, you guys cooperate, and you can have the last ten minutes to do whatever. Okay?" He looked around the room. "I can't let you just goof off."

Grumbling assents.

"By the end of the week, I want to know where each of you stands in terms of speed and accuracy. After that, I'll try to mix it up." Which didn't mean much; it was keyboarding, after all. He'd do what he could.

After they'd been at it for fifteen minutes, he got up to stretch his legs and doodle on the board, putting up strings of code in various programming languages for his next (real) class. Figuring he ought to patrol, he wandered over to the right side of the room, shuffling down the row so he could see the screens.

"Oh my God." The clacking of thirty keyboards came to an abrupt halt. Samuel waved an arm at the nearest computer and then the rest of the row. "These—this—what the hell *is* this?" He was looking at a room of neon-blue screens and pixelated white text. No frame, no operating system. It was practically DOS. "You don't have a word processing program? Like Word?"

A couple of kids in the next row shrugged. "Not really," someone said.

"FREAKING DINOSAURS." SAMUEL used the fifteen-minute break between second and third period to run a systems check on the computer nearest his desk. Glancing at the clock to make sure he had time, he went deeper, exposing the shameful innards of the outdated machine.

The computers weren't complete garbage, but they were close. Probably the best solution was to load them up with bootlegged copies of Windows XP. They'd run slow and crash occasionally, but for keyboarding, it would do. Still, how the hell was he supposed to run a serious programming class with this kind of shit?

Hearing the door open, he looked up to see Sadie, the redhead, come in. She was eating chips out of a plastic sandwich bag.

"Hey," he said. "What's up?"

She looked at her feet. "I'm in programming, too."

"Ah." No surprise that someone obsessed with an online role-playing game had an interest in programming. Her shyness was palpable, so Samuel went back to digging through the operating system, getting rid of redundant nonsense.

"Are we gonna get new ones?" She moved closer, watching the screen over his shoulder.

"What, computers?" She nodded and he laughed. "I can ask, but I kinda doubt it." The five-minute warning bell rang. Samuel picked up his crutches and headed toward his desk. "I used to play Warcraft. In college."

Sadie's eyes widened. "Seriously?"

He sat and settled back, bouncing a little. "Of course, that was the original real-time strategy. You'd laugh if you saw it now. I tried WoW for a few months when it came out, though. I liked to tank. Got up to level forty with my orc warrior."

"I play a blood elf mage. We do runs on Friday nights. I mean the programming class—we have a guild."

It was Samuel's turn to be surprised; he'd never have guessed an entire class of adolescents could keep a guild in order.

He was less impressed when the bell rang. "Uh, where is everyone?" He was looking at Sadie plus four guys. "There're twenty-three names here."

"Not anymore," said a tall, bony kid perched on the back of his chair. "Everyone transferred out after Mrs. Phelps left."

Samuel sighed. What did it matter? Teaching five kids how to program was easier than thirty, and he still got paid. "All right, introduce yourselves." He waved at the whiteboard behind him. "Give me your name and what languages you recognize."

The same kid laughed and slid down to straddle his seat backward. "I'm Marcus. And nobody here has a clue what any of that means."

The other students traded uneasy glances.

Briefly, Samuel closed his eyes. He motioned for them to continue. "Just names, then. Sadie said you guys have a guild, so tell me what you play in WoW, too."

Nick was more freckles than not, while Travis had long, stringy yellow hair. The best-looking of the bunch and the only Latino, Lemos had a first name but preferred not to use it. Sadie, as far as Samuel could tell, seemed to be accepted as "one of the guys." Marcus Menghini was classic Italian.

When they finished introducing themselves, Samuel sat back, fiddling with the pencil he'd intended to use to make notes. "As you'll figure out pretty quickly, this is my first time teaching. Until two months ago, I was Architective's senior programmer."

He hadn't expected that to mean anything, but Marcus's caterpillar eyebrows drew together. "Architective? They made, uh, uh . . ." He snapped his fingers. "That thing, um . . . it's a middleware for video games. My brother told me about this. It was part of some architectural software or something, but they realized it could be used for . . . jeez, I forget. AI? It was some total fluke—"

"Yeah," Samuel said quickly. "That company." Everyone always assumed the heuristic he'd developed for digital crowd behavior had been a lucky accident. He'd known exactly what he was doing, and that, combined with Rashid's business acumen, had launched the firm. Which was why he still owned 10 percent. "Hopefully my experience will mean I can give you some real, practical skills. On the other hand, I have no idea how to do this teaching crap, so if I'm totally screwing up, please let me know."

Nick raised a freckled hand and pointed at the upper-left corner of the board, where Samuel had scribbled his name, phone number, and address. "You probably don't wanna do that."

Samuel kicked himself mentally. Listing the info had been an automatic part of every client meeting. Rashid said it established trust, knowing the head of the project was always on call. "Thanks." He cleared his throat. "So, we have a problem. I have no clue what Mrs. Phelps planned on teaching you, but these computers are shit. Uh, garbage. We have to figure out—"

"These aren't the programming computers," Marcus interjected.

"What?" Samuel wondered if he should ask the kid to raise his hand. But with only five students, it didn't seem important.

Sadie flashed a palm. "There's a smaller lab out in the portables, way better than these. I think they run Vista."

Hallelujah. "Why aren't we having class there?"

Marcus rolled his eyes. "Because they're dumbasses? They just told us we had to be in here from now on."

Sadie shot Marcus a *shut up* look. He frowned, confused.

What was Sadie— Oh. Right. Samuel had been sitting behind the desk the entire period. "Uh, actually," he said, "I think 'they' were being considerate. Not smart, but considerate." He shrugged and held up a crutch.

Marcus was unimpressed. "Now what?"

"How about this: you guys help me reconfigure the crap in here. It'll be a good starter project. I'll find out if we can switch out some of these computers for the ones in the other lab. Sound good?"

They nodded and murmured assent.

"Okay. Let's see what you know about DOS."

"MIND IF I come in?" The classroom door cracked open an inch, revealing a wind-pinked nose and a shock of unruly brown hair.

"Uh, sure." Samuel set his backpack down. His fourth and fifth periods, inconveniently bracketing lunch, were not technically classes. Mrs. Phelps had described his duties loosely as "media co-ordinator" in the library. He'd gotten the idea he was supposed to be on hand for classes needing the equipment, but since he wasn't sure what that entailed, he'd decided to take his things with him.

The door swung in, and a slender man in a burgundy sweater-vest, beige slacks, and shiny brown loafers stepped over the threshold. "Well, hello." He used his fingers to comb back unkempt jaw-length hair, reminding Samuel of a young Beethoven. "You *are* young!"

Samuel laughed. "Nice to hear, coming from you." First Greta, now this guy—everyone knew who he was.

"I was worried." The younger man hitched up a pant leg and slid onto the edge of the desk, grinning boyishly. "I enjoy my status as baby of the family."

"Really. Mr.—?"

"Moore. Call me Greg. Samuel, right?"

Samuel nodded. "Not to be rude, but I'm supposed to be at the library."

"Oh, sure. I'll come with." Moore waited in the doorway, hands shoved deep into his pockets as Samuel shouldered his backpack and stood. Then he backstepped into the hall.

Samuel closed the door. "Don't you have class?"

"Fourth period's my prep, otherwise known as nap time." Moore pointed at the knob before raking his hair out of his eyes. "You're gonna wanna lock that."

"I'm coming back—"

"Yeah, and in the meantime, all of your dry-erase pens will have mysteriously disappeared."

Wonderful. Samuel dug the key out of his pocket and shoved it in the lock. It didn't want to turn. He took it out and turned it over; it went in either way.

"No, no, like this." Moore plucked the key from Samuel's fingers. "Divot goes up. In—not quite all the way—turn it back a little, then forward. There we go." He pulled the key out and jiggled the knob to demonstrate it had been secured. "Okay? Library's this way."

Irving had kept his distance; Moore walked too close for comfort. Samuel had to time his steps so as not to knock his companion in the shins. He didn't really mind. Nor did he mind Moore's obvious talent for carrying on a conversation almost entirely unassisted. They quickly established that, at thirty-four, Samuel was now the second youngest on staff, after Moore. This, and the fact that they were both "elective men" (Moore covered art and band) apparently made them automatic friends.

The library, when they arrived, was small and empty except for two students thumbing lazily through magazines. There were five rows of fiction. The rest was reference, including three shelves of what looked like yearbooks dating back to the Middle Ages.

"Public library's three blocks that way," Moore explained, seeing Samuel's dismay. "No need to compete."

A little woman with large hair sat behind the checkout desk. When she saw Samuel, she dropped the book she was repairing and hurried out to shake his hand. "Mr. Cooke? They said you know computers?" Her eyes flickered heavenward. "You have no idea how badly we need your help."

"I'm beginning to get the idea, actually."

The wall to the left of the entrance was empty of shelves. Instead there were four doors separated by windows looking into what appeared to be small classrooms.

"These are the media rooms," the librarian explained. "They have pull-down projection screens and DVD players and supposedly some very nice computer equipment. A lot could be done with them, but all they're ever used for is showing movies." She stopped at the fourth door and unlocked it. "Here's everything else."

Samuel peered inside. The room was piled high with junk. There were televisions, computers, and even a laser disc player, with a total of five record-sized discs stacked next to it. He sneezed, sending up a cloud of dust.

Moore, taller by a head, leaned in over his shoulder. "I didn't even know this was here."

Samuel backed out. "What idiot bought all that crap?"

The librarian handed him the key. "Some of it's donated, and occasionally someone sells Vince on some new piece of equipment. It usually ends up here, collecting dust."

"And I'm supposed to . . . ?"

Her smile was pained. "Do what you can. Maybe if we have someone who knows how it works, some of it will get used. I hate to see good resources go to waste, but the truth is they usually do." She hesitated. "I wonder, would you mind taking a look at my computer, too?"

The librarian's system was an easy fix; it had never been defragged. While they waited for the process to finish, Moore filled the time by dishing out gossip on a dozen teachers whose names Samuel immediately forgot. When Samuel suggested silence was more conducive to studying, Moore got up and ambled over to one of the kids.

The librarian, sorting through some textbooks in a small back room, poked her head out. "Mr. Cooke." He raised his eyebrows, and she sidled up next to him, glancing at Moore, who was in conversation with a student about an automotive magazine. "You're new, so be aware. Greg is . . . well, anything subtle tends to go right past him. If you want him to go away, you have to be blunt. And I mean really."

Why wasn't that surprising? "Thanks for the tip." Her warning confirmed that Moore was the kind of friend Samuel needed. The kind who wouldn't go away, no matter how often he was brushed off or turned down.

"No problem. He and Cassamajor, really, are the ones you want to stay clear of."

Moore wandered back. "How's it going?"

Samuel held up a finger. The defrag was 98, 99, and . . . "Done." He closed out and checked the time. Ten minutes until the lunch bell. The storage closet could wait; he'd rather return to his room while the halls were still vacant, rather than attempting to navigate through a throng of students. The majority of whom were disappointingly larger than he was. He conveyed his intentions to Moore as they stepped into the hall.

"I'll get my lunch," Moore said, and took off at an easy jog.

A mental replay of the trick with the classroom door, performed in reverse, got Samuel inside and seated before his companion returned. He took out a piece of paper and started a list of things he'd need to begin work in the storage room. He added a few items for the classroom as well.

"Cold out there." Moore dropped his sack lunch on the corner of the desk and rubbed the red out of his cheeks and nose. Finding no seat comparable to the one Samuel occupied, he grabbed a blue student chair and squatted on top. "Whatcha doin'?"

"Making a—"

"Shit." Moore tumbled out of the chair and was halfway to the back of the room before the door opened to admit Vince Irving.

The principal smacked the doorjamb with one hand. "Hey, how's it going?"

"Stupendously." If Samuel didn't give him anywhere to go conversationally, maybe he'd leave. In the back, Moore was trying the door to the student courtyard. It appeared to be locked.

"Just wanted to apologize for leaving you hanging last night. Hope you didn't get it too bad from Cass." Irving noticed Moore, who was studiously contemplating a tree outside one of the big windows. "Looks like you made a friend. Careful, he sticks."

Samuel forced a smile. "I'll keep that in mind." He glanced at the list he'd made. "Since you're here, there's some equipment—"

"Oh, of course," Irving said. "Anything you need. It's a legal requirement."

"Really?" In the moment before he understood the miscommunication, Samuel was impressed with the school's generosity. Then he frowned. "No, not for me. The computers. They must be ten years old." Which might as well have been a century in electronic terms. "Some updated software will get us started, but I'll need some USB and Ethernet cables, a few pairs of pliers, a soldering gun—"

Irving held up a hand. "Hold on. Mrs. Phelps never needed any of that."

"Yes, well, Mrs. Phelps was babysitting, not teaching. The programming class thinks an 'argument' is what you have when you disagree."

"She was very popular, Mr. Cooke, and she did an excellent job with the resources she had. This district doesn't have an endless budget. Exactly how much will this stuff cost?"

Ironic that there were no barriers to cost when it came to Samuel's personal needs, yet they couldn't find the money for the tools he needed to teach. It had to be fear of legal retaliation.

Samuel gritted his teeth. "Okay, look. It's partly for the students, but it's also for me." He swiveled to put his crutches in view, then indicated the cables snaking across the floor. "It's such a mess in here, I can barely get around. I want to move all the cords under the desks and bundle them together. That means I need longer cables, and I need tools." Hopefully nobody would realize that didn't require software or a soldering gun.

"Mm." Irving nodded. "Really, that's the sort of thing to put in a work request. Get the handyman in here to—"

"I'd like to have the students do it." Samuel pulled his chair up to the desk. "It will give them some valuable hands-on experience."

That put Irving completely on board. "Fantastic idea! I'll tell you what—make a list and give it to Joyce. She'll take care of you."

Samuel slid an elbow over his list. "I'll do that. See you around."

When Irving was gone, Samuel closed his eyes and sighed. "Greg," he said, "are you laughing or crying?"

Moore stood with his back to the room, shoulders shaking uncontrollably. "That—" He snorted and burst into high-pitched laughter. "That was brilliant! You just bought yourself carte blanche! Hey, there's this projector I've been lusting after for years—"

"No. Absolutely not. There's a special circle in hell for people who exploit handicaps." Samuel was already going to have nightmares of karmic retaliation for months.

Moore climbed onto the blue chair and took an apple from his bag lunch. "You're no fun," he said, the words muffled as he bit into the fruit. "But you survived a ride with Cass. That's cool."

"I guess?" Sure, she was a little scary, but so far he didn't see the monster everyone made her out to be. Although he was kind of annoyed with her for exacerbating his anxiety.

"No, seriously, she's like a volcano waiting to erupt. Last year? She thought one of the posters I designed for the tournament was offensive. It ended up on my car. In ribbons."

"Isn't that kind of . . . I mean, is she allowed to do stuff like that?"

Moore shrugged. "It's all about tenure. And she's good. As a coach, I mean."

"Huh." He pulled out his own lunch—half a deli sandwich and a soda—and popped the tab. "What's your issue with Irving, anyway?"

Moore bit another chunk out of the apple. "Shlept wif his wife."

Samuel choked. "Are you serious?" He remembered the photo in Irving's wallet. The woman was attractive, but not twenty-years'-difference attractive.

The younger man nodded. "He doesn't know it, though. Well, not for sure." He shrugged. "What can I say? It was my first month teaching, she was forbidden fruit, and man, did she want it. You know, older women can really—"

"Greg, let's consider this subject off limits for like . . . ever. Okay?"

SIXTH PERIOD WENT as well as second had, which was to say, he wasn't batting a hundred, but he wasn't curled up behind the dugout, either. There was an abnormally high number of X chromosomes in the afternoon class, mostly due to a group of tall, athletic young women who laughed at all his stupid jokes. Samuel was starting to feel weirdly pedophilic when one of them raised her hand and said, "Can I, like, listen to, like, my iPod, like, you know, while we're typing?" After that, they were just kids.

Then the bell rang, his students filed out, the door swung shut, and he had done it. He was exhausted and his head was pounding with an espresso hangover, but he'd made it through an entire day without making a complete fool of himself. Maybe Mrs. Phelps was right—this teaching thing was no big deal. Or maybe it wasn't teaching. Maybe it was him. Maybe all he needed to do was give himself half a chance.

Samuel leaned back in the swivel chair, taking a moment to enjoy his success, and groaned when a knock sounded on the door. "Come in." What did Irving want now? Samuel bent forward and started stuffing papers into his backpack. Yep, gotta get home, lots of stuff to do, no time for basketball.

He was startled when a rough female voice said, "Regretting your career change?"

Samuel straightened. Greta's appearance had not changed significantly since last night: today, instead of a sack of basketballs, she gripped a clipboard under one fleshy arm.

"Actually," he said, sitting back, "I quite enjoyed myself." An exaggeration, yes, but he had earned a bit of a gloat.

She lifted one eyebrow. "Really."

Amazing, how much that single sarcastic word conveyed. *Oh, so you're tough now? Got it all figured out? Just wait. A month from now you'll be crawling home with your tail between your legs.* Samuel might as well have rung his father on the phone.

"Yeah," he said. "Really." Because he was done with that bullshit. He flashed a self-satisfied grin. "I know you came to see if I'd melted into a helpless puddle of goo. Sorry to disappoint."

"Don't be stupid," she snapped. "I don't go around waiting for other people to fail."

"You generally take a more proactive approach, is that it?"

She struggled for words. "What— Exactly what is that supposed to mean?"

She couldn't seriously be pretending ignorance. "It means I've barely been here a day, and everyone I meet warns me to steer clear of you. And yet you've been inexplicably decent. Is there a reason why I'm an exception?" For a moment he thought she was going to swing the clipboard at his head, but he jumped in again before she could compose a coherent response. "If you're worried about these," he said, stooping to pick up his crutches, "don't bother. I can hold my own."

Greta yanked the clipboard from under her arm. Samuel cringed, but she didn't swing. Instead she ripped off a sheaf of papers and flung them into the wastebasket at his feet.

"You," she said, "are an idiot."

Samuel sat quietly after the door slammed, absorbing the sudden, sinking feeling that he'd gone too far. He licked his lips. Scooted forward. And reached into the garbage.

"Oh," he breathed. "Shit."

Lesson plans.

3

R EALLY GOOD LESSON PLANS, too. At least that's
what a cursory glance told him before he shoved them
into his backpack and headed out the door. Damn, damn,
damn.

Mortally offending anyone on his first day was bad; offending
Greta Cassamajor was particularly unfortunate. Of the faculty he'd
met, she was by far the most intriguing. He was curious about how
she ticked, and instead of taking the clock apart one piece at a time,
he'd grabbed a hammer and smashed.

He needed to do better.

Out in the hall, he turned to lock up, but he'd already forgotten
Moore's trick. The key went in, but either way he turned it, the knob
was still loose. He opened the door and shut it again, then shifted his
weight to the left crutch and tucked the right under his arm for extra
maneuverability.

Maybe Greta wasn't a total loss. He could at least apologize,
which would grant him the opportunity to seek out her classroom,
or office, or whatever it was gym teachers had. Not that groveling

was likely to help. She'd barely given him one chance; he thought an apology might get him another? Yeah, he was doomed.

"Hey! What's up?"

"Jesus Christ!" Samuel's keys and crutch clattered to the ground. He flailed and gripped the doorknob. "What the hell?"

"Oh, God, sorry!" Moore dropped to his knees, offering up Samuel's crutch like a surrendered sword. "I'm sorry, I didn't think—" He stood, fumbling the keys with his long, nervous fingers until Samuel stepped back and motioned to the knob. "Sorry," Moore mumbled again. He locked the door.

"It's fine. Next time just don't . . ." Samuel let a breath out his nose. Whatever. "Is there something you wanted?" He started for the parking lot.

Moore trotted to catch up. "I just . . . Well, it was cool how you fixed Mrs. Peterson's computer. I was kind of wondering—"

"Educated guess. Your computer's broken." Samuel was starting to think he might be violating the prime directive by interfering with the local technology. Nevertheless, they agreed on Saturday morning, and Samuel made sure to clarify that Moore should bring only his computer tower, without any of the usual accoutrements.

"Ooh, a Buick," Moore said when they reached Samuel's car.

As if he'd had a choice. Car shopping, as of seven years previous, had consisted of shoving his travel chair into trunks and seeing which one fit. At least it was black, not some shade of elderly beige. "Glad you like it. See you tomorrow."

Moore didn't take the hint. He stood on the curb, watching as Samuel levered himself into the driver's seat. When Samuel reached out to shut the door, Moore pulled his hand out of his pocket. "Um . . ."

Samuel waited.

"Just curious. Why was Cass in your room?"

"I knew it." Moore was a busybody. He had dirt on everyone

else, and now he was collecting information on Samuel. "You were spying on me."

Moore reddened, opened his mouth to protest, and then shut it again. He shrugged.

Samuel rolled his eyes. "When she gave me a ride last night? She warned me to . . . watch out for myself, I guess. I was insulted, so I pushed back." He wanted to kick himself. Her warning, and the subsequent sarcasm, had come from an entirely different point of view: her kids would have trampled him into ground beef in five minutes. Samuel's students were those too timid for shop, too inartistic or tone-deaf for Moore: in short, all the quiet, submissive drones trying to slide through school without attracting attention. One day with them, and he'd acted as if he'd scaled Everest. "I was a total asshole."

Moore draped an arm over the open door. "And she took it?"

"She looked like she wanted to hit me, but yeah." Samuel decided not to mention the lesson plans. Not just because it made his bad behavior doubly embarrassing but because it was so out of character with the woman everyone else seemed to know. Maybe they only thought they knew her. Maybe, like Samuel, she had been hoping to find someone who saw her as the person she wanted to be. And instead, he had . . . ugh.

"No offense, Cooke, but are we talking about the same person here? Big scary lesbian?"

Samuel blinked. "Lesbian?"

"Walks like a duck, talks like a duck, probably is a duck."

"Ducks don't talk."

"All I know is, any man with half a brain is scared shitless of the woman." Moore picked at a spot of paint on his shirt cuff. "You'd think she'd be easier on me, being gay, but no."

"Now *you're* gay?"

"No, but everyone thinks I am." He lifted the cuff and sucked at the paint. "Some clique decides you're gay, that's what you are."

"So Greta might not be a lesbian, either."

He let his arm drop. "Wait, who? I thought we were talking about Cass."

"Greta is her first name."

Moore's eyebrows shot up. "I had no idea. Weird."

SAMUEL HAD THE key in his front door when it swung in. "Oh!" Right, the maid. Yes, drop both crutches this time. That'll go over well.

"Mr. Cooke?" She was a wiry girl with a long black braid draped like a rope over one shoulder. She looked about twenty, which was what he'd expected, having placed the ad with the career office at the local junior college.

"I see you found the key. Maria, right?"

She nodded. "I swept, wiped down all your shelves, and started putting some things away. I found the kitchen cleaning stuff, but nothing for the bathroom."

"Oh, uh—I'll take care of the bathroom." He went ahead of her into the house, ignoring his wheelchair in the entryway. Though there were still boxes everywhere, the piles he had dumped on the floor were gone, and the kitchen was not only clean but reorganized. Good; she was bold enough to move his crap instead of just lifting and dusting underneath. "Perfect."

Well, almost. In the living room, his old leather armchair sat in front of the gas fireplace. Facing it was a cheap folding chair with a pillow on the seat. This morning there had also been a disorganized pile of paperbacks on the floor; now they were filed neatly on the shelves behind the chair. Samuel pointed. "My books? I like them on the floor."

"Oh. I'm sorry, I—"

"No, no, don't be." Great. Now she'd think he was the kind of jerk who found fault with everything. Which apparently he was. "Um. Look, move anything else around, however you want. I really won't mind. As long as I can reach it." Small as she was, she still had a couple of inches on his five-foot-*ahem*. He indicated the space surrounding the chair and the fireplace. "Let's call this area off-limits."

"Bathroom and armchair, got it. Anywhere else?"

He grinned. "I'll let you know."

She nodded and started for the bookshelf.

Social crisis averted. Barely. Samuel slipped his backpack off and sagged into the armchair, breathing in the earthy smell before heaving himself forward again. His hands moved blindly, making quick work of his shoes and the braces on his lower legs. Then he picked up his limp stockinged feet one at a time and dropped them on the folding chair. An ottoman would have been more practical, but that just seemed too . . . well, girly.

Maria plopped an armful of books on the floor to his right, then paused to organize them into four neat piles before returning to the shelf. "Long day?"

"No. Yes. Maybe. Ugh." He closed his eyes and tried to think of something calm and relaxing. Nothing came to mind, so he listened to Maria moving around behind him. In L.A., he'd had a cleaning service come while he was at work, so having someone in the house with him felt weird. Was he supposed to make chitchat, or pretend she wasn't there? He leaned over the side of the chair. "What are you studying?"

"I'm taking some prereqs, trying to get in to a four-year nursing program." She turned around, her arms piled high with the remainder of his paperbacks. "It's competitive."

"Oh." Was that why she'd answered an ad to assist a disabled guy? Practice? He stretched out an arm for his backpack, just beyond the books. His fingers didn't quite reach.

Maria deposited the rest of his books on the floor, used a foot to push his backpack within range, and turned to confront the five or six large boxes in the middle of the living room. "What do you do, Mr. Cooke?"

He pulled the bag into his lap and got out Greta's slightly crumpled lesson plans. "Just started teaching at the high school. Computer science." They were photocopied, but she had used a blue pen to make additional notes in the margins. He thumbed through the stack. There were notes on most of the pages. Once again, damn.

"Two of my brothers go there." Maria spoke over one shoulder as she rifled through the contents of the first box. "I don't think they're taking computers this semester, though."

"Oh." He watched her pull out a colander and a C++ manual. "Two little brothers, huh? I only have one, and he drove me crazy enough."

"Three brothers, total. And two sisters. I'm the old—" She turned to look at him and grinned. "Mr. Cooke, you don't have to talk." She waved at the lesson plans. "Read your papers. I'm here to work."

Samuel felt himself go a little red. "Um. Right. Thanks."

Maria gathered an armful of kitchen implements and disappeared around the corner. Samuel swallowed his chagrin and returned to the pages on his lap. How could a gym teacher's lesson plans possibly be applicable to computer science? Greta's first note, scrawled in all caps, answered his question: "Health and Nutrition." So she understood that jumping jacks and push-ups were not analogous to algorithms and procedure calls. Still, health and nutrition didn't seem much closer.

He scanned her notes and realized subject matter wasn't the point. She had marked out the sixty-minute period in a neat structured format; typically she warmed up with a question or brief activity, moved into the meat of the lesson, and brought it to a close two thirds of the way through the hour. The remaining time was reserved for illustration—a demonstration, group work, or occasional guest speaker. Time frames shifted depending on the thrust of the lesson and peripheral activities.

Greta's examples were similar to what he'd found online, though he appreciated having more templates to choose from. Of greater value were her comments regarding the students. "Not a good idea to let them work alone for more than 20 min.," she had written. "No patterns—variety important to keep them engaged." "Student-student dialogue better than student-teacher." "If a good question comes up, don't be afraid to go off topic." "Wing it."

Maria materialized in front of him, rubber gloves dripping soap. She held her hands up like a surgeon scrubbing for the OR, water running down to her elbows. "Mr. Cooke?"

Abruptly, his subconscious informed him that she had already attempted to gain his attention several times. "Uh, sorry. What did you . . . ?"

One side of her mouth tugged upward into a quizzical smile. "I was just looking for some dish towels. To dry."

"Ah." Samuel gave her directions to the cupboard to the left of the refrigerator. A minute or two later she came back in the living room, hair tidied, cell phone in one hand. Samuel used an elbow to push himself up straight and said, "Thanks for coming. See you on Thursday?"

"Thursday." She started toward the door, patting the back of his chair as she passed. "Good luck with your job."

"Thanks." All right, he'd jumped over his last social hurdle of the day. Now on to dinner, otherwise known as boxed mac and— "Hey, Maria?" He leaned around the side of the chair, hoping to catch her before she shut the door, and was startled to find himself face-to-face with his own wheelchair, no longer in the entryway. Maria stood behind it, purse strap over one shoulder. "Oh. Thanks. Um, I was wondering. You don't cook, do you?"

It turned out she did, and yes, she would be interested in an extra fifty a week. It was a bit much, but it beat eating out. Samuel had already discovered quality drive-throughs were few and far between in Healdsburg. Los Angeles did have its perks.

"Great," he said when they'd worked out the details. "Thursday, then?" Oh God, he'd already said that.

Maria mirrored his wince. "Get some sleep, Mr. Cooke." She tapped the back of the wheelchair and turned to go. Again.

"Hey, Maria?"

"Yes, Mr. Cooke." Her hand was on the doorknob.

"You'll be good at it. Being a nurse, I mean. And I've known quite a few."

Maria said nothing, but as she turned to close the door, Samuel saw her blush.

SLEEPING IN A clean, freshly made bed was heavenly. Waking up to his alarm was hell. Samuel had vowed to get to school well before class—Greta's class, technically, since first period was his prep—and apologize.

He had no idea where she might be, so he parked in the mostly empty lot and started the long trek to the main office, where he assumed they kept track of such matters. The morning was so cold that every breath came out in a white puff.

The heavy aluminum door was unlocked, but it was also stuck. Nobody answered when he knocked. Samuel was on the verge of throwing himself against the door when a girl in gray sweats and a red gym shirt marked "Biggers" sauntered by. "Excuse me. Could you—" He had been about to ask for help with the door but changed his mind midsentence. "Do you know where Ms. Cassamajor's room is?"

The girl, tall and slender to the point of awkwardness, studied him as if unsure how to answer the question. "She doesn't really have one." She gestured vaguely. "She's got an office over that way, though."

"Thanks."

The girl shrugged and started away. She'd gone five or six paces when she turned, hands on nonexistent hips. "Cass won't be there now. She has a zero-period PE class, which is where I'm supposed to be." She took a step toward Samuel. "Do you, um, want to come?"

Lending a student an excuse for her extreme tardiness? Not a great way to get back into Greta's good graces. "No, it's not important. Will she be in her office before first period?"

"I dunno. It's on the other side of the gym, by the storage portables out there. I don't know what number it is or whatever, but I think there's a basketball schedule on the door."

"Thanks." He watched the girl start away again, breaking into a jog. Then the office door grated open. He turned to find the smiling secretary; what was her name?

"Mr. Cooke! Did you need something?"

Joyce. She was *way* too perky for seven-thirty in the morning. "Not anymore."

"If you have a minute, I've got a stack of paperwork with your name on it."

Samuel groaned, but turned around and thumped up the ramp.

She held the door. "You know, you don't have to come all the way out here every time you want something. Just dial zero-one on the phone in your room."

Now she told him. "Thanks," he muttered, probably with less enthusiasm than she expected.

"Not at all, dear."

WHEN HE'D FINISHED scaling the mountain of bureaucratic trash, Samuel glanced at the time; it was twenty minutes into first period. So much for catching Greta before class.

At lunch, he hiked out and found her office more easily than expected. Beside the schedule the student had mentioned, her last name was stenciled on the door.

When he knocked, a sharp "Come in!" rang through the paneled aluminum. The door was as heavy as the one at the main office, but it opened inward, so he leaned on it until it gave.

Greta's space was more closet than office—just enough room for a desk and a couple of big canvas bags that looked like overflow sports equipment from one of the adjacent sheds. Her desk was cluttered, and various event schedules and calendars were pinned on the wall. Smaller, to one side, hung the unframed portrait of an attractive woman in her thirties. Well, damn. She really was a lesbian.

Why did that matter?

He squinted, and in spite of the vast difference in build and demeanor, the family resemblance became obvious. A sister, then.

Greta sat with her back to the door, bent over a stack of attendance sheets. "What is it?"

Samuel licked his lips. "Uh," he said, and stopped as she turned. There was more surprise than anger in her expression. Suddenly he was sweating. He made another effort to shove the spring-loaded door and succeeded in getting one foot over the threshold. "Um," he began again, "I wanted to apologize for—"

She returned to her paperwork. "Don't bother."

It was over, then, whatever "it" might have been. He felt like crawling out the door and hiding under the first rock he found. On the other hand, if she was going to be pissed off no matter what he did, he had nothing to lose. "No," he insisted. "I was entirely out of—"

She swiveled to face him, pen in hand. He was half afraid she would stick him in the eye. "I do have a reputation," she snapped. "And I did come to see if you'd crashed and burned."

"Oh." Samuel looked at his feet. Did that make things better or worse? "That's, uh . . ."

She grabbed the door handle, pulling in so he wasn't forced to lean. There wasn't enough room for him to come in and close the door, at least not unless they wanted to be *really* uncomfortably close, so she planted a foot on the floor like a doorstop and sat back. Waiting.

Samuel was having difficulty parsing her words. Was she taking responsibility for yesterday's altercation, or should he still apologize? Was this one of those situations where the woman said exactly the opposite of what she meant and he was supposed to know intuitively or telepathically or by whatever means women communicated that men were deaf to? Then again, Greta seemed nothing if not straightforward. Her frown was making him desperate.

"Please don't put me on the list."

Her frown deepened. "List?"

Oh God, he'd said it out loud. He couldn't possibly be that stupid, could he? Samuel didn't know what to do other than finish the thought. "Of, um, idiotic men."

Greta let out a humorless bark of laughter. "Nobody makes it on the list," she said, voice laden with sarcasm, "without earning it first."

"Which is exactly what I did, I know, but I—I mean—dammit—"

"Forget it." Greta turned back to her desk.

The door, minus her foot, treated Samuel to a full-body slam.

His lungs emptied with a solid *oof,* and the only reason he didn't collapse into a wretched little pile of skin and bones was because the edge of the door pinned him against the frame. To his credit, he hung on to his crutches this time.

Greta spun, lurching out of her chair with a look of wordless horror.

"I'm fine, I'm fine," he panted, trying to regain his air before—
She pulled the door back. He sagged into his crutches, abdomen
throbbing where the handle had skewered him. But he didn't fall.

"I—apologize," she said, the syllables stilted. She looked angry,
whether at herself or at him, he couldn't tell.

"Don't worry about it. Really." Samuel straightened and brushed
the line of dust that ran down the right side of his shirt. There was
probably a matching pinstripe on his back. "That was sort of inevitable, I guess. Please." He gestured. "Sit down."

Greta sat.

The door might have won the round, but its attack had bought
him one more chance to make things right. "Thank you for the lesson plans. I'm sorry I was rude. Can we reset?" Wonderful. Use some
geeky computer terminology, and she'll realize how smart you are. "I
mean, restart?" That didn't sound right, either. "Start over?"

She lifted an eyebrow. "I know what you meant. And there's no
need. You haven't made it on the list yet. Which is unisex, by the
way."

"How comforting." He couldn't tell for sure, but he thought
Greta seemed vaguely amused. "Then we're . . . everything's . . .
okay?"

"Fine."

She still seemed angry. "Are you sure?"

"Very."

Now she was definitely getting irritated. Best quit while he was
ahead. "Okay. Bye."

ANY ORDINARY MAN would have required at least a week to
sort out even the basics of such a relational mess, assuming he attempted at all. Samuel got three hours.

As the tallest girl in his sixth period filed out, he heard a "Hurry up and get on the court, no wasting time in the hall," and knew instantly it was Greta. He had about thirty seconds to compose himself before she stepped into his room.

"Still alive?"

He gave her what had to be a deer-in-the-headlights look. "I think so?" The uncertainty in his voice had nothing to do with his students. Students were easy. Relatively.

She gave him a wry, world-weary smile, which was probably as close as she ever came to the real thing. "The girls like you. You'll do fine." She slapped the doorframe with an open palm and was gone.

Relief washed over Samuel. He really wasn't on her list, or if he had been, he was off, free and clear.

Not until he was in his car, driving home, did he allow himself to wonder why that made him so happy. It wasn't just that he'd made a friend. (Sort of.) Nor was it that he'd faced Greta's fury and triumphed. (Sort of.) While it felt good to know he could handle someone like her, that wasn't the reason for his euphoria.

Samuel pulled into the driveway, set the emergency brake, and eyed himself in the rearview mirror. "You," he said, "are attracted to her."

And then the words sank in. "Oh God," he whispered. "I'm *attracted* to her."

4

GREG MOORE'S MOUTH WAS open before he stepped through Samuel's front door. "I heard you went to Cass's office!"

In his wheelchair, Samuel rolled back and gestured for Moore to put his computer tower on the kitchen table. "Word travels fast." Seeing as he didn't have a chance in hell with a taller, older, intensely physical woman—even if he wanted one, which he shouldn't— Samuel had been hoping to avoid talking or thinking about Greta pretty much indefinitely.

Moore eased his burden onto the table with a grunt. "Are you kidding? That took two days to get to my class." He folded his arms and turned a full circle, taking in Samuel's living/dining room. "So? What happened?"

Samuel shrugged and headed for the spare room, where most of his computer equipment was boxed up. "I apologized, that's all. And I think we're okay."

His chair jerked as Moore, coming up from behind, gripped the handles and leaned forward. "You didn't get chewed out? Nothing?"

"Nothing," Samuel said. "Hands off, please."

"So, now what, you're friends?"

He reached for the light switch. "I wouldn't go that far. In fact, I wouldn't even glance in that direction." He surveyed the boxes stacked in front of the bare, upended mattress and pointed. "That one, I think."

An hour later, Moore had learned how to hook up his own computer, and Samuel had ruled out human error. Even after a complete re-install, the system blue-screened every time it booted, which was not good. He tested the RAM, but it checked out fine. Another half an hour, and the computer's guts were exposed, coming out one organ at a time under his expert hand.

Moore stood a few steps back with a hand-vac cradled under one arm, unnerved by the sight of his disemboweled machine. He had been truly horrified by the amount of dust inside the tower. "Is it dead?"

"Hm? Oh, no. Might need a couple of new parts." Samuel glanced up. "Make yourself comfortable."

Moore set the vacuum on the table and pitched himself into Samuel's leather armchair, where he began rifling through the pile of books on the floor. "Didn't you want me to do something?"

"Actually . . ." Samuel grabbed a screwdriver and went for the power supply. It had been the most likely culprit, but you never knew for sure unless you checked everything else first. "I was wondering if you'd mind a slight change in plans." He pulled back from the table and rolled into the living area, holding up the boxy unit. "You need a new one of these, and I need a bunch of crap for school. Want to go shopping?"

"What about your pictures and stuff?" Moore picked up another book and flipped open the front cover.

Samuel waved a hand. He'd only suggested a trade so Moore wouldn't tell everyone he was free tech support. "What are you doing, anyway?"

"Reading the first and last pages of all your books."

He snatched the paperback out of Moore's hands. "We're going. My car or yours?"

"Oh, I didn't drive. I live two blocks away! Cool, huh?"

"READ THAT ONE again."

Moore squinted at a box on the top shelf. "Four hundred eighty watts, twenty millimeter fan, twenty-four pin . . . ?"

Samuel closed his eyes and mentally paired each power supply with the equipment in Moore's computer. "Let's go with the Antec." Moore looked confused, so he pointed. "All right, now the other stuff." Briefly, he consulted the list in his shirt pocket and then started for the next row.

While Samuel sorted through Ethernet cable options, Moore wandered down the aisle and pushed buttons on the display of digital multimeters. Most of them were already broken, but when one let out a piercing beep, he snatched his hand back.

"You might as well be one of my freshmen."

Moore smiled. "Trust me, I'm a lot nicer." He swapped his shopping basket from one arm to the other. "You're smart, you've been here a week. Spotted your troublemakers yet?"

Samuel shrugged. "There are a couple of idiots. One wannabe gangster who offers wiseass comments every time I call on him. His buddies think he's hilarious." He shifted on his crutches and pitched a packaged length of cable toward the basket, landing the shot neatly.

Moore looked down at the cable and blinked. Then he shrugged and sauntered back toward Samuel. "That doesn't bug you?"

"I have better comebacks." He tossed another cable into Moore's basket and headed for the next aisle. "The one who's getting on my nerves is this kid in programming. Bright guy, but seems to have forgotten how to raise his hand." He pointed to a soldering gun on the top shelf. Why did everything he wanted have to be out of his reach? "Let me see that one."

Moore laughed. "That's right, you have Marcus." He handed down the box.

Uh-oh. Samuel added the package to Moore's basket. "Is he a problem?"

It wasn't so much Marcus as his lawyer parents and an uncle on the school board. Moore's bitter tone pointed to more than hearsay; when Samuel asked, Moore shoved a hand into a pocket and glowered. "Yeah. Marcus sucks at drawing. But art is subjective, did you know that?"

"Great." The next item on Samuel's list was thermal paste. He shuffled to the end of the aisle and found two wispy-haired toddlers blocking the way. An unshaven man, presumably Dad, was combing through CPU fans. "Excuse me."

"Oh!" The man grabbed the younger kid's arm. "Out of the way, girls. Sorry."

Moore ambled after him. "I wouldn't worry. Marcus isn't stupid, he just didn't take my class seriously. If he likes computers, he'll earn his A."

Samuel stopped in front of a rack of silver tubes. He picked through a few possibilities and compared prices.

"Do I have something on my face?" Moore asked.

Samuel followed his eyes to the end of the aisle. The two little girls were staring openmouthed. "Your face is fine. I'm dragging myself around with a couple of ski poles."

"Oh, right." Moore stuck out his tongue, and the girls giggled. "Why don't you just use your wheelchair? It'd be faster."

"And shorter." Apparently the only person in Healdsburg who

minded her own business was Greta Cassamajor. "Forgive me if I don't want to live at eye level with everyone's crotch."

"Mm. Point taken. Anyway, with Marcus, pick your battles. He knows the only leverage you have is his grade, and if you get serious, you'll find yourself in front of the school board, trying to explain flunking a kid for speaking out of turn."

"Please tell me the good ones make this job worthwhile." Samuel picked out two tubes of Arctic Silver and tossed them into the basket with everything else.

"Sure, but those only come along every five years or— Okay, you didn't even *look* that time."

"What?"

Moore lifted the basket. "You haven't missed once."

"Oh." Samuel shrugged. "I'm from a family of ballplayers. Guess it's hereditary." Moore looked interested, so Samuel made a quick redirect back to the previous topic. "Great students are rare, huh?"

"Absolutely." Moore followed Samuel toward the checkout counters. "Speaking of which, my best one is visiting in two weeks. Olivia's first flute in the San Francisco Symphony. We e-mail now and then, but I haven't seen her since she graduated. I'd love to see her play. Hey, we could go together! You wanna—"

Samuel turned. "No offense, Greg, but anyone ever mention you come on a little strong?"

Moore looked sheepish. "Sorry. I can never tell when it's too much."

"For your future information, I'm not big on going out . . . places."

"Really? Why?"

Samuel opened his mouth to make a sarcastic comment about how many hours it had taken them to get through the store, then stopped. "I don't know. Maybe I should get out more."

"So do you wanna go to—"

"No."

BACK IN THE car, Moore fastened his seat belt and opened the glove compartment.

Samuel lifted an eyebrow. "Looking for something?"

"I just thought you'd have a bunch of, you know, gadgets. GPS and stuff." He bent and reached under the seat, pulling out the small black canvas bag Samuel kept underneath. "What's—"

"Put it back." All at once Moore's total lack of respect for personal space was not amusing.

"Why? What's inside?" His fingers reached for the zipper.

Samuel grabbed the bag and flung it into the backseat. "Greg, I don't give a fuck how stupid you are. Violate my privacy again, and you can forget we ever met."

Moore's eyes got very large. "Sorry?"

Samuel cranked the key in the ignition. "Whatever." He twisted to look out the rear window as he levered the gas and backed out. God. He wanted to erase this entire day. It almost didn't matter that Moore hadn't opened the bag. In Samuel's imagination, the zipper was pulled and the plastic tubing and sanitary wipes had tumbled out onto Moore's lap and he was asking what it was for and— Oh God, stop it. Just stop.

"Sorry," Moore said again.

Samuel levered the brake and shut his eyes, tight. Okay. Nothing had happened. The bag didn't exist. And Moore was probably totally bewildered by his massive overreaction. "Just . . . don't do it again."

"'Kay." The car was filled with tense silence for about half a minute. Then, as Samuel turned onto the freeway onramp, Moore blurted, "You don't even have a cell phone, do you?"

Jesus Christ, he never stopped. "I don't like to be any more device-dependent than necessary."

Moore grinned. "Computer geek and Luddite?"

"I'm not a Luddite. I . . ." Samuel just had major issues. Which would have been obvious to anyone even slightly less dense than Moore. "I like simplicity."

"Sure," Moore said, accepting the explanation without question. "Hey, you're scary when you get mad, you know that? You sound just like *her*."

"Who?" As if he didn't know.

Moore rolled his eyes. "Cassamajor. Are you sure there's not more to the story?"

Absolutely. "Look, I apologized. She accepted. Roughly. In fact, it took me a while to figure out I had been forgiven."

"That's the thing," Moore returned. "She doesn't forgive. *Anyone*."

"I have no idea what that means. I barely know the woman."

Moore was silent for the remainder of the ride, and Samuel did not feel compelled to share his feelings about Greta, nascent and convoluted as they were. Oddly, however, Moore's words filled him with hope.

No. No, they didn't. Shut *up*.

TWO WEEKS INTO his teaching career, Samuel's second-period keyboarding class began to giggle. Not all at once; it tiptoed around the room like a contagious disease. At the end of the period, he went to the board and listed the information they needed to collect by Friday. Next week they'd start on résumés. At his back, classroom chatter rose to a crescendo. Someone laughed and said, "What a fag!" Samuel didn't need to see Fernando to recognize the lazy sneer.

When Sadie returned at the end of break—she was always the

first to appear for third period—Samuel studied her face and asked, "What's going on?"

She turned bright red. "Uh, nothing, Mr. Cooke."

He was about to try teasing the information out of her when Lemos entered, along with a blast of frigid air. Samuel gestured in his direction. "Lemos, tell me why Sadie won't tell me what everyone is talking about."

Lemos dumped his backpack on a chair, swore lightly in Spanish, and rolled his eyes. "Some dumbass girls are saying you and Mr. Moore are together."

Samuel burst into laughter before he could check himself. Moore *had* warned him.

"So it's not true?" Sadie's voice was small.

He snorted and reached into a desk drawer for his water bottle. Nick and Travis tumbled in, followed by more freezing air. It was damn cold. "Uh, no. As lovely as Greg Moore is, I'm very heterosexual."

The guys snickered and slouched into their seats as the bell rang.

"Aaand Marcus is late again." Samuel tapped his pencil on the desk. It was the fourth time in as many school days. He hadn't drawn a line with the hand raising, and now Marcus was pushing the limits even further.

"Um." Sadie looked more nervous than usual. "He's coming. I saw him, um, talking to his second-period teacher."

She was covering for him. And not very subtly. "Well," Samuel said, "we can't wait, if we want to get these computers swapped out today." He pulled his keys out and tossed them at Lemos. "You know my car?"

"'03 LeSabre?"

Teenage guys always knew. "There's a red toolbox in the trunk. Grab it." Lemos left; Samuel turned to Nick and was about to speak when the door opened again. "Marcus, nice of you to join us." Christ.

Two weeks and already he'd metamorphosed into an honest-to-God teacher, complete with sarcastic quips.

"Sorry." Leaving the door hanging wide, Marcus tried to slide into a chair behind Nick. He looked peaked and pale. Just like Samuel's brother after a night on the town.

"Don't get comfortable," Samuel said, too loudly. Marcus winced. Jesus, Tuesday morning and the kid was hung over. "Run to the office for me and grab the key to the other lab."

Marcus dragged himself to his feet and plodded out without a word.

Sadie stood. "I'll go with him." She rushed after Marcus before Samuel could object.

He sighed and wafted a hand at Nick and Travis. "Head to the lab. If Marcus gets it open before I catch up, start unplugging the machines you want."

THE CLASSROOM WAS arctic by the time they returned with the computers. A call to the office confirmed that the boiler in the main building was out. "The portables are fine, though," Joyce assured.

Very helpful. Fortunately the librarian took pity when she found him shivering in the junk room and directed him to the teacher's lounge.

Which was how he discovered where Greta ate lunch.

5

SAMUEL FOUND A CLUSTER of teachers camped on and around a frayed, sunken couch, raking an absent drama instructor over the coals for his fall production choice (something about vampires). They invited Samuel to join, but he declined—aside from a complete lack of interest in the topic, he'd never escape the couch with his dignity intact. He settled himself at the round table in the center of the room and pulled out a book.

Five minutes after the lunch bell, Greta strode in. Samuel glanced up, felt his eyes widen, and forced a relatively calm "Good afternoon." Her face was flushed with a mix of exertion and windchill, as if she'd spent the morning outdoors. Perhaps she had.

His greeting gave her little choice but to join him. She gave him a curt nod and sat, pulling out an apple, a sandwich wrapped in waxed paper, and a water bottle.

Were they not going to talk? He had to say something. "Um. Thanks again for the lesson plans."

"Forget it." Coming from anyone else, those two words would have been a modest deflection. From Greta, it was an order.

Samuel fiddled with his half-eaten tamale. He was peripherally aware, via the sixth-period girls, that the basketball team had been traveling. "So, off to anywhere interesting this weekend?"

Greta's expression soured. "San Francisco."

"I didn't know you guys went that far."

Her frown deepened. "We don't. My sister's getting married."

Ah. He'd hit a personal note. At least it confirmed his guess about the photo in her office. "Are you going with anyone?" Holy shit. Where had that come from?

She gave him a glance he interpreted as *You're on thin ice.* Crap—was she married? It hadn't even occurred to him. She wasn't wearing a ring, but that didn't mean anything these days. Even if she weren't attached, she'd doubtless be insulted by his assumption. He braced himself for backfire.

"No," she said.

Samuel blinked. "What about me?" Oh Christ.

She cocked an eyebrow. "What *about* you?"

"I could, um . . ." He fumbled the soda can. What was he doing? He had to back out now. Just back the hell— "Go with you." This was going to end badly. Very, very badly.

The twin lasers of Greta's eyes bored into him. He could tell she didn't know what to make of his offer, whether he was expressing interest or attempting to be friendly in his own bizarre, socially retarded way.

"I'm the maid of honor," she said at last.

"Oh." Did that mean she couldn't have a date? Maybe it meant nobody on God's green earth was going to see her in a frilly pink dress. He glanced at the women around the couch, but their discussion had become heated, and none of them was paying attention. Just in case, he lowered his voice. "How about dinner, then?"

She slid back and gripped the edge of the table, but didn't get up. "I don't take these things lightly."

"Do I look like someone who does?" He was certainly taking *this* too lightly. He should have planned, should have thought it through before—well, no. He had thought it through, and he'd decided to do nothing, because this was stupid. Except here he was. The truth was, he had nothing to lose. When she refused, they could avoid each other until judgment day. And if their paths did cross, she could do little beyond treating him with the same contempt as every other man on staff.

She still hadn't answered. He had a feeling she was trying to look angry, but it wasn't working. This was getting awkward. "What about Friday?"

She stared.

He cleared his throat. "Seven o'clock? My place?"

This time she did stand, gathering her uneaten lunch. And then—"Fine."

She left, and Samuel sat frozen as her heavy footsteps sounded down the ramp outside. When the sound didn't die away, he realized he was listening to his heart. Slowly the conversation on the other side of the room found its way back into his brain. He shot another surreptitious glance at the teachers. The gossip session seemed to have come to an end, and a couple of the women were returning chairs to their original places. Nobody was giving him any funny looks.

Good. If this got out, it would spread like wildfire. He wasn't prepared for that. He wasn't prepared for anything. He was shaking.

"MARIA, I WAS wondering, could you come on Friday instead of Thursday this week?"

"Yeah, no problem." Her arms were up to the elbows in soapy water as he, sitting at the breakfast bar, downed the potato-and-cheese casserole that had just come out of the oven. She glanced at him over one shoulder. "Why?"

"I seem to have . . ." Oh, God. "Met someone. She's coming for dinner."

She turned. "Mr. Cooke! ¡Qué romántico!"

"I don't know about romantic." He laughed, winding a string of cheese around his fork. "You haven't met my date."

Concern clouded her eyes. "How can you say not romantic? How can you ask her if you do not—"

Samuel put up his hands. "Hold on, hold on. It's more complicated than that."

Maria stared at him, waiting.

He sighed. "Unfortunately, as you get older, romance just gets more confusing." Like he was some sort of expert. He planted an index finger on the counter. "I can't think of a single reason why I should be attracted to this woman, and yet I am."

Concern gave way to a skeptical frown. "Why? What's she like?"

He opened his mouth and then closed it again, frowning. "You won't tell—"

She pulled off one dish glove and put the bare hand on her hip. "Mr. Cooke, my brothers don't even know you're a teacher."

He shrugged and returned to his food. "For starters, she's at least five years older than I am. About twelve inches taller, too, but then that's not unusual. And big. When she smiles, she looks like a shark about to devour its prey."

Maria's expression went blank. She whispered something in Spanish. "Mr. Cooke, this is *not* Ms. Cassamajor."

"It is," he admitted.

"No." She shook her head. "No, Mr. Cooke, you could not—with such a—" She replaced the unspoken invective with a gesture of frustration. "This woman was the curse of my life for two years. I have never failed any class but hers."

"Come on, she can't be that bad."

"She is merciless, Mr. Cooke. She has no respect for anyone who cannot perform physically."

He winced. "Well, then, Friday night should be interesting."

6

SAMUEL SURVIVED THE WEEK largely on Cheerios, the blandest item in his kitchen. It seemed marginally healthier than puking his guts out every time Greta crossed his mind, but by Friday evening, black spots clouded his vision when he stood. He wanted to shut himself in his room and bolt the door; instead, he sat at the breakfast bar, holding a book he wasn't reading, rambling in Maria's direction.

"What was I thinking? She must think I'm crazy. Maybe I am. I haven't been on a date since—" Jesus, not since that desperate paraplegic in college, the incident that had convinced him he was better off alone. And here he was, ignoring his own better judgment. This was going to be exactly the same. Only worse.

He needed to do something, so he got up and made one last inspection of his abode. He didn't even have to leave the room. There was his armchair and the sprawling pile of paperbacks covered with spaceships, guns, and buxom women in scanty clothing. Not that he read them for that reason (in particular), but they definitely looked bad.

"Maria?" She came around the end of the bar, and he gestured.

"But your private space—"

"I know, it's my fault. They can't *be* here."

"I'll put them on the shelf, Mr. Cooke, but the pot will boil over if—"

"I'll do it. Get the books." He stumbled into the kitchen, grabbed the wooden spoon, and stirred like it was all that stood between him and drowning.

Maria stayed until six-thirty, when even she got nervous. Everything was ready, the table set, food warming in the oven. "Don't worry," she said. "If she agreed to come, she must like you very much."

The remark didn't sink in until Maria had gone—and then it opened a heretofore unexplored region of fear: what if Greta didn't show? He should have looked up her number, called to say he was ready if she was willing. What if she thought he had forgotten?

Even worse, what if *she* had forgotten?

Was the porch light on?

When he got up to check, his knees buckled, and he had to find his wheelchair. Oh, this was brilliant. Good evening, Greta. No, nothing's wrong, I'm just too nervous to *stand* in your presence. Excuse me while I go puke.

Maria, bless her, had turned on the light. Samuel rolled back and forth in front of the hall window, feeling stupid but not stupid enough to stop. He contemplated switching back to crutches and decided against it. Maybe he got some sort of pathetic mental boost out of being on his feet, but to anyone else, crippled was crippled.

He went into the kitchen and realized there was no way he could get the food to the table standing up, anyway. Why hadn't that occurred to him earlier? They should have gone out. He could have driven, paid. All the benefits and no hassle.

Samuel glanced at the clock. It was seven.

She wasn't coming. She'd forgotten or, more likely, decided not to bother, and he would sit here and eat everything himself because he hadn't learned his lesson the first time and clearly he needed physical reinforcement to prevent him from ever trying this again. *You are an idiot,* she'd said.

Yes. Yes, he was.

Samuel was just opening the oven when she knocked. He froze, not sure he wasn't hallucinating. The sound came again. He let the oven door snap shut and sped into the living room.

Wait. Was he presentable? Shirt tucked in, fly zipped. Hair, whatever. Did he smell all right? Yes, just enough cologne. He grabbed the doorknob and pulled.

She stood on the walkway in khaki pants and a light blue dress shirt, cradling a bottle of wine.

Samuel's heart surged into his throat. She was holding *a bottle of wine*. They would open it over dinner, loosen up—

She thrust it toward him. "I don't drink, but I thought you might. Everyone gives wine around here. I've got cases."

Oh. "I see. Thanks." He took the bottle and put it in his lap. "Come in." He pivoted away from the door and led her into the dining area.

Samuel survived the first few minutes on autopilot. He invited her to sit, told her the meal was in the oven, hoped she was hungry, and mentioned Maria's role, lest she assume too much about his cooking skills. He could feel himself talking too quickly, possessed with a heady sense of euphoria born mostly out of relief that she had *come.*

Then he got the enchiladas out, pulled up to the table without bothering to switch to a chair, served her and himself, and remembered at the last minute to grab a couple of drinks.

Then they looked at each other.

Silence.

He dug around on his plate. "So where are you from?"

"Why did you ask me to dinner?"

Samuel swallowed, feeling like an eight-year-old in the principal's office. *Why did you pull Susie's hair?* Instead of remaining calm and acting like an adult, he shot back a smart-ass "Why do you think I invited you?"

Greta's face darkened. She put her hands on the edge of the table and slid her chair back. "Mr. Cooke, I did not come here to—"

"Wait, wait." Jesus Christ. Did she seriously not get this? His anxious chatter would have clued in a vegetable. For whatever reason, she flat-out rejected the notion that he might sincerely want her company. Tough as she was, maybe someone had hurt her once upon a time. If he didn't put her off her defenses, and fast, she was going to leave.

So he was honest. "I'm attracted to you."

She opened her mouth and closed it again, although they both knew the word she had strangled was "Why?"

She knew she wasn't lovely. Oddly, the thought stung. As much as he wanted to offer reassurance, nothing seemed appropriate.

Greta grabbed a fork and returned to her meal with militaristic discipline. "Maria is a good cook," she pronounced.

Samuel nodded, relieved. "I think so, too. Obviously, or I wouldn't be paying her." He took a bite and chewed slowly. Dare he ask? "How was your sister's wedding?"

She glanced up. "Fine."

"Good weather?"

"Overcast but no rain."

He tried a smile. "I hear that's all you can hope for in San Francisco."

She nodded.

As Samuel had predicted, there was little that could be called "romantic" about the evening. He spent the next half hour pumping Greta for information about the wedding. Though her sentences remained largely monosyllabic, Samuel gathered that her younger sibling occupied an important position in her life. From there, he segued into a few other safe topics: teaching methods, grad school, local politics. He wasn't brave enough to delve deeper. That was all right, it was only the first date. If he could call it that.

After dinner, she insisted on doing dishes.

"*No.*" Samuel grabbed the edge of the salad bowl as she attempted to carry it away. "Please. Don't. I'll—"

"Will you?"

He felt himself color. "Maria will. I pay her to—"

"When will she be back?"

"Tuesday. But I don't mind," he added quickly. "Leaving the dishes won't bother me at all."

Greta snorted and tugged the bowl out of his hand. "Men are never bothered by filth."

"Oh, believe me, I am. But dirty dishes don't turn into filth for four days; five if you set the thermostat below sixty-eight."

She stopped, turned to give him a puzzled look, and laughed. Then she plugged the sink and ran the water.

The laugh was enough. Samuel could see arguing with her was pointless; Greta wouldn't give in once she'd made up her mind. Ever.

So he followed. "At least let me dry."

Afterward, she sat on the couch and he risked joining her, seating himself at the opposite end with plenty of space in between. They chatted a little more, avoiding eye contact.

Then she said, "I should go."

He glanced at the clock. It was nine on the dot. "I'm glad you came," he ventured.

"It was nice." She stood.

Samuel sat forward, hoping she couldn't hear his heart banging around in his rib cage. "Does that mean—we can do it again?"

Greta sat. She stared at the opposite wall, hands on her knees. Then she turned to him. "Exactly what do you mean by that, Mr. Cooke?"

He didn't have the guts to tell her she could use his first name. "I guess what I mean is—are you interested in . . ." Oh God, it sounded so final. So soon. "Pursuing a relationship? With, um, me?"

She studied the floor between her feet. The moment stretched, and Samuel had a terrifying suspicion she was trying not to laugh.

She looked up. "Mr. Cooke, do you know how old I am?"

He cleared his throat. "Older than me, but if you think I'm going to guess, you're wrong."

"I am forty-six."

"Oh." Wow. She really was in good shape. "I'm fine with it if you are." The age gap wasn't the first difference people would notice.

Greta took a deep breath and seemed on the verge of saying something more. She let the air out soundlessly and stood. "I can't give you an answer right now." She put a hand out. "But we can have dinner again. If that's what you want."

He looked at her hand. What, like this was some sort of business transaction? When he put his palm in hers, she hauled him upward. In the next moment, he was over the wheelchair and sitting down.

Samuel blinked. Had she just done that? Quickly he pulled his feet onto the rests and followed her to the door. He was missing something here. Aside from his physical therapists, not even his own mother had ever handled him so casually.

Why not just ask? He was more embarrassed about his disability than she was, if she'd even noticed it at all, which was starting to seem doubtful. "Hey, um—"

She turned, hand on the doorknob.

Oh, what the hell. "Do you have some sort of experience? With handicaps?"

She shrugged. "Kinesiology was my BS."

"I see." What the hell was kinesiology? The word was familiar, but its meaning danced just out of reach. Now he really felt like an idiot, as if he hadn't before.

"Good night, Mr. Cooke. Thank you for dinner."

"Good night." His voice felt thin and distant. From the doorway, he watched her stride to the curb, get in her car, and drive away.

SAMUEL EXPECTED TO be up all night while his mind dissected everything that had passed between them that evening. Instead, he passed out as soon as his head hit the pillow. He'd never have known, except that, ten minutes later, the phone jolted him out of a deep slumber.

He fumbled for the cordless receiver and started to speak when he realized it might be Greta, and his throat constricted into a wordless croak.

"Cooke?" It was Rashid. "Are you—"

Samuel cleared his throat. "Still alive." He felt hot and sweaty. His body must have gone into overdrive to digest the much-needed meal. "What's up? No, wait; let me guess. Trung is whining because he can't figure out my physics."

"Whining? He came into my office today—I swear to God, he was about to cry. I've started interviewing, but damn, your shoes are hard to fill. Do you mind if he e-mails you? No more than once a week."

Samuel had made it perfectly clear when he left that he was available for consultation. He could hardly justify part ownership otherwise. "This is why you called?"

Rashid harrumphed. "Thought you might hang up on me if I didn't have a pretense."

"You know me too well." Samuel stuffed a pillow under his shoulders and shifted onto his back. He hadn't imagined he'd miss anyone in L.A., but as he listened to the pleasantly rounded syllables come through the line, he realized there was one exception. "How's it going?"

"Me? I'm not the one who ditched his career for the crappiest job on earth."

"It's not . . . Okay, it's kind of horrific." He contemplated telling Rashid about Greta, then decided to keep quiet. Half of him didn't want to jinx it; the other half didn't want to earn Rashid's pity when it failed. "The lesson plans I was promised never showed up, the kids are jerks, and the equipment's crap, but I'm dealing."

"And you're all right? With classroom stuff?"

Samuel knew what Rashid was trying to ask. "No, I haven't been puking my brains out. Not that it would be any of your business if—"

"All right, all right. Sometimes I worry that you don't care enough about yourself." Rashid hesitated. "Did I just say that? Christ, you've turned me into my mother."

"Usually I only have that effect on women. Must be branching out." The phone made a polite beep. "What the hell? I just charged the damn thing—" It beeped again.

Rashid laughed. "Cooke, you're getting another call."

"I didn't even know I had that function." Probably paying extra for it, too. "Hold on, let me see if I can do this without hanging up." The portable phone did, in fact, have a hold button. "Uh . . . hello?"

"Bro! How's it going?"

Shit. It was October. The end of baseball season. "Hey, Chris. Hold on a sec, will you? I've got Rashid on the other line." He flipped back. "Rashid? Chris wants to spend the next hour giving me a play-by-play recap of the entire season." Like he did every single fall.

"God forbid I stand in the way of the great American pastime."

"I'd beg you to save me, but he'd just call back." Samuel sighed. "Take care."

"You, too. And Cooke? I thought you'd lost your mind when

you quit, but I was wrong. It takes serious guts to leave everything. Honestly, I didn't think you had it in you."

"Honestly? Neither did I."

SAMUEL CAME HOME on Tuesday afternoon to find Greg Moore sitting on his doorstep, one elbow draped over the computer tower at his side.

Samuel leaned out of the car. "Did it break again?"

Moore shook his head and held up a CD case. It was Photoshop. "Need help installing this."

Samuel gestured to the door. "It's open."

"You leave your door unlocked?" Moore got up and brushed off his pants before picking up the tower.

"My housekeeper does." Samuel followed Moore inside, narrowly missing a backpack and a pile of books by the door. "Maria?"

"Mr. Cooke!" She came out of the guest bedroom and hurried to the door. "Sorry, I forgot to put my stuff in the kitchen."

"No harm done." He put a hand out. "This is Greg Moore. I don't know if you had any classes with him when you were in high school, but . . ."

"No, I didn't." She started to attempt a handshake around her armload of textbooks, then realized Moore was similarly burdened and settled for a nod. "Nice to meet you."

Greg set the tower on the dining table. "I like your name. Do you want to clean my house?" He combed his hair away from his face.

"Ah . . ." Maria's eyes darted to Samuel for assistance.

"He has boundary issues. Greg, please try not to scare my housekeeper." Samuel sat at the dining table. "And go get my crap, you know where it is."

Maria pulled one of the chairs out from the breakfast bar and piled her things on top. "So? How did it go?"

Samuel shook his head minutely and attempted to say *later* with his eyes.

She grinned and busied herself straightening the kitchen counter. "Sorry again about leaving my stuff out," she said a little too loudly. "I know it's crazy, but if I left my textbooks in the car and someone broke in, my chances of getting into a nursing program—"

"Is nursing school hard to get into?" This came from Moore, returning with a box of cords. He set them next to the tower.

"The four-year programs, yes."

Samuel waved Moore toward the hall. "Monitor, too."

"You're not telling him?" Maria whispered as soon as they were alone.

"I can't. He's the local gossip. Now will you please—" Moore's steps sounded in the hall. "You know, if you need a quiet place to study, you're welcome to use the house while I'm not here."

"Are you sure?" Her eyes were bright. "I may take you up on that."

"Of course." He gave her his best *shut up or I will kill you later* look.

She smiled sweetly. "I'll go change the sheets." She disappeared into the back of the house, humming.

"What was that about?" Moore set the monitor down and took a seat at the table. "Is something going on between you two?"

Samuel laughed, relieved not to have to lie, and popped in the first CD. "Not a thing. Ask her if you don't believe me, but I'd appreciate it if you didn't creep her out any more than you already have."

Moore shrugged. "Just didn't want to miss anything interesting."

"By which you mean scandalous." Samuel was definitely not going to tell him about Greta.

Photoshop wasn't the simplest installation, but it was nothing Moore couldn't have handled on his own. Samuel leaned an elbow on the table. "You came over because you were bored, didn't you?"

"Is that bad?"

He imagined Moore materializing during his next dinner date, assuming there was one. "Greg, you're welcome to come over whenever. Just call first, okay? I'm not usually busy, but I'm not big on surprises."

"Sorry. I was busy at lunch today and I missed you, so I thought I'd stop by." The sentiment would have been sweet if it hadn't bordered on stalking.

"I wondered where you were." It had been the first time Moore *hadn't* shown up. Samuel clicked "yes" for the fiftieth time. "Here, input your name and address."

"Basketball tournament's coming up, this annual thing. Teams come from all over. Not only does the band have to play, my art classes have to do all the team banners for the gym. It'll eat my time until December, but it's fun."

Samuel took the keyboard back. "And your student came on Friday, right?"

Moore's face lit up. "Olivia. It was great. She's beautiful, funny, makes all the kids want to be her. Heck, I wanted to be her. She plays—amazing. Makes me feel like a total idiot, but in a good way."

"Sounds like you have a crush." Not that he'd know anything about that. At all.

Moore shook his head. "I'm just some old fart who used to be her teacher."

"Old? Greg, you're what, thirty?"

"Twenty-nine. She's twenty. Still a kid."

"Ah." That was a big difference. Although, come to think of it, not as big as thirty-four and forty-six. Ay. The install had completed, so he took out the last disc and put it in the case. Absently, he started deleting all the useless shortcuts on Moore's desktop.

"So what did you do this weekend? Read?" Moore glanced at the floor next to the armchair. "Hey, where'd they— Oh." He spotted the books on the shelf.

Samuel had prepared for this question. "The highlight was a long, annoying call from my little brother." He shut down the computer and started unplugging the tower.

"You have a brother?"

"A minor-league ballplayer, no less." Or more, as their father saw it.

That topic kept Moore busy until Samuel ushered him out the door. Alone, he sagged into the armchair, closed his eyes, and reached for a book. His fingers grasped air.

"I'll get it, Mr. Cooke."

He opened his eyes to see Maria emerging from the hall, a knowing smile spread across her face. She plucked one of Asimov's Foundation books from the end of the shelf and handed it to him. "So?"

Samuel covered his face with the dog-eared paperback, moaned, and let it drop. "There's not much to say. We ate, we talked, she left. I'm not sure what she thought, but she said we could do it again."

"This Friday?" Maria plopped down on the chair he usually used for his feet. "That gives us time to plan. What should we make?"

Samuel cleared his throat. "I appreciate the help, but I haven't even called her back."

Maria blinked and counted on her fingers. "Four days, Mr. Cooke? Are you joking? You can't leave a woman hanging like that. Even Ms. Cassamajor."

He put a palm up, blocking her laser glare. "Okay, okay, I'll call. Tonight."

Maria marched into the kitchen, long braid thumping against her back, and returned with the phone. She placed it firmly on the arm of the chair. "*Call.*"

Samuel sat staring at the receiver for a few minutes after she left.

He'd looked up Greta's number on Saturday morning, and the digits were etched across his brain. He turned the phone on, listened to the dial tone, and turned it off again.

His throat was dry.

He put down the receiver and breathed. This was ridiculous. One call was Not a Big Deal.

Unless the guy making the call hadn't entertained the thought of real-world romance in a decade. Friday night had been an impulse, riding on the high of his moderately successful debut at school. Now reality was sinking in: namely that he had no fucking clue what he was doing. Dinner hadn't gone well enough to overpower him with confidence, and he had been avoiding this call because he was terrified she would reject him. And doubly terrified she wouldn't.

If he did nothing, he'd lose her anyway. Before his brain had a chance to argue, he dialed. It rang twice.

"Hello?"

"Hi. It's me. Uh, Samuel." Oh God. He rested his forehead against the wing of the chair.

"Mr. Cooke," she said, making his name a greeting.

"I'm, uh, not interrupting anything, am I?"

"Why would you think that?"

"It's dinnertime? I thought— Well, never mind, I guess not."

She was silent.

Right; he had called, it was his responsibility to talk. He took a deep breath. "On Friday—night—you said it would be okay to have dinner?" He waited, but apparently she didn't think that warranted a response. "Is it still okay?"

Pause. "Yes."

"Good. How about Friday again?"

"Fine. My house."

"Really? Great! Um . . ." He didn't know what to say, and if he stayed on any longer, he was going to make an idiot of himself. "Um, see you then!" He hung up and pressed the phone to his chest, breathing carefully.

It rang. Samuel's heart leaped out of his throat and landed on the floor, flopping. Well, almost. "H-hello?"

"Thought you might want my address."

7

GRETA LIVED IN AN older subdivision in the hills on the north side of town, where the houses were spread out and the landscaping had been decades in the making. Though it wasn't far, Samuel gave himself half an hour just to be safe. Which meant he was twenty minutes early. The porch light wasn't even on.

He looked at the cellophane-wrapped bouquet sitting on the passenger seat and sighed. Four days he'd spent trying to think of something unique, but everything his Internet trawling had turned up was laughably saccharine. There were no top-ten gift lists for un-sentimental middle-aged women.

Still, he couldn't show up empty-handed, not after Greta had brought wine, so he'd wound up at the supermarket flower display. He'd settled for a collection of yellow carnations because red roses were definitely premature, and pink . . . pink wasn't Greta. At all.

The bouquet had cost him a whopping four bucks and change. At least with the first dinner, he'd been able to provide the food and setting. This, on the other hand, was just pathetic. Had his father been witness to this sorry little tableau of inadequacy, he would have enjoyed a good hearty laugh.

A light came on somewhere in Greta's house, dimly illuminating the drapes in the front room. Now or never, Mr. Cooke.

Although he had already groomed himself in detail, Samuel pulled down the visor mirror to double-check his hair and collar, pulling out his shirt to make sure he smelled decent. Then, before he could reconsider, he shoved the driver's-side door open, stuck the flowers on the roof, and hoisted himself out of the car. He managed a reasonably secure hold on the bouquet by gripping the stems along with a crutch handle.

He realized it wasn't going to happen when he reached the four steps up to her front porch. Not unless he wanted to crawl. He was trying to decide whether to drop the flowers in the bushes or take them back to the car when the porch light snapped on and Greta strode out. She took the bouquet in one hand and his arm in the other, and in a moment they were standing inside her front door.

He shrugged his shirtsleeves down. "The flowers," he said, a little out of breath. "For you."

Greta looked at the bouquet in her hand as if seeing it for the first time. "Oh," she said, and took it into the kitchen.

Samuel saw at once that his choice was all wrong. Greta didn't know what to do with flowers. She wasn't that kind of woman. She liked—

What *did* she like?

She had left him in the entryway, so he shuffled forward and peered into her living room on the right. What he found was sparse. Not at first glance; there were pictures on the wall, a few books on a shelf, and a coffee table. Knickknacks sat under the glow of an end-table lamp, and a plaid lap blanket had been draped over one arm of the couch, although it looked unused. The only thing that stood out was a row of trophies collecting dust on top of a bookshelf.

Somehow he knew none of it was hers. They were gifts or items purchased at the behest of whoever had taken her shopping once upon a time. Everything but the trophies existed as a polite acknowledgment of someone else's desires—he would have been willing to bet on it. And his flowers would temporarily be added to the collection.

He looked for something, anything personal, and found an arrangement of family portraits on the wall to his left. The most recent photographs were of Greta's sister and a few other people, maybe elderly aunts and uncles or grown cousins. A couple of older photos in the center might have been parents. As there were none more recent, he assumed them dead. There were no images of Greta at all.

"Coming?" She stood in the open doorway of the kitchen.

"Just looking. Your house is nice." It was bigger than his.

She shrugged and disappeared without comment, lending credence to his theory that she had no emotional attachment to the place.

Samuel started after her. "So how long have you— Oh, wow. Wow, that smells good." He'd half expected a meal from Greta to be hearty and robust; something traditional, like steak and potatoes. Either that or dry, bland foods with high nutritional content, which he'd be expected to eat whether he wanted to or not. The smells that overpowered his senses as he stepped into the kitchen proved both of his guesses wrong. He had no idea what it was—spices or sauces or oils—but his stomach responded with an eager rumble.

It was also immediately obvious that the kitchen was where Greta *lived*. The black granite countertops were immaculate, all of her pots were top-quality copper, and implements he didn't even have names for hung from a wrought-iron rack overhead.

She was standing next to the stove, a lid in one hand, looking at him expectantly.

He had started to say something. "Oh. How long have you lived here?"

She stirred something and put the lid back. "Depends on how you count."

"What do you mean?" Feeling awkward standing in the center of the kitchen, he glanced over one shoulder and found a breakfast table set with plates. And, to his chagrin, his carnations in the center.

Greta bustled around him and whipped out a wooden chair, indicating with a brusque gesture that he should sit.

He lowered himself onto the seat. "You, um, don't have to, uh . . ." He gestured lamely at the flowers.

She moved them to the counter. "My parents bought the house a few years before I went to college. After my father died, I came back to take care of my mother."

So it was her parents' place. That explained why the furnishings weren't entirely hers, but not the detachment. He watched as she got out an oval dish and began to lay down a bed of lemon-yellow rice. "Is that why you—"

"Took a job at my own high school?" She poured the contents of the copper pot on top of the rice, giving it a firm shake to make sure it had emptied completely. "Yes."

Actually, he'd been about to ask if that was why she was such an expert cook, but this was more interesting. He propped his crutches against an adjacent chair and dragged his legs under the table as inconspicuously as possible. "Not where you expected to end up, eh?"

She crossed the floor and dumped the dish in the middle of the table, adding emphasis to her "no."

He laughed. "High school was that bad?"

"Worst four years of my life."

Even three decades later? Yikes. Samuel could see how she might not have been part of the in crowd, but the way she bent over the oven, her face angled away, signaled something beyond social awkwardness. Whatever it was, it wasn't up for discussion. That was fine; he had plenty he didn't want to talk about, either. If they got serious, there were certain physical realities he needed to divulge, but there was no reason to expose himself now, before he was sure of passing muster.

Greta straightened, bearing two more dishes, and brought them to the table before returning to the fridge. While she had her back turned, Samuel leaned forward to examine the food. The first dish, the one on rice, looked like curry with some black lumps. He had no idea why the rice was yellow.

Greta set a tall glass of milk at his elbow. "Curried chicken with raisins and saffron rice."

Samuel drew back, embarrassed at having been caught, but she didn't seem offended.

She sat across from him and pointed to a bowl filled with green mush. "Lentils, carrots, and spinach with seasonings." Her finger moved to the final item, a bunch of golden cubes on a plate. "Fried tofu with cashews and chili sauce."

She hadn't given him a choice of beverage, but it soon became clear why: Greta didn't pull any punches when it came to spice. He made it about halfway through the meal before he needed a refill.

But it was good. So very, very good. Even the tofu. He told her so, then asked where she had learned to cook.

She shrugged. "It's a hobby. I also minored in nutrition."

He pretended outrage. "You're telling me it's healthy, too?"

She gave him a thin smile. "Aside from the chicken, this is a basic vegetarian meal. It accounts for everything you need. Except fruit, but that's dessert."

"I'm a convert. You should teach a class on this."

"Sometimes I do."

"Oh, that's right." Some of her lesson plans had addressed basic nutrition.

"Health focuses on human biology—food, exercise, and sex ed."

He grabbed his glass of milk and took a long drink, trying to clear the mental image of her putting a condom on a banana. "Interesting."

"I do a unit on cooking, but food like this is too mixed."

"That's the best part!"

She shook her head. "Toddlers prefer their foods separated, so they can identify what they're eating, and then gradually branch out as they mature. If all they're ever given is burgers and fries, they never venture beyond basics. Most teens would be reluctant to try any of this."

He laughed. "That would be tragic if it weren't so bizarre. But," he added, in case she didn't agree, "you probably take it more seriously."

She shrugged. "I'm not going to have a coronary at fifty."

"Cynical." He swallowed and smiled.

"Tell me what you think when you've been teaching for two decades."

Samuel didn't buy her indifference for a second. He hadn't known her for long, but one thing was obvious: she didn't put up with bullshit. If teaching held no value, she wouldn't be doing it. Unless it hadn't been long since . . . "When did your mom pass away? If you don't mind my asking."

"Seven years ago."

Plenty of time to find a new career. "And you're still—"

"I got used to it."

He grinned. "You like it." He used his fork to point at her. "You get involved with them, don't you? The students." She certainly wasn't in it for her coworkers.

Greta used a butter knife to push a bit of food onto her fork. Bulky and stern as she was, she ate with the comportment of a queen. "You try not to. It happens."

"I could never do your job. I mean gym, specifically."

"Being physically fit is not a requirement."

He resisted the impulse to point out that he *was* pretty fit, given his limitations. "I meant in terms of our students. Your class is like mine—the kids have to take it for . . ."

"Two years," she supplied.

"Right. Then they can keep taking it as an elective." Typing was a single-semester requirement. "So our classes are skewed toward the kids who choose to be there. I get the quiet kids trying to sneak by without being noticed. You get the aggressive jocks."

"True." She lifted her napkin from her lap to her lips briefly. "We teach the students who suit us. I wouldn't know how to motivate thirty uninterested teenagers. And you—" She stopped.

"With your kids?" Samuel laughed. "My own private hell."

Greta didn't laugh, but she didn't disagree, either.

"How do you get them to respect you? As a teacher, but a woman, too?" In other words, how had she learned to scare the shit out of people? Samuel wanted that superpower.

She pushed her empty plate to one side and leaned back, crossing her legs beneath the table. "You never let your guard down. Ever. If you show them any vulnerability, they'll exploit it."

So while Greg Moore simply ignored his students' bad behavior, Greta avoided giving them anything to work with in the first place. "You make it sound like war."

"PE is usually where gang activity emerges."

"Are you serious? In this little town?"

She finished off her milk. "They cut class—the idiots go in their gym clothes, don't ask me why—and go out to fight. Mostly fists, sometimes knives."

It had never occurred to Samuel that he might be teaching adolescents with weapons. It seemed so barbaric. "Should I be worried?"

"Probably. Attacks on typing instructors aren't unheard of."

Because she didn't smile, it took Samuel a moment to realize she was joking. He snorted. "Funny." Then he frowned. "You know I teach programming, too, right? I wouldn't have taken this job if—"

"I know." Apparently that had been part of the joke. "Third period."

"Wait, how did you know that?"

Samuel expected Greta to point out how small the school was, or to say Mrs. Phelps was a friend, but she hesitated. "Vince put out a memo a couple of days before you started."

"What, about me?"

She nodded once, and the thin line of her mouth told him he didn't want to know what it had said.

He shut his eyes. "Oh my God." She didn't need to elaborate; he could guess. Likely Irving had issued some helpful reminder about maintaining political correctness around the cripple, presented as an informational bulletin for good legal measure. No wonder everyone knew his name—he'd been walking around with a big neon sign plastered to his back. And here he'd thought it was small-town spirit.

"Vince only embarrassed himself," Greta insisted. "The man's incompetent. It will catch up with him eventually."

Samuel wanted to hack the man's PC, steal his identity, and drain his bank account, but she was right: the only thing retaliation would achieve was a lot of frustration. Irving was too stupid to understand how offensive his actions were, and even if Samuel went the legal route, the principal would be protected by the district.

He drew in a breath and let it out again. "Oh well." It happened. Life went on.

Greta stood, gathering their plates. "Not 'oh well.'"

He slid sideways on the wooden chair, tracking her as she went around him to the sink. "What, I'm supposed to hold a grudge until I die?"

She dumped an empty plate in the sink and got out a roll of plastic wrap for the rest of the chicken. "No. But you remember. You learn. And you don't trust him—or anyone like him—ever again."

Grim. As he watched her work over the sink, Samuel couldn't help thinking her advice came from some hard-learned lesson in her own life. Was this what high school had taught her? Irving was an ass, but Samuel wasn't going to assume the same for anyone who happened to share Irving's good-old-boy grin and penchant for asking invasive questions.

Okay, maybe Greta had a point.

"Hey," he said, turning to the half-empty table, "don't I get to do the dishes this time?"

"No. I'll bring dessert into the living room when I'm done."

Samuel knew better than to argue. He seated himself on the couch by the plaid blanket, smoothing it with one hand. It was scratchy. Wool. Not soft, but warm. Maybe Greta had picked out the blanket after all. It was certainly functional.

And that, he realized, was the kind of woman Greta was. She valued function. Efficiency. Utility. Color and shape and texture were irrelevant—all that mattered was that each piece of furniture fulfilled its purpose.

Which left him where? He fingered the handgrip on a crutch. Functional was the last word anyone would use to describe him. Then again, he managed with what he had. He was tidy. The only fetish he indulged was his paperbacks, and when he accumulated too many of those, he took them to a used bookstore and traded them in for another stack. That was efficient, right?

Or maybe the whole thing was ridiculous. What if she did happen to like him? She'd be better off with some muscle-bound jock who could run with her or spot her weight lifting or whatever she did to keep in shape.

But she'd been serious when she implied that it was up to her students whether to eat bad food. Maybe she did what she liked and left everyone else to their own devices.

Still, what did they have in common?

Greta interrupted his recursive loop of self-doubt by bringing in two bowls of peaches with real vanilla ice cream. Having already stuffed himself to the point of nausea, Samuel swallowed hard when she handed him a bowl. He didn't want to offend, so he shoveled a bite into his mouth.

Greta settled herself on the opposite end of the couch, toeing off her sneakers before stretching out her legs. "Make yourself comfortable."

Samuel looked at her feet, as blunt and squared off as the rest of her under white sports socks. Given that he couldn't feel a thing below his knees, it made little difference whether his shoes were on or off, but he didn't want to seem uptight. So he set the bowl aside, bent over, and slipped out of his loafers. He tugged down his pant legs, trying to be casual about it, but the cuffs didn't cover his braces. He felt exposed. Which was silly, so he pulled one knee up onto the couch, turning to face her.

"You shouldn't be embarrassed," she said.

His face grew warm. "Yeah, well, that's my problem." He felt he had been about to say something, but her comment robbed his brain of words. It was all right. She filled in.

"I told you last week I couldn't answer your question."

His stomach performed a sickening flip-flop. "Right." Her directness was refreshing, yes, but also terrifying.

"There are certain things I need to make clear."

He nodded and waited for her to continue, but she looked uncertain. "The question is definitely still on the table," he said. Yes, he wanted to be with her. Whether he was in his right mind was another question entirely.

"Do you believe in God?"

"Um . . . what?" Seriously? This kind of bluntness could go a long way toward explaining why, at her age, she was single. Twelve years' age difference, okay, but religion was moving a little fast. He laughed, and it sounded forced because it was. "Aren't we supposed to discover these kinds of things as we go along?"

She frowned.

Oh Jesus. He hadn't expected dating Greta to be so conditional. Perhaps he should have. She'd told him she didn't take these things lightly, and neither did he. Getting to know someone was difficult and risky. Maybe Greta wasn't interested in waiting while he tried to figure her out. Maybe she was putting her cards on the table now, so they'd both be clear about the deal-breakers from day one. No room for misunderstandings three months down the road.

Her face said this was a serious issue. Which meant he had to be honest. He cleared his throat. "My mother was Jewish. She converted in college, before I came along. She was pretty, uh, devoted." Fanatic. "We went to a Baptist church. I stopped going when I was fourteen. Never went back." Never wanted to. Ever.

"I'm not interested in your attendance record."

"Oh." What *was* she looking for? If this was a test, he was failing miserably.

"I want to know if you believe in the Judeo-Christian God."

He folded his hands around his foot. "Sure, I guess. I'm just not sure he believes in me." Samuel had the feeling she was studying him, weighing his words. This wasn't fun anymore.

"Meaning what?"

So. Here was where it ended. He closed his eyes and drew in a breath. Might as well get it over fast. "You know that verse about how God works for the good of those who love him?"

"Romans 8:28."

Shit. *Shit.* "Yeah. I think it's a load of crap." He waited for Greta to say something. To tell him sorry, this wasn't going to work out. There was only silence. He looked up.

"What if you're wrong?"

"What if I am?" If God had ever offered a helping hand, Samuel hadn't noticed, although the Alpha and Omega had been happy enough to cut him off at the knees.

Greta shifted and let out a short breath. "Mr. Cooke, I'm not interested in forcing you to believe something you don't. But I promised myself I would never involve myself with anyone who would not sit next to me on Sundays and keep an open mind."

Translation: church. She wanted him to go to church. The place his mother had been convinced would fix everything. The giant snake pit of people who loved to pity him, pray for his miraculous healing, and "assist" him with things he could do perfectly well himself.

Then again, Greta wasn't like that. At all. Her church might be different, too. Or maybe if he went with her, she'd tell everyone else to piss off.

Part of him wanted to say fuck it and let it end right here, before it started, before anyone got hurt. He didn't know what the other part wanted, or why, but it must have won, because he didn't move.

Greta was watching him.

He couldn't look her in the eye, so he focused on her feet. "I can't promise anything. Except to give it a try." It was honest. It probably wasn't enough.

It was. She nodded.

Samuel rubbed his forehead and sighed. He couldn't blame her; if you believed something, you believed it, that was all. And he'd been worried about whether they could work out together. Dating called for some bigger changes than he'd anticipated.

What had he expected, if not change? Being connected to someone else, another life, had to be radically different from singleness in every way. If a relationship wasn't about growth, it was little more than two people putting up with each other.

Samuel wanted more than that. At least he thought he might.

"Another thing." Greta folded her arms over her chest. "This is going to sound premature, but you need to know. I don't believe in sex outside of marriage."

Given the fact that he hadn't expected sex at all, Samuel could live with that. He started to agree, but she cut him off.

"And I'm not a virgin."

Samuel thought she was trying to tell him she was divorced. Then he saw her face. It was a source of shame for her. Now she was the one waiting for rejection. Suddenly it seemed silly. He laughed. "I certainly am. Do you care?"

"What?" She looked unpleasantly startled.

"Greta"—oh God, he'd used her name—"we're how old, here? I'd have to be crazy to expect a woman your age to have waited. I think it's pretty pathetic that I haven't—"

"I don't think it's pathetic," she snapped.

"Then we have a difference of opinion. It works out well enough, doesn't it?"

She said nothing.

Samuel wondered if he should apologize, but he couldn't think what for. So he waited, studying the bridge of her nose as she concentrated on her hands. Although her virginity was irrelevant to him, the admission had obviously cost her a lot to make. If so, why had she confessed? Was she testing to see if he would run? Well, he was better than that. And he certainly had his share of revelations—

Ah, crap. All he wanted to do was call it a night, go home, and bury his head under a pillow until his alarm rang. But now that she'd trusted him enough to come clean about her own personal demons, holding out was going to make him look like a total douche. And if he didn't spill his guts now, he would spend every date after this worrying about finding the right opportunity to confess. And the right moment would never come, because there was no right moment to say something like this, and then inevitably he'd have an accident, and wouldn't that be a delightful way to break the news?

Suck it up, Samuel. Better to know if it's a problem here and now.

He sighed and cleared his throat. "While we're at it, there's something you should know, too."

Greta looked up, which didn't help, because then he got nervous.

It was going to be excruciating if he didn't make it quick. He drew in a breath and let it out. "I'm sure I don't have to explain this to you in detail, but basically—well, I wear a catheter."

There it was.

Samuel's most persistent insecurities told him he should be humiliated. He was surprised to find himself only mildly embarrassed. The bag had been a fact of his life for so long that he could no longer summon the appropriate response.

And when he looked for the flicker of disgust in Greta's face, he found blank indifference.

"So?" she said.

Samuel frowned. *So?* Though he hadn't wanted her to recoil in horror, he'd expected some kind of reaction. Obviously she didn't understand how it was supposed to go. "Frankly," he said, leaning on the sarcasm, "some people would find it a little revolting to know I walk around with a bag of urine strapped to my leg." Himself included. More than anything else, he hated the smell.

"Urination is necessary," she countered brusquely. "There's nothing you can do about that."

Of course. So there was a problem with his plumbing. The catheter fixed it, and life went on. Easy for her to say.

No. What the hell was wrong with him? Did he want her to find him repulsive? Or was that how he felt about himself? He had no right to argue if all she said was "so." For all he knew, she did think it was disgusting. Maybe, in spite of that, she didn't care.

Still, her indifference was hard to swallow.

"You really don't care?"

"How else would you like me to put it, Mr. Cooke?"

"Oh— No, I get it." Right. She meant what she said. "Well. Now that we've had that happy conversation . . ."

"It needed to be said."

"I know." No casual dating for rejects and cripples. Half an hour ago they'd been little more than acquaintances. Now they knew things about each other that, if publicized, could cause a lot of pain. Oddly, that didn't frighten him. Perhaps the potential to inflict pain was also the foundation of trust.

Greta got up and took the dessert bowls to the kitchen.

Samuel bent to put his shoes on and nearly deposited his dinner on the floor. He straightened and swallowed, hard. "I don't think I've ever eaten so much in my life."

Greta returned. "I was wondering when it would hit." She handed a small glass over the back of the couch.

"What's this?" It was fizzing.

"Drink."

He obeyed. It tasted something like Alka-Seltzer and grenadine. It settled his stomach, and he felt instantly better. "Thanks." He handed back the empty glass, and she disappeared again. When she returned, he rose to meet her. "Thanks for dinner. It's been . . . interesting."

She nodded, and he followed her to the door. The steps were still there, but he got down without falling. Then he turned around.

What he wanted to do was kiss her good night. Nothing scandalous, just a kiss. Possibly not even on the lips. He just wanted her to know he cared.

It wasn't going to happen. Not unless he managed to grow a foot in the next thirty seconds. She was up there, he was down here, and the whole thing would be ruined if he asked her to bend over. He didn't think she was going to take her cue from the puppy-dog longing in his eyes, either.

"Thank you for coming, Mr. Cooke."

"My pleasure." He hesitated. "You can call me Samuel, you know."

"I'll keep that in mind."

8

SUNDAY FOUND SAMUEL WIDE awake at five in the morning. They hadn't made plans for church, so he didn't know when to expect Greta, if at all. He bathed and put on his best suit and waited on the couch with sweaty palms. At eight he started to wonder if he should call. If church was at, say, ten, he didn't want to wake her up. He decided a ring was reasonable at nine, but she didn't pick up. Asleep, maybe, or in the shower. At ten he called again, with the same result. If she had been asleep or in the shower the first time, it was possible she was coming to get him right now.

At eleven he convinced himself she wasn't coming. He didn't know whether to feel relieved or despairing.

MONDAY MORNING WAS a welcome distraction—until Fernando got up and walked out.

"Excuse me," Samuel said. "Might I ask where you're going?"

Fernando turned in the doorway, shrugging to make his baggy

white T-shirt fall *just so*. "Yo, man, I'm goin' to the bathroom. This room smells like *piss*. You got a problem with that?"

"By all means, relieve yourself." Samuel waved a hand and continued his lecture on résumés, ignoring the second interruption when Fernando returned.

When the bell rang for break, Samuel rushed to the staff bathroom, locked the door, and stripped.

No leak, no detectable odor. Nothing.

He sat on the toilet with his head in his hands, breathing.

When the urge to vomit passed, he reached for the pants crumpled around his ankles and pulled them up to his knees. "Fuck," he whispered, and forced himself to look at the bag strapped to his thigh. It was warm, just starting to fill. He used the right leg because it was stronger, with a thin, intermittent line of sensation down the inside of his calf, and sometimes he could feel when there was a leak. He had nightmares where that line disappeared permanently.

There. Was that enough masochistic introspection? Could he get dressed, go back to pretending this didn't exist, and get on with his day?

Samuel tugged his pants over his thighs and leaned to one side to slip the belt under his rear. He switched sides, zipped his fly, and reached for his crutches.

Ignoring this—everything—was how he survived. If he couldn't do that, he didn't know what he had. If anything. "This isn't going to work," he said aloud. "Is it."

SAMUEL'S PULSE QUICKENED when lunchtime brought a knock at his door. Moore stepped in.

"Oh," said Samuel.

"Well, hello to you, too." Moore whipped a seat around and assumed his usual squatting position.

"Sorry." Samuel flipped through the papers he'd collected in programming, their first big project. "Having an off day." More like an insecure meltdown.

Moore plucked a paper clip off the desk and began to unbend it, raising his eyebrows in question.

"The little prick in my second period. You were right. He found another way to get on my nerves. Walked out for fifteen minutes today—said he had to use the bathroom." Samuel flipped through the projects a second time, frowning. Something felt familiar. He pulled out Marcus's and Sadie's papers and positioned them side by side. "Damn."

"What?" Moore got up and came around the desk. "Wow, what is this?" He picked up a page and squinted at the code.

"Just a basic algorithm. Tic-tac-toe. And these two look identical."

"Uh-oh. Fail!"

Samuel shook his head. "I didn't say they couldn't work together. I just didn't expect these two to cooperate, and I wouldn't be surprised if she did most of it." He sighed. "I honestly didn't think . . ."

"They'd cheat?" Moore laughed. "Didn't you go to high school?"

Barely. Samuel put his head on the desk. Greta, Fernando, Sadie, Marcus, even Irving. He couldn't deal with this right now. He wanted to go home.

Moore cleared his throat and shifted from one foot to the other. "I'll, uh, see you later?"

"No, no, please. I'm sorry." Samuel straightened and rubbed his face. "Greg, does my room smell?"

Moore sniffed thoughtfully. "Mm, stale rain and . . . your cologne. No offense, it's nice and all . . ." His eyebrows drew together. "What's going on?"

"Nothing." Samuel sighed and waved him back to the plastic seat. "You looked like you had something on your mind."

Moore climbed onto the chair, grinning. "Olivia called. She said she had a good time the other day, and she wondered if we could hang out."

"Olivia. Your former student? The one you told me was an immature kid?"

"We're going out on Friday. I made reservations at—"

"Greg. Are you not hearing yourself? She's your *student*. A decade younger than you."

Moore scuffed the sole of his shoe against a bubblegum stain on the floor. "Yeah, I guess you're kinda right. I can't call it off, though, I—"

"Greg, I'm not telling you to cancel. Just be careful. Don't get carried away." Samuel was such a hypocrite.

SAMUEL WATCHED HIS sixth-period students file out of the room. Then he sat watching the second hand tick around the clock. Tennis shoes squeaked and voices called out in the hall. He closed his eyes.

How could she *not care*?

Obsessing was pointless. Samuel shoved his chair back and rubbed his thighs to get the blood moving. Then he slipped his backpack on, locked up, and headed for the gym.

He stopped inside the door, noting the pair of banners that had gone up over the stands, no doubt the product of Moore's art classes. It took Greta a minute to notice him, but when she did, she strode across the floor, shouting over one shoulder for the girls to continue their layups.

"What's wrong?" she demanded, as if his appearance were equivalent to yelling *"Fire!"*

"Nothing. I just wanted to—to see you." Samuel hadn't even invented a reasonable pretense. Could she tell he was falling apart? Like, completely?

"I have practice for another hour."

Apparently not. "I know. I'll watch. Is that okay?"

She led him to the stands and held his backpack while he sat. "Correct papers or something. Otherwise the kids'll think you're perverted." She walked away.

As if they didn't already. Samuel slid to the end of the bench and turned sideways, leaning against the wall as he worked. Keyboarding focused more on form and function than content, although decent grammar was always a plus, so it wasn't difficult to divide his attention between his papers and the court.

Greta ran the girls ragged, suffering no excuses or complaints. The young women (there were nine) started with one-on-one drills and built up, adding two players each round until they were staging a complete five-on-five, with Greta stepping in as the missing guard. She wasn't fast on her feet and didn't go out of her way to impress them, but to Samuel's untrained eyes, she looked like she knew what she was doing.

"Well, hello," an all-too-familiar voice said from behind. "Didn't expect to find you here."

Samuel experienced the sick, sinking feeling of a child caught shoplifting. He looked up to find Irving looming over him, hands on hips as he surveyed the court.

"Uh, hi." Samuel's first impulse was to run a crutch through the man's gut, but protecting his relationship with Greta was more important than retribution. For the moment. So he fought the rush of fury, mind racing to invent some halfway coherent explanation for his presence. Okay, *any* explanation. "I'm just . . ." He tried not to look at Greta, but his eyes betrayed him. This was going to be a disaster.

Greta, turning to pass the ball, caught sight of Irving. She stopped midstride and pointed to a spot over the principal's shoulder. "Vince, this is the last time I'm going to say it. Set foot in this gymnasium while we're practicing, and you can find a new coach."

Irving patted the air with his hands, looking bemused. "Now, Greta, I do have some authority here—"

She didn't move. "Want to test my tenure? Let's take this to the school board."

He lifted his palms in surrender. "All right, I'm going. I don't see why I can't watch, but if you say so . . ." His voice faded as he wandered out the door.

Samuel breathed a sigh of relief. On the court, the girls traded glances and silent giggles.

Greta turned on them. "Get back to it," she barked, and they did.

Samuel dared not stare now, but he returned his attention to grading with an inward smile. Though the animosity between her and Irving was apparently long-standing, Greta had been particularly vehement just then. Part of him wanted it to have been for his sake; either way, the look on Irving's face had been pleasure enough.

When Greta called an end to practice, the girls grabbed their water bottles and warm-ups and headed for the locker room. Greta crossed the gym and waited while Samuel put his papers away, shouldered his backpack, and got up. They started for the door.

She held it open and followed him through. "You can't do this every day."

"No, of course not. I just wanted"—needed—"to come today." Simply standing next to her was enough to calm him down. She didn't hate him. She had meant what she'd said. Probably. "Thanks for telling Irving off, by the way."

She frowned. "That had nothing to do with you."

"I know. But it was fun to watch."

She let out a short "hm" that was almost a chuckle. "Try it some-time."

He raised an eyebrow, considering. "No," he decided. "He gets plenty from you, and I'm pretty good at living vicariously."

Greta did laugh that time.

He nodded toward his car, and they angled that way. "Why do you hate him so much?"

Her answer was matter-of-fact, as if she didn't object to supply-ing the information but would rather not discuss it at all. "He taught until a few years ago. He was careless. Crass. Still is, if you let him talk. He wants so badly to be a buddy to these adolescent boys, he's forgotten how to set an example. He behaves like one of them."

"You really think he would—"

"He'd never do anything obviously inappropriate." Her voice was heavy with contempt. "But his misogynist attitude and sexist jokes make young men think it's acceptable for them to do what he wouldn't."

"I see." Kind of.

"It's good for the girls to see me stand up to him. Too often they think they have to give in."

"You're a good role model."

She shrugged off his appraisal. "It would be better if I were more appealing."

Samuel stopped to catch his breath but also to look at her in amazement. Greta wasn't beautiful, yet her sole desire for worldly charm stemmed from a wish to set a good example. "*I* think you're appealing," he said.

Her eyes narrowed. "That's beside the point."

Samuel started forward again, feeling himself go warm. She didn't want flattery; she wanted to be taken seriously. "You're right. Teachers do have a big influence. I guess I should be more careful."

They came to his car, and Greta leaned a hand on the trunk as he fished the keys out of his pocket. "I wouldn't worry about it," she said. "Your jokes may be stupid, but they're not offensive. Or so I hear."

In the process of getting his keys into the door, Samuel's brain didn't register her words for a moment. "Hey!" he objected belatedly, casting an accusatory glance over one shoulder. "You're supposed to be nice to me."

She stepped around him and held the door as he got into the driver's seat. "Why?"

Samuel looked up, feet dangling over the pavement. "Well, because—" He hesitated, too embarrassed and uncertain to say the words on the tip of his tongue. "Because—"

Greta took his crutches and slid them behind the seat. "Come over tonight. We'll eat."

Her invitation surprised him, but he was ready with a reply: "Why don't we go out this time? I'll pick you up, seven o'clock."

Greta nodded once, waited for him to get his legs inside, and slammed the door. He watched her walk back to the gym, then backed out of the parking spot and headed for the street.

"Because," he whispered. "You're my girlfriend."

THE SENSIBLE THING to do, when he parked at the bottom of her driveway, was honk. Sometime in his college days, he'd overheard a girl declare, "If a guy can't be bothered to come to the door, as far as I'm concerned, he's not there." Samuel didn't know why the sentiment had stayed with him, but there it was. So he got out of the car and started slowly up the drive. Greta appeared before he reached the steps, a light jacket slung over one arm.

Samuel turned around and walked back to the car.

She got in on the passenger side. "Honk next time."

Despite his best efforts to the contrary, Samuel's brain had spent the afternoon constructing an elaborate fantasy that involved saun-tering down the street by Greta's side, watching complete strangers do double takes as they wondered what the hell he was doing with her. Or, conversely, what she was doing with him.

If he'd had any hopes of living out this fantasy, she let him down, or at least Healdsburg did. Since he had little dining experi-ence in town (he'd gotten takeout from Denny's, but he'd bite off his own tongue before suggesting that), he left it up to Greta. She directed him to a street branching off the square—and there was, honest to God, an actual town square—but on a Monday night, it was deserted. He had no choice but to pull up right in front of the hole-in-the-wall Chinese place. Even if he could justify parking in the handicapped spot down the street, nobody was there to witness their perambulation.

It didn't matter. He was content to be with her. In public. Oddly, going out with Greta felt more intimate than an evening at home.

Seeing the buffet killed his buzz. Okay, there had to be a way to manage this so she didn't end up carrying his plate. Could he get away with saying he wasn't hungry? Not without passing out half-way through the meal; he was famished.

Samuel was still trying to work it out when their hugely preg-nant waitress seated them. He couldn't help thinking it would be a lot easier if he'd actually eaten in a restaurant any time in the past decade. Damned drive-through.

Greta reached for a menu, propped between the soy sauce and salt-and-pepper shakers. "Let's order a couple of dishes. The buffet looks like it's been out for hours."

Samuel wanted to kiss her feet. "That sounds great."

They decided on chow mein, a vegetable dish, and Mongolian beef. When the waitress returned, Samuel glanced at Greta, wonder-ing whether she'd be offended if he took the initiative. She looked back, inscrutable.

Samuel ordered.

The waitress retreated, waddling ponderously, and Samuel relaxed. Greta didn't seem to have a problem with silence, but it made him feel weird, so he'd prepared a few questions in advance. "How are your sister and her husband doing?"

"Fine."

"They live in San Francisco?"

She shook her head. "Vallejo. My sister always wanted to get married at the Palace of Fine Arts. When we were young, my father would take us to the Exploratorium, and afterward we'd have lunch on the grass by the lake."

"You grew up there, then."

"For the most part. We moved here when I was thirteen."

She didn't sound very happy about it. "I suppose it was hard to make the transition?"

"For me, yes. I was . . . willful."

Samuel grinned. "Why doesn't that surprise me?" He was teasing, but Greta didn't smile. She straightened her silverware with the same concentrated, introspective focus she'd had when she'd spoken about her virginity, or lack thereof. There were a hundred questions Samuel wanted to ask about Greta's past, but everything in her posture and attitude bristled *Don't go there.*

Fortunately he had another question left in his mental pocket. "What would you recommend seeing in San Francisco?" As if he'd ever venture there on his own. But the question steered the conversation toward safer waters. Then the food came, and they dissected each dish. Greta had a talent for guessing ingredients.

Still, Samuel craved more information. He didn't want to upset her by prying in the wrong places, but he had no idea where the boundaries lay, and she obviously wasn't going to volunteer any information. She was either too polite or too indifferent to ask about his background. The only solution he could see was to start talking about himself and hope she decided to reciprocate.

"I come from Long Beach originally," he announced.

Greta didn't look particularly interested. She didn't look *dis*interested, either.

"My dad was an electrician. Mom had a degree in literature, but she stayed home with us, me and my annoying brother, Chris." Ah, there was a safe topic. "He's five years younger than me. We moved into Orange County when he was born. He plays minor-league baseball, by the way. The Inland Empire 66ers. You've probably never heard of them, but—"

"I have."

"Really?" Now, there was a first. If she was some kind of fanatic, he was going to shoot himself. And if, God forbid, she knew who Chris was, something more self-flagellating might be necessary.

"I used to coach softball. Baseball isn't my favorite sport, but I kept track of teams."

Whew. Samuel and his self-respect would live another day. "My whole family is obsessed with baseball. Well, the obsession is my old man's. For the rest of us, it was more like 'resistance is futile.' I'm not just talking about going to games or wearing team colors. Dad played when he was younger, never made it to the majors, but he was convinced it was some sort of family destiny. Believe it or not, he lied about my age to get me into Little League when I was four."

Greta's left eyebrow went up.

"I know, pretty sad, right? I learned how to play baseball before I could—" Oh, fuck. That wasn't what she'd been about to ask. Most people assumed he was the product of a birth defect, which was almost always the case with spina bifida. Most of the time that was what he let people believe. It was easier. Maybe he could slide over it. "So, yeah, my family, obsessed. Mom passed away when I was seventeen, and the old man's still living the dream through Chris." He glanced up. "What was your family like?"

Greta didn't meet his eyes. "Average. My father worked in construction, my mother was a nurse." She moved some chow mein around her plate.

Hell. She knew he was hiding something, so she was clamming up. "Baseball was . . ." Samuel took a deep breath. "My old man's passion, not mine. But you know how those things are. It was all I knew how to be. I was about twelve before it stopped being fun. I was good, but it wasn't in my blood. I liked math, science, computers. So I try to tell Dad. He blows up, completely, like I've betrayed him and I'm a horrible son. Mom, pacifist that she was, hustles me off and tells me to pray. So I ask God to get me out of this somehow.

"Six months later, midseason, I start tripping over my own feet. Wetting the bed at night. Feels like someone is ripping my spine out. Mom wants to get me to a doctor, Dad gets drunk and insists I'm faking. Beats the crap out of me. Mom patches me up, but she waits until the bruises are gone to smuggle me to the hospital. Next thing I know, they're saying my spinal cord is tethered because I have a 'mild' case of undiagnosed spina bifida, and they have to operate to cut it loose. Too bad I didn't get help sooner, they say, because they can't reverse the damage that's already been done."

Just thinking of it brought the smell of the recovery ward to his nostrils. Some charitable nurse had smuggled an early Macintosh in on a crash cart—his only respite from utter boredom and the burgeoning frustration of immobility. His father, visiting, had taken one look at him over the computer, frowned, and said, "Guess you got what you wanted."

Chris, only seven, had been waiting with his hat and glove in the hall.

Samuel's hand hurt. He looked down and saw he had a death grip on the butter knife. He let go and forced himself to breathe. "Sorry."

She must think he was a complete mess. At least he'd stopped there, halfway through the wretched story. Now he was afraid to look at her—afraid he'd find pity in her eyes. Why hadn't he been more careful? He wanted her to see him as a man, not some pathetic puppy. He rubbed his eyes. "Please," he mumbled, "pretend I didn't say all that."

The waitress came by, and in his peripheral vision, Samuel saw Greta stiffen as the woman paused to top off her water. He lifted his head. Had she heard anything he'd said?

Greta picked up the glass and set it down a moment later, an inch emptier than it had been. "Are you coming to church this Sunday?"

He blinked. What, like that would fix everything? Pray to God and it'll be all right? Just like his mother. That was nice in theory, but it didn't do much for the daily humiliations that composed his life.

"Mr. Cooke?"

He couldn't believe he'd thought that. Though his life was a challenge, it wasn't humiliating. No. He was happy with who he was, what he did. He appreciated the truly important things in a way most people never could. If he had to choose between his life and what might have been, he chose to be here. Now.

He was also completely full of shit.

Okay, calm down. Greta was definitely not his mother. Maybe he should stop freaking out and reserve his judgments until he had something to judge.

"Yeah," he said. "I'll come."

Greta bristled. "If you don't want to—"

She thought he was going back on his word. "Look, it's not about . . ." Was he really going to admit this? No. It was stupid. But he was. "Okay. Until I took this job, my entire adult life existed at work or online. This—" He swept a hand over the restaurant, hesitated, and then allowed his fingers to include her. "This is new. And it's not as simple as I thought it would be."

Greta looked at a spot somewhere over his shoulder, and then at her mostly empty plate. She seemed to be searching for words, but all that came out was a distant "I see."

GRETA SHOWED UP at ten on Sunday, wearing much the same outfit she had on their dates. Samuel looked at his suit. "Am I overdressed?"

"Yes."

He sat and removed his jacket and tie.

"Better."

He dreaded finding a white chapel with a flight of steps up the front, but Greta's church looked more like a multipurpose building. At the doors, which were ground-level, they were greeted by a bouncy woman in a floral-print dress. She exclaimed, "Good morning!" and gave Greta a hug, which was returned stiffly.

"This is Samuel Cooke," Greta said, stepping back to include him. "He—"

"So you're Samuel! We're so glad you could come. My name is Karen. I won't keep you, but do stay afterward! We have cookies and coffee."

"Um, thanks." Samuel wanted to turn and flee; instead he followed Greta into the sanctuary. The woman knew his name. She hadn't spotted him instantly, which meant Greta hadn't described him, but he was clearly on the radar. Who was this Karen? Did everyone here know Greta was attempting to win him back to the flock? He felt cornered and moderately duped. If Greta valued him only as a potential convert, he wanted out. Right now.

They sat at the end of the fifth row. "Is, uh, Karen your friend?"

Greta flipped through the bulletin. "She's in my Bible study. I mentioned you'd be coming."

"Oh." That was normal. Samuel rubbed his sweaty palms on his pants and told himself to relax. There was a hymnal tucked into the back of the pew in front of them, so he took it out and wandered through the pages until the service started.

It turned out Greta was Episcopalian. Everyone stood in straight lines, greeted with handshakes, and stood up at appropriate intervals (as indicated in the bulletin). The median age was somewhere around sixty. All of which was fine with Samuel. Not everyone shared his mother's lust for chaotic fervor.

Greta's more orderly, conservative approach suited her strict, no-nonsense personality, giving structure to proceedings she might otherwise have scorned as overly emotional. He wondered why she hadn't chosen Judaism, with its law-based orthodoxy. Christianity might share a similar set of mores, but in the end Jesus forgave anyone who asked. Samuel wasn't sure Greta would approve of that.

Father Hayes, a kindly-looking man with a wavering tenor, taught on confession: when it should be public, with a concerned party, or between the individual and God. About five minutes into the sermon, Greta pulled a slim leather Bible out of her purse and opened it but did not offer to share. Samuel didn't mind; piecing the references together kept him just on the sane side of utter boredom.

Around what he hoped was the middle of the sermon, Samuel glanced at Greta and realized she had moved. What had started out as a few inches between them was now a gaping two feet.

His first panicked thought was that he smelled. A hand run quickly under his thigh revealed no dampness, and when he leaned forward under the guise of tucking the hymnal into its spot, he smelled nothing. His fly was zipped, his shirt tucked in, his hair too short to ever qualify as out of place. He tried to catch her eye, hoping for a clue, but she kept her focus trained squarely on her Bible.

Samuel spent the rest of the service trying to figure out what he had done, to no avail. When the doxology ended, he expected some sort of confrontation, but Greta stuck her Bible into her purse, stretched, and looked at him with her usual frank appraisal. Maybe he was imagining things.

They slipped under Karen's radar on the way out, steering away from the snack table by silent mutual consent. In the parking lot, when Greta moved to help him into her car, Samuel waved her away. He'd finally figured out how to mount the big machine.

With the door closed, Greta turned the heater up and waited for the windshield to defog.

"Well." He cleared his throat. "I could tolerate that once a week." He smiled hesitantly. "I, uh, hope you aren't expecting me to have some sort of revelation, because—"

"I'm not."

He loved her bluntness, her refusal to be anything other than straightforward. It was more refreshing than a thousand cups of coffee from smarmy Karen. "There should be more Christians like you."

Greta reached out and turned up the defroster. The condensation on the windshield began to clear, a hazy radius expanding from the dash. She said nothing.

Samuel felt he had said something wrong. The silence was taut. He searched for something innocuous. "Were you always Episcopal?"

"I wasn't always Christian."

Greta: undisputed master of the conversation killer.

She put the Suburban in reverse and backed out of the parking space, performing a perfect three-point turn before heading out of the lot.

Samuel couldn't tell if she was trying to avoid an uncomfortable subject or stalling conversation altogether. "Want to get some lunch?" There. That would—

"I'm busy."

"Oh." He swallowed. He'd done something. Definitely, definitely done something. The church wasn't far from his house, and she was already turning down his street. He tried to think fast. "If I said something—"

"You didn't do anything." Greta pulled to a stop at the end of his driveway. "I'm just busy."

He opened the door, wincing at the blast of chill air, and hesitated. "Dinner?"

"Friday."

"I was thinking . . . Could we do it on Wednesday or Thursday?"

"Why?" She seemed impatient. She wanted him out of the car.

"I thought if we go to church on Sunday, and have dinner on Friday, that's like a week before we do something again. If we eat midweek, that's only three or four days." He felt a little childish, but his mind couldn't tolerate six days of separation. It started picking everything apart.

"Fine. Thursdays." She pulled away as soon as he got out of the car.

Samuel stood on the empty sidewalk for a long time. On a cold September Sunday, the street was deserted. He felt desperate and small.

He looked at the phone lines overhead, sagging between poles.

"Look. I know you don't make deals. So I'm not promising anything. But I'm telling you—I'm just letting you know—I want her. You probably don't care; you never cared before, but there it is. I want her. That's a request. I'm asking. Okay?"

He hadn't expected a flash of lightning or a booming voice. Which was good, because he didn't get one. Nothing dropped out of the sky, no ominous raven flew overhead. Nothing.

Samuel went inside.

9

O N MONDAY, SAMUEL SKIMMED the daily bulletin and discovered an announcement for a lunchtime rally, supposedly to kick off the basketball tournament. "Lunchtime" being loosely defined as third and fourth periods.

"What is this?" he asked his programming class as they waited for the entire ten minutes' worth of class to expire. "What exactly do you do for an hour and a half?" He had spent Sunday afternoon picking over their projects, designing a lesson to address some of the more egregious logical flaws. Only to be preempted by organized, school-sanctioned mass hysteria.

"Watch people do stupid things for applause," Marcus supplied.

Sadie, always the gentle pragmatist, added, "Technically it's only an hour. They give us an extra half hour for lunch."

"McDonald's!" Nick crowed. Travis gave him a high five.

Samuel looked between them. "What does that mean?"

"We have time to go off campus for lunch!"

And they chose McDonald's. Samuel sighed, glanced at the clock, and waved the offending bulletin. "Okay, guys, get out of here."

Nick and Travis bolted. "You're not coming?" Lemos asked.

Drag himself halfway across campus to sit on a hard bench for an hour? "I think you guys can take care of yourselves. Just don't kill anyone, okay?"

Lemos shrugged and started for the door, followed by Marcus and Sadie.

Samuel saw his chance. Though he didn't relish the task, the next window of opportunity might be far more awkward. "Sadie."

She stopped by his desk. Samuel folded the bulletin in half and then in half again, giving the boys time to get out of range. Then he looked into the girl's pale blue eyes. They were beautiful, and someday when she filled out and got rid of her acne, she'd be beautiful, too, in a kind of warm, busty way. She gave him a questioning look.

"Sadie, I wanted to talk to you. About the project." He had already handed it back, so she knew he'd given her a B+. "I couldn't help noticing yours and Marcus's were very similar."

She was immediately on the defensive. "You didn't say we couldn't work together."

He put up a hand. "I know. If it were an issue, he'd be standing here next to you." He waited, and she relaxed. "I just wanted to make sure he was pulling his weight."

Her eyes widened. "He is!"

The lady doth protest too much. At Samuel's request, the librarian had introduced him to the school's online record system. Marcus stood at the top of his class, with Sadie not far behind. "Good," Samuel said carefully. "I was worried he might be . . . using you. To boost his grades."

And then Sadie got angry. She *blazed*. "What, because the only possible reason he'd want to hang out with me is so I'd do his work? Because I'm not good enough for him?"

Samuel realized he had tapped a frustration that had been growing for a long time. He let her stand there and breathe for a minute. "No," he said quietly. "Because you're too good. You know Marcus better than I do, but what I see is a guy who stumbles into class hung over, does no more than he needs to get his A, and takes half of his courses at the JC so he can get the extra grade points. He's not interested in learning. He wants to be valedictorian, and he'll cut whatever corners he needs to get there. I'm just wondering why you would want to give him that when you could have it yourself."

Sadie's lips trembled. She blinked, and tears spilled over her plump cheeks.

Oh God, no, no, *no*! "Sadie—"

Her face crumpled. "I don't care, I don't care!"

He wanted to put his arms around her and hug her like the brokenhearted child she was, but he was pretty sure that would get him fired. She just stood there, sobbing. He didn't know what to do except go on. "I— Maybe it doesn't make a difference, but does he care about you?"

"Yes!" She hiccupped. "He—he has to!" Her hands clenched into small, hard fists. "You don't understand. What it's like. To be me. He's the only—the only—"

Samuel rummaged through the desk drawers. There had to be something. There. He pulled out a roll of rough paper towel and tore off ten inches. She took it and blew her nose noisily.

How could he explain that, in another year, this would all be over? That if she hung on, put in her time and her applications, she'd find herself in a world swarming with possibilities she'd never even dreamed of?

He couldn't. She couldn't see that far from where she stood.

He sighed. "Sadie, I'm not telling you to stop hanging out with him. But listen to me. Stop helping him, and see if he doesn't change his tune." He closed his eyes. "And in the meantime, please, *please* don't have sex with him."

"Yeah," she said miserably, her voice muffled by snot and tears, "like he'd ever sleep with *me*."

Samuel raised an eyebrow. "You'd be surprised."

THE RHYTHMIC *THUMPA-THUMPA-THUMP* of blaring techno followed him into the library storage room. Wary of the shuddering walls, he sidelined his delicate dissection of the digital projector and began to sort through the detritus lining the far wall. Even after a month's work, he had only made it about halfway through the room.

By the time the music stopped, he'd found a few interesting tidbits, so he kept digging.

When a throat cleared in the doorway, Samuel spun on the swiveling office chair, putting a hand out to stop himself before he went all the way around. It was Irving.

"You've got quite the little workshop here," he observed, smiling genially.

Samuel might have found such scrutiny unnerving a week or two past; now all he could see were the man's blocky fingers slowly pecking out a *memo*. He wanted to knock Irving's head off his shoulders. "Minuscule," he agreed. "Not to mention the garbage I have to work with. Most of it was shit even when it was new." Maybe he couldn't hit the man, but he could skewer him with words. "To be completely honest, I think something fishy is going on. Like the guy who bought this stuff was making a little on the side. He takes some crap off of someone's hands, charges the school, gets a kickback. I'm making a list of expenses that could have been avoided, if you're interested. I know the school board will be."

Irving looked distinctly uncomfortable. "The school board? I'm not sure that's necessary." He laughed. "How about you run it by me first? Looks bad if I don't know what's going on in my own school, eh?"

"Oh, of course." Samuel nodded and tried to look appropriately naive. "I mean, why would the whole school board listen to a guy who's only been around for a month, right? I'm sure I'll need your help."

Irving was quick to jump on that one. "Absolutely! We'll get it figured out. Just give me a holler."

"Great. Speaking of which, I still haven't been reimbursed for the supplies I purchased. Could you mention that to Joyce?"

The principal frowned. "Hm, yes. We'll take care of that."

Samuel couldn't tell if Irving knew he was being played—more likely, he was running scared—but Samuel didn't care. So long as Irving stayed out of sight.

No such luck. The principal had just stepped out of the storage room when he turned, slapping the doorjamb. "Almost forgot why I stopped by."

Samuel raised his eyebrows. "Yes?"

Irving seemed to backpedal mentally, choosing his words with care. "The assembly today. I got the impression . . . It seemed like you weren't there."

"I didn't think five well-behaved kids needed a chaperone."

"You see, Cooke . . ." Irving coughed. "Rallies are a requirement. We need teachers to keep things from getting out of hand. Just sit with them and watch."

As tempted as Samuel was to turn the screws some more, he'd already gained the upper hand. "All right," he allowed. "Next time I'll go. Anything else?"

"Uh, nope. That about does it."

"Good afternoon, then." He nodded firmly in dismissal. It felt good.

SAMUEL RANG GRETA that evening.

"Yes?" she answered in her usual brusque manner.

"Hi, it's me." Hopefully she knew his voice by now. "I realized we didn't set a time or place for Thursday. Do you want to go out again?"

"I'm busy."

"Really?" His stomach sank. "Why, all of a sudden—"

She interrupted him with an exasperated sigh. "Mr. Cooke, I coach the basketball team. The tournament begins this weekend. If that weren't enough, I need to find housing arrangements for the visiting teams. I have responsibilities, and if you can't—"

"Okay, okay," he relented. "I get it. I can deal. Sort of. But stuff like this is going to freak me out, because if you hadn't noticed, I'm a teensy bit neurotic."

She let out another heavy sigh. "Mr. Cooke. I will inform you, explicitly, if and when I am done with . . . this. Will that suffice?"

He swallowed. "Yeah, actually, I think so."

"Good."

Although her tone indicated the conversation was over, Samuel wasn't ready to let her go. "So you're organizing housing for the teams? I read the blurb in the bulletin. You still need beds?"

"Quite a few. I've been calling down a list of parents."

"What about me? I can take a couple."

"You're a single man." Her voice was flat. "It wouldn't be appropriate to put the girls—"

"What, boys don't need somewhere to sleep?" He laughed. "Greta, I realize you're not enamored with the opposite sex, but I do happen to be a member of the party. They won't eat me."

She gave him the details, and he hung up with a puzzled grin. Did she even think of him as male?

Next he dialed Moore. "Hey. I have to pick up some kids on Friday night. You want to go to the game?"

WHEN MOORE CAME out of the apartment complex, he was trailed by a girl who looked all of sixteen. Samuel, waiting in the car, swore quietly.

Moore and Olivia argued for a minute about who should take shotgun. Finally Moore relented and held the back door. She slid in. "Hi."

"Uh, hi." Samuel glanced at Moore as he got in the front and buckled up. He had the nerve to grin.

"He minds," Olivia said.

"Do you?" Moore was genuinely surprised. "I didn't think you would."

"It's fine." Samuel glanced at his rearview mirror as he pulled into traffic, and found himself looking straight into her eyes. The whites contrasted sharply with her skin, which was the kind of deep black you saw in native Africans. "Just not big on surprises." Or dating children.

Moore frowned. "Oh, right. Sorry. Dang it."

Samuel looked at Olivia again in the mirror. "You might have to squeeze on the way back. I'm picking up two or three teenage guys."

The high school parking lot was packed, as were the streets in either direction. Not for the first time, Samuel was thankful for his blue sticker.

"Uh," Olivia said when he pulled up in front of the gym, "we can't park here. This is a handicapped spot."

Samuel looked at Moore. "You didn't tell her."

He shrugged.

"Jesus, you're an idiot." Samuel twisted to face Olivia. "You do realize he's as dumb as a post?"

She grinned. "A cute post."

An idiot and a kid. They were meant for each other. Samuel gave it three weeks.

The gym was as crowded as the parking lot; perhaps more so, since many families appeared to have come on foot, bundled in jackets. Casual groups gathered inside, under the low-ceilinged open foyer.

Olivia, who had been clinging to Moore's arm, broke away and trotted ahead. She spun briefly. "I'll find us some seats!"

Samuel grabbed Moore's elbow. "Don't you dare disappear," he hissed.

"Relax." Moore cleared a path through the foyer.

Samuel's heart sank when he saw the crowd. This was no simple home game. It was the opening night of the tournament, and the place was packed. Even the smaller stands, where he'd sat last time, were full.

"There she is." Moore pointed to a spot halfway down the court. Olivia was standing and waving from the fourth row up.

"I'll wait in the car," Samuel said.

"Are you kidding?" Moore tugged him toward the court. "Come on, we'll get you up there."

It was a toss-up between peer pressure and his desire to avoid public humiliation. Sadly, peer pressure won, though Samuel told himself he was doing it for Greta. As if she'd notice him in the crowd. As if she'd care even if she did see him.

He got to the bottom of the bleachers without tripping or slicing off anyone's fingers. Then Moore crouched and patted a shoulder.

"You're not serious," said Samuel. "One of my students could see me!" He looked around. Actually a lot of his students could see him.

"And you think my kids aren't here? Hurry up and get on my damn back."

Samuel got. For a moment he clung helplessly to Moore's neck, but then Moore handed the crutches up to Olivia and hooked his hands under Samuel's knees. Two seconds later they were seated in the fourth row.

"Here." Olivia passed the crutches back over Moore's lap.

"Thanks." It was too cramped to put them behind his seat, so Samuel propped the aluminum poles between his knees.

He had just gotten settled when the locker room doors opened and the girls thundered out. The pounding feet on the waxed wooden floor seemed more pronounced from where he sat, amplified by the struts beneath the bleachers. Samuel kept his eyes on the locker room until Greta emerged, lumbering along behind her girls.

"Oh, man," Olivia groaned. "I can't believe she's still teaching!"

"Hey, she's not *that* old," Samuel said. Although from twenty, Greta probably seemed ancient.

"Cooke has a soft spot for her," Moore said.

Olivia laughed. "Seriously?"

Samuel folded his arms around his crutches and rested his chin on top of a cuff. "I just don't think she's as horrible as everyone makes her out to be."

Olivia leaned forward conspiratorially. "I had her when I was a freshman. There was this girl in my class who always went to the bathroom right after we changed into our gym clothes? Then she'd run out to get on her number." Samuel frowned, and Olivia pointed to the row of numbers along the wall. "That's how she takes roll. This girl would always get there just as Cassamajor walked by. And Cass marked her late every single time. This was like a straight-A student, and Cass gave her a D. They had this whole parental conference and everything, and she wouldn't give in. Finally they agreed to take it off the girl's record if she retook the class."

"And was she late?" Samuel asked.

"The second time? No way."

He smiled. "So she learned something."

"*Maybe*." Olivia shook her head. "Anyway, as a girl? It's so much better to have PE with a guy. At least they go easy on you when you're on the rag. Cassamajor? No pity."

Moore's face was red. "Um, so how do you like the banners?"

GRETA WON. OR her team did, which was all the same to Samuel. By the end of the fourth quarter, his hands were sore from clapping.

"I didn't realize you were into basketball," Moore said, standing and stretching as the stands began to empty. A voice blared over the loudspeaker, instructing host families to meet by the scorekeeper's podium to collect their players.

Samuel rubbed his hands on his pants, massaging out the tingling sensation. "I'm not, really. It's just more exciting in person, I guess."

"Oh my gosh!" Olivia leaped up and waved at a group of girls. "It's Lacey and Tania!" She glanced at Moore. "I'll be back in a few minutes, okay?"

Samuel watched her hop down to the floor and jog across the gym. He looked at Moore. "You realize some of those kids are in my class."

Moore sat, scratching an eyebrow. "Mine, too." He looked at Samuel. "I really like her, though. What would you do?"

"It's your life, Greg. But I will say, for a guy with maturity issues, dating a kid is not the brightest idea."

Moore sighed. Then, abruptly, he smiled. "Well, I won't worry about it tonight." He got up and bent over. "Ready?"

"I think I can get it." Samuel stood and mapped his course mentally. If he was careful . . . "Just grab me if I fall, okay?"

He slipped once, but Moore caught his arm and steadied him. Then he was safely on the ground, where he intended to stay for the foreseeable future. He would come early next time, convenient parking or not.

Moore left to retrieve his date, and Samuel started for the podium. It seemed like Healdsburg's entire population had emptied onto the floor, and it took him a while to navigate. Moore and Olivia found him again as he reached his goal.

"We're gonna walk home," Moore said. "You mind?"

Samuel sat below the podium and waved them off. "Go ahead. I'll see you tomorrow."

They disappeared into the crowd, Olivia tucked under Moore's arm.

"You! Clean that up!"

Samuel followed the familiar bark to see a small boy darting away from Greta. She rolled her eyes and reached into the gym bag slung over her shoulder, pulling out a small towel. Putting a hand to one knee, she lowered herself to her haunches and wiped at a puddle of sticky soda.

Samuel waved as she stood. "I think you successfully scared the crap out of him."

"Someone could slip." She tossed the dirty towel into the seats behind him.

"Good game." He smiled.

Greta planted a foot on the bench next to him and balanced the duffel bag on her knee. "I'd appreciate it if, in the future, you did not attend."

"What? Why?"

She dug through the bag and pulled out a notebook. When she spoke again, her voice was quick and low. "Your presence is . . . distracting."

Samuel's smile turned into a grin. "I didn't think you saw me."

Greta let the bag slide to the bench, turning to face an approaching figure. "Mr. Tappin, good to see you." She extended a hand to the tall man, shook, and then gestured to Samuel. "This is Mr. Cooke, our newest teacher. He'll be taking a couple of your boys."

SAMUEL HUNG HIS keys on the hook inside his door, hitting the light switch in the same motion. "Straight to the back, first door on the right. Make yourselves at home, gentlemen."

Pierce and Danny bustled past him to the spare room. They were lean and muscular, with hair buzzed off close to the scalp. Samuel came to just below Danny's armpit, and Danny was the shorter one.

While they were settling down, Samuel slid up onto one of the chairs at the breakfast bar. They emerged a few minutes later, shuffling like shy toddlers as they peered at his things, no doubt anxious about staying at a teacher's house. Samuel motioned them into the kitchen. "I assume you're hungry. Enchiladas in the fridge. Soda, milk, whatever you want to drink." He pointed. "Dishes down there, silverware there, microwave there. Eat as much as you like; I had my housekeeper make extra. Seeing as I don't do the dishes, I don't care where you leave them as long as it's not on the floor."

Danny hesitated. Pierce said, "Awesome," and dug into the fridge. A few minutes later, they were at the dining table, shoveling food into their mouths.

"Where are you guys from?" Samuel asked.

Pierce swallowed an enormous mouthful in one gulp. "Portland."

"Really! You did travel quite a bit. And you're playing tomorrow?"

They nodded. Still shy.

"Good luck."

"We're playing your team," Pierce pointed out.

"Oh." Samuel waved a hand in dismissal. "Good luck anyway. I only care about the girls."

Danny gave him an odd look and returned quickly to his plate.

"It's nothing weird," Samuel assured them. "The coach—the one giving out room assignments? She's my girlfriend."

Pierce choked on his milk, then grabbed a napkin and covered his face.

10

"HEY, MR. COOKE? MY mouse is broken."

"Mine, too!"

Samuel stood up to see the two girls in the back. "What do you mean, broken?"

"Like, nothing happens when I move it."

There was a chorus of agreement, all from the far-right corner. Samuel started around the desk and then stopped. "Hold one up." He pointed at the first girl. "You. No, the other way."

She held up the mouse and flipped it over.

He sighed. "All right, who took the tracking balls?"

Everyone looked at him, wide-eyed and innocent. Right. Well, it had to be someone in the corner. "Come on, you guys, it's Monday morning. Don't make me search you."

"How do you know it was us?" the second girl piped up. "Someone could have gotten in over the weekend."

They weren't going to make this easy. "How plausible do you think it is," Samuel said, "that someone took the time to sneak in and then took *only* the track balls in the far-right corner of the room—

which, I might add, is the region farthest from the door? There're a dozen other things in this room that could easily be carried off. Stealing balls is quick, and it's annoying. Odds are, it's one of you."

A few kids tittered at the nominal double entendre. Children. "Yeah, balls are hilarious." Samuel moved in front of his desk and slid up onto the edge, piling his crutches beside him. "All right, one by one. Come up here and empty your backpacks and your pockets."

They groaned. "Seriously?" someone said.

"Unless someone *seriously* wants to return the track balls, yes." He pointed to the girl who had spoken first. "You. Up here. You don't have to show everyone, just open it and let me look inside."

He got through four students before someone objected. Naturally it was Fernando, his number one suspect in any case.

"You don't got no right to search me," the wannabe gangsta said. "You wanna see my bag, get a fuckin' search warrant." A couple of his buddies grunted agreement.

A quick call to the office confirmed that Fernando was right. General inspections were out, and if he wanted to search a particular student's bag he needed more than a hunch.

"Well." Samuel sat and folded his hands together. "Your ten minutes of free time at the end of the period are officially revoked. I—"

"That's not fair!" whined a girl from the front row. "Just because one person—"

"You're not entitled to that time," Samuel interrupted. "Until this problem is resolved, you'll be typing or you'll be doing nothing. No talking, no iPods, no cell phones. And forget about our weekly competition. This class doesn't have to be fun."

Fernando snorted. "Dumbass games."

"Yeah, you cultivate that attitude." Samuel opened the center drawer in his desk and pulled out a newspaper. He unfolded it, shook it a little, and settled back to read.

The paper was two months old, left behind by one of the substitutes who had preceded him. None of the students knew that. All they knew was that their mildly entertaining class had become an hour-long time-out. It wasn't long before the whispering began.

Let them talk. Maybe if they got irritated enough, the tracking balls would mysteriously appear. If not, who cared? It gave him an excuse to buy some optical mice, which couldn't be so easily emasculated.

Samuel sank farther back into the chair, skimming an outdated editorial without absorbing the content. It was hard to be truly pissed off when he was in such a good mood.

He'd finally said it. He'd told someone he was dating Greta. No matter that his witnesses happened to be a couple of teenage boys struggling frantically for an appropriate response. She was his *girlfriend*. Fernando could have punched Samuel in the gut, and he would have smiled.

The bell rang.

"See you guys tomorrow," he called without moving. Chairs scraped and bodies scuttled out the door. He didn't want to look at their miserable faces anyway.

When the room sounded empty, he peeked over the top of the paper.

And nearly fell out of his chair. "Jesus Christ!"

Someone had tacked a strip of slightly crumpled butcher paper over the whiteboard at the back of the room. It had been—the only word Samuel could think of was *violated*—with a bright red marker. A crude, misshapen caricature clearly intended to be Samuel straddled Moore's back, sodomizing him with a crutch.

"Wow, is that us?"

Samuel thanked God it was Moore who had come in and not one of his students. Or Greta. He grabbed the nearest object within reach—an eraser—and flung it at his friend. "Get rid of it. Now."

Moore clambered across the room and sidled up to the board.

Instead of pulling the paper down, he picked a black marker out of the trough, uncapped it, and started making corrections. "This kid needs to take my class. Worst technique I've ever seen."

"*Take it down!*"

"Chill, dude." Moore tugged the paper free and wadded it into a ball. "Toldja your troublemaker would find another way to rattle your nerves." He ambled back to the front of the room and dropped the ball into the trash.

"As far as he knows, he hasn't, and if I can help it, he never will." He'd go out this afternoon and pick up optical mice for the entire class. Business would continue tomorrow as usual. He rubbed his eyes and glanced at the clock. "Sadie is going to come through that door in about fifty seconds. Did you have something to say?"

"Oh yeah. I told Olivia maybe dating wasn't such a good idea."

"That's surprisingly mature, Greg." Samuel felt a little guilty for triggering the breakup, but when he thought of Olivia giggling with the girls from his sixth period, the feeling went away.

"That's what *I* thought. Then she gave me this lecture about caring too much what other people think. Particularly people who are thirty-five and still single."

"Really."

Moore scratched the back of his neck. "She had to go back to San Francisco, so she told me to take a week to think it over."

"She told *you* to think it over? She's more mature than I expected."

"Does that mean I can—"

"Absolutely not." The door swung in. Samuel didn't bother to look. "Hello, Sadie."

AT LUNCHTIME HE used the classroom phone to ring Greta's office.

"Do you have a reason for calling?"

"I know this is a long shot, but how about dinner tonight? I can grab takeout and bring it to your place if you've got a lot of work." He'd already checked the tournament schedule, so he knew she didn't have a game.

"Hardly appropriate, with two teenage girls in my guest room and three on the living room floor." She said it as though it should have been obvious.

"How was I supposed to know? Mine went home Sunday. After all," he teased, "I'm not allowed at the games." He considered. "Seriously, what would it hurt if I came over? They don't go to school here—"

"Mr. Cooke." The way she said his name meant *no*.

He decided not to mention what he'd told the boys. "When's the tournament over?"

"Friday night. But my sister and her husband are coming for dinner on Saturday."

He sat forward. "Really? That's great! I can't wait to meet them!" It was impossible to imagine Greta as a child, let alone having a little sister, and he was wildly curious to see what the woman was like. "What time? I'll help with dinner if you want." Ha, ha.

There was a long pause. Finally Greta said, "Five-thirty."

That was earlier than their usual meeting time. Did her sister warrant more quality time than he did? Oh, no. Samuel put his foot down mentally. He was not going to be jealous of his girlfriend's family. "Five-thirty it is. Oh, and Greta? I really did mean it when I said you could call me Samuel. Like, really."

HE DRESSED NICELY, put on a tie, and drove to Greta's house fifteen minutes after five. She came out to the porch to meet him, glancing at his attire before helping him up the steps. "What's the occasion?"

"Uh . . . nothing."

His anxiety about his status relative to Greta's sister was un-founded; it turned out Greta had taken him up on his offer to help with dinner. She sat him at the kitchen table, took his crutches, and shoved a large bowl of potatoes at his chest. She gave him a peeler before returning to the counter to chop carrots.

Little passed between them in the next forty-five minutes, but Samuel settled into a rhythm and discovered potato peeling was rather relaxing. When he finished, Greta chopped them and tossed them into a pot of boiling water. Samuel hooked his arm over the back of his chair and sampled the aromas coming from the stove..

"This isn't like what you made last time."

She shook her head. "Hazel prefers more traditional meals."

"Hazel," he said. "That's a nice name."

"Her husband is Derek."

He wanted to ask what Hazel did for a living, how many years apart they were, which parent they resembled most, but he decided "wait and see" was the best policy. Greta was quiet even for Greta, probably nervous, and he didn't want to make the evening more awkward than necessary.

They came at six. Greta rinsed her hands and bustled to the door, leaving Samuel stranded at the dining table. Such oversight was un-like her, but it was an easy fix. She'd propped his crutches against the refrigerator, so he slid from one chair to the next until he reached the opposite end of the table. Tip chair backward, plant hand against wall, grab crutches, and he was up.

He got to the front door just as they entered. Hazel came first, complaining about traffic to Greta over one shoulder. She was a shorter, softer, more feminine version of her sister, with shoulder-length brown hair in large curls framing her face. Her husband was slightly taller than Greta, broad-shouldered and overweight in a way that seemed more robust than self-indulgent.

Hazel turned and caught sight of Samuel. "Oh—hello." She glanced at Greta.

"This is Samuel Cooke," Greta said. "A coworker."

Something inside of him broke.

"I see." Hazel gave him a broad smile. "Good evening, Samuel."

He felt light-headed, as if his blood were draining out the soles of his feet. He managed to shift his weight to one crutch and put his hand out, and he saw the pity in her eyes as she reached out to meet his grasp. "Nice to meet you." His voice sounded hollow. "Mrs.—"

"Oh!" She giggled. "It's Whitehall. I'm still getting used to it. Did Greta tell you we were married last month?"

"Yes." He couldn't look at Greta. "She did."

Derek gave him a careful handshake, and they all sat at the table. But for Samuel, the evening was over. Everything was over. He managed to limp through the meal by agreeing with whatever Hazel's husband said.

Afterward he excused himself, citing work waiting at home. When Hazel begged him to stay, he treated it like the courtesy it was and refused. Greta rose to accompany him to the front porch, but he assured her he could manage by himself.

SAMUEL FOUND HIMSELF standing in front of his house with no clear idea how he'd gotten there. It was drizzling, and when he put a hand to his face, it came away damp. His car sat in the driveway, intact, so presumably he hadn't run into anything on the way home. He located his keys and let himself in, turning slightly as he stepped over the threshold.

"Thanks," he said to the empty street, "but no thanks."

He shut the door.

11

SAMUEL CALLED IN SICK on Monday. Then he pulled a pillow over his head and tried to retake the dreamless slumber he'd been pursuing all weekend.

He was not going to quit, not going to run back to L.A. Tomorrow he would pull himself together and go on with life as if nothing had ever happened. Probably.

Today, this morning, he couldn't face getting out of bed.

At least not until he heard footsteps in the hall.

The bedroom door swung open and Samuel sat up, flinging the sheets aside. It was one of those purely reflexive moments when his body took over, and his body still thought it was ten years old and functional. So instead of leaping out of bed to confront the intruder, all he managed was a decent thrashing.

Fortunately it was Maria.

"*Madre de dios!*" And then when she realized it was only Samuel: "Oh my God, Mr. Cooke, I'm so sorry!"

Samuel clawed the blankets over his body. "What the hell are you doing here?"

"You—you said I could use your house to study and I have a big test today and I've been in the kitchen for an hour. I saw your car but I knocked and you didn't answer so I thought Ms. Cassamajor gave you a ride or something . . . I just thought since I was here I would see if you had any laundry." She fumbled for the doorknob. "I'm sorry. I'll go."

"Wait, Maria. Please. Stay. Study as long as you want. It's fine."

"But . . ." Her eyebrows drew together. "Are you sick?"

Samuel flopped back into the pillows and pulled the blanket up to his nose. "Something like that."

SHE KNOCKED NEXT time. Samuel considered not answering, but he figured she'd come in anyway to make sure he wasn't dead. "What?"

The door swung in. "I made soup."

As if he didn't feel horrible already. Here, have a helping of guilt with that self-loathing!

Maria balanced the bowl and a glass of orange juice on a cookie sheet because he didn't own any breakfast trays. Having it dumped in his lap wouldn't make him feel any better, so he cleared a spot on the nightstand. She'd even folded the napkin.

"Thanks. You didn't have to, but thanks."

The corner of her mouth tugged down. "You aren't sick, are you." It wasn't a question. "Did something happen? With her?"

Samuel closed his eyes and sighed. Maria would know if he lied, and if he told the truth, he'd start blubbering. "Maria, as your employer, this is officially something I don't want to discuss. Right now. Okay?"

Her frown didn't go away. Neither did she. "Mr. Cooke, I'm worried for you. Is there someone you can talk to?"

Jesus Christ. "Maria, you're a saint. But if I were even close to suicidal, you'd already be mopping my blood off the bathroom floor."

AFTER MARIA LEFT, Samuel crawled into his wheelchair and went to the bathroom. He hadn't bathed or shaved since Saturday morning, and he looked like shit. He picked up his razor, decided it was better to avoid blades for the time being, and started the bathwater instead. After detaching his overfull urine bag and emptying it into the toilet, he transferred to the edge of the tub and wriggled out of his boxers. Only then did he hear the faint jingle. He reached for the faucet and cut the flow in half. It was the phone.

"Dammit." He hefted himself into the chair and rolled backward out of the bathroom, just far enough to reach the nightstand. "Yeah?"

"Cooke! Rashid. Got a minute? I think I found your replacement, but I don't want to make an offer until I run his credentials past you."

"Yeah, hold on." Samuel grabbed the doorjamb and propelled himself into the bathroom. He set the receiver on the sink and lifted his legs over the edge of the tub. The water was so hot it hurt as he slid in, but it felt good. He fumbled behind his head for the phone. "So. You found a programmer, or is that just today's pretense?"

"Both. How's it going up there? Still surviving?"

"Mostly."

"What does that mean? Tell me you're taking care of yourself."

Samuel sighed. "I'm just experiencing some PR issues. It's not a big deal. My classes are fine, I'm fine, everything's fine."

Rashid hesitated. "If this were anyone but you, I'd be asking if this is about a woman."

Samuel closed his eyes and sank beneath the water, holding the phone safely above his head. Was he really *that* transparent?

When his air ran out, he surfaced to hear Rashid's voice calling a quizzical "Hello?"

"Yes," Samuel said. "Okay? It was a woman. Who didn't like me nearly as much as I imagined. You have no idea how badly I want to beg you to forget this new guy and let me come crawling home."

Rashid laughed. "Absolutely not. You're doing great."

"Are you listening? I made a fool of myself."

Rashid laughed again, a high, pleasant sound. "Ten years I've known you, and I've never seen you do anything you didn't plan. You . . . Where do I begin? Every day you park in the same spot. You take the elevator upstairs and the same route to your office: around the corner to the right, through the double doors, past Ted's cubicle and the conference room. Anyone would expect you to fall on your ass now and then, but I've never even seen you trip, except for the couple of times you passed out in the john. You never go out, you get your groceries delivered—man, you won't even come to dinner without asking what we're having first. You hate your father, but you go to his house every single holiday—"

"Rashid. No offense, but coming from a guy with his own company, a wife who could be a supermodel, and—"

Rashid cut him off with a snort. "Your memory is very selective, my friend. Don't you remember how many months it took to convince Sheena to go out? Or how many miscarriages we went through before Priya? Or how many boots I licked to get the start-up money for Architective? Here is the truth, Cooke: in real life, you spend a lot of time on your ass. Get used to it."

"HEY, I GOT it to work! Check it out! Uh—Mr. Cooke?"

Samuel blinked and looked at Sadie, sitting next to him at the computer. Winter had precipitated a series of cold sores for the poor girl, making it painful for her to talk too much or smile. But right now she was grinning, gesturing to the diamond shape puttering around the screen as she pressed the WASD keys.

He returned the smile, hoping it looked genuine. "Sorry, zoned out. It looks great! Now you can add some obstacles." The bell rang. "Tomorrow."

"Thanks, Mr. Cooke. I totally get it now." Sadie helped him out of the plastic student chair, then pushed in all the other chairs on her way down the row.

It was his role in life to bring out the mother in every woman. Except one.

Three weeks since that night at Greta's. It still hurt.

He didn't blame her. He realized now that she hadn't wanted him to come to dinner. He'd invited himself, just like he'd initiated every other step in their so-called relationship. Greta hadn't reciprocated; she had merely tolerated his clumsy advances, trying to let him down easy. How else could any rational person explain her refusal to use his first name, excusing herself repeatedly as busy—hell, she'd flat-out asked him not to come to the games. How he'd twisted that into an affirmation, he didn't know. Clearly he couldn't take a hint.

Well, it was over now. Their paths wouldn't cross unless he put himself in her way, and he saw no reason to twist the knife.

Moore didn't materialize during fourth period or lunchtime, so Samuel pulled out his sandwich and ate alone.

When school let out, he made a few notes on his lesson plans while the crowds dissipated. Only when he stacked the pages and slipped them into his backpack did he notice the twice-folded square of binder paper on the corner of his desk.

He reached for it, unfolded it once, and, finding "Cooke" written in neat black capitals, opened the page to its original dimensions.

I hear you and Cass are an item. I mean—wow. Seriously? I
was planning something else, but this is better. Think I'll just sit
back and enjoy the show.

Samuel stared at the note, unseeing. The murmur of student
chatter faded, drowned out by the blood rushing in his ears.

Somehow, dismally late, the news had gotten out. Supposed
dalliances with Moore were easily laughed off, but this . . . this hurt
too much. Everyone would see the truth written on his face. Moore
would dig until Samuel spilled the entire humiliating story, which
would doubtless make its way to every last man, woman, and child
on campus.

He was "intelligent, tech-savvy guy with crutches and wry sense
of humor" no more. For as long as he remained in Healdsburg, he'd
be that poor cripple with a strange, hopeless crush on a woman nobody wanted.

Oh, Christ. Greta.

She was going to think it had come from him. His stupid attempt at retribution for the hurt he'd received. She would kill him.
Possibly literally.

Samuel packed up and headed for the car. Students loitered in
the hall, forming bored clusters or stepping apart to summon rides
with cell phones. As he passed, they glanced up and moved out of
his way. Had they heard? Were they spreading the rumor even now?
Samuel avoided looking at any of them directly. He didn't want to
see the laughter in their eyes.

The short bus was double-parked behind him, but reaching his
car was enough for the moment. He got in, locked the doors, and
rested his forehead on the steering wheel.

He listened to the whine of the hydraulic lift and the loud, overly
cheery tones of the bus driver as she asked how her drooling passen-

ger's day had gone. Then came the creak of the folding door and the engine's grumble, fading as the bus lumbered away.

Other than Greta, he'd done all right. He couldn't go back to L.A., but it wasn't the only place on earth. He could start over somewhere else, armed with the knowledge that romance was out. Period.

"Hey!" There was a knock on the driver's-side window. "You okay in there?"

God, not now. Samuel gave Moore a cursory wave and reached for the ignition. It was too late.

"Hold on!" Moore mimed rolling down a manual window. "We need to talk!"

Samuel started the car and keyed the switch, giving him an inch of open space.

Moore bent to speak through the crack. "Cooke. Sorry. I tried to get to you at lunch, but I forgot the art club needed—"

"Is this a matter of life or death?"

"Uh." He considered briefly. "No?"

"Then we'll talk later." Or maybe not at all. Samuel left Moore standing in the vacated parking spot, looking confused and forlorn.

If only the way out of the lot hadn't wound past the gym, he might have escaped. But as Samuel passed the seventies-era murals adorning the south side of the building, he saw a couple of Greta's players loitering outside the rear exit. One drank from a water bottle while the other stretched fingers to toes. Both were smiling, laughing as they chatted.

He didn't know they were talking about Greta. He didn't know they weren't, either.

The car in front of him stopped to let a third vehicle out. Samuel willed them to hurry, his fingers tapping out a syncopated rhythm on the brake lever. What form would the rumor take with Greta's students? Would they say she was so shrewish and ugly that she had to settle for him? And when it became obvious they weren't talking, that she couldn't even do that much?

How much more abuse would she have to shoulder if he disappeared?

He tried to tell himself she could handle it; surely experience had inured her to ridicule. Still, the image that appeared in his mind's eye was not her commanding glower but a bulky silhouette balanced on the edge of her couch, waiting for the reproach she expected her confession to yield.

When she heard this rumor, if she hadn't already, she'd be waiting for the other shoe to drop. For him to publicize her past promiscuity, secrets only hinted at but ripe for extrapolation.

"Dammit." Samuel cranked the wheel to the left and pulled around behind the gym. No matter how embarrassed he was or how much it hurt, he couldn't leave her with that. For a moment he wondered if he could summon the courage to get out of the car. Then the girls spotted him, traded knowing smiles, and hurried inside.

He would do it quickly. And afterward—if he faced her, if he got the words out—he could do whatever he wanted. Quit. Hibernate for a month. Get in his car and drive until he felt like stopping. Which might not be ever.

He shuffled up to the double doors, drew in a breath, and slipped inside.

The gym was thunderous with pounding feet. The girls were running what he remembered Greta calling lines, starting from one end of the court, sprinting to the free-throw mark, back, then to half-court, back, the other free-throw line, and finally all the way from one end of the court to the other.

Greta stood on the sideline with her back to him, stopwatch in hand. "Twenty-seven," she shouted as most of them stooped to touch the second free-throw line. "Thirty-five . . . Keep going, keep going, we're not done here! This is the slowest you've been all month!"

They were slow because each time they turned to run back to the starting line, a couple more noticed him standing inside the door. It occurred to Samuel that he had not, perhaps, picked the best time or place to approach Greta. Too late now.

He started toward her, skirting the edge of the court, and was about ten feet away when the clack of his crutches made her turn. Her piercing gaze caught him, and in that instant he understood that the rumor had already reached her. She wasn't surprised to see him in her gym.

Samuel imagined he saw anger in her face, but whatever Greta truly felt was veiled behind the mask of scornful indifference she wore through life. He wondered, briefly, if he had ever truly seen behind that facade.

Abruptly she broke eye contact. "Five minutes!" she barked, and her team staggered to the bleachers, reaching for water bottles. Greta shoved the stopwatch into a pocket and eliminated the space between them in three strides.

"It wasn't me," Samuel blurted. He forced himself to look up, to let her see the truth in his eyes. God, she was tall. "I haven't said anything to anyone, and I never will. I'm sorry."

She frowned. "I know."

"You do?" Not entirely the response he had expected.

"I—" She cut herself off, eyes moving to focus somewhere behind him.

Samuel followed her gaze to Moore, who was standing in the doorway, beckoning urgently.

Samuel turned back. Greta was already walking away, calling out instructions to her players.

"Cooke," Moore hissed, "get over here!"

Samuel was going to kill him.

When he got to the door, Moore grabbed his arm and pulled him outside. "Are you *crazy*? I thought you were going home!"

"What difference does it make?"

"I am trying to save your ass! I think." Moore ran a hand through his hair and glanced at the open door of his Karmann Ghia, which sat idling next to Samuel's car. "Dammit, this was why I was trying to catch you at lunch."

"Whatever you were going to say, just say it." Not like it made a difference now.

Moore touched his hair again, then buried the nervous hand in his pocket. "Jesus Christ, Cooke, she scared the shit out of me. Cornered me over by the portables at break. Said you were going out. Like, you and her. I thought—she's fucking crazy, right?"

In the space of several seconds, Samuel's brain crashed. Unable to process information. Please restart. "Sorry, *who* said this?"

"Cass! She must be—I dunno, playing some sort of mind game? I was going to find you at lunch, but then I got commandeered by the art club and— Jesus Christ, you aren't, are you?" Moore took a step back, suddenly uncertain. "I mean, *are* you?"

"I . . ." Samuel shook his head, hoping something would click into place. "I don't know. I don't . . . I don't know what's going on." He felt . . .

"Whoa there." Moore's hand closed around his arm. "You okay?"

No, Samuel was not okay. Why would she do this? Why now? Why at all? It made no sense.

"Cooke, let's find you somewhere to sit."

"No, I'm fine." He straightened, shrugging off Moore's support, and started for the car.

Moore paced him easily. "Seriously, Cooke, what the hell? Is it true?"

"No. I don't know. Just—leave me alone." Samuel got to the driver's side and wrestled with the lock.

Moore reached over him and held the door open. "But you—"

"Are you deaf? I said leave me the fuck alone!"

THE WASHER AND dryer were running when Samuel got home, and he could hear Maria in his bedroom, likely changing the sheets. He wanted to turn around and walk back out the front door, but if he disappeared, she'd probably call the police and report him missing.

That was another thing he was going to do differently next time. No romance, and no getting personal with the maid.

He hung his keys inside the door, collapsed into his armchair, and buried his nose in a paperback. Hopefully that would be enough to indicate his desire for isolation.

As if his luck could ever be so good. Maria came into the living room a few minutes later. "Oh, hi, Mr. Cooke, I didn't hear you come in. Hey, if you're not busy . . ."

"What?" he snapped.

"Ah—never mind."

Samuel winced and peered over the top of the book. She had retreated to the kitchen table, wiping it down with a sponge. He wanted so badly to leave it at that. Or to tell her to go home. "Sorry," he said instead. She'd already put up with enough moodiness from him during the past three weeks. "Really, really bad day. What is it?"

She pulled out a chair, bending to wipe the seat. "I was wondering if you could help me with something, but it can wait."

There was only one reason anyone ever asked him for assistance. "Computer problems?"

She looked back over one shoulder, seemed to decide he wasn't going to blow up in her face, and turned around. "I've been applying for nursing programs, but one school only accepts them online. The site stops working halfway through, and I have to start over. I wouldn't bother, but it's my top choice. I probably won't even get in."

"You don't know that." He set the book aside. "Which browser are you using?"

She had no idea. She didn't even own a computer, though how that was possible in this century, he didn't know. Her phone sufficed for daily use, and she used the computer at the library for writing papers and submitting applications. All the files she needed were stored on a thumb drive attached to her keys.

Samuel went into the kitchen and slid up onto the stool at the breakfast bar. Maria brought his laptop and stood next to him, resting an elbow on the counter as the screen blinked to life. She was unusually quiet.

"Sorry for snapping at you," he said. "My bad day doesn't have to be yours." Truth to tell, she was offering a welcome distraction.

"Was it really that awful?"

"Yes." He opened Internet Explorer, Firefox, and Chrome. "Which one did you use?"

She pointed to the first window. "Want to talk about it?"

"No." He closed Firefox and Chrome and pushed the laptop toward her. "Here, find the website. She told the entire school we were dating."

Maria's fingers froze over the keyboard. "But I thought you two were . . ."

"Finished? Yeah, me, too."

"I don't get it."

"Welcome to the club."

"Oh, here." Maria logged in to her account and passed the laptop back to Samuel.

The interface was a generic data-entry client, not sophisticated enough to handle what the school was using it for. Some administrator had probably thought it was a good deal. Samuel reopened it in Chrome and plunked through the first few windows, immediately spotting the crossover in their logic sequence. "Ah. Here we go."

Maria studied his face as he worked. "What do you mean when you say she told everyone?"

"She told Greg, which is essentially telling everyone, because he can't keep his damn mouth shut." He pushed the laptop toward her. "Try it now."

"And she knows what he's like?"

"He's the goddamn campus intercom."

She tapped through the windows. "Hey, you got it!"

"Thank me when you get to the end. I'll dig deeper if necessary."

A crease of concentration appeared between Maria's brows as she began to fill out the online forms. "This will take a minute." Her lower lip disappeared between her teeth. "I click this one?"

He leaned over for a better view of the screen. "Yeah. Don't use these arrows to navigate, they're screwed up."

She nodded. "I know you didn't," she said between keystrokes, "want to talk about it, so forgive me for asking, but what happened?" She cast a furtive glance at his face. "To end it?"

Before, he'd been afraid of falling apart if he even so much as spoke Greta's name. Now he was so damn confused, he didn't know what to feel. "I thought we were keeping the whole thing under wraps so it wouldn't get around at school. Then her sister came to visit and . . ." He swallowed. "Oh my God."

"What?"

"I have to go back." He slid off the stool. "I'm sorry, I'll see you Tuesday. I have to go."

12

IT WAS AN APOLOGY.

Only Greta didn't do things in words, or flowers, or greeting cards. She acted.

She had failed to acknowledge him in front of her sister. He had been devastated. And so she had set it right—and then some—by telling *everyone*.

It was a completely lunatic thing to do, and he loved her for it.

He pulled up in front of the gym five minutes shy of five, which was when practice let out, and used the visor mirror for a quick check of hair and teeth.

And wondered what the hell he was doing.

Even assuming his interpretation of Greta's actions was correct, she had hurt him. Badly. And even assuming neither of them fucked up the next few minutes, there was no guarantee it wouldn't happen again. He should walk away right now. Go somewhere else. Live his life. Because next time, it might not be so simple. Next time it might really be the end of his world.

Samuel got out of the car.

A green iron bench was bolted to the ground out in front of the gym, next to a disemboweled pay phone. He sat, his back to the building.

Almost on cue, the door burst open behind him. The footsteps were light, and a moment later a trio of girls schlepping duffel bags passed the bench, headed toward the student parking lot. The one on the left sneaked a glance over her shoulder, then leaned toward her companions to report.

This scenario repeated itself several times in the next few minutes. And then silence, save for a couple of scrub jays squabbling in the redwoods towering alongside the gym. Samuel wished he'd had the presence of mind earlier to count the number of players at practice. His hands grew damp.

The door opened again, more slowly this time. There was only one set of footsteps. He waited, holding his breath as he listened to the soft rattle of keys. Then the steps started forward—and faltered.

Samuel turned, hooking his arm over the back of the bench. Greta stood midway between the bench and the building, a large purse slung over one shoulder and a duffel bag dangling from the other arm. He swallowed. "So, um . . . What would you say to an early dinner?"

She looked at the ground. Turned half away. Then, abruptly, came around the end of the bench and sat next to him. Well, two feet away. With her purse between them.

"I should apologize," she told the pavement.

"No, please don't." As suddenly as that, Samuel's pain was irrelevant. She was a middle-aged woman with a younger, prettier social butterfly of a sister. Of course she'd been embarrassed to introduce him as her boyfriend. It hadn't been him in particular but the fact that she was dating anyone at all. It seemed so obvious now. "You, um, you needed more time."

She leaned forward, resting her elbows on her knees, and pressed her palms together. "I'll call Hazel."

"Greta, I . . ." If she had beaten herself up even half as much as Samuel had, it was enough. "You're here. That's further than anyone has ever come, and that's what counts." He snorted. "You'd think I, of all people, would be past caring what others think."

"No." She frowned, struggling for the words. "It matters."

Her gruff embarrassment was charming. "Maybe it does. But if you had something to prove, you did it today. You'll tell Hazel eventually. Just wait until you're ready." He gave her an encouraging smile, groaning inwardly at the irony: he'd spent the last three weeks wallowing in self-pity, and here he was, reassuring her. "I promise I won't hold it against you."

She didn't say anything.

"Hey, let's do something before dinner." Samuel slipped his forearms into his crutches. "Are there any nice drives around here? I haven't seen much of the countryside yet."

"Quite a few," she allowed. "It's an excellent area for biking."

"That's definitely out." He slid to the edge of the bench and leaned forward. When he glanced at her, he realized she wasn't following his cue.

"You," she said, her voice low, "have been candid. With me."

Samuel let out a breath and sat back. "Look, it might seem that way, but there's a lot you don't know. Don't feel like you have to spill everything immediately. Why don't we just relax and enjoy ourselves tonight?"

She ignored him. She had something to say, and she was going to say it. "When we moved here, I rebelled. By the time I was sixteen, not even my father could control me." She spoke sternly, as if reprimanding him—or perhaps herself. "There was a boy."

"Greta, stop." He didn't need to hear this. Didn't want to. "You don't have to—"

"Let me *finish*." She pressed her lips together. Swallowed. "I would have done anything for him. He said. If I—if I really—I'd let his friends—" Her voice broke. "I—"

Oh Jesus. He'd imagined that, whatever it was, the years had magnified its significance in her mind. But if she was saying what he thought she was saying . . . "I'm sorry." He was ashamed on behalf of his entire sex. Bastards. All of them.

He put out a hand, meaning to touch her leg, but she stood and turned her back to him. "Mr. Cooke, I—"

Samuel couldn't bear to let her struggle through the rest of it, as she clearly intended to do. "Greta, I understand."

"No. I—"

"You got pregnant," he finished. He didn't quite know how he knew, but it fit.

She was silent for a long moment. One hand reached up to brush something away from her face, and when she spoke again, her voice was measured and even. "By the time I found out, the father could have been anyone on the football team."

"I'm sorry," he said again, feeling the vast inadequacy of his words.

This was why she had been so distant. She had been struggling to tell him, to get it out, and he hadn't helped by spilling his guts that night at the Chinese restaurant; he'd only made her feel worse for not reciprocating. And then that whole sermon about confession—no wonder she'd practically shoved him out of the car. After that, the tournament had provided an excuse to avoid him while she tried to screw up her courage. Or decide if he was worth the pain of confessing.

He was glad she had deemed him worthy. The awful thing was that it didn't mean nearly as much to him as it did to Greta. What had happened to her as a teenager—or whatever she thought she had done—didn't change his feelings at all.

He wanted to crack a stupid joke or make an ass of himself—anything to distract her, make her forget the pain, and never, ever come back here again. If only it were that simple. The best he could do was help her get it all out now, so at least she didn't have to bear the additional guilt of hiding something, justified or not.

"The baby?" he asked quietly.

Greta sat and pulled her purse onto her lap. She dug through it and handed him a piece of stiff paper.

It was a photograph; Greta was young, so very young, but he would have recognized that stern, emotionless mask anywhere. Though the infant in her arms was swaddled in pink, Samuel could see its tiny face was gray.

"She lived four days."

"What . . ."

"Heart defect."

"I'm sorry." Couldn't he think of anything better to say? "I'm . . . so sorry." Yeah. Much better.

Samuel had a sudden urge to take the precious photo and tear it up. She would never have forgiven him, so he placed it on the bench between them, facedown. On the back, someone had scrawled *Greta and Amelia, b. Feb. 14*. He swallowed, hard.

Greta picked up the photo and tucked it into her purse. Then she stared at the ground between her feet, unmoving.

Samuel shifted. He moved himself closer until his shoulder brushed hers. He wanted to offer words of comfort, of reassurance. What came out was "Can I kiss you?"

There could not have been a more inappropriate moment to ask. Samuel expected Greta to slap him.

Instead she glanced at the deserted parking lot with an expression of vague disgust. "Just do it if you're going to."

"Oh." He felt the blood drain from his face. He bit his lip and studied his knee for a minute.

And then he did.

Samuel's personal history was littered with awkward moments, but this topped the list. He made a kind of lunge to reach her face and missed the mark (he was afraid to really look at her), and it took his lips a panicked moment to find her mouth, which was tight and closed. But it was too late to turn back, so he kissed her in the way he thought a woman should be kissed, which was longer than a few seconds. Once he was there with his eyes closed, he touched the side of her face, too.

Then, quite suddenly, she was kissing *him,* pushing him rather violently against the iron bench, robbing him of breath altogether. Her fingers closed around his biceps, and her body was heavy on top of his.

After perhaps an eternity, she paused for air.

A gallon of pure oxygen flooded Samuel's lungs, and with it he gushed, "Greta, I want to—"

She pulled back. "What?"

He wanted to make love to her. Right now. Possibly several times.

"Nothing," he said.

But she knew. Carefully, she disengaged herself, leaving about a foot of cold, empty space between them. Samuel wanted to reach out and pull her back. If a few weeks of dating could produce a kiss like that, he wanted to know what thirty years of abstinence had built up inside of Greta.

He ran a hand through his hair and straightened his collar. "Well, uh, I guess . . ." He trailed off as Greta stood, collecting her purse and duffel bag. "Where are—"

"Good night," she said. And strode off toward the staff parking lot without so much as a backward glance.

"That's a no on dinner, then?"

13

SILLY AS IT WAS, Samuel took extra care to make himself presentable the following morning. He was used to being the object of surreptitious glances, but he would be enduring an extra measure of scrutiny while people got accustomed to the idea of him and Greta. And if they were going to stare, he might as well look his best.

When he arrived, the cluster of students outside his door scattered as if he were ten feet tall and wielding a spiked club. Samuel handed the key to Sadie, who didn't even say hello. Everyone shuffled in, sat down, and stared.

It was more than shock; Greta was scary, and the effect had rubbed off on him. He grinned. "Good morning, guys!"

Normally he'd have to wait while the aimless chatter died, call out for quiet once or twice. Today, when he put his bag on the desk and sat, the crack of his knees was audible in the silence. "Since this is the last week we have before Christmas break, I thought we could do some holiday-related stuff. So today we're going to format some Christmas cards—"

"Yo, man, I don't do Christmas."

There remained one student who didn't fear him and wanted everyone to know. Samuel gave Fernando a withering look. As usual, the boy was wearing a gold pendant embossed with a Catholic saint. "You're telling me you don't celebrate Christmas?"

"I'm an atheist, man." Several students snickered.

"Then you can make an atheist card."

"Are you mocking my faith? I could totally sue for that."

"First of all, atheism is not a faith, it's an anti-faith. Second, Fernando, if you can find a lawyer to represent you, be my guest."

"See, man, that's the problem with the system. I don't got no access to no lawyer, so I don't got my rights protected. I bet you know like three who could back you up."

"Five, actually."

"See? Brown man always gets the raw deal."

"Yes, Fernando, I'm certain any court in California would, in fact, consider being forced to make a greeting card 'raw.' But until you and all the Hallmark employees get your class action suit together, I'll be basing a good five percent of your grade on this activity. I'll let you decide whether you need that five percent to pass my class."

Fernando snorted and sat back in his seat. "Whatever, man."

"Thank you." Samuel went through the roll quickly. Whatever intimidating aura he'd had at the beginning of class had worn off, because the usual shuffles and whispers returned. Oh well. He opened the top drawer of his desk to retrieve a dry-erase marker.

His pens were gone. The drawer was empty except for a single sheet of binder paper. It bore a crude sketch of him and Greta . . . copulating. Except she was pictured as the man, and Samuel was on his knees. The style of the artwork was all too familiar.

He slammed the drawer shut and gestured to a boy on the left side of the room. "Lance, throw me one of the pens on the board over there." Samuel refused—refused—to let this rattle him. Lance tossed a pen over, and Samuel levered himself out of the desk chair, moving to the whiteboard to outline the formatting he wanted them to use.

The room went silent.

Then Fernando snorted and laughed. "Dude, you shit your pants!"

14

SAMUEL TURNED. "EXCUSE ME?" Then he saw his chair. The seat was smeared with something brown; obviously not his own excrement, or the smell would have gotten to them first. He propped one crutch against the wall, touched the stain, and held the finger to his nose. "Chocolate. Brilliant." He wanted to scream.

Very, very calmly he sat down. "Someone isn't very interested in Christmas cards." He shot an accusatory glance in Fernando's direction; the boy wouldn't meet his eyes. "So we'll just go back to typing for the rest of the day."

Samuel didn't take out the newspaper this time. He sat behind his desk, staring bullets at his students. The ringleader was obviously Fernando, but there was no way he had done it alone. Samuel let his eyes pinpoint each kid in turn, searching for knowledge, for culpability. And, most important, motive. Why were they doing this? He wasn't a bad teacher; the class wasn't unbearable. Was it as simple as being new and inexperienced and therefore vulnerable?

By the time the bell rang, all of his students were incredibly uncomfortable, and he had no leads. Maybe it wasn't anyone in second period or in his classes at all. Somehow Fernando had gotten a key to the room or knew someone who had access. A janitor, perhaps.

Samuel held out his car keys when Sadie got up. "There's a black bag under the driver's seat. Get it, would you?"

She nodded and hurried out the door. When she returned, the room had emptied.

Samuel took the bag. "Thanks." At least there was one student he could rely on. He didn't have to ask if she knew anything; several weeks previous, she'd tipped him off that Travis carried a pocketknife, not that Samuel cared. If she had information, she'd be the first to tattle.

Still, she looked embarrassed. "Mr. Cooke, I'm really sorry—"

"Sadie, you didn't do anything. Pranks are a hazard of teaching, right?" He waved her out. "Take your break. I'll see you in a few minutes."

When she was gone, Samuel slid his chair over to the door and locked it. Quickly he dragged one of the blue student chairs behind his desk, where it couldn't be seen from the windows. He slid to the floor, opened the black bag, and pulled out a pair of pants. Thank God he kept a change of clothing with his catheter kit. He wriggled into the clean pants, then shoved the soiled pair into the bag and dumped it in the bottom drawer. He pulled himself onto the blue chair, grabbed his crutches, and lurched to his feet.

And promptly found himself on the floor.

"*Shit!*" Hoping he had simply overbalanced, he dragged himself onto the chair again and stood, more carefully this time. His right knee buckled.

Goddammit, this wasn't happening. His knee was not giving out. It couldn't be. Well, it could, but . . . *goddammit.* He rolled up his pant leg and prodded the joint with his fingers. It didn't look swollen. "Fuck," he whispered.

The warning bell rang. Five minutes until class officially started.

It was just a sprain. He rolled the pant leg down. He'd look again when the day was over and it would be swollen and he'd go home and ice it over the weekend and wear a neoprene knee brace for the next month and it would be fine.

The door shuddered, followed by a muted exclamation of frustration. Samuel grabbed the edge of the desk and pulled. Though the student chair didn't have wheels, the floor was reasonably slick, and he managed to slide about a foot. By leaning back, he could reach the doorknob, barely, and unlock it.

"*Thank* you." Marcus shouldered into the room. "It's freaking cold out there." He looked at Samuel, who was panting slightly. "You okay?"

Sadie followed him in. "Marcus," she pleaded.

"I'm fine. And you're right, it's freezing. Please shut the door." Samuel shoved the ruined office chair aside and jerked himself toward the desk. His armpits were level with the top. Travis and Lemos, drifting in, eyed him curiously. Samuel didn't know whether it was his choice of seating or because they had heard about Greta.

He resented the fact that Fernando and his cohorts had robbed him of this small pleasure. Deeply. If that was what they wanted, they had won. He felt helpless, angry, and frustrated that they could have so much power over him. He felt frustrated and helpless for other reasons, too, but he wasn't going to think about that right now.

He *wasn't*.

Samuel sighed. "You know what? Scratch today's lesson. Just work on your projects."

WHEN THIRD PERIOD ended, Samuel rang the librarian. She was kind enough to bring his storage room chair without demanding explanation; when she saw the seat, she murmured a sympathetic "Oh dear" and took it away.

Samuel adjusted the chair to the height of the desk and shifted over, careful not to put any weight on his knee. Jesus, how was he going to get home? He tugged up the pant leg. The knee looked a little swollen. Maybe.

He could make it to the car. He had enough upper-body strength to get himself that far, and if he were careful, the left leg would be enough to balance.

He was still brooding when Greg Moore mustered the courage to knock.

Samuel closed his eyes and took a deep breath, clearing his head. "Come in."

The door swung in a few inches. "I swear," Moore said, "the only person I told was Ms. Baker, because she said—"

"Forget it." Samuel motioned him in. "Hasn't it occurred to you why Greta picked you to . . . pick on?"

"No, thank you, I was too busy having the crap scared out of me to really, you know, process." Moore slipped into the room and took a cautious seat on the other side of the desk.

Samuel was too tired to put it delicately. "She knew you'd tell everyone, Greg."

Moore took a moment to digest that. "Oh," he said finally. "Wow. That makes me feel so much better."

Samuel felt a little guilty. "You are who you are. Don't worry about it."

"Dude, I don't know what to think. You, her? I mean, when?" Moore frowned. "This didn't just happen. This has been going on. Hasn't it?"

"Sort of," Samuel admitted.

Moore raked back his hair. "And she's older than you. Like, by a lot."

"So?"

He dug into a pocket, pulled out his cell phone, and dialed. "If you can date Greta, I can sure as hell go out with Olivia."

Samuel covered his eyes.

There was another knock at the door, and Greta leaned in. "Oh, hi," said Samuel. "We were just talking about you."

Greta graced Moore with a curt nod.

"Hi," he said in a small voice.

Samuel ignored him. "Any student trouble?"

Greta cast another glance in Moore's direction. "A little." Her face hardened. "I took care of it."

Ah, the virtue of physical education: disciplinary problems could be solved with heavy physical labor or the threat of it.

"You?" she asked.

"Sure," he lied. "I'm fine."

She nodded again and slammed the door.

Moore wilted. "Cooke . . ."

"What?"

"You're insane."

15

NEVER HAD SAMUEL BEEN more thankful for a holiday than when Christmas break arrived. It ought to have been because he would have more time with Greta, or at the very least get away from Fernando, but mainly he was relieved to be off his knee.

When Sunday arrived, he had enough confidence in the malfunctioning joint to accept Greta's invitation to church. He was less certain when, at the close of the service, she extended the invite to lunch at her house. But he pulled himself into the passenger seat, silently reassuring his knee that it would get all the rest it needed during the following week, which he planned to spend on the couch.

"Are you all right?" Greta asked, turning out of the church parking lot.

"Oh, uh, yeah." Ground control to Mr. Cooke. He cleared his throat. Make idle chitchat. "So, what are your plans for Christmas?"

"I'm going to my sister's. Our aunt is flying in from Dallas."

"Oh. I guess what I meant was, what are you doing over the

vacation?" He had sort of assumed she would spend December 25 with him.

She shrugged.

It would be his first Christmas alone. Traditionally he stayed the night with Chris and the old man on Christmas Eve, or if he was smart, he'd pop in on Christmas Day. Traveling six hundred miles instead of six would mean being stuck, for at least a couple of days, in his father's house. Samuel would rather have a root canal.

Greta's house came into view. "Hey," Samuel realized, "I've never seen your place in daylight." It was pale yellow, the same shade as the carnations he'd given her.

She didn't comment. With anyone else, Samuel might have repeated himself, but Greta rarely responded to anything not phrased in the form of a question. She hit the garage door opener.

"Um," he said. "You have a motorcycle."

"I told you this was a good area for biking." She pulled into the right half of the double garage, killed the engine, and got out.

Samuel slid down to the slab floor and circled the front of the car. Greta stood next to the moderately chromed machine, given a matte finish by the overcast horizon.

"You have a motorcycle," he repeated.

"'83 Honda Nighthawk. My father loved working on bikes, so I always had one." She picked a helmet off a rack on the wall. "I'll take you around the block."

"Oh," he said, backing away, "I'd rather not." He glanced at the three steps that led into the house and wondered if he could make it without her help.

Greta's invitation was not so easily declined. "Have you ever ridden?" She took hold of the cruiser-style handlebars and aligned the wheels.

"No," he admitted. "I don't think I can."

She rolled her eyes. "Come here."

Reluctantly Samuel shuffled forward.

"Put your hand on my shoulder." She took his crutch and started to bend down.

"Greta," he protested, "ordinarily I'd be thrilled to have you grope me, but at this point in our relationship, I don't think I'm ready to—"

She reached under his thigh, picked up his leg, and pushed it over the leather seat. Blood rushed into his face, but Greta didn't seem to notice. She took the second crutch and handed him the helmet. "Put it on."

What else could he do? She fastened her own helmet and slid her leg over the gas tank. "Feet here." She tapped one footrest with her heel and waited while he fumbled to get his unresponsive limbs into position. "Ready?"

"No."

She kicked the stand. The engine growled beneath them, and Samuel didn't have to be told to hold on. He cinched his arms around her waist, squeezed his eyes shut, and buried his face between her shoulder blades.

They rolled down the driveway and onto the street. Samuel knew his balance was terrible, his knee was being especially uncooperative, and he was terrified one of his feet would slip, hit the ground, and be torn to bloody shreds.

But she didn't seem to be trying to set the land speed record. He opened one eye and then both. Though it was unnerving to see the ground rolling away beneath him, his feet were still attached. Greta had set her heels snug along his toes, holding them in place. Every few moments, she glanced down to confirm their position.

Under any other circumstance, having his arms around her would be thrilling—in a good way—but all he could think of was escape. He tried to memorize the feel of her: the solid circumference of her waist; the slight give of her muscular bulk, cushioned by a comfortable layer of padding. Later, he would retrieve the memory and savor it. If he didn't spoil everything by throwing up.

They rode around two blocks and coasted into the garage. She kicked the stand down, removed her helmet, and helped him off. He was shaking.

"We were only going thirty." Her eyes darted over him with curious amusement. "You really are scared."

"And this surprises you?" Samuel snapped. "Sorry, forgot to mention I'm a spineless coward. I know that's hard to understand, since obviously you've never been afraid of anything in your life."

"You're wrong." Greta dumped both helmets into a bin on the wall.

"Says the woman who continues to live and work in the place she was—" He closed his mouth over the words *gang-raped*. Dammit. Too far.

She was still, her back to him. "I stay," she said finally, "because going anywhere else would be running." Her shoulders rose with an intake of breath, and she turned around.

"Sorry," he said.

"I am afraid." She passed him and went up the steps to the laundry room. "Of men."

Samuel snorted. "Coulda fooled me."

She offered a hand. "That's the point."

IN THE DAYS before Christmas, Greta introduced him to several more local restaurants. Samuel would have pressed for more time before she departed, but his desire to spend every possible moment with her was tempered by concern for his knee. He called to say hello once a day and hoped that was enough. If it wasn't, she didn't say.

Telling her about his knee was completely out of the question. Or, he amended, completely unnecessary. Everything would be fine by January.

And Christmas alone? Not so bad. At least, judging by how he felt on Christmas Eve, he didn't think it would be. He spent the morning doing some extended lesson planning, made himself a ham sandwich, turned the fire up, and settled into the couch to answer a couple of e-mails from his replacement at Architective. All in all, he was proud of the calm, rational way in which he was handling his solitude.

Of course, his constant internal monologue about how well it was going indicated that the point wasn't altogether moot.

When he finished up online, Samuel switched to his chair and went to check the status of his closet. Maria had taken the week off, and if his clothing stock wasn't going to last until her next visit, he might as well see if he could figure out the washing machine.

He was picking through his shirts when the bell rang. He coasted back into the living room, opened the door, and found Greta standing on the mat.

"You're still here," she said. Before he could thank her for stating the obvious, she turned and marched back to her Suburban. She opened the passenger door and pulled out a large cardboard box.

Samuel backed out of the way and followed her into the kitchen. "Uh, shouldn't you be heading to Vallejo?" Foodstuffs meant for Hazel and Derek and Greta's nameless aunt were coming out of the box. "We'll celebrate when you get back. Your sister—"

"Is married." A large ham went in the fridge.

And poor little Sam was all alone. Right. Now he got it. "Greta, I've spent most of my adult life by myself. Being alone on December the twenty-fifth is not going to kill me. Hell, I'm technically a Jew. Besides—"

"Shut up."

Samuel blinked. Shut up? That was her argument? No, Greta didn't argue. She acted, and damn the torpedoes. Well, this was his house, and she wasn't going to get away with that. "Greta," he said firmly, "there is no reason for you—"

"Get out of the kitchen."

"You can't order me out of my own—"

"Go do something useful."

Samuel went to his room and slammed the door.

The worst thing was, Greta was right. Intellectually he might hold the high ground, but privately he was relieved she had come. Which proved her point. Which was infuriating.

When he finished sulking, Samuel ventured into the living area, stopping short of where the breakfast bar divided the dining table from the kitchen. Greta gave him a warning glance and continued combing through his cooking utensils. Samuel took the hint and backed up. Then he noticed the small travel bag sitting next to the box of food. "Are you staying the night?"

"You have a guest room, don't you?"

"Um, yes." Was the mattress even sheeted? Maria wouldn't have left something like that undone. He checked. Everything was fine. Except now his heart was pounding.

They weren't going to have sex, so no worries there; Greta had been very specific. But her, in his house, all night seemed like a big deal.

It also seemed like a long time. It was just after two; assuming Greta went to bed at ten, that left eight hours. Eating whatever Greta was starting to cook would fill up an hour, max. That left seven hours. What on earth were they going to do?

He glanced at the television and cursed his decision not to get cable. He had a feeling she wouldn't be thrilled with his bootlegged copies of *Battlestar Gallactica, The Next Generation,* and every film

Sigourney Weaver had ever made. He could probably do a quick download of some old Christmas movie, though the thought of watching *It's a Wonderful Life* or *A Christmas Carol* made him want to puke.

"Here." Greta handed him a wine goblet, quite possibly never used, and poured him a glass of the wine he'd never opened. "Do you have any Christmas music?"

"Music. Yes!" That he could do. Fortunately he had the correct cable in a sufficient length to reach from the television to his laptop at the kitchen table. A few sips of wine and a little techno-fiddling later, and his speakers were blasting the opening bars of "O Holy Night." "Sorry!" he shouted, and conducted a panicked search for the remote.

Once the music was playing at a reasonable range of decibels, he told Greta to let him know if she disliked any of the songs, since he was using Pandora. Her blank look necessitated an explanation of digital music services. Which led to media streaming and BitTorrent and somehow cloud computing.

Several hours later, amazing aromas were emanating from the kitchen, and Greta was seated next to him, watching as he demonstrated his grading setup in Excel. She did everything on paper, which he found totally unacceptable. He had just gotten into layout when she pulled out a pair of reading glasses and began to take notes, frowning like a studious schoolgirl. It was adorable.

He had a second glass of wine with dinner and stuffed himself shamelessly.

"Now I know why you don't cook," Greta noted.

He felt himself flush. "I, uh—" He clapped a hand over his mouth to stifle a belch. "Sorry."

"Don't be." She took his empty plate and stacked it on top of her own. "Cooking for someone else is more rewarding." She slid back and cocked an eyebrow at him before standing. "And you could do with a few more pounds."

"Yeah, yeah." He'd heard the same thing from every doctor he'd ever seen, and he *so* did not want to have that conversation with her. "Hey, do you play cards?"

After several rounds of gin rummy, Samuel decided it was safe to break out his hard-core German board games. Greta had never heard of Carcassonne or Settlers of Catan, but when she pulled out the rulebook for Twilight Struggle, her eyes widened in appreciation.

"MR. COOKE."

Samuel snorted and brought his arm down, along with half the sheets. "What the—" He squelched an exclamation of surprise as the bedroom door opened and Greta leaned in. It was morning. She was still here. She had spent the night. In the next room.

She held out the phone. "Your brother."

He squinted to bring Greta's face into focus as she delivered the receiver. "Thanks." As quickly as she had come, she was gone; Samuel took a moment to clear his throat and his head before putting the phone to his ear. "Hello?"

"Merry Christmas!"

"Merry—" He glanced at the clock on the bedside table. "*Seven?* What the hell are you doing up?"

"Dude! Who's the lady?"

Samuel groaned inwardly. He didn't want to have this conversation; not right now, not with Greta in the next room. He lowered his voice. "My girlfriend, all right?"

Chris let out a triumphant whoop. The phone clattered, and his voice went tinny and distant. "Dad! Sam hooked up!"

"Okay, okay, will you shut up?" Jesus, now he knew what Greta felt like, trying to tell her sister.

Chris's voice returned. "So who is it? Your maid?"

"Her name is Greta. She teaches." Samuel hesitated, and then added: "Gym."

He savored the moment of shocked silence like a drought of fine wine.

"Gym? You—you're dating a *gym* teacher?"

He smiled thinly. "That's what I said."

When Chris's voice came again, it was quiet, like it got whenever he was afraid of upsetting someone. "Isn't that, you know, weird? With, you know . . ."

Samuel was tempted to say, "No, I don't know, Chris, what do you mean?" But hell, it was Christmas. "Kind of," he admitted. "To tell you the truth, it hasn't really come up."

"Damn," said Chris. "She must be some chick."

Samuel wondered what Greta would do if she ever heard anyone refer to her as a "chick."

"So she's at your house, bro! Congrats! You get to open your 'present' early or what?"

"She spent the night in the guest room."

Chris let out a low chuckle. "Uh-huh."

"Trust me, Chris, if I had gotten laid, I wouldn't feel the need to hide it from you. She's a conservative Christian, which, if you've totally blanked on every Sunday sermon Mom ever dragged us to, means she doesn't believe in sex before marriage."

Chris snorted. "Come on, man, that's for teenagers. You guys are like . . ."

It was Samuel's turn to laugh. "What, too old not to have sex? You realize I'm still a virgin, right?"

The line went silent.

"Chris?"

"Hey, I, uh, I'm sorry." Chris cleared his throat. "I didn't know."

SITTING IN THE bathtub, Samuel turned the handheld attachment to the highest pressure setting and pointed it at his face. Virginity past thirty: in Chris's mind, a tragedy of epic proportions. Samuel wanted to strangle him. Or scream.

When the urge subsided, he turned the showerhead on his feet and watched the water rise around his ankles. His legs weren't disfigured, just rail-thin and not very functional. And his upper body was nicely toned. Was it reasonable to hope Greta could be attracted to that? The only feature that might be really off-putting to a large, bulky woman like her was the fact that he was small. Not *that* area in particular but in general. Standing up, he was barely over five feet, and his hands, feet, and facial features were all proportional. Which was to say small.

If they ever did have sex, she would crush him. Samuel smiled. He rather liked the thought of that.

When the tub was half full, he soaped up, washed his hair, and shaved quickly. Then he let the water drain and used the handheld to rinse off.

There was a rap, loud and firm, on the bathroom door.

Jesus! Samuel lunged for a towel. Did she have no sense of personal space? "What?"

"Breakfast!" Her heavy footsteps tromped back toward the hall.

Samuel sighed. He'd half expected her to barge into the bathroom. Which would have settled the matter quickly. After performing his daily check for potential pressure sores, he pulled himself onto the edge of the tub, dried off, and reattached an empty urine bag. Technically it was time to change the catheter, but it wasn't going to kill him to wait one more day. Probably.

He dressed to the waist, including the knee support, then located his crutches and took an experimental turn around the room. His knee seemed fine—maybe it had been a simple strain after all—so he threw a shirt over one shoulder and went into the kitchen.

"Merry Christmas," he said. "And good morning. Sorry if the phone woke you; Chris is not exactly renowned for his thoughtfulness."

"I was already up." Greta turned around, a glass of orange juice in each hand. "Aren't you cold?"

He sat and pulled the shirt over his head. It was chilly for short sleeves, but he'd survive. He blew out a breath as he examined the spread on the table. "Geez, Greta, I can't promise to do this justice. I'm still full from dinner."

Although breakfast was large, it wasn't heavy: mainly fruits and a raspberry-jam pastry. Samuel had put away twice as much as he thought he would when he noticed the envelope sitting at his elbow. He picked it up. "For me?"

"It has your name on it."

"Right. Oh, I totally forgot. Your present is in my trunk."

"So is yours."

Samuel grinned, perfectly aware of her strategy. Uncertain whether her gesture would be reciprocated, Greta had brought in only the card. If he hadn't gotten her anything, the present would go safely unmentioned. Fortunately, he had. He slipped an index finger under the flap of the envelope and tore it open, wondering what a card from Greta might say. She was a woman of few words and even slimmer sentiment.

It was a postcard, printed on both sides, informing him that an unspecified sum had been given to a pregnancy crisis center in his name.

"I give them to my family every year," she explained.

"Oh. Thank you." He was disappointed not to find anything in her handwriting, but he liked the idea of being included in a family tradition. "I'm honored."

She stood and collected the dishes.

"Come out to the car. I want to get your present while it's not raining." Samuel let himself outside and popped the trunk. Greta appeared behind him. "Greg," he said. "Greg helped me wrap it." Just so she wouldn't think he was completely insane.

"I see." She pulled the box out and carried it inside, emerging again to open her own car while he was halfway to the door. Inside, she waited for him to sit in his armchair, then handed him a package about half the size of a shoe box.

"Open yours," he prompted, more concerned about her opinion of his present than the reverse. Moore had questioned his judgment when they'd gone Christmas shopping, but Samuel had written him off after he'd gotten Olivia a vacuum cleaner.

Greta pulled up the folding chair Samuel usually used for his feet and put the big box in her lap. She didn't try to save every bit of wrapping paper, but she didn't tear into it, either. Once the box was visible, the contents obvious, she refrained from comment until all the paper lay in a pile to one side.

The wok had been an easy find, the English-Chinese cookbooks less so. Not having a distinct Asian community in the area was odd. "I hope you don't have one," Samuel said. "A wok, I mean. I noticed we always go out for Chinese. And I thought it might be fun for you . . ." He realized he was being annoying and shut his mouth.

She picked up one of the cookbooks and flipped through the colored photographs. "I'll have to experiment." She nodded. "Thank you."

He studied her face and decided she was being sincere. Greta wasn't rude enough to dismiss a gift outright, but he'd hoped to get her something that wouldn't end up on a shelf alongside most of her other belongings. Greta appreciated functionality, and a wok had seemed useful.

She looked at him.

"Oh." He turned his attention to the box in his own lap. Forest-green paper embossed with tiny silver trumpets concealed a simple white box, which he opened to reveal a wallet the color of wine. He ran his fingers over the smooth, supple leather. "This is nice. Really nice."

"Thought you could use a new one."

He scooted forward and reached into his back pocket for the frayed canvas specimen he should have trashed years ago. "No kidding." She must have seen his wallet only a handful of times, but she'd remembered. Smiling, he began to transfer his credit cards.

A jangle alerted him to the fact that the box had slid between his knees and turned over on the floor, spilling a second item. Leaning over, he discovered a stainless-steel keychain, the kind with a belt clip and a retractable cord.

"Thought you could use that, too."

He caught the wry note in her voice. But he had dropped his keys in front of Moore, not Greta. "Please tell me Greg didn't—"

She shrugged. "Once he starts talking, it's hard to shut him up."

"My own personal fan club."

"At least he's not malicious."

Samuel's mind went to the drawing in his desk drawer but quickly pushed it away. "True." He smiled. "Merry Christmas."

Greta stood up, circled his chair, and bent over him.

They shared a kiss. It wasn't wild or desperate or clumsy, not like the first. This time it was comfortable. Warm. As if they'd been doing it for years.

"I love you," he whispered.

It seemed so natural, he almost didn't notice he'd said it aloud.

But Greta took a clumsy step back. She stooped to pick up the wrapping paper and went to throw it out, crumpling it in her hands.

Samuel strangled the urge to apologize. He wasn't sorry. He got up and followed her into the kitchen. She was bent over the refrigerator, a hand resting on the open door. "Greta." He put his hand on hers and pulled the door wide enough to see her face. "I mean it."

She closed the refrigerator, pulling away. She didn't seem to know what to do with her eyes or her arms. And then she lunged forward, catching his head between her hands, and pressed her lips to his.

Samuel dropped a crutch, but somehow she backed him against the counter and he slid up on the edge. The other crutch clattered nicely. He was slightly above her, and he used the height advantage to explore her nose and forehead. Her close-cropped hair was softer than it looked. She had one big hand around his ribs, and he was dimly aware that the other was on his knee. It ended when the bottle of juice tipped over and splashed the toaster.

Greta broke away and looked under the sink for a sponge.

"Left," Samuel breathed, "side."

She wiped up the mess without looking at him. Then she screwed the cap on the juice and rinsed the bottle off.

Samuel watched from the countertop, amused by her abrupt withdrawal. At least until she left. He leaned around the bar. "Hey, don't leave me here!"

Greta returned, eyes riveted to the floor. She picked up his crutches and thrust them in his direction. "Sorry."

"Are you kidding? I've been waiting for that since the first time. My whole life, maybe."

She stood in the center of the kitchen, still not looking at him, her face flushed with something between embarrassment and anger. The expression was familiar, and Samuel realized it was how she'd looked when he first invited her to dinner: on the verge of simply walking out the door.

He anchored his crutches and slid down. "Hey, hold on. You don't have to be like that." He touched her arm, gently. "Look, I enjoyed it. I hope you did, too. We'll do it again sometime. Now, how about we go for a drive?"

"I have to go. They're expecting me."

"Oh, you're going to see Hazel and Derek?"

"And my aunt."

SAMUEL STOOD IN the open doorway long after her car had disappeared, envying her family the time they had with her. He told himself he would have put the hours to better use, but that didn't matter. What mattered was that she had spent Christmas with him, before anyone else. What mattered was that he loved her, and it seemed like there was a pretty good chance she felt the same way about him.

Eventually the cold sank in and he closed the door. He chewed his lip, stared at his books, and then, abruptly, went to his bedroom and opened the walk-in closet.

A few storage boxes were stacked under his hanging pants and shirts; he slid the clothes to one side and spotted the box he was looking for tucked behind the others, under a couple of folded blankets and his detested full-leg orthotics. There was no graceful way to do this: he dropped his crutches, grabbed the doorframe, and half-slid, half-fell to the ground.

He pushed the old braces aside, resisting the perennial temptation to smash them against the wall until the metal hinges were bent beyond recognition. He had not succumbed to them this time; that would have to be enough. Instead he tugged the box forward. It was cardboard, nothing special, and he lifted the lid without effort.

Instantly the musky odor of his grandfather's tallit filled the closet. A quarter of a century dead, and the man's cigar smoke still clung to everything he'd owned. Smiling, Samuel lifted the blue and white shawl out and set it aside. Underneath were his mother's Tanakh, Bible, and a yellowed envelope with the letter she'd left when she died. He opened the envelope, tipped it to one side, and teased out the other item it contained.

The filigreed gold band fell into his palm, heavier than he'd remembered. The diamond embedded in the front glinted as he tilted his hand.

It had been his grandmother's ring. In the letter, his mother confessed her father had charged her to give it to Samuel on his thirteenth birthday. Samuel imagined she'd held it all those years, longing to give it to Chris, her only son with a hope in hell of passing on the family name. Some measure of deathbed guilt had prompted her, finally, to fulfill her father's wish.

Unlike the old man, she never would have admitted it even to herself, but Samuel knew she hadn't believed he would marry. Or rather, that anyone would choose to marry him. Until recently he would have agreed.

But maybe not. Maybe she was wrong.

16

JANUARY POURED. THE DRIZZLE that had come and gone since September came, stayed, and then rained buckets, overloading storm drains and swelling the Russian River so that Samuel held his breath every time he drove over the bridge. Umbrellas and crutches were mutually exclusive, and his raincoat only sufficed when he was standing up, so he was treated to a free shower every time he got in or out of the car.

Maria ran out and held an umbrella over him when she was home; the school librarian dug out an old space heater and installed it under his desk. Two weeks into the year, he pulled up before second period to find Sadie standing on the sidewalk, umbrella in hand. She showed up every day after that. Greta, who for some unfathomable reason liked to ride her motorcycle in a downpour, didn't comment on his perpetually foul mood. But she left him alone when he got too cranky, and for one reason or another, their weekly dinners always ended up being at his house.

He managed not to catch any of the plagues circulating around his classroom, although he did develop an infection. He spotted the cloudiness in his urine, dug out his horde of illicit Mexican antibiotics, and got it under control before the shaking started.

It was a week into February before someone mentioned Valentine's Day. Slightly panicked, Samuel tried to sound Greta out, whereupon she turned to him and announced, "I do not celebrate that holiday, nor do I want to see you on that day."

Samuel remembered the date on the photo in her purse, and the still, gray face of the only child she would ever have, and decided not to push the issue.

Maria disagreed.

"Mr. Cooke," she said, shaking out the umbrella and propping it inside the front door, "sometimes a woman *thinks* she doesn't want something when really she is secretly hoping you will surprise her."

"I understand, Maria, believe me, I do." He dumped himself into the waiting wheelchair, peeled off the damp, fingerless gloves he used for traction, and tossed them onto the hearth before rolling after her into the kitchen. "I can't explain without betraying her confidence, but trust me, she doesn't want candy and roses."

Maria looked thoughtful. "Then we'll have to think of something else. It's this Saturday, right? So we have two days. How about—"

The phone saved him. Samuel slid back and plucked the receiver from the counter. "Hello?"

"Bro! It's me."

"Uh, hi." Chris only called for major holidays and emergencies, sometimes not even then. "What's up?" Had something happened to the old man? Not that he cared.

"Nothin' much, just getting ready for spring training. Gonna be an awesome season."

"That's . . . great." Maria gave him an odd look, so he mouthed "brother" and rolled into the living room, receiver pinned between his shoulder and ear.

"So, we got this preseason publicity game up in Oakland,

thought I'd call to see if I could crash at your place for a night or two."

"Oh—sure."

"Awesome. We'll be there in about an hour. See ya!"

"Hold on, what?" The phone was dead. "Shit."

Maria leaned around the corner. "Everything okay?"

"Perfect." He sighed. "An hour" meant Chris had called from Oakland. More significantly, "we" meant he was bringing a girl-friend. Samuel could handle that, but advance warning would have been nice. If Chris had let him know a week ago, or even, say, yester-day, Samuel could have had Maria make some extra food, fix up the couch—

He snorted. The couch. As if they weren't sleeping together. Greta was definitely rubbing off on him.

Greta. He had forgotten. She was coming over tonight. Some-how Chris would manage to insult her or offend her or just act like a total douche. Belching at the table, using words like "piss" and "chick," scratching his . . . Oh, God. All Chris had to do to make this a disaster was act like *himself*.

Maybe Samuel could keep them from meeting altogether. He couldn't think of any lies Greta would believe, so finally he dialed her number and told her the truth. "My brother is a chauvinist asshole," he finished. "I'll lock him in the house and we'll pretend he never existed and I'll see you Sunday morning. All right?"

"I want to meet him."

Samuel kneaded his forehead with a knuckle. "You say that be-cause you never have."

"I'm not going to judge you based on your brother's behavior."

"Gretaaa," he moaned, "why do you have to say nice things?"

"I can handle him, Mr. Cooke."

He sighed. She could. "Well, Chris called like five minutes ago, and I don't think we have enough food." He ignored Maria's gestures to the contrary. "Can we at least put dinner off until tomorrow?"

"If you insist."

"Come tomorrow. It will be miserable and disastrous and horrible, but come."

TWO HOURS LATER, Chris stood in the living room, picking things up and putting them back in the wrong places. His bleached, dyed, and moderately tattooed girlfriend looked at the ceiling as she popped her gum. "I need a beer," she noted, and yawned.

"Place looks good, bro," Chris said, head bobbing in approval. "Woman's touch, hm?" He ribbed Samuel, but Chris was so much taller that his elbow hit Samuel's shoulder.

"Yeah," Samuel returned, deadpan. "My housekeeper's."

The girlfriend, whose name was Toni, tugged on Chris's arm. "There was a gas station near the overpass. I could swing by and get some beer."

It was hard not to call her Tammy, which had been the last one's name. As far as Samuel could tell there was no significant difference, except this one had a butterfly tattoo where he'd remembered a rose. "Actually," he said, "I'd prefer you not get wasted in my house."

She looked down at him, biting a fake nail as her eyes wandered from his feet to his crutches and arrived, finally, at his face. Then she glanced at Chris. "Baby . . ."

Chris slid an arm around her and squeezed her ass. "So, whatcha got to eat?" As usual, he would play the mediator.

It was going to be a long night.

SAMUEL INSISTED ON going to bed promptly at ten, mainly because he was tired of pretending not to notice while they sat on his couch and pawed each other like teenagers in heat.

"Aw, come on," Chris cajoled. He sat forward, disentangling himself from Toni. "We could watch TV or something."

"I don't have cable." Samuel got up from the kitchen table, feeling slow and clumsy. He always did around Chris. "Anyway, tomorrow's a school day." He gave a short wave. "See you guys in the morning. Or afternoon, if you're not up when I leave."

Samuel had no intention of going to sleep at the insanely early hour of ten. He shaved and bathed his upper body at the sink, then got into bed with a book. Around eleven, he heard Chris and Toni shuffling down the hall.

"This is like staying at my grandma's house," Toni whispered, too loudly. The comment was followed by stifled laughter.

Samuel rolled his eyes and tried to keep his mind on the page instead of the giggles and inane murmurs of "No, *you* are!" that came muffled through the wall. Sometime around midnight he finished the book, turned out the light, and lay in the dark, listening as his guests began making noises of a kind he would rather not have heard coming from his little brother.

Samuel thought of his grandmother's ring, sitting cold and heavy in his nightstand drawer. Even if Greta did want to make love to him someday, he knew it would never be as effortless as the self-absorbed rutting on the other side of the bedroom wall.

WHEN SAMUEL ROSE at seven-thirty, not even a rustle came from the next room. He might have hoped they'd up and gone in the middle of the night, but Chris's battered truck was still parked on the curb when Samuel left. For once, it wasn't raining.

At school, he spread a pile of graded homework along the edge of his desk for his keyboarding class to pick up as they filed in. Half the kids looked asleep.

A girl named Alma was the first to settle into her seat, jiggling her mouse to activate the screen. "Uh, whoa," she said. A few others sat down and glanced at Samuel uncertainly.

Fernando, sliding past Alma, stopped and whistled a lewd note. "Nice rack." He laughed and looked at Samuel. "Brave, man. She's gonna kick your ass, though."

The bottom fell out of Samuel's stomach as stifled snickers rippled around the room. He clattered to his feet and circled the desk. By the time he got into a position to see the class's screens, he was looking out across a sea of identical desktop backgrounds.

It was a photo of Greta in the process of removing her sweatshirt: back arched, normally unremarkable breasts thrust forward. The picture had been altered with a fisheye-lens effect, rendering her chest bulging and obscene. White letters below the photo stamped out the words GIRLFRIEND FAIL.

"Out," Samuel whispered.

The room was silent.

He tore his eyes away from the screen. The students were staring at him, wide-eyed. "Out," he said again. "Get out. All of you."

A few kids shuffled toward the door. "Where do we go?" someone asked.

Samuel pointed to the senior court outside the big windows. "There. Go sit. Talk. I don't care. Stay there until I call you in. At which time I'll be taking roll."

"It's cold—"

Samuel turned on the unfortunate boy. "Do I look like I give a fuck about the weather?"

When they were gone, Samuel collapsed into the nearest chair. He changed the background on the computer and then expunged the file from the hard drive. He shifted to the next computer and the next.

Lewd caricatures, okay. Chocolate, fine. In a sense, it came with the territory. This, though. This wasn't about Mr. Cooke, keyboarding instructor. It was personal. It was Greta. It was a good thing he didn't have a license to carry.

Half the period had gone by before he finished purging the image from his classroom, but Samuel didn't care. He knocked on the big window and motioned to his class. They straggled in, subdued and shivering.

He said nothing as they settled in their seats. He didn't know whether to lecture them all for the sake of the one or simply ignore the incident. Finally he settled for saying, "When I catch the person responsible for this, there will be consequences."

He looked at Fernando, who smirked.

SAMUEL HAD BEEN walking the programming class through the basics of Java. But when they arrived after the morning break, he said, "New project. We're going to get another computer from the other lab and set it up on my desk. And then we're going to network every machine in the classroom to mine."

They all blinked at him, except for Sadie, who studied her fingers. Samuel felt a rush of gratitude toward her for not telling the others—and guilt for having made her sit outside.

"What about Java?" Lemos asked. "And our midterm?"

Travis shushed him, too late.

Samuel was no longer interested in challenging them. "I'll shorten the test and make the project part of it; we'll pick up Java again afterward. I want this done ASAP."

"Why?" Marcus this time. "You want to spy on us or something?"

"Yes."

* * *

SAMUEL HADN'T SEEN Greg Moore in weeks. He'd assumed the man had fallen into the gravity well of his own little love affair, but Samuel needed to talk.

A call to the band room yielded no response, and the art room wasn't wired, so he set out over the gravel. When he reached his destination, he was confronted with a spring-loaded aluminum door like the one on the office. He whacked it with a crutch until it swung out in an angry arc.

"What the *hell* are— Oh, it's you." Moore stepped out and held the door.

Samuel shuffled into the dimly lit room. High tables swathed in butcher paper crowded the floor like a herd of angular cattle. Paint-spattered cabinets with broken hinges covered one wall, and the back of the room dissolved into heaps of miscellaneous materials. "Wow. Remind me to check with the Health Department before I visit your apartment."

Moore sniffed. "Who said you were invited?"

Samuel laughed and pulled out the nearest stool, wincing as it grated across the bare concrete. He pulled himself onto the seat, feet dangling, and deposited his crutches on the tabletop. The aluminum poles crossed numerous games of tic-tac-toe, sketches of comic book monsters, and scattered profanity. He was about to launch into his student woes when he realized something had changed. Moore had been in a state of euphoric anxiety since he and Olivia had resumed their relationship, but now he was subdued. "Is something wrong? I haven't seen you in a while."

Moore seated himself across from Samuel. He studied the decorated butcher paper. "She dumped me."

"What?" Samuel sat forward. "When? Why didn't you say something?"

Moore fingered a fold at the edge of the paper. He tore a piece off and began to rip it into confetti. "I dunno, I thought you were busy. I know how everything disappears. When you're in love."

If it hadn't been a supremely unmanly thing to do, Samuel would have hugged him. "Jesus, I'm sorry. What happened?"

Moore's eyes wandered. "She said I came on too strong. Said she wasn't ready for that much commitment."

"What did you do, propose?" Briefly Samuel's mind went to the wedding ring in his nightstand drawer. "You did, didn't you."

Moore shook his head. "She'd already said she was too young. So I asked her to move in."

Samuel closed his eyes.

"I didn't think she would freak out like that!" Moore put his hands out, palms up. "I don't get it. We've been sleeping together like every—"

"Spare me the details, please. Look, maybe it wasn't meant to be."

He put his head on the table and let out a heavy sigh. "She was so pretty. So, so, so pretty."

Samuel didn't know what to say. You'll find someone else? You're better off alone? If Moore had said anything like that when he thought he'd lost Greta, Samuel would have bitten his head off. So he kept his mouth shut.

After a few minutes, Moore straightened. "You didn't come out here for this, did you?"

Samuel had almost forgotten. Almost. "Just hoping to get some advice on a student issue. Remember that drawing? You know, us . . ." He gestured, and Moore nodded, sparing him the need to elaborate. "Yeah. That wasn't the end of it." He summarized.

Moore was aghast, his own grief forgotten. "How long has this been going on?"

"A while. It stopped after Christmas, so I thought it was over. Then today."

"And you have no idea who's doing it?"

"Oh, I know exactly who it is. I just don't have any proof. I don't even know how he's getting into my room."

Moore stood. "Let's find out."

FIFTEEN MINUTES LATER, Moore had scrutinized every inch of Samuel's classroom, concentrating on the doors and windows. He put his hands on his hips and let out a puff of air, blowing his hair away from his face. "This is not a forced entry," he pronounced.

"I figured he had a key."

Moore sat in one of the student chairs. "Easy enough to get. You haven't left yours anywhere?"

Samuel held up his key chain, attached to his belt. "I would have known. Still, this place isn't exactly a prison. If he had access to the office or knows a janitor . . ."

"Hm." Moore studied the ceiling. "We could set a trap."

"Okay, Greg? When I asked for help, I didn't mean like James Bond help." Or Wile E. Coyote. "Thanks for searching my room, but I was hoping you could tell me how to, you know, make him stop."

"Oh." Moore looked disappointed. "Maybe you could scare him? Tell him you have evidence and you'll turn him in if he doesn't stop."

Samuel shook his head. "He'd know I was bluffing."

"Would you be? I'm pretty sure the administration would consider this a Big Fucking Deal."

"Which Irving would handle with as much finesse as he did my arrival. Recall getting a memo about me, by any chance?"

Moore winced. They sat for several minutes, thinking. Finally, he said, "Have you told Cass?"

"No. And I'm not going to."

"Why not? *She* could scare the crap out of him."

Samuel held up an index finger. "First, I'd rather not mix my personal and professional lives." He put up a second finger. "Also, I, uh, really don't want her to think I'm a wuss." At least not any more than she already did.

"Ah." Moore nodded thoughtfully. "I can see how that might be a concern."

SAMUEL HALF EXPECTED to step into his house that afternoon and find his guests sprawled out amid empty beer bottles. He was pleasantly surprised to find nothing more than a couple of shopping bags on the couch. "Hello?"

"Hey!" Chris came out of the kitchen. "I was surfing on your laptop, hope that's okay. There's not much else to do."

"Sure. Where's, uh . . . Toni?"

He crooked a thumb over one shoulder. "Back porch. I told her she couldn't smoke in the house. Right?"

"Definitely not."

"How was your day?"

"Less than thrilling." Samuel shuffled over to the couch and peeked into the shopping bags. They were from a couple of hideously overpriced clothing stores on the plaza. "So, Greta is coming over tonight."

"Seriously? Awesome!"

"Right. Anyway, we need food. I can go by myself or—"

"Naw, man, I'll help. Just a sec, I'll ask Toni if she wants to go." Chris ducked out the back door and returned a moment later, smelling like an ashtray. "She's staying. My car or yours?"

"Mine." As they turned to leave, Samuel glimpsed the girl on the porch, probably freezing her ass off in a miniskirt. "So, what, this is like the second week?"

Chris closed the front door behind Samuel. "Almost three, man. How'd you know?"

"You always get them stuff at first."

"Dude, have a heart! Don't you ever get Greta anything?" Chris got in on the passenger side.

The conversation paused as Samuel levered himself into the driver's seat. "Sure," he continued, backing out of the drive, "but we're both independently wealthy, or close enough. I mean, you don't have money. Do you?"

Chris frowned. "I'm working on it. But what I got, that's hers, too, you know?"

They rode the rest of the way in silence. At the store, the lot was half empty, which meant Samuel could avoid the time-honored argument about whether he needed to park in the handicapped spot.

As they walked along the curb to the entrance, Chris thumped Samuel's shoulder. "Dude, you're not usually this quiet. C'mon, tell your bro what's wrong."

He wasn't trying to be condescending, but standing next to him always made Samuel moody. Five years' seniority never seemed to compensate for the fact that his brother was a foot taller and twice as broad. "Nothing," he muttered.

Chris pulled out a shopping cart. "Now, Samuel John . . ."

Oh, for Christ's sake. If he wanted truth, he could have it. "Yes, *Christian,* I'm just afraid you're going to wake up one morning and realize you've wasted your life. And then it will be too late."

Chris seemed genuinely puzzled. "What's wrong with my life?"

Samuel sighed. He glanced over his shoulder; only the mildly retarded parking lot attendant was around to hear. "Chris, look at you. Every season you think *this* is going to be your year to make the pros, but goddammit, you're pushing—no, you *are* thirty—"

"Hey, go easy!"

"See? Thirty isn't old, but you still can't face it. You run around with girls like you never left high school. It doesn't last, Chris. This one will hang on for another month or two until she realizes you aren't the star she thought you were, and then she'll be gone and you'll find someone else to take her place. Except someday there won't be any more. And then it'll be you and a bottle, and you'll look in the mirror and see Dad."

Chris studied him soberly. Then he shrugged and gave Samuel an easy grin, thumping him on the back again. "Hell, I can take care of myself—no need to worry about me, huh?"

That was the worst part. Chris could never believe that life would be so unkind as to deal him a critical blow, and when it came, it would catch him completely off guard. He'd think he was a victim of fate rather than its willing accomplice. Until then he'd simply pick himself up, dust off the scratches, and continue onward with that stupid, innocent grin. It was impossible to stay angry with him.

Chris grabbed a cart and flexed his arms over the handle. "Let's go for it, man. Draft me."

So Samuel followed his brother down the aisles, calling over his shoulder as unobtrusively as he could when they passed something that needed to go in. They stopped side by side at the meat display, a waist-high refrigerated bin. Chris picked through the yellow Styrofoam, tossing aside cuts he considered inferior or not sufficiently fresh.

"You have a barbecue, right? Chicken or steak? Wait, it might rain; is there an overhang on the porch? We could do it under there." He glanced at Samuel, eyes shining with the same puppy-dog eagerness he'd had since childhood. "What do you think?"

"It sounds fine." Samuel regretted having said anything. They only saw each other a few times a year; Chris was going to live however he wanted no matter what Samuel said.

Chris grinned and snatched up a couple pounds of tri-tip. "Trust me, you'll love it. You have steak sauce, right? Never mind, there's only one good kind. I'll show you."

Samuel put a hand on his brother's arm. "I'm glad you came." And he was.

"Aw, geez." In a rush of affection, Chris swung one long, muscled arm around Samuel and hugged him against his chest.

"Shit—" Samuel gasped. People were staring. In a second someone was going to ask if he needed help escaping the enormous blond ogre. "Put me down, you idiot! Jesus, if you don't—"

Chris dropped him.

Samuel caught himself on the meat display, breathed an uneasy smile, and shrugged his shirt down.

Chris scratched the back of his thick neck, where his haircut turned into prickly stubble. "Sorry."

"Do you have the meat? Let's go."

Chris pushed the cart next to Samuel. "You're mad, aren't you?"

He glowered. "No. I just— Christ, why do you have to do things like that in public?"

Chris shrugged and made a correction as the cart veered left.

"I'm five years older than you," Samuel muttered. "You treat me like a fucking kid."

"You are mad." Chris looked chagrined.

"No, I'm— Forget it." Samuel didn't want to deal with this, not now, not ever. It was pointless. "Sorry. I had a really crappy day."

"I don't understand."

"Never mind."

"Okay," Chris said quietly.

SAMUEL GAVE HIS brother a short lecture on behavior before Greta arrived. "No scratching," he said.

"What if I have an itch?"

"Not scratching; *scratching*." He gestured.

"Oh. Right."

"And no swearing."

Toni snorted. Samuel didn't bother to talk to her. If he convinced his brother, Chris would wheedle her into a compromise.

"*You* swear," Chris pointed out. He poked at the steaks and peered at the clouds moving overhead.

"Yeah, but not . . . Just try to keep it clean, all right? And don't say disrespectful things about women."

"Hey, I respect women more than anything."

Yeah, because they had vaginas. "What I mean is"—how could he put this in Chris's language?—"they aren't chicks or babes or whatever else. They're women."

Toni rubbed herself against Chris's thigh. "I'm a babe, baby." He gave a low laugh, and they kissed obscenely.

"I know how difficult it must be," Samuel said, "but I'd appreciate it if you could restrain your carnal impulses for a couple of hours."

GRETA ARRIVED AS the steaks came off the barbecue. She looked defensive, which was good. If she'd taken Samuel's warnings to heart, she had come prepared for the worst.

"Greta, this is my brother, Chris, and his girlfriend, Toni. Chris, Greta."

"Hi," said Toni, and went back into the kitchen.

"Glad to meet you, Mr. Cooke," Greta said, nodding to Chris.

Samuel wondered how that was going to work, two of them with the same name.

Chris just stood there looking dumb.

"Can you talk?" Greta asked.

He cast an anxious glance at Samuel.

"Go ahead." Maybe he had cautioned his brother a little too much.

"Um, hi," said Chris.

Greta put out a hand, and Chris looked at Samuel again.

"For the love of—" Greta cut herself off. "I'm sure Mr. Cooke told you not to do all sorts of things, but please, be yourself."

Samuel felt himself turn red.

Chris grinned. "Awesome. Hope you like steak, 'cause we got a ton. Want a beer?"

"Orange juice would be nice."

"Oh." Chris looked puzzled. "Bro, do we have any—"

"In the refrigerator. The orange bottle, strangely enough."

"Please relax, Mr. Cooke." Greta was now addressing Samuel.

"Me?" His brother was about to piss her off royally—Samuel didn't know how, but he was going to. And when Greta found out what was going on in his class, she was going to tear his head off. For all he knew, someone had already told her and she was waiting for him to confess, but he couldn't, because if she *didn't* know, she'd think he was a complete pansy for letting it go on this long. "Relax? *Why?*"

She took off her jacket and draped it over his armchair. "Your brother is who he is. I won't be offended."

Samuel didn't believe her. If Vince Irving offended Greta with his spurious remarks, there was no way she was going to overlook a guy who swapped women as often as he rotated tires.

Then her words sank in: He is who he is. Chris wasn't pretending to be respectable, and he certainly wasn't responsible. He admitted his faults, and if women got hurt, they couldn't say they hadn't seen it coming. It didn't mean Greta would like Chris, though she might be able to tolerate him for a few hours. Samuel relaxed. A little.

She helped him get the vegetables together, and they sat down to eat. Chris discovered the leftover wine from Christmas, insisted they finish it off, and took great pride in portioning out the meat, waiting with bated breath as everyone sampled his "secret" sauce.

"It's good," pronounced Greta.

Chris shot Samuel a triumphant grin and turned to Greta. "So," he said coolly. "Sam says you're a gym teacher?"

"Yes."

He nodded. "You definitely look like one."

Samuel tried to kick Chris under the table. It didn't work. He settled for a glare, vowing to drown his brother in the bathtub as soon as Greta left. Toni pressed a napkin to her mouth, but her eyes were laughing.

Greta only raised an eyebrow. "Partially the reason I chose my profession."

"Oh," said Chris, belatedly realizing his faux pas. "I didn't mean—"

"You strike me as a first baseman," she added.

"You follow baseball?"

"When I was younger. Used to go watch the Giants with my father."

"Sweet! Hey, do you remember this guy who played third base for . . ."

Samuel watched Toni pick at her vegetables as Chris and Greta dished on baseball, their conversation gradually filling the room. Later, they moved on to sports medicine and weight lifting. Samuel had nothing to say, nothing to contribute. His fears about Chris offending her were groundless; they could have gone on for hours. All Samuel could think was that Chris had more in common with Greta than he did.

He had known this would happen. This was what he had really feared.

After dinner, he found himself on the porch with Toni while Greta and Chris did the dishes. He sat on a patio chair and prepared to sulk.

"So," Toni said. "That's your girlfriend."

She had finally gotten bored enough to speak to him directly. "Yeah."

"Interesting." She tongued the mouth of the beer bottle. It was her third. "She's older?"

"Yeah." Duh.

"Seems like they hit it off pretty well." She paused to take a sip. "Don't worry. He's decided she's another guy. That's how he talks to guys."

Samuel snorted at the implication that he might be worried Chris would steal Greta. "Thanks for the reassurance."

She sniffed. "It's my fault? As if."

He hadn't a clue what that meant. She seemed like the sort of person who parroted lines she'd heard in chick flicks and reality TV.

She took another sip. "So you like her."

"I am completely, pathetically in love with her." Samuel decided he shouldn't have had the entire glass of wine.

Toni laughed. "That's sweet."

Yeah, just adorable. God, he wanted to punch someone.

"Sometimes . . ." She pulled out a cigarette and lit it with one hand, beer bottle dangling from the other. "Sometimes I wish Chris was like that."

"Try someone with a heart instead of a body." Even as the words came out of his mouth, he knew he was being unfair. "Jesus, forget I—"

She shot him snake eyes over the lip of the bottle. "You're kind of an asshole, you know that?"

He shrugged.

"Chris isn't a bad guy. He likes me. But . . ." She glanced from her beer to the stars. "It wouldn't hurt him, not really, if I left."

"Sure it would." For about three days, Chris would be crushed. Then he'd shake it off and move on. She was right; he wasn't heartless, he just wasn't needy.

She shrugged. "He'd find someone else. He always has. It's not like I can complain. I'm 'someone else,' too."

"So why do you stay?"

Toni finished off the beer and stooped to set the bottle on the deck, treating him to an unsolicited view of her cleavage. "He's nice. Doesn't treat me bad, takes me out places. We have fun."

"Fun. That's what you want?"

"More than that, eventually. I'm not ready for anything serious."

"When does 'eventually' come?"

She thought about it. "I think I'll know it when I see it. If it even exists."

"And if you don't?"

"Then life sucks. Big surprise." She dropped the glowing butt of her cigarette, aiming for the empty bottle of beer. It missed; she crushed it with a heel. "Why do you care?"

"I don't, I guess."

She yawned and turned to go inside.

"Do you think she loves me?" he blurted.

Toni let out a bark of surprised laughter. "How should I know?"

Samuel was definitely, definitely off alcohol from now on.

"GRETA IS AWESOME," Chris pronounced after she had gone. "Personally, I wouldn't go for her, but—"

"But for me, she's all right?"

Chris followed Samuel down the hall to the bedroom. "You know I didn't mean it like that. She's hard-core, like a martial arts master or something."

Samuel forced a laugh. "What?"

"Like all serious and honorable and stuff."

"That's called integrity, Chris." He pushed in the door and flicked on the light.

"Yeah, okay. But man, she knows her ball. Basketball, too, did you hear?"

"I'm aware of her interests."

"God, if I could find a girl like that, with a body like Toni—"

Samuel turned. "How can you *say* that?"

Chris took a step back. "I didn't—"

"With your girlfriend in the next room—"

He rolled his eyes. "Aw, she went out for another smoke, she can't hear."

"Does it matter? You're thinking it. Even as you're—you're *fucking* her."

"Hey, she knows we're not serious, like marriage or anything. I'm not leading her on, you know I don't do that."

"Does it make a difference? You're honest, but you're still using her. And she's taking it—her and all the girls like her—because she doesn't think there's anything more. She's never seen what love can *be,* and if she ever does, she won't believe it's real. Just by doing what you're doing, you cheapen it, Chris."

Samuel knew immediately he'd gone too far.

Chris's hand covered the thin line of his mouth and then fell, slicing through the air. "Okay. You know what? I'm done. Mom made me promise to look out for you, but she's gone, and I am done with your shit." He squeezed his eyes shut. "You act like you're so much better than everyone. Maybe that's what you tell yourself, and maybe you believe it, because everyone else plays along. But your bullshit doesn't work on me."

Samuel felt like he'd been stabbed in the gut. Like he couldn't breathe. Funny, how someone could do that even from the grave. "Mom—Mom asked you. To take care. Of me." Blood pounded in his ears. Then the boiling fury cooled and hardened, and his tongue lashed out with the violence his body could not. "And you—" He laughed bitterly. "You took her seriously? I wouldn't trust you to pick up my goddamn dry cleaning. Consider yourself officially relieved of any shit-eating obligations." He held up a finger. It shook. "And for the record, I am not better than everyone else. I am better than *you*."

Chris took a threatening step forward. "News flash, Sam: you left your career to teach *high school*. That doesn't exactly say 'job satisfaction' to me." His hands balled into fists. "Meanwhile, your little brother—your dumb, stupid, idiot brother—is out having the time of his life. Admit it: you don't think baseball sucks. You'd trade places with me in a heartbeat. The only reason you say you don't want to play is because you *can't*."

"Oh, right. Yeah." Samuel didn't back down. They stood face-to-chest. "Secretly I fantasize about being a subpar player who can't even hit a breaking ball on some crappy second-rate team. Way to go, Mickey Mantle. You're really living the dream."

"You think I'm wrong? It's the same with women. Do you seriously expect me to believe you wouldn't drop your pants for the first girl who offered? And the next? You're not better than me. There's just nobody who'd take you."

"Excuse me if I'd rather be celibate than sleep with any of the walking STDs you like to fuck."

Chris snorted. "You never said jack shit about my sex life until now. Some crusty old lesbian takes pity on you, and suddenly you think you're in love. But it can't just be any love, no, it has to be real love, and everyone else's has to be fake."

Samuel shoved a finger at his brother's chest. "Say what you want about me. But don't you *dare* say Greta isn't real."

"Oh, please. You don't have a fucking clue. You want to know what Greta is? She's Mom." He laughed. "You went out and found another goddamn Mom to protect you from the big bad world. How pathetic can you—"

Samuel threw himself at Chris. It was no contest, but he didn't care. He grabbed Chris's shirt and landed one firm blow to his jaw before he fell to the floor in a clatter of plastic and aluminum.

17

W HAT THE HELL WAS that supposed to be?" Chris put a hand to his face, looking more surprised than angry. "Are you nuts?" He gave a puzzled laugh and bent, offering a hand.

Samuel lunged for his arm.

"What the—"

He clawed himself up to Chris's shoulder, wrapped an arm around his neck, and plunged a fist into his stomach. Goddamn, it felt good.

Chris's surprise melted into a wordless exclamation of fury and pain. "You crazy little bastard!" He gathered Samuel's collar in one fist and drew the other back—

"What are you *doing*?" Toni stood in the doorway, mouth open.

"Do it," Samuel urged. "Hit me, you worthless piece of shit!" It was too late. He saw himself reflected in Chris's uncertain eyes; watched as the elder brother dissolved into helpless cripple.

Chris's grip relaxed. The threatening fist unfolded, and he hooked his arm under Samuel's, lowering him carefully to the floor.

Samuel shoved him away. "Get the fuck out of my room."

Chris opened his mouth, but nothing came out. Finally he shut it and nodded. "Yeah. Sure." He slammed the door.

Alone, Samuel sat on the floor, legs twisted beneath him. "Shit," he whispered. "You worthless little shit."

After a few minutes, he crawled to the bed and pulled his pant legs up, checking for injuries. There were none.

He'd never fought like that with Chris. Ever. Not just physically but with that much venom. When it came to their father, Chris had always stayed out of the way, and Samuel had interpreted that to mean his brother was at least nominally on his team. Apparently Chris's easygoing attitude had been an act, an attempt to placate his pathetic cripple of a brother.

Now Samuel knew the truth. So much for family.

There was a knock at his door.

"What?"

"Phone." Chris leaned in and chucked the receiver at Samuel.

Samuel caught it midair. He opened his mouth to throw back a sarcastic comment, but his brother had already gone. "Hello?"

"I forgot to say I'd bring breakfast tomorrow."

It was Greta. "Breakfast?"

"To the game. We can eat in the car."

Now he was lost. "Game?"

She sounded impatient. "We agreed to go to your brother's game tomorrow. Saturday. In Oakland. Remember?"

He didn't, not really; he hadn't exactly been paying attention. "Oh." Crap. "I kinda doubt he'll be happy to see me there."

Greta was silent, digesting his subtext. "What happened?"

How did one abridge twenty years of bottled-up bile? He pulled one leg up to unbuckle the brace. It fell out of his pant leg onto the bed, an empty shell in the middle of the white down comforter. "I hit him," he said, perfectly aware how ridiculous it sounded.

There was no pause of disbelief, no incredulous snort. "Why?"

"We argued. I don't know, it was stupid." He sat back, holding the phone between shoulder and chin, and pulled the other leg onto the bed. "I accused him of being careless. With, uh, romantic situations. And then he sort of blew up. I never realized he resented me that much. And then he said something that just—I—God, I just lost it."

"He doesn't resent you. Go apologize."

Samuel was silent. "Are you saying that to get rid of me?" He imagined her standing by the phone in the kitchen in her . . . whatever she wore to bed. He tried on a nightgown, but that wasn't right, and neither was underwear. Sweats? Probably sweats.

"No," she said.

"He resents me." He unbuckled the second brace and started to massage his foot. It looked swollen. Hopefully it wouldn't turn into anything dire.

"If he's resentful of anything, it's his inability to win your approval."

He stopped. "Uh. What?"

"He bragged all night—"

"He always brags."

"It wasn't me he was trying to impress."

Samuel closed his eyes. She couldn't be right. That was absurd. "Greta, you didn't hear the things we said to each other."

"I don't have to. You're his older brother."

"The last time that impressed him, I was eleven."

Greta was quiet. And then she said, "It doesn't matter what you can or can't do. He still looks up to you."

He swallowed. "Are you sure?"

"Yes. Go apologize."

"But—"

"If you want my advice, that's what it is."

"Oh." Not that he'd asked for it. But still.

"I'm going to bed."

"Wait, Greta, listen. I'm sorry if I checked out tonight. The two of you got along so well—"

"I told you I could handle him."

"You were 'handling' him?" Samuel was confused. Oh, very confused. "But . . ."

"Having common interests does not mean we think alike." She sounded very definite. "I'm going to bed. I'll come by at eight."

"Um, okay."

She sighed. Heavily. "Mr. Cooke."

"Yeah?"

"I like you better."

He didn't say anything.

"Did you hear me?"

"Yes."

"Go apologize. Good night." The phone went dead.

Samuel didn't know if she was right about Chris. She seemed so *certain*. Like it was completely obvious to everyone but him.

It didn't feel obvious. Chris's accusations were already circling inside his head, stirring doubt and confusion. Samuel couldn't see it rationally; he just wanted to hit Chris over and over again.

Greta was coming at eight. If he didn't make an effort, she'd be angry. And if the choice was Chris or Greta . . . well, he wasn't picking Chris.

Samuel looked at his braces and sighed. Sometimes it was such a pain. Instead of putting them on, he grabbed a crutch and used the handle to catch the back of his wheelchair. He pulled it over to the bed and got in.

For reasons Samuel didn't care to dwell on, the wheelchair made Chris visibly uncomfortable. As if he could pretend everything was normal so long as Samuel was standing up. Too bad. If Chris wanted an apology, he'd have to deal.

Samuel went into the hall and knocked on the guest room door. There were muffled voices and a thump as Chris's feet hit the hardwood floor. The door cracked. "What?"

"I want to talk."

"Can we do this later?" He was in his boxers.

"No."

"Fine." Chris squeezed out the door, closed it, and strode down the hall to the kitchen. Even at thirty—middle-aged in baseball years—he had the body of a young god, powerful and perfectly toned. He sat at the table. "Say what you have to say."

Samuel pushed a chair aside and pulled up to the edge. "I want to apologize." He sighed. "For hitting you. And what I said. Everything. I'm sorry. Your life is yours."

"Yeah." Chris gave him a sullen look.

Samuel had sort of expected a reciprocal apology. Oh well. "I never knew—I never thought you felt that way. About me."

Chris shrugged, avoiding Samuel's eyes. "Only sometimes."

Samuel laughed softly. "I guess that's allowed. I hate you sometimes, too." He gave his brother a crooked smile.

Chris traced the grain of the table with one finger. "Just sometimes?"

"Chris . . ." Samuel reached for his arm. "Of course I don't hate you. Jesus, tell me you know that much!"

He shrugged.

"Jealous, God, yes, but you're my brother. Maybe I've been too critical, but it's because I worry about you, understand?"

"I dunno."

"Chris." What did he want Samuel to say? What else could he say? "Please."

"I don't hate you, either."

Samuel sighed. "Thank you."

Chris got up. "Did she tell you to say that? Greta?"

Samuel smiled sheepishly. "She told me to apologize. I couldn't get anything else out of her."

"She's smart." Chris smiled a little, too. "A good match for you."

"I hope so." Samuel pulled back from the table. "Um—Chris. I want you to know, um, that I, uh, I'm proud of you." There. He wasn't sure if it was true, but he'd said it.

Chris colored. "Really?"

Holy crap, Greta was right. "Sure. Your childhood was at least half as awful as mine, and look where you are. It's not what I'd choose, but it's good for you."

"Hey, it wasn't that bad." Chris stepped to one side of the wheelchair and then the other. He seemed to want to touch Samuel without knowing quite how.

It took all of Samuel's willpower to force himself to say through clenched teeth, "Push me to bed?"

Chris seized the handles. "No problem."

Samuel crossed his arms and tried to relax as his brother propelled him down the hall and into the bedroom.

"Is there anything you want me to—"

"I'm good, thanks."

Chris stood there watching as Samuel moved from the chair to the bed. "Sam?"

Samuel winced. "Yeah?"

"Why did you want me to hit you?"

He laughed. "I dunno. I guess I wanted you to take me seriously."

"I didn't want to hurt you."

"Chris . . ." He sighed. "Pain is a relatively small price to pay for a little respect."

Chris looked at the floor. He gnawed on his lip. Then he took two long steps to Samuel's side, grabbed his shoulder, and slugged him in the gut.

"Oh—God—" Samuel doubled over, clutching the explosion of agony in his middle.

"Happy?"

Samuel reached for the bedpost, catching himself before he slid off the edge of the mattress. "Um—yes." He laughed, or managed a breathless equivalent. "Thanks."

"Night, bro." Chris slipped out the door.

Samuel pulled his legs onto the bed and lay in a fetal position, moaning quietly, for some time.

18

IT WAS A CHARITY game.

"I hate these things." Samuel shuffled into the row of seats and sat next to Greta.

Toni, who had gotten up to let them in, sat down on his other side. "You okay? You're walking funny."

"I always walk funny."

"Funn*ier*."

"I'm fine." His stomach, not so much. If Chris ever decided to give up baseball, he could probably swing a career in boxing. Samuel scowled at the row of kids in the rows behind home plate. "I really, really hate these things."

Greta took his crutches and propped them on the empty seat to her left. "It's for a good cause."

"It's disgusting. Look at them." They all had wheelchairs, walkers, missing hair, or something. A couple of players walked back and forth in front of them, shaking hands and signing balls. "The kids worship those guys."

"They're role models," Toni pronounced, clearly including Chris in her estimation.

"A role model is someone you emulate. You think any of those kids will ever be out on the field? Not a chance in hell. Their parents should be teaching them to admire Van Gogh, Itzhak Perlman, Stephen Hawking. Instead they're here, wishing they could be Christian Cooke." And what an aspiration that was.

"Big deal," Toni said. "It's just a metaphor or whatever, anyway. Nobody becomes what they dream of as a kid."

"I always wanted to be a programmer."

"Yeah, well, you're weird."

Greta was quiet for another minute. Then she said, "Van Gogh isn't raising money for research."

She had a point. Nothing drew money like sports. It was still sick, and he didn't have to like it.

Chris found them before the game started. He was enormous and spectacular in his freshly bleached uniform, drawing stares from everyone in their section. He perched on the arm of a chair behind them and pointed out various features of the stadium, a firm hand on Samuel's shoulder. Samuel smiled and nodded and focused on not exploding.

"Do you take after your mom?" Toni asked Samuel when Chris moved down a couple of rows to sign autographs for a group of Cub Scouts.

Samuel laughed. It was an obvious assumption; next to his brother, he looked like a child. And Toni had likely met their father, who was nearly as big as Chris. "Actually, aside from Chris's hair, we're both male copies of Mom." Toni gave him a skeptical look; he sighed. "I had to take a lot of drugs. For stuff. It stunted my growth." Frequent nausea and upchucking probably hadn't contributed much to good nutrition, either.

"Oh." She shifted awkwardly. "Sorry."

"Why?"

She blushed. "Well, I mean, you know . . ."

"What, you think I'd rather be a six-foot-three, two-hundred-pound cripple—"

Greta put a hand on his thigh.

Samuel glowered. Feeling damned uncomfortable, he'd tried to make someone else squirm, and Greta had seen right through the attempt. He took her hand and she squeezed, which made him feel a little less like going on a murderous rampage.

Then the Jumbotron turned red. Hearts fluttered across the giant screen. It spelled out HAPPY V-DAY in seizure-inducing flashes.

Greta withdrew her hand.

"Oh God," he whispered. It was Valentine's Day. Greta had *come*, and he had forgotten. Maria was right, and Samuel had no card, no gift, no candy. He swallowed and darted a glance at Greta.

She glared at him, but it wasn't an incredulous *you forgot* look. Her stony expression said, *Pretend this isn't happening and I will spare your life.*

Saint Valentine? Never heard of the guy. "Great weather, huh?"

The game wasn't bad; Chris's team lost, but it didn't go on the season's stats. Samuel concentrated on the field, ignoring the section of kids cheering by home plate. He bought two hot dogs and ate them both because neither Greta nor Toni would touch the second one.

Afterward, Toni disappeared, making a beeline for the locker room. Greta waited with Samuel until the stands emptied, then helped him extricate himself from the stadium seats.

The kids—and a gaggle of reporters—had the same idea. Several dozen loitered near the team merchandise shop, directly in front of the exit to the handicapped parking area. They were trapped.

A woman with a camera and an electronic notepad rushed forward. "Sir, it's wonderful that you've come out to support today's game. Do you suffer from cerebral palsy?"

"I don't suffer from anything."

That set her back. Not for long. "You have lymphoma?"

"Yeah, these crutches really help with the cancer." He tried to brush past.

She trotted after him. "You've come out to support today's game, haven't—"

"I have nothing to do with anyone." He wished Greta would turn around and give the reporter one of her death glares, but she just walked next to him, hands in her pockets. "I came to watch my brother play. Now I'm going home."

That got the woman really excited. "Your brother is a player? Sir? May I ask his name?"

"No."

She gave him what she clearly imagined was her most winning smile. "Why don't you tell me which team?"

"Why don't you go fuck a cactus?" Samuel said. She went away.

"That was uncalled for," Greta said.

"See what you think after it's happened another five or ten times." *Baseball hero plays for crippled brother* was every journalist's wet dream.

Greta suggested lunch; though Samuel appreciated the not so subtle change of subject, he didn't feel like eating, not after the hot dogs. "Can we just go home?"

"If you want."

Something in the tone of her voice—which might have been coolly irate or simply indifferent—reminded him of Maria's admonition about Valentine's Day. Had Greta's suggestion been more than a subject change? Was she hoping for a romantic meal? He cleared his throat. "Unless you want to go out; we could totally do that. If you wanted."

Greta's look said she didn't need to be treated with kid gloves any more than he did.

"Or we could just go home."

She offered to drive, so he explained how to work around the hand controls, and she circled the parking lot twice before heading back the way they had come. On the other side of the bridge, through the twists and turns of the freeway, Samuel started to feel queasy.

Greta had evidently been keeping an eye on him, because when he heaved, she was already pulling over. He spilled halfway out the door and deposited the contents of his stomach on the ground. He waited, gasping putrid air, until his body convulsed again and purged his system completely. Feeling Greta's hand on his back, he glanced over one shoulder to see that she'd gotten napkins out of the glove box and a bottle of water from who knew where.

He used the napkins, tossed them into the dirt with the rest of the mess, then sat up and accepted the bottle of clean, cool water. He spat out the first mouthful and swallowed the rest.

Greta reached over him, and his seat fell back with a bang. "Here, this will help." She dug a pink digestive tablet out of her purse.

Samuel felt like throwing up again, but if he chucked the water, he was going to get all wacky and dehydrated. He forced the tablet down, smiling weakly. "What else do you have in there?"

"Classified."

"Anything hallucinatory?"

She snorted and pulled into traffic. Two seconds later, a vintage telephone ring sounded from her purse. Greta fumbled blindly, pulled out an iPhone, and glanced at the face before handing it to Samuel.

The display read *Chris Cooke*. "My brother has your number? Do *I* have this number?"

"Answer."

Chris was calling to say that he and Toni were heading home rather than spending another night, which was fine with Samuel. He must have telegraphed his lack of disappointment, because Chris said, "You liked the game, right? It was fun?"

"Sure. You guys put up a good fight." Samuel decided not to comment on the hot dogs.

"You'll never guess what happened after. This lady reporter, pretty hot—she comes into the locker room asking if one of us had a brother at the game. I say yeah, and she describes you, and I say, 'That's my bro, Sam.' Then she does this whole interview on me and, like, what it's like to be brothers. So now there's gonna be an article in the *Oakland Tribune,* no kidding, with my picture! She woulda taken us together," he added, "but she said you were busy or something. Is that cool or what?"

"Yeah." Samuel sighed inwardly. "Cool."

"All right, we gotta head out before it gets too late. Thanks for the food and stuff, it was great. Tell Greta she was awesome, too."

Samuel dropped the phone into the open maw of Greta's purse. "Hear that?" Chris always yelled into the receiver, so it was a good bet she had. "Oakland gets to read about my pathetic life, and you're awesome. Oh, God—"

This time there was no water, so he had to make do with napkins and a breath mint that didn't erase the sour taste of stomach acid. "Wow," he said. "Happy Valentine's Day."

Greta pulled back into the slow lane. "I've had worse."

Jesus. "Sorry. I shouldn't have . . ." The words evaporated somewhere between his brain and his mouth. He felt light-headed. "Um, Greta? If I pass out, don't take me to the ER. I'll come around."

"What?" Her eyes flicked from the road to his face, alarmed.

"I'm losing fluid, and there's nothing in my stomach."

She frowned. "You should—"

"Yeah. I know." He knew the lecture inside out: he needed to put on more weight, so a lapse in blood sugar wouldn't hit him so hard. But any weight he put on was extra weight he had to drag around. He needed to drink more fluids, because his urine wasn't being stored in his bladder for his body to recirculate. But more fluids meant he had to empty the bag every couple of hours. "Trust me, I know."

She shook her head, as if to express general disgust with men who did not take care of themselves, and merged into the fast lane. "Keep talking."

"Um . . ."

She asked him how he liked Healdsburg. It felt like the middle of nowhere, but as long as he had the Internet, he was fine. Did he miss L.A.? No. Teaching? Also fine, unless you counted the horrific things his students were doing to him. Not that he was going to mention that. Did he see his brother often? No, not as long as he could help it. He swallowed hard, fighting the nausea as it passed, wavelike, over him.

Greta cranked the fan up and angled a vent at his face. "Does he know what happened?"

"What?" The blast of cold air and her question caught him off guard. "Oh. You mean with the old man."

She nodded.

"No." Samuel let out a quiet breath of laughter. "Chris thinks it was a medical fuckup." Oh shit, he'd said "fuck." It wasn't fair, asking him this kind of crap when he was half out of his head. "My folks said if I told him, or anyone else, what really happened, the cops would lock them up and I'd end up in a home for retards."

Greta fell silent, her half-humorous attempt to keep him lucid fading to, what, horror? "You stopped believing that at some point," she said.

"Yeah. I dunno. I guess." Samuel shrugged. "It wasn't the first time he hit me. Dad. But he never laid a finger on Chris."

Greta raised an eyebrow.

He sighed. "Chris got the good father. I can't take that away." He didn't know where this was going, but it felt weird. If he kept talking, he was going to say things he didn't want her to know. "Thanks for coming today. I know you had other plans, so I appreciate it."

Greta looked like she might force the conversation back; then her face softened minutely, and she sighed. "It was time."

Samuel wanted to ask her what that meant, and perhaps he did. But his next conscious memory was a slight jerk as she parked the car. He blinked, feeling disoriented, and saw that they were in front of his house. "Did I pass out?" It was February 14. He was thirty-four. He lived at 442 North Street. Mental state: reasonably lucid.

"Sleeping, I think," she said.

Whatever had happened, he felt like crap. Slowly, very slowly, he got out of the car. The world spun lazily. Greta had his keys, so she let them into the house.

"I'm not sure what possessed me to eat those— Shit." He went into the bathroom and did some pointless dry heaving. When he emerged, Greta was making soup. That didn't go down well, either.

"*Relax,*" she told him over the kitchen sink.

He hooked an elbow over the edge and looked at her. "You think this is mental." Of course; that was why she had asked about his old man.

Greta turned, resting her backside against the edge of the counter, and folded her arms. "You just spent three hours digging your nails into your thighs."

Which naturally meant he was a basket case. "Right, because there's no possible way I could be puking my guts out over reconstituted pork by-products." How had this followed him? Six hundred miles, and still his father loomed.

"I've never seen you so anxious."

God, could she not just— "I can't *help* it!"

Apparently she decided he did need help, because she leaned over and kissed him.

"Oh, God," he gasped. "I can't believe you did that!"

"Your mouth is clean."

He bent over the sink again.

She rubbed his back. "Well. Not anymore."

19

"I TALKED TO HER last night. She said she'd think about it." Greg Moore paced in and out of the library storage room, biting a hangnail.

"Greg, you can't obsess like this."

"Clearly I can, because I am. I have to get her back."

Samuel set down the soldering gun. He'd repaired everything that could be fixed in the media room a month ago; since then, a steady stream of staff computers had migrated his way.

"You continue to do this, and she's going to freak out again. You have a chance, and you're going to blow it if you act like a stalker."

Moore moaned. "I totally am."

"So don't. Relax." If only he could handle students as easily as computers. He'd arrived that morning to find the top of his desk covered with derogatory comments about Greta—in permanent marker. The old newspaper, unfolded, had covered most of it, but he'd be spending the afternoon with a bottle of acetone. Worse, Fernando had opted to stay in his class for a second semester. Had his private life not been faring rather well, Samuel might have taken it as concrete proof that God hated him.

Moore chewed his lip. "Really?"

Samuel shrugged and spun the office chair. "I dunno, that's what Greta keeps telling me." Not that it worked, but it was a good idea.

"No offense, but if I'm taking relationship advice, it's not gonna be from—" Moore stopped and cocked his head to one side, listening as the library door opened. "Speak of the devil."

"It's not Greta."

Moore picked up a potentiometer and fiddled with the knob. "Who else would it be?"

"Fifty bucks says it's Irving."

He dropped the meter. "Shit!"

"Oh, relax." Samuel laughed as Moore hurried out, ducking his head to the principal as they passed.

Irving paused in the doorway, taking a visual inventory of the room. "Morning," he said.

"What's up?" Samuel knew perfectly well what was up. Although he hadn't heard a thing from the man since before Christmas, there was a rally tomorrow. Which meant Irving had come to an impasse. He feared Samuel would expose his spending habits, but he had an almost pathological need to feel that his staff was one big happy family. If Samuel avoided rallies, the illusion of unity would crack—and shatter altogether if, God forbid, any other teachers followed his example.

Irving stepped into the room. "I see you've got some new equipment."

Samuel followed his eyes to the computer tower sitting open in front of him. "This? It's from Mr. Langford's room." Was Irving attempting to catch him doing some of his own discretionary spending? Please.

"Oh. Good, good." Irving leaned against the wall. "Just wanted to remind you about the rally tomorrow—"

"I'll be there."

"Good." Rather than taking the hint to leave, Irving smiled. "On a personal note, I've been hearing some interesting rumors. I don't usually put much stock in hearsay, but—"

"It's true." Samuel shrugged. "We're dating."

Irving looked mildly surprised. "Really. You and Cass. Interesting." He chuckled. "She's a handful, eh?"

A screwdriver sat on the bench next to Samuel. He resisted the urge to pick it up and hurl it at Irving's face. "Anything else? Because I'm done discussing my love life."

The principal held his hands up. "'Nuff said." He backed out, wearing the same condescending smirk his brother had at that first basketball game, when—

When he'd mocked Greta.

Samuel stared at the space Irving had vacated. For a moment, the library beyond the doorway was a blur; then his eyes focused, and he realized he was looking at the shelf of old yearbooks.

He grabbed his crutches and lurched across the library.

Greta was forty-six, she'd said. So three decades . . . He skimmed down the row until he hit the right year. He pulled it off and dumped it on the nearest table, then added the year before and after. He sat and began flipping. General photos, senior photos, activities— sports. Basketball. Girls. There was a photo of the entire team; he studied each face one by one. Greta wasn't there.

No, of course not. Not if she was pregnant at sixteen. He reached for the previous year and opened to the same section.

Her hair was in a ponytail. Though she stood in the back row, partially hidden, her broad shoulders and square jaw were instantly recognizable. At fifteen, she had to be one of the youngest players, but she was bigger than the other girls, built for action. She had probably mowed down everyone on the court. Samuel smiled at the defiant challenge in her eyes, then remembered what he was looking for.

He flipped past boys' basketball and found the football team; the faces in the group shot were too small and blurred to make out. On the following page, they had been photographed by year. And there he was, with the juniors. Samuel let the book fall open on the table. The name under the photo read *Paul Irving*. But it was Vince's brother, Butch. And he wore that same infuriating sneer.

THAT AFTERNOON, AS he scrubbed his desk clean, Samuel wasn't thinking of Fernando. All he could think about, all he could see, was the knowing grin on Irving's face. And it filled him with white-hot fury.

He had jumped to the obvious conclusion: Butch was the bastard who had manipulated Greta; Butch was responsible for her pain; Butch had to be punished. He didn't know if it was true. Even if it wasn't, at the very least, the Irving brothers knew what had happened. At the very least, they laughed at her expense. He despised them.

Samuel couldn't touch Butch, but all he needed to hit Irving was a certain memo. Greg Moore probably had one squirreled away in his art room. Samuel had one weapon, and he would use it to bury Irving.

20

"SADIE, YOU DON'T HAVE to stay with me. Go on ahead."
Samuel felt foolish, having this teenager keep him company as
he trekked across campus to the gym.

She stuffed her hands, chapped and nail-bitten, into the pockets
of her hoodie. "I don't mind."

"That's not the point."

Sadie shrugged and said nothing. Stubborn.

Samuel sighed. Somewhere along the way, he had lost authority
with her. She wasn't taking advantage of him, thank God, but their
relationship felt more like friendship than the appropriate student-
teacher dynamic. It was an obvious freshman blunder; still, he didn't
know how to regain the impersonal distance without being cruel.
And he didn't have the heart to do that to Sadie, who didn't have
many friends to begin with.

"That midterm was pretty easy," she said.

Samuel laughed. "And you're admitting it?"

"Just saying. We all got A's."

"It was easy because you know your stuff. All five of you have learned a lot, and I know you have. I don't need to be sadistic for the sake of a curve."

She replied, but her words were drowned out by the sudden blare of music. Samuel could feel the thumping bass in his chest. "Lovely."

"What?"

He shook his head and motioned for her to precede him. He'd given himself a ten-minute head start, so there were plenty of seats on the bottom row. Sadie climbed up to join Marcus and the other guys at the top of the stands. The whole setup seemed to defeat the purpose of his presence; exactly what was he supposed to do if one of them started throwing spit wads or something?

At least Greta was there. She leaned against a concrete pillar on the far side of the gym, arms crossed as she glowered at her rambunctious group of freshman, relegated to the floor.

The festivities consisted of a couple of students giving out school-funded gift certificates to whomever could stomach a few wriggling worms, a parade of sports teams along with some chanting by each class in turn, and . . . Vince Irving.

As the principal got up in front of the student body and gave a rousing speech about starting off the new semester with a bang, Samuel silently willed the man to have a heart attack; a stroke; an aneurysm. Irving got laughter and applause.

Samuel realized he was holding his breath and forced himself to expel the air. It was okay. He'd asked Moore about the memo; Moore was sure he had a copy somewhere, and if he didn't, there were several other pack rats on campus he could ask. Irving's days were numbered.

Someone sang the anthem, didn't hit the high note, and the rally was over. Irving held them in for another two minutes, watching the clock and ignoring boos and catcalls until the lunch bell rang. The principal left first, through one pair of open double doors.

Suddenly Samuel wanted Irving to know. He wanted to tell the man what he was going to do. He wanted him to sweat. He got up as students scattered around him, and headed after Irving.

Too late, he realized his mistake.

The gym had been host to about six hundred students. Two sets of double doors meant three hundred students each, all frantic to escape. Samuel tried to backpedal, but there were already too many kids behind him. When those directly behind him tried to stop, they were shoved forward. Samuel could only go with the flow, hoping to be carried out with the tide.

As the door loomed closer, the crowd thickened. Students jostled him apologetically, then awkwardly, and then it didn't matter how they did it, they were all around him and he couldn't get out. A couple were shouting, but it didn't matter because everyone was yelling, confused, like cattle in a stampede. Samuel hung on to his crutches for as long as he could, until one caught on someone's clothing and jerked away. For a moment he was held erect by the crush of bodies on all sides.

Then he lost the other crutch and he was stumbling in nightmarishly slow motion, clutching at backpacks, and the last thing he heard was a girl's high voice behind him, shrieking, "Back off, assholes!"

He couldn't breathe.

21

HE WAS ONLY OUT for a second or two. When he returned, he was on his hands and knees, surrounded, engulfed, so close to the door that he could see it through a forest of legs, impossibly out of reach. Someone trampled on his hand and he cried out.

Then she was there. The image that imprinted itself on his mind afterward was of her wading through the crowd, shoving children to either side as she plowed toward him like a battleship in the midst of a raging sea.

Greta hauled him up by the back of his shirt, wrapped one powerful arm around his chest, and dragged him back, back through the crowd into the strangely vacant gym. She pulled him to the stands and let him down abruptly.

Samuel collapsed against her, gasping, so close to sobbing that he couldn't because all he needed was air. He clutched at her shirt, not worrying about where her breasts might be because all he could think of was *getting out*. Suddenly, so easily, he was helpless and terrified and knowing it for the first time in a long while. The panic wouldn't let him go.

He was only dimly aware when Irving appeared to offer help and Greta told him, rather uncharacteristically, to fuck off. Samuel stared at his hand and listened to the blood roaring in his ears.

Greta held him. She put her arms around him and squeezed until he choked and began to breathe normally. She didn't let go.

After what seemed like a long time, the roar began to subside. He was exhausted and clammy with cold sweat.

Greta felt his brow. "I'll take you home."

He nodded dumbly, and his hands fell away from her shirt, the tips of his fingers throbbing. She stood, and he thought she had left him, but she returned with his crutches and managed somehow to get him to his car, his house, his bed. She took his shoes off and covered him with a blanket before going into the bathroom for a glass of water.

"I—I can't."

"Drink." Her tone left no room for argument.

His hands shook so badly, he spilled half of it down his shirt.

Greta took the glass and set it on his nightstand. Then she bent over, tucking him in like a child. "You're in shock. Try to get some sleep." Her footsteps cross the room, and she paused by the door. "I'll come back after school."

"I can't."

"Can't what?"

He couldn't stop shaking. "Can't—do this anymore. I can't. I'm done with teaching." He'd convinced himself he was doing all right, that Fernando's pranks were little more than a nuisance, that he was pretty good at this teaching thing. It wasn't true. He hated Irving and the run-down facilities and the way even the smallest request turned into an infuriating bureaucratic sinkhole. He wanted to go back to his office, his nice clean office, and the business that ran like a well-oiled machine and people who knew what the fuck he was talking about. Most importantly, he never wanted to see the inside of a classroom again.

"I see." Greta bent to retrieve her purse. "We'll talk later."

"MR. COOKE, WAKE UP."

Samuel resisted consciousness, clinging to his fitful dreams like a prisoner desperate for escape. He didn't want to go back, didn't want to face his responsibilities in the real world.

A hand shook his shoulder. "Mr. Cooke, it's me. Maria."

He opened his eyes. He was curled on his side, his back to her. "She called you." As if being trampled by the entire student body weren't enough, Greta had to tell Maria, too.

"She said I had to make sure you weren't hurt. That you needed to check your legs." Her hand moved down his side.

"Don't touch me!"

She jerked back. "Mr. Cooke . . ." Her voice dropped to a whisper. "She made me promise, Mr. Cooke."

Samuel wanted nothing more than to lie in bed until everyone went away. Until Maria stopped bothering him, until they hired someone else to do his job, until the state came and took his house. If only he could just fade away.

"Mr. Cooke—"

"I'll do it."

"Promise?"

"Yes."

Maria left. Samuel pulled the blanket over his head.

What must Greta think of him now? She had glossed over his performance at the baseball game, and maybe she had even believed her own words. But how could she possibly view today's disaster as anything other than absolute proof of his cowardice? He had clung to her like an infant.

She could never respect him, not after this.

And he had imagined he would avenge her. By taking out Irving. What a joke.

He held up a hand. It was shaking, and there was a dark welt forming across all four fingers. Nothing broken.

He worked off his pants and sat up to remove his braces and examine the damage.

It wasn't nearly as bad as the time he'd fallen down the stairs. Both knees, which he could feel in a dim secondhand way, were already bruising. There was a nasty scratch on his shin that could use disinfecting. More worrisome was the smallest toe on his left foot, which appeared to have been crushed, possibly by his own crutch. He would have to keep it elevated overnight, make sure it didn't get worse.

Nothing needed immediate tending. He rolled onto his side, pulled the blanket up to his chin, and settled in to contemplate his own worthlessness.

Maria knocked.

"I'm fine!"

She came in anyway. He ignored her, hoping she would leave when she saw his pants and braces on the floor, but she sat on the end of the bed. Through a fold in the sheet, he saw her put a hand on his foot.

"Please leave me alone." He was a thirty-four-year-old man, she was a child, and he didn't need her sympathy.

She nodded, but did not look at him. "I want to tell you. About something that happened a few months before I met you."

He said nothing.

Maria drew in a deep breath. "I used to work for some other people, cleaning, like here. One day, the husband, he . . . caught me in the bedroom and—and tried to rape me." She studied her fingers, her face a mask of barely restrained pain. "His wife came home . . . in time."

Slowly, Samuel sat up on one elbow. "Jesus. I'm sorry. This must seem pretty insignificant to you."

"You don't understand." She looked up, her eyes like two black holes. "I know what it's like to feel helpless and humiliated."

The word dropped off his lips, almost accidentally: "Oh."

"I was afraid for a long time." Maria shrugged. "But I need to reach my dreams. The risks are the same if I become a nurse. I couldn't let him—what he did—stop me. Or he would still have the power. You understand?"

"Yeah." For a long time, he'd felt similarly: that he couldn't let his father win. But his father was not here. He shook his head. "Not that I'm making any comparison, but, well, at least you have someone other than yourself to blame."

Maria considered this. A ghost of a smile tugged at her mouth. "For you, Mr. Cooke . . . I think maybe your body is not the same person as your heart."

SAMUEL HAD ASSUMED Maria was long gone when she knocked again at his bedroom door. Maybe she had stayed to do some studying. He mumbled an invitation to enter, knowing she'd come in regardless.

The door opened, and the footsteps that crossed to the center of the room were not Maria's.

"Feeling better?" Greta asked.

He didn't move. "No."

He heard her pick up the glass on his nightstand. A moment later the water in the bathroom ran. She came out. "You panicked. It happens."

"Not to you."

Greta set the glass down with a thump and went to the window. The blinds rattled, and ocher light spilled across the bedsheets. "You'll feel better tomorrow."

"No." Samuel lifted his head. "No, I won't. I meant it, Greta, I can't do this anymore. Dump me if you're going to, I know I'm a coward, but I can't take it. I can't stand being picked at and stolen from and trampled and mocked, and I especially can't handle it when they're making fun of *you*."

She turned toward him. The afternoon sun slanted through the window at her back, making it impossible to read her expression. "What are you talking about?"

He spilled everything. From Fernando's first sarcastic comment to the marker on his desk. It came out in a desperate, manic rush and he didn't care. Not anymore. What difference would it make? He'd already proven himself utterly spineless. By the time he finished, he'd worked himself into a kind of frenetic rhythm. "I'm tired, Greta, I tried to handle it on my own, and I can't, I'm done. I quit. I quit. I quit." The words wouldn't stop, and he had to slap a hand over his mouth to shut himself up.

Greta turned toward the window. The dying sunlight illuminated her profile, still stiff and stern. "When we met, you swore you'd finish out the year."

"I know, but . . . This job isn't right for me. I didn't realize it would be so . . ."

"What, difficult?"

He knew he was supposed to object to her sarcasm. He didn't. He wasn't fooling himself anymore. "Yes. Difficult. I'm not strong enough."

"Strange." The sharpness in her voice fell away. "How those who have endured the most think themselves weakest."

"Are you kidding?" The sheer stupidity of the aphorism transformed his despondence into fury. "Are you *blind*? Look at me!" He threw the blanket aside, revealing all of himself, his smallness, his all but lifeless legs. The half-full bag of urine showed below his boxers. Well, let her look. Let her *see*.

Greta turned, taking him in, and made a throwaway gesture. "You know that makes no difference to me." She sighed, as if wearied by the need to explain the obvious. "Everyone is under the delusion that they're in control. Nobody is. Understanding the truth is not a weakness. 'We fix our eyes not on what is seen, but on what is unseen. For what is seen is temporary, but what is unseen is eternal.'"

She was quoting *scripture* now? Unbelievable. "This is my life, Greta, not some—some theological debate!"

"I didn't say it was."

"So tell me. What, exactly, do you see here? In me?"

Greta came to the edge of his bed. She glanced at his legs before meeting his eyes. "Tenacity."

Samuel laughed bitterly. What a cliché. The crippled guy was either the Machiavellian schemer or suffering saint. She'd decided on the latter. "If that's what you think, you don't know the first thing about me."

"I know stubborn when I see it." She bent, unfolding one arm, and hooked a finger under the strap of one of his braces. "I know no physical therapist in his right mind would recommend this little support for someone carrying most of his weight on his arms." She tossed it onto the bed. "Which means you haven't seen a specialist in years."

So he hadn't been hiding anything from her. The realization stung. But she was wrong. She thought he clung to his mobility out of pride. "It's not courage, Greta." He gestured to his legs. "I told you this happened when I was twelve. Did I mention I locked myself in my room for the next five years? My mother was so guilt-ridden, she waited on me hand and foot until cancer ate her from the inside out. And I let her. The only reason I can walk is because my father—my *father*—mocked me for using a wheelchair. Told me I was weak, that I was an embarrassment to myself and my family, and fuck if that isn't all I can think when anyone sees me in that thing. College? I went because it was easy and free. I could've been in and out in three years, but I put off graduating until my funding ran out. I was going to move back home until the idiot who got stuck with me on his senior project decided to start a company." When Greta opened her mouth to object, he held up a finger. "Oh, but I didn't stay there, right? I was big and brave and moved up here. After a decade. But I don't feel liberated or accomplished. I'm *fucking scared*. I wake up in the morning and I'm scared to go to class because I don't know what horrible surprise I'm going to find. I could probably do something about it, but I'm too scared to confront the asshole I know is responsible.

"Most of all, Greta, I'm scared of you. I live in constant fear that you'll leave. Every time you call, every time you speak to me, I think, Here it is, it's over. Every moment we spend together, I'm wondering when you're going to realize what a loser I am and walk out. In fact, I'm sure that's going to happen today, and I'm almost relieved because it means I'll be able to crawl back into my hole and lock the door forever."

He expected some sort of reaction—anger, scorn, outright disgust—but Greta merely looked thoughtful. She went to the door and flipped on the overhead light, washing out the dusky orange glow. Back by the bed, she bent over his legs and carefully fingered the cut on his shin. "Hm," she said, and disappeared into his bathroom. He could hear her opening drawers.

Samuel clung to his despair, but she was making it really hard not to be pissed off. "Did you hear anything I said?"

"I heard you." Greta reappeared, carrying his first aid kit. She pushed Samuel's legs over and sat on the edge of the bed.

"You know, it's polite to ask before—"

"Shut up." She tore open a disinfectant wipe and swabbed the cut, bandaged it neatly, and then set the first aid kit aside. She pulled the blanket over his legs. "You're no coward."

"Oh, really."

For his sarcasm, she gave him a sour frown. "Tell me this. Why did you leave your father's house?"

"He's an asshole."

"The real reason."

"That *was* the real—" Her raised eyebrow silenced him. He looked at his hands. Chewed his lip. And said in a low voice: "He wouldn't take me to the hospital. When Mom died."

She put a hand on his leg. "And why did you leave your job?"

"I . . . I wanted more. And I knew I'd never get it by staying there." It was vague, but it was as honest as he could be right now, both with her and with himself. He ran a hand through his hair. "Are we done?"

"Why did you ask me to dinner?"

"Oh, God." He looked at the ceiling, breathing carefully.

Greta moved closer.

"Because I had nothing to lose." He swallowed. "And I guess I thought it would be better to let you laugh in my face than waste months fantasizing that you might not. But then you—well, you— Oh, hell."

"Come here." She coaxed his head into her lap.

Samuel did not let himself cry. "Don't do this," he begged. "Not you."

"Do what?"

He buried his face in her thigh. "You're not my mother."

Greta was very still. Then he felt her hand in his hair. Gradually her fingers traced the line of his forehead, around his ear, down to the nape of his neck. Her body rose and fell with a silent sigh.

"All women," she murmured, "are mothers first."

He must have fallen asleep then, because when he woke, she was gone.

22

GRETA BARGED INTO HIS room at eight in the morning. "Don't you ever lock your door?"

"Holy sh—" Samuel whipped the sheets up to his armpits. "Don't you ever knock?"

"Don't you ever get out of bed?"

"Potty breaks are optional for me, thanks." With a few spare bags and plenty of space under the bed, he could last for days. He sat up as she opened his closet and began to dig around. "What are you doing? Don't you have zero period?"

"It's over. First is my prep. Hurry up or we'll be late for second."

Two shoes landed in the center of his bed. He caught them as they bounced. "No, not 'we.' You. I told you, I quit. I'm not going anywhere." She wasn't listening. "Greta?"

She turned around, holding a pair of slacks and a shirt on a hanger.

"Those don't even match."

She tossed them after the shoes. "Get dressed."

He raised his eyebrows. "*No.*"

Her hands contracted into silent but altogether eloquent fists. "Don't make me do it, Mr. Cooke."

"I'm not going."

In two long strides, she was at his side, hand clamped around his arm. She dragged the sheet aside.

"Okay, okay!" She was fucking serious. "A little privacy, maybe?"

Greta rolled her eyes and stepped into the hall.

Samuel struggled into his pants, seething.

"Are you done?" The door started to open.

"No! Almost! Okay, there."

She came in as he was slipping into his shirt.

"Socks would be nice."

"Where?"

He pointed, and she returned with a pair. "You're the most stubborn woman I've ever met, you know that?" He pulled on the socks and rolled them to his knees, then gestured impatiently toward the braces on the floor.

"Woman?" She bent and handed them up.

He blinked. "No, you're right. Person. You take the cake, Greta."

"Just put your shoes on."

"You find this amusing?"

She glanced at her watch and let out a belabored sigh. "Not really."

"I'm gonna need a minute in the bathroom before we go. Unless you plan on coming to my rescue again."

"Make it quick."

Though he was tempted to lock himself in and wait it out, he made a quick bag change and returned, stabbing at the floor as he followed her to the car. "You couldn't have given me one day?"

She spoke over one shoulder. "I told Irving you'd be back. Comb your hair. Keys?"

He pulled out the string on the chain she'd given him and let it snap back. Greta nodded and helped him into the passenger seat.

Samuel sat in silence during the ride to school, glaring out the window.

There was a pause when they pulled into the parking lot, a moment when neither one moved.

"You know what I hate?" Samuel said. "Knowing I'm going to thank you for this later."

"Don't thank me. Just get to class."

"I can't believe you had the gall to tell Irving I'd be back. I can't believe he took your word for it. No, wait. I can." He slid to the ground and slammed the Suburban door.

"There's the first bell. Come on."

Samuel was out of breath by the time they got to the main building. "They're all going to stare at me. They won't be listening to the lesson, they'll be wondering—"

"So teach them something they will listen to, Mr. Cooke. I'll ring your room at lunch."

"In case I try to make a break for it?"

"Yes."

He wanted to say he hated her, but it wasn't true. Instead he muttered "Fine" and stalked off to class.

"TODAY WE'LL START on documentation—footnotes, citations, bibliography, all that. Completely useless in the real world, but you'll need it for most of your assignments in college. Word has some tools for making this fairly automatic, so you don't have to reorganize the whole thing if a footnote changes pages."

Samuel's second-period class stared at him, clearly not sure whether to be curious or afraid. Either way, they hadn't heard a word he'd said.

Push through.

He swiveled to face the whiteboard, uncapped a pen, and rose to write the details on the board so they would have something to refer to after they'd finished examining him. As he raised his arm to write, he realized he was giving them an excellent view of the livid bruises across the back of his hand. For all he knew, the foot that had crushed his fingers could belong to one of these kids.

The pen was dry. Samuel muttered a curse and opened the drawer where he kept extras.

Only they were gone, and he was staring at a grotesque rubber penis. Underneath, written in permanent marker on the bottom of the drawer, someone had scrawled, *You'll need this if you want to satisfy her.*

Samuel slammed the drawer shut. "Fuck this."

Every head in the room snapped to attention.

He wanted to hit something, break something, kill someone. He settled for hurtling the dry pen at the clock on the far wall. It hit dead center and dropped to the floor, leaving a crack in the aged plastic faceplate.

Mouths fell open.

"Fuck," he said again, because it made him feel better. He was done pretending not to care. "I'm finished with this stupid shit. With all of you. I know you hate this class, I know you think it's as stupid and pointless as I do, and you're right. This crap might save you some time, or get you a couple of grade points in college, or land you a nice secretarial job if you plan on spending the rest of your life making a buck over minimum wage. Big fucking deal."

Samuel could have gone on yelling for the rest of the hour, but he had to pause to take a breath. Could everyone else hear his heart beating?

I quit. That was what came next. The little bastards had won; they would never have to see him again. Then he glanced at Sadie.

She was staring at him, her eyes big and round and wet. Christ, was she *crying* for him?

A boy behind her shifted, and the noise was loud in the pin-drop silence of the room. "Are you all right, Mr. Cooke?"

Something inside of Samuel exploded. "Have you heard a single fucking thing I've said? No, I am *not* all right! And you know what?" He ripped the drawer open, grabbed the dildo, and slammed it on the desk. "This hurts. Okay? I'm tired of pretending I don't care. I'm thirty-four goddamn years old, and Greta Cassamajor is the first girl-friend I've ever had. She's the only person I've ever met who sees the world the way I do, and I am *not* about to let some moron's sadistic pranks ruin our relationship."

He pointed at Fernando. "Anything like this ever happens again, I'm calling the cops."

Fernando shrugged and looked out the window.

Samuel dropped into the chair. He put the dildo in the drawer, shut it, and cleared his desk. The class waited in stunned silence. He waved a hand. "Do your typing program. Talk. Do whatever the hell you want. Lesson over."

He drummed his fingers, pointedly ignoring the awkward si-lence that filled the rest of the period. Then the bell rang and every-one shuffled toward the door, leaving a wake of relief hanging like a curtain in the air.

"Hey, yo."

Unbelievable. Samuel turned to face Fernando. "All right, what game are we playing now?"

"No game, man." Fernando shrugged his shirt back and touched his belt as if to confirm his pants were still in the vicinity of his hips. "I dunno what you think I done, but I ain't have nothing to do with this stuff. That shit on your chair and the computer screens and whatever else. I don't even know how to make a computer do that."

"Right."

"Seriously, man. You seen how much my typing sucks."

"Perhaps you can understand why I'm having trouble believing you."

Fernando gestured impatiently. "Look, man, I give you a hard time. But I respect you, all right? I got a cousin in a wheelchair. Everyone treats him like a baby, but he's a smart-ass little *pendejo*. Gets away with stuff my mom would smack the shit out of me for. But he knows he ain't gonna put nothing over on me. You understand? I see you, I think, This asshole gets it easy. I just wanted to bother you a little. Most other teachers would send me to the office for the stuff I said. You come right back at me, no hesitation. No fear. I respect that. You all right, man."

Samuel had been preparing a salvo of defensive sarcasm, but it knotted in his throat. Easy? Fernando thought he had it *easy*? "Why," he choked stupidly, "why didn't you say anything? Until now?"

"I dunno, it was kinda funny you thought it was me. Made me look kinda . . . I dunno. Cool."

"But then who . . ."

"Shit, I dunno. Everyone in class likes you."

"Really."

"Sure."

"Given the fact that nobody's said jack about anything that's happened, I find that hard to believe."

"No offense, man, but . . ." Fernando shrugged and looked at his feet. "You kinda seem like you'd take a shot at anyone who offered to help."

"I'M AN ASSHOLE." Samuel lay his head on the desk, cradling it in his arms. Greta sat on the edge, one leg dangling. "You're positive he was telling the truth?"

"I only thought it was him because he was so damn brazen. I doubt he's capable of subtlety."

She put a hand on the back of his head. "Let's go."

He got up and followed her out the door, pausing to lock up. "I don't know why I even bother."

"You should have the lock changed. Put in a work request."

He closed his eyes and rested his forehead against the door. "Why couldn't I have thought of that three months ago?"

"You don't think straight when you're upset. Next time, tell me."

He winced. "I guess you're mad about that."

"Don't I have a right to be?"

"Yeah. I guess so." They started down the hall toward the parking lot. A few loitering students moved aside as they passed. "I just . . . I wanted to take care of it by myself."

"Well, you're *not* by yourself."

She was right. As painful as it was, having other people in his life meant letting them in even when he had totally lost control. Maybe especially then. "I'm sorry. I should have said something."

She dug her keys out of a pocket and thumbed through the ring. "I didn't decide to teach until my last year of college, after I ruined my knees. An English professor told me it was a rewarding profession but that I should be prepared to suffer through the first year. It's hell, he said."

"Was it?"

"Of course. It is for everyone."

"Greg never mentioned that."

She rolled her eyes. "He may be the exception—only because he's oblivious."

"The exception, huh? How do you think this guy's first year went?" Samuel nodded down the hall: Irving had come around the corner and was making a beeline for them.

"Wonderful," Greta muttered.

Samuel wanted to take Irving down in hand-to-hand combat, but even if he could have, he had a feeling it wouldn't impress Greta. Still, he could hurt the man in other ways, and he might decide to do so eventually. That was good enough for now. He grinned. "Watch this."

Irving was breathless by the time he reached them. "Cooke," he said, nodding briefly in Greta's direction. "I want to say how sorry I am about what happened yesterday, and if there's anything we can do—"

Samuel silenced him with an upheld hand. "I'm sorry. My lawyer's advised me not to talk to you. He'll be in touch. Come on, Greta."

They left Irving standing white-faced in the hall.

Greta didn't speak until they reached the parking lot. "Done living vicariously, I see."

SHE SHOWED UP that evening with a bag of groceries.

"I do have food, you know."

"I get tired of the same thing."

"You have gastronomic ADD." Samuel followed her into the kitchen. "Anything I can do?"

"It's quicker if I—"

"Yeah, yeah." He took his usual place at the kitchen table. "So here's the question. If Fernando isn't responsible, who is?"

"How should I know?"

"Rhetorical question. Honestly, I can't think of anyone else who would really *hate* me, unless it's Irving, and he's too dumb."

"Mmm," Greta said, agreeing. She pulled a head of lettuce out of the paper grocery bag and peeled off the outer leaves.

Samuel cleared his throat. "Incidentally, can I get in trouble for swearing in class?"

"What exactly did you say?" She turned on the tap and submerged the head.

He told her. Mostly.

She looked over one shoulder and then turned to face him, her eyebrows rising. When he finished, she passed a damp hand over her eyes and sighed.

"Hey, I thought I was going to quit, okay?" His face was hot.

"You didn't?" She turned to the lettuce and started pulling the leaves apart.

He shrugged. "Should I?"

She shot him a withering glance.

"Greta, mostly I love you, occasionally I hate you, and sometimes I understand exactly why guys wet their pants when you walk by."

"Good thing you don't have that problem."

"Oh, now you're going to make me cry." Since he had come clean about, well, *almost* everything, he felt free. Giddy. He still hadn't mentioned finding Irving's brother in her yearbook, but that could wait for a more appropriate moment. "So, am I in hot water?"

"You may get a couple of angry parent calls. Anything worse will have to go through Irving."

"Ah. Good. We're okay, then."

"You could look at it that way." Greta leaned forward, peering out the kitchen window. "Someone—" The doorbell sounded. "Are you expecting company?"

Samuel grabbed his crutches. "So help me, if this is Greg, I'm going to kill him. I've told him five hundred times to call before he shows up." He hauled himself to the front door and took a moment to unfasten the lock and bolt. Greta had a habit of battening down the hatches wherever she went. "Greg, if you—"

He shut his mouth. Standing on his doorstep, Sadie was a mess of mascara and tears. When she saw him, her face crumpled. "Mr.

Cooke, I'm sorry, I'm so, *so* sorry. I didn't realize. I didn't think—" She took a ragged breath and dragged a sleeve across her nose.

"Sadie?" he said stupidly. She had disappeared after keyboarding. "Marcus said you went home sick." He backed up. "Um—come in. Please, come in."

She stumbled over the threshold, but when he gestured to the couch, she shook her head, tears rolling slowly down her cheeks. In the kitchen, the water shut off, and Sadie's eyes widened when Greta strode around the corner. "Oh, I—"

"How did you get this address?" Greta demanded.

"Mr. Cooke, um, at school he . . ." Her voice wavered and fell to a miserable whisper. "I'm sorry, I shouldn't have—"

Samuel held up a hand. "It's all right. You're welcome in my house. Now, why don't you tell us what's going on?" He indicated Greta. "Whatever it is, she's going to find out."

Sadie's eyes passed from Samuel to Greta and back again. She swallowed.

He gave her an encouraging nod. "Go on."

"It was Marcus."

23

SAMUEL FROWNED. "WHAT WAS Marcus?"

Sadie studied the ground, biting her lips. "Everything," she whispered at last. "The—the track balls. The drawings, the—everything." She covered her face. "He said—he said it wasn't a big deal. That you'd just be annoyed. And you seemed okay, so I thought . . . I thought . . . I didn't realize until today!" She dissolved into sobs again, muffled by the sweatshirt sleeves drawn over her hands. "I'm sorry, I'm sorry."

Samuel stared at her in mute horror. If there had been one student he trusted . . . He felt Greta's hand on his shoulder. "Why?" he managed finally. "I don't understand. Why?"

"Grades," Sadie blurted, as if it were an invective. "His stupid grades. He freaked when you gave him a B on that first project, and he wasn't getting Java, even after I helped. So when you started going hard on us or announced a test . . ."

She was right. Every time something happened in second period, Samuel had responded by letting up on third. He'd tried to make the programming class more enjoyable to compensate for the drudgery of keyboarding. In comparison, the kids had seemed so smart, so talented, so well behaved. "And you knew this was going on? Sadie, how could you help him?"

"Because I love him!" Her wail wavered between fury and despair. "I love him, okay? I'm stupid and pathetic and ugly and—"

"Stop." Greta stepped between them and folded a firm arm around Sadie's shoulders. "Excuse us."

Samuel nodded. Sadie looked frightened, but she let Greta steer her into the guest room. "Drink some water," he heard Greta say. There was a pause, and then she closed the door.

Samuel paced to the front window. He felt like putting a fist through the glass, but his hand had already suffered enough damage. Instead he closed the shades with a jerk and planted himself on the couch. He leaned forward, elbows on knees and head in hands. How could he have been so *stupid*?

When Sadie returned to the living room, she was no longer hysterical. It looked like she had scrubbed her face with one of the guest bathroom washcloths, leaving only faint mascara tracks over too-pink cheeks. She kept her eyes on the floor.

Greta stepped around her. "I'm going to take her home." She opened the front door. "Come on, your parents will worry."

That was doubtful, based on Sadie's wince. She started after Greta, but halted halfway across the floor.

"Come on," Greta prompted.

Sadie bolted for the couch. Samuel only had time to put his hands up as she threw herself at him, wrapping her arms around his torso and shoving her face into his shoulder. "You were right, Mr. Cooke, you were right. I told him I didn't want to help him anymore and he did try to get me to sleep with him and I said I wasn't ready and I still wouldn't help him and he said really, really horrible things." She gasped for air. "And I'm so glad I didn't, Mr.

Cooke, I'm so glad you told me not to sleep with him because I didn't and he's horrible! I know I'm horrible, too, and you can't forgive me but I still—"

"Hey. Hey." Gently Samuel pulled her away. "Sadie, it's okay. I forgive you. I'm just glad you're safe. All right?"

She stumbled back and rushed out the door.

Talk about unexpected. Samuel straightened his shirt and was reaching for his crutches when he felt a draft.

Greta stood in the open doorway. "Thank you," she said, and shut the door.

WHEN SHE RETURNED, Greta strode to the kitchen table, leaned over Samuel, and kissed him full on the lips. For a long time.

He was embarrassed. "It's not like I saved anybody's life."

"You don't know that."

He cleared his throat and looked for a subject change. The smell of french fries provided an easy outlet. "Takeout?"

"It was getting late." She set the bag on the counter.

"You, Greta Cassamajor, actually went to a drive-through and purchased a meal from—" He leaned sideways to see the lettering. "Burger King? I'm shocked, Greta, absolutely stunned."

She chucked a burger at him, along with a sardonic grimace. "Hope you like onions."

"I'll deal." He peeled back the thin paper wrapping, already half soaked with oil. "I assume you got Sadie home all right."

"If you mean without hysterics, yes." She retrieved a bowl from a lower cabinet and filled it with fries before setting it on the table. She joined him a minute later with her burger, two sodas, and a bottle of ketchup.

"Will she be all right?"

"Eventually. I gave her my number and a card for a crisis line. It doesn't sound like she's in any danger from herself or him. She's just upset. "

He sighed. "And here I was worried she saw me more as a friend than a teacher. I guess that theory's been debunked."

"Not necessarily. Teenage life is complicated."

He waved a fry dismissively before popping it into his mouth. "You're the expert."

"She gave me some details."

"Oh?"

"Some time ago, you sent Marcus to the office for a key?"

"Dammit." He could have kicked himself. "To the other computer lab."

"Evidently he told them you had broken your classroom key. They gave him a replacement without question."

"I remember—Sadie followed him. It never even crossed my mind." He shook his head. That was also the last time Marcus had been late. She must have warned him not to attract attention. "You think you can trust someone, and then—"

"She stood watch for him once or twice. That was all. Don't judge her too harshly."

It was easy to see why Greta's sympathies lay with Sadie: the innocent girl ensorcelled by the charms of a suave, manipulative bastard. Maybe Greta was right. It was hard not to be moved by those desperate tears.

"This is disgusting." Greta got up and dropped the remaining half of her burger into the trash. "In any case, it should be easy enough to catch Marcus with the key. You can alert campus security tomorrow morning."

"Number one, you should get your taste buds checked, because that was delicious." Samuel crumpled his own empty wrapper and tossed it after Greta's. Her eyebrows went up in approval when it hit the open lid and dropped in. "Number two, I think I'd like to have a chat with him first." Now that the shock of Sadie's involvement had sunk in, the helpless fury he'd lived with since September was dissipating. Anonymity had given Marcus the upper hand; no more.

24

MARCUS POKED HIS HEAD into the classroom. "Uh, what is this about? My first period is kind of important."

"Oh, I'm sure it is." Samuel extended a hand toward the chair he had positioned on the other side of his desk. "Have a seat."

The teenager dumped his backpack on the floor and sat, face betraying nothing except guarded caution. "Well?"

Samuel studied him, trying to see what it was Sadie desired in this cocky, opinionated kid. He was good-looking, or at least he had clear skin and washed his hair regularly. "I'm sure you can guess what you're here to discuss. You'll get back to class faster if you admit it."

Marcus rolled his eyes heavenward. "That bitch." His lips curled into a sour smile. "That little bitch. She folded."

"Mm. About that. My girlfriend has gotten attached to Sadie, so I'd advise against calling her names."

Marcus snorted. "I didn't think you'd be so open about hiding behind Cass's skirts."

"As far as I know, she only wears pants." Samuel opened the topmost drawer and sent the dildo rolling across the desk, forcing Marcus to catch it before it landed in his lap. "Thought you might want that back. I'm actually still a virgin, so you'd know how to use it better than I would."

Marcus's eyes widened, and he let out an incredulous laugh. "I can't believe you admitted that."

Samuel shrugged. "It would be pretty sad if I used my sex life as a measure of my manhood, now, wouldn't it?"

"Funny." Marcus leaned forward and dropped the dildo in the wastebasket. "You think you got me by the balls, but there's nothing you can do. You've got no proof unless you're recording me now, and that would be inadmissible in court. Which I know because my parents are lawyers. And my uncle is on the school board. The administration loves me. So if some new teacher starts—"

"Spare me the lecture. You've got connections."

"You knew?"

Samuel grinned. "Anyone as cocky as you either has money or reliable backup."

"So why are we here?" Marcus spoke with his usual bluster, but there was a hint of confusion in his face.

"Because I have money." Samuel was sorry to end the pissing contest. Although he was confident he could outsmart-ass Marcus any day of the week, working him into a blind rage would be counterproductive. "I know there's nothing I can do to hurt you in the long run, but I could make your life pretty miserable until June."

"Not unless—"

"Not unless I want to lose my job? I'm not overly attached to this dump. Maybe you didn't know, but I'm independently wealthy. Actually, you *should* know. You were the one who recognized the name of the company where I worked. Did you ever ask your brother what that was about?"

Marcus shook his head cautiously.

"Hm, too bad. He would have reminded you that Architective launched with a certain program, a middleware for crowd behavior, which is now considered rather critical in the gaming industry. I designed that program, and I still own ten percent of the company. So I don't need this job, and I don't care if screwing you costs me my . . . Well, teaching's not so much my career as it is a hobby." A fairly masochistic hobby, come to think of it.

Marcus flushed. He sat forward, trying to maintain his cool and failing. "You think so? We'll see how—"

"Let me finish." Samuel couldn't let him say anything he wouldn't back down from. Marcus wasn't going to win here, but if he got angry enough, he might turn kamikaze. "You push me, I'll push back. I'd rather we deal. Listening?"

Marcus's gaze dropped to the desk and then flashed back to Samuel's face. "I'm listening."

Samuel detailed his demands. First, no more nonsense. Obviously. Second, Sadie was off limits. Greta would be watching her like a hawk, so it was in the kid's best interest to stay the hell away. Third, Samuel wanted his damn key back.

Marcus waited. When there was nothing further, his eyes flickered up. "That's it?"

Samuel allowed himself a thin smile. "Number four has already been arranged. I called Mrs. Ortega earlier this morning and had a nice long chat with her. Mrs. Ortega," he added, "oversees the full-inclusion program."

"The what?"

"Full-inclusion. You know, the program for cripples and retards." He sat back. "I explained the trouble you're having in class; how you desperately need some extra credit to maintain your four-point-oh. When you volunteered to help with the special-needs students, I was so thrilled, I couldn't refuse. If only I'd had friends like you when I was in school."

"This is bullshit."

"Mm. How convenient that you have a free fourth period. Mrs. Ortega will be waiting for you in . . ." He consulted the scrap of paper he'd written the information on. "Room twenty-three. I suggest you take a moment to think this over carefully before you refuse."

"Bullshit," Marcus muttered again. He sat very still, picking pensively at the seam of his pants. No doubt trying to figure out if there was some catch he wasn't seeing. Finally he nodded and shoved a hand into his pocket. He pulled out a key, held it up, and tossed it onto the desk.

"Smart." Samuel pulled out his own chain and made a quick comparison. It was the same cut. He slipped the key into his shirt pocket.

"Well? I'd like to get back to class."

Samuel laughed. "You have a spine, I'll give you that." He leaned back and laced his fingers together over his stomach. "All right, we're done. But I want you to remember. When you get wherever it is your daddy wants you to go—whenever you reach that million-dollar sinecure—I want you to remember that you walked over a cripple to get there. Worse, you made a beautiful girl cry."

Marcus stood and shouldered his backpack.

Samuel grabbed the edge of the desk and used it to push his chair out, blocking the door. "Did you hear me?"

"I heard."

"Why don't you repeat it back to me? Just so we're clear."

Marcus's face darkened. "Fuck you."

"Or I could call the office—"

"I walked over a cripple to get here," he said, smashing the sentence into one long word. "And made a beautiful girl cry."

Samuel nodded. "See you in two hours. Be prepared to work for your grade."

Marcus jerked the door open, muttering to himself.

"What was that?"

He sneered. "I said, she's not exactly beautiful."

Samuel chuckled. "Marcus, fifteen years from now, you'll be drowning your second marriage in booze. Sadie? She'll be just fine."

25

THERE WAS SOME SORT of parade. Samuel wasn't clear on the details, but it was the first time Greta had ever taken the initiative on planning a date, so he agreed. Which was why he was now peering out the Suburban's passenger window with growing apprehension. Most of the pedestrians flowing around the car toted seating of some sort; a little girl just outside carried a pink Cinderella lounge chair under one arm as she trotted after her mother. His eyes followed the girl's trajectory and seized upon the orange cones at the end of the block. "Street's closed off up ahead."

"Peggy's place is there." Greta pointed to a white and blue house on the corner.

"Oh." He hoped he didn't sound as disappointed as he felt, but when the car came to a halt, he felt Greta's eyes on his back. Reluctantly, he turned to face her.

"Are you all right?" she asked.

"Sure." Not freaking out about the crowd at all. Nope, not at all. He smiled and rubbed his sweaty palms on his pants. Unfortunately that only served to remind him of his grandmother's ring, sitting weighty as a lead brick in the bottom of his pocket. Foolishly, he'd been carrying it around since the night Sadie appeared on his doorstep, though it wasn't like he was hoping for an opportunity to pull it out and pop the question. When he did, eventually, it would be well planned. Special. To make up, just a little, for all the other things Greta sacrificed by being with him.

Greta let up on the brake, making a gradual right turn through the crowd and into Peggy's driveway. She managed not to flatten anyone and got out to meet her friend, who was hurrying barefoot down the front steps.

Samuel slid to the ground and circled around the front of the Suburban, glancing warily at the street. He'd hoped the crowd would thin out by the time they made it to Peggy's, but it wasn't looking good.

"Mr. Cooke!" Like Karen, Peggy was a member of Greta's Bible study. Unlike Karen, she was bearable. "Greta says this will be your first taste of small-town nightlife."

"You call this night?"

She laughed. "Six o'clock is about all we're good for around here. Mark and I are finishing dinner, but we've got the chairs set up right around the corner. Go get settled, and we'll be out in a few."

Greta lifted a hand in thanks as Peggy jogged up the steps. Samuel followed Greta to the sidewalk, where she waited for a break in foot traffic before stepping in. When he joined her, nobody stampeded or slammed into them. In fact, everyone gave him and his crutches a pretty wide berth. He breathed.

The four folding chairs were the only empty seats on the strip of sidewalk running along the back of the house. The rest were occupied by families who had clearly been waiting for some time: there were ice chests and picnic blankets, and the ground was littered with little silver rods that Samuel couldn't place until he saw a child run down the street with a sparkler in hand. It was like a giant tailgate party.

Greta took a zigzag route around the family clusters already gathered, until her way was obstructed by an elderly man in a lawn chair. She said, "Excuse us," and he stood, picking up his chair to let them through.

"You're Cassamajor, aren't you?" When she nodded, he grinned and put out a hand. "George Sirocco. Jenny—my granddaughter— played about three years ago. Studying to be a doctor now."

Samuel shuffled past Greta into the street, meaning to settle himself while she made small talk, but the chairs were so low and flimsy there was no way he'd get into one without falling flat on his face. He looked around, feeling conspicuous.

"I remember." Greta stepped back, planted her heel on the chair rung, and leaned against the side, using her weight to anchor the frame to the ground. "One of my best players."

She hadn't missed a beat. Samuel wanted to kiss her. He backed up to the chair, gripped the arm, and sat.

"Man, wasn't she? Could've played college, got a scholarship, all that, but she says she wants to concentrate on her studies. What can you say, eh?" The old man shrugged and put his chair back, testing it with a hand before seating himself. "You know, I still remember the year you took us to the state championships."

When Greta paused and said, "That was a long time ago," Samuel realized the old man was referring to something she had done as a player back in her high school days. He wished he had looked more closely at the yearbooks.

Sirocco laughed. "We still talk about that season at the coffee shop. Us old guys are glad you decided to stick around. Having a decent team gives us something to brag about."

"I do my best." She gave him a polite nod and sat next to Samuel.

"Thanks," he said.

"For what?"

"For, uh, you know." She gave him a blank look; he sighed. "So what now?"

Greta listened for a moment. "Shouldn't be long. I hear drumming. The parade stops at the corner there, so we're nearly at the end."

Samuel settled in for some people-watching. Across the street were mainly elderly folks and families with small children, though a few groups of vaguely familiar teens wandered back and forth on the sidewalk behind the folding chairs. A friendly mix of English, Spanish, and Spanglish filled the air. Toddlers pranced out on the tarmac until the faint drumming became music and the first float came into view, at which point parents darted out to whisk their children away.

"Hey, sorry we're late!" Peggy's voice came from behind. "My mom called."

Greta got up to let her in, making a quick introduction between Samuel and Mark before the music drowned them out.

The first "float" was a flatbed farm truck stacked with bales of hay. Greg Moore's band students were seated on top, playing a rousing march. Moore stood on the highest bale, propped up against the cab. He conducted with gusto totally disproportionate to the enthusiasm of his students—or lack thereof.

Samuel laughed and pointed as the truck rolled past. "That's Olivia! They must be back together." She sat over the trailer hitch, legs dangling, as engrossed in playing as Greg was in conducting.

Next came a women's horseback club, riders and animals both done up in western-style sequins and braids. Trailing them was a miniature pony pulling a miniature cart with one rider, inciting children to cry out in delight. Once Samuel understood that the parade was a demonstration of community pride, none of the entries were surprising: a preschool with kids dressed as flowers; the mayor and his wife in an old Fairlane; a group of karate students and instructors; a fire truck; red-fezzed Shriners beating drums; the high school cheerleading squad. Every community organization had turned out in one capacity or another, and it was clear that the citizens on the sidelines were acquainted with many of the participants.

Still, he was surprised by the sewer truck. When he looked to Greta for an explanation, she shrugged. "Anyone can enter."

The end of the parade was signaled by a lone clown pulling a battered aluminum trash can strapped to a hand truck. Children ran after him, stretching out hands for . . . Samuel squinted. Tiny garbage cans?

"Candy inside." Greta stood and brushed off her pants before offering him a hand. "He's from the recycling plant."

"I see. Kind of." He backed up as Greta gathered their chairs.

"Oh, Mark will take care of those." Peggy had to raise her voice over the crowd, which had begun to surge after the fractured parade. The preschool truck pulled over at the end of the block, parents crowding around the bed. Peggy passed the chairs to her husband and then led them back to the safety of her driveway, where she issued an invitation for dessert.

Greta glanced at Samuel. "We haven't had dinner yet. I thought we might get something at the fair." She seemed to be looking for confirmation, so he nodded.

"Well, knock later if you've got room for blackberry pie." Peggy gestured to the crowds. "With all this commotion, we'll be up past ten." She gave Greta's arm a friendly pat and followed her husband inside.

"Fair?" Samuel had assumed the Friday off was some miscellaneous federal holiday.

She nodded. "The Future Farmers fair. It's at the ballpark. I'll drop you off."

He looked at the car and then at the crowd. The fire engine was creeping past. "You want to drive me through all this mess, come back here and park, and walk by yourself?"

She shrugged and pointed down the street. "It's four blocks that way."

He snorted. "It'll take you an hour to get there and back. I'll walk." He'd made it through the parade without incident. His palms were dry. Everyone seemed willing to give him plenty of room. Four blocks was a stretch, but not impossible.

Greta got her purse out of the car, and they joined the river of people heading for the park. Kids in karate uniforms and flower headdresses were everywhere, hopped up on sugar and attention. Dusk had fallen, but as they reached the end of the first block, there was an enormous mechanical clapping, and field lights blazed in the distance, casting weirdly distended shadows down the street.

A horn honked a friendly rhythm, echoed by another somewhere behind them. Children's voices chanted in unison until the fire truck relented and let out a foghorn blare. A group of band students with brass instruments answered with a few bars. The crowd grew denser as people funneled in from side streets.

Suddenly it was hard to breathe.

"Mr. Cooke?"

Only when she said his name did he realize he wasn't moving. Greta had assumed a kind of defensive stance, one leg behind him to ward off accidental blows as pedestrian traffic flowed around them. He swallowed and forced himself to take a deep breath. "Sorry."

She nodded to the left side of the street. "Walk next to the cars."

That was a good idea: Greta on one side, parked cars on the other. If something bad happened, he could climb on top. No. That was crazy. Nobody was going to push him over. Nothing was going to happen. He was not going to panic, not again. Not here. He started toward the nearest car.

And failed to see the pothole.

He sprawled forward, instinctively dropping his crutches to break his fall with his hands. The tarmac bit into his palms.

"Mr. Cooke!"

"Hey, are you okay?"

"What's going on?"

"Do you need an ambulance?"

Samuel rolled over to find himself imprisoned by legs and feet. He couldn't breathe. His heart felt like it was ready to explode. Out. He had to get *out*.

Greta's voice cut through the crowd. "Give him some space."

The bodies receded, but he still couldn't breathe. He felt Greta at his side, kneeling over him.

"Mr. Cooke, should I call someone?"

"No." He struggled to sit up, wheezing. "No, I'm fine. I just—I just need—" He looked for a break in the crowd. There was nobody behind him, by the car. It was black. He started to crawl toward it. "I need to get *out*."

Other people were saying things. Greta talked to them. Samuel reached the tire. He clung to it. There. There. That was solid. Oh God, just breathe. He put his back against the tire, pulled his legs up, and rested his head on his knees. Breathe. Breathe.

Greta was beside him again, holding his crutches. "You're sure you're all right?"

"Yes. Just let me. Get my. Breath."

"I'll get the car."

"No. Please. Stay here."

The tarmac gritted as she sat, a barrier between him and the flow of human traffic. She slid his crutches out of sight, underneath the car, and put a hand on his shoulder.

He jerked away. "*Don't!* Touch me. Sorry. Just . . ." Breathe.

Samuel stared at the ground between his legs. Okay. He had space. Nobody was going to touch him. Or make him do anything he didn't want. Greta was here. She liked him. Loved him, even. Maybe.

Gradually his heart descended from its hummingbird flutter into a heavy, rhythmic *thu-thump*. His pulse was thunderous in his ears.

How long had it been? Was everyone gone? He lifted his head and then dropped it quickly. No. He would not be sick here.

"Mr. Cooke . . ."

He swallowed. "I'm okay." As if the words would make it so. He turned his head slightly and looked at Greta. Now that the all-consuming panic was ebbing, he could see he had scared her. "I'm sorry."

She touched his arm again, and when he didn't pull away, she moved her hand to his back. Feeling his heart rate, he realized. After a moment she began to brush off the back of his shirt.

"I must be a mess." He held out his palms, noting peripherally that the crowd had begun to thin, and cataloged a couple of minor scratches. He rubbed the dirt off on his pants— "Oh, Jesus." The left knee was torn and bloodied.

"Let me—"

He waved her off gently. "It's okay. I can barely feel it." Now that his heart had settled, the injury registered as a dull throb. He rolled up the pant leg, bracing himself mentally, but there was no bone or gushing blood. The pavement had grated the skin off, that was all.

Greta opened her purse and pulled out a pack of tissues and a bottle of water.

Samuel couldn't help smiling. "Always prepared."

"Comes from working with kids. I have aspirin, too, if you want it."

"Nah." He doused the knee, picked out the bits of sand and tarmac, and used a tissue to blot the wound. Blood had seeped down his sock, which was folded over the top of the brace. So much for that pair.

"I'll get the car now."

"Wait." He forced himself to look at the street. There were people, though not as many as before, or maybe the suffocating throngs had been mostly his imagination. He rolled his pants down and retrieved his crutches. "Let's have dinner."

"Mr. Cooke . . ." Her expression suggested he might have misplaced his brain.

He reached for the car's side mirror, tested his weight briefly, and pulled himself up. "I'm not in pain, and I'm not going to bleed to death. There are very few perks to being defective, but this is one. I might as well enjoy it."

Greta stood and caught his arm, steadying him as he found his balance. "This is not a good idea."

He sighed. "Also, I'm going to feel really, really bad if I've ruined tonight."

She hesitated.

"Unless you object to my being filthy?"

Greta rolled her eyes and shouldered her purse. "Come on."

In spite of his (entirely false) bravado, Samuel picked his way down the street, staying close to the line of parked cars. It was fully dark now, so the only light came from streetlights and the ballpark.

Greta walked next to him, her usually purposeful stride oddly broken. It reminded him of the time he had watched her practice with the girls—that slight crouch. She was guarding him.

"Greta . . ." He didn't know what to say. *I don't need a bodyguard?* The truth was, he kind of did. "Never mind."

The fairgrounds were a combination baseball/football field. The baseball diamond had been sectioned off with iron gates, and the livestock housed in stalls to one side suggested that it would become an auction ring at some later point. Beyond, temporary booths around half the football field advertised food and children's games.

"Do you want to look around?" Greta asked.

Samuel was tempted to say yes, but the panic attack had drained him, and collapsing in the middle of the field was not how he wanted to end the evening. "Isn't there something you like?"

She pointed to a booth done in whitewashed plywood and blue lettering. "That one's pretty good."

By the time they reached Foursquare Teriyaki, Samuel was shaky. There was a tented pavilion with tables a little farther on, but most of the chairs were occupied. People with paper plates and sodas were strewn out on the grass all around.

"I'll find you a chair," Greta offered.

He imagined her walking over to the tent and yanking the seat out from under the first teenager she encountered. "Uh, no. Here is fine. Just, um . . ."

Greta took his arm and lowered him to the ground. "I'll get the food."

As she strode away, instantly resuming her usual brisk pace, Samuel slid a shirt cuff over his hand and wiped the cold sweat off his forehead. Okay. That hadn't been a *complete* disaster. Perhaps the evening was salvageable. He stretched his arms and rubbed his thighs. The shakes were partly low blood sugar, so if he ate quickly and carried the conversation long enough to digest . . .

Yeah, right. He was going to have to send her for the car.

He watched Greta at the back of the line. She stood alone, shoulders square, face set in a mask of concentration. In a fight, she could have taken any man in line, and she looked like she was prepared to. The women around her were fashionable even in casual jeans and blouses; Greta wore nothing that accentuated her figure. She could have been a guy from behind. She was, in almost every sense of the word, more of a man than he was. And he liked her that way. Did that, in some weird backward way, make him gay? Whatever.

A couple of small children raced past, nearly tripping over his crutches. He pulled them closer as a strawberry-blond toddler stumbled after, shrieking with delight as she tried to catch her older siblings. The chase ended a few yards away, where a gaggle of kids had gathered around the trash-can clown from the parade. He was making balloon animals.

Samuel watched until Greta returned, bearing two plastic bowls. She handed one to him, then nestled the other in the grass before sitting, grunting as she straightened her legs. "Not as flexible as I used to be."

Samuel had tucked his legs neatly beneath him. His feet were probably completely asleep. Not that it mattered.

Greta shifted again, settling for one leg straight and one bent. She looked uncomfortable.

He couldn't have articulated why that made him want to hug her, but it did. "I love you."

She gave him a puzzled frown. "Where did that come from?"

Samuel shrugged. "I just do." He was disappointed not to have the sentiment returned, but it was okay. He could wait.

They ate, listening to the chatter around them, punctuated by the screams and laughter of children. Every now and then the tableau was interrupted by a distinctive barnyard breeze and an emphatic *moo*. Samuel felt the need to make conversation, but the only topic that came to mind was one he didn't want to discuss. Still, if he didn't do it soon, he was going to find himself in hot water. Greta had essentially given him a free pass over the debacle with Marcus; he doubted she'd be as forgiving a second time.

He picked at the grass. "In the interests of full disclosure, I need to make a confession."

Greta raised one eyebrow. "What now?"

"Well, in the library, there are . . ." He swallowed. "I found your high school yearbook."

"Oh." She looked confused.

Brilliant. She was going to make him spell it out. "What I mean is, I—"

Greta shook her head. "I know what you mean. I assumed you had done it months ago."

He blinked. "Really?"

She shrugged.

"Nice to know what you think of me."

She allowed a small smile. "I appreciate your honesty, in any case."

He waved a hand. "Right. Whatever." So she had wanted him to connect the dots about Butch Irving. Easier, he supposed, than saying the words. Fair enough.

"Mr. Cooke." She used her fork to indicate his knee.

"Damn." The stain on his pants was growing. He put down his bowl and leaned to one side, tugging the leg out. Greta grasped his heel and pulled. "Thanks. Napkin?" He rolled up his pants, took the wad she'd gotten from the teriyaki booth, and pressed it against his kneecap.

She winced at the sight of his mangled flesh, fully illuminated by the field lights. "You really can't feel . . . ?"

"Right knee, yes. This one, no." He pulled his leg up and slipped a hand underneath. "I can feel the back of both knees, which is how I get by with just the ankle braces." He felt shy, suddenly, as if he'd said too much. "Never told anyone that." He peeked under the napkins. "I think I stopped bleeding."

"Keep putting pressure on until—" Abruptly Greta's attention snapped to a point somewhere on his left.

Samuel followed her eyes to the clown. Some sort of commotion had started: kids shouting, clown looking around with a helpless confusion only barely discernible beneath his painted red smile. The clown said something, looked down through the cluster of children, and then said it again, louder. "Help! Someone? Please help!"

Greta rolled to one knee and pushed herself to her feet. Before Samuel could ask what she was doing, she started across the grass, breaking into a heavy jog. As she drew near, she waved her arms, scattering the kids. Only then, as the crowd broke, could Samuel see the cause of the commotion: the toddler who had passed him earlier, lying in the grass.

Greta dropped to her knees beside the child, snapping a command to the clown as she checked for a pulse, then holding her hand an inch or two above the little mouth. The clown headed away, hurrying as fast as he could in his big shoes toward a booth with a big red cross on the other side of the field.

"Oh my God!" someone shrieked. A large woman barreled toward Greta, bust heaving as she staggered under her own weight. One of the toddler's siblings trailed behind her.

Greta stuck her fingers in the little girl's mouth. The curse her lips framed told Samuel she met with no success. She rolled the child onto her stomach and performed a quick, violent Heimlich. The mother of the child, only a few feet away, let out a bloodcurdling scream. Someone grabbed her arms to prevent her from doing anything stupid.

The girl's pink skin was mottled with purple.

Samuel looked for—something. Anything. He couldn't get up without help. The only other thing he could do was start crawling toward Greta, but what would that accomplish? Other adults were looking on, faces slack and pale. They didn't know what to do any more than he did; Greta seemed far more competent to handle the situation.

A young man with curly black hair sprinted from the direction of the first aid booth, a kit tucked under one arm. He pulled up short when he saw the child.

"Are you a doctor?" Greta demanded.

His mouth worked, fishlike. "No, I—I'm just helping."

"Where's the doctor?"

"I don't know, he had to—"

"I need a knife," she announced. Still on her knees, she straightened and raised her voice to a bellow: "I need a knife!"

Samuel blinked. He had a knife. A pocketknife on his key chain. He clawed it out of his pocket. It was attached to his belt, but he took the line in both hands and jerked. The wire bit into his fingers and snapped. "Greta!"

She turned. He hefted the ring of keys once, to get the feel of it, then drew his arm back and pitched the loose mass of metal. It was maybe ten yards, but his aim was sure.

Greta caught it, gave him a firm nod, and thumbed the blade on the pocketknife. "Someone *get me a straw*," she shouted, and bent over the child.

Samuel watched along with everyone else, aghast as Greta pulled back the girl's strawberry-blond head and slid the knife into her throat.

26

THE MOTHER'S SCREAM REACHED an unending crescendo. Someone else began to weep. At least one person had the presence of mind to hand Greta a Slurpee straw. In one swift motion, she pushed it into the incision and slid out the knife. The little girl's chest rose.

"Hold her," Greta said. Hands reached out to grip the child's arms and legs as consciousness returned, with panic.

Everything happened in a rush after that. The paramedics must have been nearby, on call for the parade, because they arrived moments after Greta had performed the makeshift tracheotomy. As they were strapping the kid to a stretcher, a heavyset, tidily dressed man in his early fifties jogged up, looking chagrined; he had to be the missing doctor. He was followed by firefighters and then cops. The cops wanted to talk to Greta, but they let her go after several bystanders interrupted to express breathless admiration.

Greta wandered away from the crowd as the paramedics hurried off. Her eyes scanned the field, as if searching for something without quite knowing what. The second time her gaze swept by, Samuel put up a hand and waved. She blinked and shuffled toward him. Samuel's key ring, knife still extended, dangled from the index finger of one bloodstained hand.

"Greta, I— Wow." She stopped over him, and he leaned back to see her better. "That was the most amazing thing I've ever seen." And she'd acted like he was a hero for telling some teenager not to sleep with a boy. Pretty pale next to snatching a child from the brink of death. His heart was still pounding. When she didn't respond, he realized she was a little shell-shocked. Who wouldn't be? "Here, let me take that." He picked up a napkin and used it to pluck the keys from her hand.

She stared at her palms. "I need to wash. Will you—"

"Yes. Yes, I will absolutely be fine right here. Go."

As she started to turn, the doctor approached. "Excuse me, ma'am? Excuse—" He started to hold out a hand, then withdrew it when he saw the blood. "Oh. I'm sorry, I won't keep you, I just wanted to say how impressed I was with what you did. My name is Dr. Mihalik— Uh, Jim."

Greta stared at him, her face blank, until she registered what Samuel already had: this was the guy who should have been on call at the first aid booth. She frowned. "Where were you?"

He gestured to the hill beyond the far side of the field, topped by a squat brown building. "They called me up to the boys' club. An elderly woman having trouble breathing." He paused, examining her face. "Are you a nurse or something?"

"No." Her voice was cold; clearly she didn't find his excuse compelling. If she'd been more collected, Samuel guessed, she would have taken offense at his guess of "nurse" rather than "doctor."

"Where did you learn to perform a trache? If you don't mind my asking?"

"I teach at the high school. A few years ago I nearly lost a student who choked on an orange slice. I asked a paramedic what to do if it ever happened again."

Mihalik's eyebrows went up. "Even knowing how, not many people would have had the presence of mind—or courage—to do what you did."

Greta shrugged. She looked impatient but apparently hadn't regained enough mental presence to formulate an appropriately acerbic response.

Samuel was about to do the honors—craning his neck to see was getting old—when the man patted his pockets and produced a wallet. "As I said, I admire your courage. If you ever want to . . ." His immaculately manicured fingers fumbled out a business card. He offered it, then realized anew that Greta's hands were covered in blood. "Well, I'd love to have dinner with you. If you're up for it."

He was *hitting* on her. Samuel had honestly never anticipated finding himself in such a position. What the hell did he say? Greta was supposed to be . . . safe.

Her frown returned, deeper this time. "I'm with Mr. Cooke," she said, gesturing.

Samuel breathed out and managed a thin, humorless smile.

"Oh." Mihalik let out a nervous laugh as his eyes darted over their half-empty bowls of teriyaki. "I don't mean tonight. Just sometime."

He didn't get it. Because who would ever associate the cripple stuck on his ass with a heroic baby-saving Amazon? Particularly when Greta still wouldn't use his damn first name? "Look," Samuel began. "We're—"

"Oh, gosh, I'm so sorry," Mihalik blurted, tapping his forehead. "I'm such an idiot." He gestured to Greta's hands. "Go clean up. Please, don't let me keep you." He stepped aside and motioned, with a slight bow, toward the restrooms by the old baseball stands.

Greta glanced at Samuel and raised an eyebrow, as if to ask whether he wanted Mihalik barbecued or fried. Under different circumstances, Samuel would have been thrilled to see the show, but he was exhausted, and so was she. Better just to get home. He shook his head minutely and motioned for her to go.

Mihalik shifted from one foot to the other, looking anxiously after Greta as she headed across the field. "Did I just make a complete fool of myself?"

"Pretty much, yeah." Samuel's irritation gave way to amusement. The idea of someone else lusting after Greta ought to have alarmed him, but her knowing look had delivered ample reassurance. Concerns ameliorated, it felt good to know he possessed something another man could not have. He almost felt sorry for the guy.

Mihalik's hand returned to his forehead. "Oh no, I didn't even think— She's not married, is she?"

"No, but—"

"Thank goodness. That's the first time I've done anything like that since my wife passed. I wasn't even planning—and well, when I saw—wow. You know? Wow." He looked down at Samuel. "I'm sorry, where are my manners? Are you okay?"

Samuel gave up trying to clue the guy in. What the hell. Now that someone else had recognized his wealth, he felt benevolent. "I'll live." He rolled the pant leg down over his bloodied knee, covering the brace. "I could use a hand up, though."

Mihalik leaned over and grasped him under the armpits. "SCI?"

Samuel gathered his crutches and pulled the extended leg back so he was in a nominal kneeling position. "Spina bifida."

"Ah. Here we go." With a grunt, he hauled upward and steadied Samuel as he regained his balance. "Got it?"

His arms felt like Jell-O, but his unexpectedly lengthy stay on the grass had given his muscles time to regroup. Not that he'd make it to Greta's car, but he could probably get to the street. "I'm good." Although he was going to be unbelievably sore tomorrow.

Mihalik stepped back. "You, ah, work with her?"

"Among other things."

Mahalik looked toward the bathrooms again. "I don't know whether I should go over there and apologize again or what."

Samuel bit the inside of his cheek. "Not your best bet with Greta."

"Greta. That's her name?"

He nodded.

"What's she teach?"

"Gym. Coaches the girls' basketball team, too."

"Oh. Wow." He cleared his throat. "If I left my card with you, would you give it to her?"

Samuel didn't have the heart to disappoint the guy. He accepted the printed cardstock with diplomatic silence.

"Tell her . . . tell her I . . ." Mihalik winced and shook his head. "No. Just give her the card. Here." He thumbed out a second copy. "I head up the ER here in town. If you ever need anything, let me know."

Now Samuel felt guilty. "Look, don't be surprised if you don't hear from her." He tucked both cards into his pocket, briefly fingering his grandmother's ring. "I get the idea she likes her independence."

Mihalik darted another glance at the bathrooms and sighed. "Yeah. Well. A guy can hope, right?" He flashed a smile at Samuel. "Guess I'd better get back to my post. Have a good night." Mihalik headed for the first aid booth, his stride breaking momentarily as he shot one last glance toward the restrooms.

Samuel felt he ought to be angry. Mortally insulted, in fact. Either that or massively depressed. He knew he wasn't exactly Prince Charming, but the fact that a rational, decent human being had made it through an entire conversation about Greta without entertaining the thought that they might be an item was . . . Well, it ranked him rather lower on the scale of desirability than even he had imagined. Which was very low indeed.

For once it didn't matter. Any negative feelings he might have had were completely overwhelmed by pride. Pride at being with a woman who didn't flinch from circumstances that demonstrably scared the crap out of most adults. Pride that, for once, nobody could deny how awesome she was. And pride that she had chosen to be with him.

Now if he could just make it to the damn bathrooms. Which were, fortunately, next to the exit to the street. He propelled himself forward largely by willpower, ignoring the protesting muscles in his arms. Right crutch forward, left foot; left crutch forward, right foot. Repeat. Don't fall. Repeat.

He was so focused he didn't notice Greta joining him until he saw her shoes next to his. "Oh—there you are. Are you okay?" Her hands were clean, and there were a few wet spots on her shirt where she had tried to wash out bloodstains, more or less unsuccessfully.

"Fine." She tilted her head. "You?"

They had passed the bathrooms. No point in prevarication; his arms were shaking. Visibly. "Not that you needed to do any more rescuing tonight, but no, not really."

Greta put a hand under his arm. "If you can make it to the curb, there's a bus stop."

"Oh, good." He hobbled to the bench and seated himself under the burned-out streetlight with a sigh. She looked him over once, probably to confirm he wasn't about to pass out, and started away.

"Greta, wait." Samuel reached for her hand, bringing her down to his level. "I definitely don't deserve you." He kissed her softly on the lips. He wanted to give her so much more than that, but for now it would have to do.

He expected her to pull away, but for a moment she only looked at him steadily. He flinched, surprised, when her hand touched his face. Her fingers traced his cheekbone, his temple, and brushed the top of his head. Then she straightened and set off at a brisk walk.

Samuel leaned back, exhaling his desire, and smiled at her receding silhouette. Someday . . .

Overhead, the bullhorn crescent of the moon shone through the gnarled branches of a half-bare oak tree. It was quiet out here, in the shadow of the ancient wooden baseball stands. At ten years old, he would have been rabid to explore the innards of the old hulk; even now he contemplated a visit to the livestock auctions on Sunday afternoon, to sit on wide benches worn smooth with use and age. So long as they weren't playing ball.

Bending to check his knee, he discovered it was oozing blood again, at least from the feel of it. Tonight's outing would exact revenge on his body for days, if not a week or two. But it had been worth it.

Tenacity. That was what Greta had said she'd seen in him. Even if it wasn't true, not really, tonight he had proved that it could be. Yes, he had panicked. Yes, he had tripped. But he hadn't quit or run home or fallen into a bottomless pit of self-loathing. He had simply picked himself up, dusted himself off, and gone on.

Less than a year ago, his life had consisted of his apartment, an office, and his car. And he'd called that sufficient because it was all he could handle without, well . . . Samuel glanced down at himself. That very small world was all he had been able to handle without ending up covered in blood, grass stains, and tire grime. Now that he was here, dirty, exhausted, he understood it wasn't the end of the world. It was the beginning.

He leaned to one side and slid his hand into his pocket, feeling for the ring. When he pulled it out, one of the doctor's business cards came, too, fluttering to the ground before he could snatch it out of the air. He considered picking it up, but that would involve bending over, and even as dirty as he already was, he didn't want to end up on the pavement. So he left it at his feet.

The filigreed band glittered in the faint moonlight. He slid it over his thumb—his hands were small, and his grandmother had been a plump woman—and turned it so the diamond faced out.

He had hoped to change his life by moving to Healdsburg and teaching, but that wasn't why he was sitting on this bench tonight. If not for Greta, he would have crawled back to L.A. months ago, tail between his legs. Being with her had altered him in some fundamental way. Digging his grandmother's ring out of the closet was proof of that.

Samuel wanted Greta more than anything he had ever wanted in his life. So deeply and desperately that he usually tried to avoid lingering on the matter. Plunging into that well of longing was dangerous; it meant that if he lost her, he might break, permanently, and in a worse than physical way. Nevertheless, the well existed. And he wanted her so badly that even the probability of drowning seemed worth the risk.

True, she hadn't said she loved him, but he wasn't sure the words themselves were particularly significant. Greta's heart was in her actions, in the curious, gentle way she had touched his face. If actions were what she understood, then that was what he would give. He didn't have much, but what he did possess belonged to her.

He looked at the moon. "You hear that?" he said quietly. "I will give her everything I can."

He did not expect a reply, but one came—softly, and from the deepest recess of his heart.

You already have.

Samuel looked at his feet. His knees. His crutches. He twisted briefly, glancing over his shoulder at the ballpark. Much as he didn't want to acknowledge the truth, there it was: he had already given Greta everything he had to offer.

This, here, with her—this was the best he would ever be. Not tonight, exactly, but Samuel Cooke, thirty-four, was unquestionably topping the summit of his life. He had three or four years, possibly a little longer, before his knees gave out. Then he'd be stuck in the cumbersome full-leg braces, or more likely the chair. And he couldn't keep cathing himself 24/7 like he did now; they'd been warning him about that for years. His tissue would start breaking down, or he'd get bladder cancer, or he'd miss a UTI and kill his kidneys. He had decent sexual function, but that wasn't likely to last, either.

Greta liked to think she didn't care, which was nice, but it wasn't only physical. Psychologically, tonight was a personal milestone. But on the grand scale, or even a petty small-town scale, it was nothing. He'd made it four blocks. He'd enjoyed dinner. He hadn't flipped out. Too much.

Greta? Greta had saved a child's life. That wasn't an anomaly, it was her identity. She was involved in her church, her community. She was aggressive when necessary. She was bold. Certain. She rode a *motorcycle*.

Next to her, Samuel might as well be sticking colored stars on a chart. His so-called fresh start had amounted to one friend and six months of teenage bullying. And Moore would hang out with anyone who'd take him. Never, not in a million years, would Samuel ever be Greta's equal. Being with him would always be a compromise for her. She would have to slow her pace for him—more so as time went on.

He wasn't positive Greta loved him, but she was loyal. For God's sake, she hadn't batted an eye at the doctor's advances. She would stay with Samuel as long as he didn't do anything unforgivable, and eventually she would grow to love him. She would never say or even think to herself that he was not enough.

But he would know.

Samuel wanted more for her than *him*.

Headlights glared briefly, and he looked up to see her Suburban round the corner.

He knew what he had to do. Before he had time to second-guess himself. Before cowardice got the better of him.

He shoved the ring into his pocket. When she got out of the car and offered a hand, he gave her the card instead.

"What is this?" She squinted in the dim light.

"Dr. Mihalik's card. He wants to have dinner with you. I think you should."

Greta's brow furrowed. "What?" she said finally in a tone that suggested he have his cerebellum dry-cleaned.

The words stuck in his throat, but he couldn't continue to deprive her of so many better alternatives. Surely her time with him had convinced her she had both the confidence and the right to share her life with another human being. She had managed with him; now she could do it with someone worth her time. At least he had given her that.

"I'm sorry." He couldn't say her name. "This. Us. We. Are over. It's not going to work." He stopped, feeling like he should say more but not knowing what. "I'm sorry."

Greta examined him for a long moment, her eyes searching his face. Samuel looked elsewhere.

"But I love you," she said.

27

SHE MIGHT AS WELL have ripped him open, sternum to navel, with his own pocketknife. He knew in that instant all he had to do was apologize, back out, and they would hug and kiss and he would explain how stupid he had been and she would forgive him and they would be in love. But he would *know*.

"You think you love me." His voice came out very quiet. "Only because you haven't realized you could do so much better. You don't have to settle."

She was starting to look angry. It was almost a relief. His rejection would not break her. Of course it wouldn't.

"I'm not your only option," he reiterated, with more force.

Her hand closed around the business card. When she spoke, her words sliced through the air like a knife. "In three decades, Mr. Cooke, do you honestly think you are the first man to express interest in me?"

He closed his mouth on the word, but he knew *yes* was written in his eyes. "I—"

She flung the crumpled card away. "I don't need you to tell me what my 'options' are."

He cringed. "I'm sorry. I didn't—"

"You are not my only choice. Maybe that's how *you* feel. Is that what you think of me, Mr. Cooke? That I am *your* only option?"

"Yes," he whispered.

Her hand moved, and Samuel flinched at the flash of pain across his face.

"If I'd known that," she hissed, "I never would have spoken to you."

Greta stepped off the curb and circled to the driver's side of the Suburban. She didn't spare him so much as a glance as she drove away.

Samuel put a hand to his cheek. It was warm.

Somehow it seemed right that this was the last touch she would ever give him. How arrogant he had been to imagine he deserved anything more.

He wasn't aware of having put his hand in his pocket, but gradually he realized he was staring at the ring again, held between a thumb and forefinger. His mother ought to have given it to Chris after all.

"Mr. Cooke? What are you doing out here?"

Samuel straightened, shoving the ring deep into his pocket and reaching for his crutches. Then he recognized the voice and the plump silhouette. "Oh. Sadie." He was surprised by her approach; she hadn't spoken to him voluntarily since she'd appeared at his door on Tuesday night.

She sat next to him, clearly absorbed in her own thoughts. Then she glanced at his knee and did a double take. "What *happened*?"

Even in the wan moonlight, he was apparently quite a spectacle. He cleared his throat so his voice wouldn't fail. "It's been a rough evening. You don't, ah, have a car, do you?"

She shook her head. "I walked."

"Phone?"

She shrugged and pulled an old flip-phone out of the pocket of her sweatshirt.

Fortunately numbers stuck in his mind like gum under a desk. He dialed Moore's cell.

"Hello?" Classical music played in the background.

"I need you to come get me. I'm at the bus stop outside the base-ball stands."

"Cooke?" Muffled rustling filled the line, and when Moore's voice came back, the music had gone. "What's going on? Where's—"

"Look, either pick me up or give me the number for a cab."

"Okay, okay. Give me a few minutes?"

"I'm not going anywhere." Samuel shut the phone and handed it to Sadie. "Thanks."

She slid it into her pocket without looking at him, obviously embarrassed by his predicament.

He sighed. "Don't feel like you have to wait around." Although, granted, her presence was the only thing between him and a complete meltdown.

She risked a glance at his face. "Well, I . . ." She swallowed. "I wanted to say I'm sorry again. Especially for coming to your house and crying and stuff. I feel really stupid for freaking out."

Samuel could sympathize. "Don't. Just because you realize later that something isn't important doesn't mean it wasn't at the time."

"I guess so. Anyway, sorry."

"Apology not really needed but accepted. Can I expect you to start participating in class again?" As he said it, he realized he was planning on going back. Greta or not. He'd finish out the year. Just because he wasn't enough for her was no reason to self-destruct.

Really?

Really.

After that—well, after June, he'd decide if life was worth living.

She smiled sheepishly. "Yeah."

"Good. It's been pretty dead without you. I feel awkward asking questions when I know nobody is going to answer."

She stifled a giggle. "Should you be saying that?"

"Probably not." For some reason he couldn't fathom, he reached into his pocket and pulled out the ring.

Sadie's mouth opened slightly. "Mr. Cooke, are you going to . . ."

He took her wrist, pressed the ring into the center of her soft palm, and closed her fingers around it. "Take it."

Her eyes went wide. "*What?*"

"Sell it and put it toward your college fund. Keep it. Toss it in the trash. I don't care. I've been torturing myself with that thing since Christmas, and I'm done."

"But what about Ms. Cassamajor?"

"It's over."

"Did she—"

"No. I did."

Sadie stared, uncomprehending. "I don't understand. I thought . . . I thought you really liked her."

"It's complicated," he said.

"I'm not stupid."

"Sadie." He sighed and rubbed his temples. "Look, it's not your—"

"Mr. Cooke, you just gave me a wedding ring!" She held it up to punctuate the point.

He put up a hand. "Fine." He took a breath and let it out again slowly. "I just . . . She deserves better than me. That's all."

He didn't look at Sadie, but he could feel her eyes on him, disapproving.

"God," she said abruptly. "That's the stupidest thing I've ever heard."

Samuel resisted the urge to point out what a romantic genius she was. "You're entitled to your opinion."

She stood, glaring down at him, hands clenched at her sides. "Who do you think you are? How do you know how she feels?"

"It's not about feelings. Emotions are irrational. Eventually she'll realize I was a mistake and find someone else."

"What if she doesn't *want* someone else?"

He shrugged. "Then she's better off alone."

Sadie made an exasperated noise. "You think you're being all noble or something, but really, you're just scared." She pushed the ring into his hand. "If you love her, let her make up her own mind."

He looked down at his open palm.

She kicked a leg of the bench, sending a dull vibration through the wood slats. "Stupid," she spat, and walked off.

Samuel sighed. Sadie made a certain amount of sense if you assumed Greta prioritized her own needs. But her sense of worth lay in serving others, whether at school or church or in her personal life. She was loyal and dependable and would always allow both of those qualities to take precedence over her own desires. And Samuel didn't want Greta's loyalty. He wanted her to be happy.

He put the ring away. Trying to give it to Sadie had been foolish; he would get rid of it tomorrow on eBay.

When Moore pulled up in his canary-yellow Karmann Ghia, Samuel felt relatively in possession of his faculties. It was perhaps an indication of what was to come when the first thing the car made him think of was the yellow carnations he had given Greta once upon a time. It wasn't even the same yellow. Thank God he had the next three days to himself. Maybe he could get drunk.

The passenger door opened and Olivia got out, looking petite and lovely in a ratty old sweater of Moore's. Though she never wore makeup and her hair was cut close to her scalp, she seemed disheveled somehow, and Samuel realized the sweater was inside out.

And suddenly he was trying very, very hard not to cry.

She gave him an apologetic smile and slid quietly into the tiny backseat.

By that time Moore had gotten out and rounded the car. His shirttails were hanging out. "Holy crap," he said. "What happened?"

"I tripped."

"Jesus. Where's Cass?"

"Gone." And, when he saw pity flood Moore's face, "I ended it." The fact that everyone would assume he had been dumped was a concise summation of why it couldn't go on.

Moore looked incredulous. "No offense, but have you lost your fucking mind?"

Actually, he felt more lucid than he had in quite some time. But he didn't want to sit here arguing with Moore. "Can you just take me home?"

Sitting in the cold had stiffened Samuel's joints; he struggled to get up, and Moore all but carried him to the car. Inside, the vehicle smelled faintly of patchouli and motor oil.

The silence, as Moore navigated down the darkened neighborhood streets, would have been bearable had Olivia not been sitting in the backseat. Samuel could feel her radiating with an intense, almost palpable desire to speak.

"*What?*" he demanded finally, tossing the word over one shoulder.

"Huh?" Moore glanced at him and then overcorrected, swerving into the other lane. Fortunately there was nobody else on the road.

Olivia cleared her throat. "Why did you do it?"

For God's sake, did he need to put it on a T-shirt? He looked out the passenger window and started counting electric poles. "Not that it's your concern, but I realized I couldn't let her spend the rest of her life babysitting me."

The car went silent, and Samuel was glad nobody tried to tell him he was being silly.

He massaged his knee as they rounded the corner to his house, hoping the car heater had warmed him enough so he could make it to the door without collapsing.

"Hey," said Moore, "what's that?"

A box sat on Samuel's doorstep. "No idea." He opened the passenger door and slid his crutches out. "If you could give me a hand . . ."

Moore was already out of the car, heading for the package.

Samuel sighed and left his legs in the car; as long as Moore was going to dick around, they might as well get a little more heat.

"Sorry," Olivia said from the backseat.

Moore stopped and looked down at the box for a good long moment before picking it up and bringing it back to the open passenger door. He tipped it forward, displaying the contents.

It contained a wok. Specifically, *the* wok Samuel had given Greta for Christmas, purchased while shopping with Moore. Tucked beside it were the cookbooks he'd gotten online and a couple of CD cases, programs he'd ripped to show Greta how much easier it was to grade on the computer than by hand. Scattered over the top of everything, the broken remains of what had been a bouquet of dried carnations. Yellow.

He reached into the box and picked up one of the flowers. It crumbled in his hand. Jesus Christ. She'd *kept* them.

"Now what?" asked Moore.

It didn't matter. Greta was angry. Samuel had known she would be. He swallowed. "Now you help me up and go mind your own damn business."

Moore's brow wrinkled. "Mmm, no. Wrong answer." He dumped the box in Samuel's lap, shoved his crutches into the car, and slammed the door.

"Hey! What the hell are you doing?" Samuel fumbled for the door handle around the big box, but Moore was already getting into the driver's seat. "Greg, this is not funny."

Moore stepped on the gas.

Two minutes later, he pulled up in front of Greta's house.

"I don't know what you think you're doing," Samuel said, "but it's not funny."

"I think it's a great idea," Olivia said.

He twisted to see her over one shoulder. She was grinning. "Nobody asked you." He turned to Moore. "Look, jackass, this is not some stupid romantic comedy where you can make everything better with your idiotic high jinks."

"Your choices." Moore held up a finger. "One, we do this peacefully and I help you to Greta's porch. Two, I drag you out of the car and leave you in a pathetic little pile on the curb."

"And exactly what am I supposed to do once you're gone?"

Moore shrugged. "Up to you."

"You realize I don't have a cell phone. And I can barely stand."

"What'll it be? Option one or option two?"

"Fuck you, Greg. Fuck. You."

28

SAMUEL WATCHED MOORE GET into the car with Olivia and putter away, leaving him on Greta's front porch like an anonymous gift. Or a paper bag full of shit.

He stood there fuming for a minute or two, vowing vengeance upon the guy he'd thought was his friend, but the night had gotten cold, and procrastination wasn't going to help anything. The sooner it was over, the better. He sighed and jabbed the doorbell with a thumb. The chime sounded inside.

He waited for a minute or two, arms trembling with fatigue and cold, before trying again.

To the right of the door was a narrow stained-glass window with an oval of clear glass in the center. He stretched his neck to peer through it. As far as he could tell, there were no lights on inside.

Great. Moore had marooned him on the porch of an empty house.

It couldn't have been later than eight or nine. Where else could she be? Samuel contemplated checking his watch, but he was no longer confident he could hold himself up with one arm. God, it was cold.

He knew she would move on eventually, get over him. But Greta was a realist. What if she thought pining for someone who didn't want her was a waste of time? He imagined her dumping his sad little collection of gifts on the doorstep and driving away, her face relaxing from fury to stoic indifference—and then a recollection that she needed to pick a few things up from the supermarket.

Then he heard something. A faint but definite rustle from inside.

He shifted his weight and rapped a quick one-two-three. "Greta, are you there? I'm kind of—"

The light in the front hall snapped on, followed by the porch light. He heard the lock turn and then the door opened. Just a crack.

"Go away," Greta said.

"I'd like nothing better." He swallowed. "Unfortunately I'm kind of stuck, so if you want me off your front porch, I'm going to need a phone."

She slammed the door. The hall light went off and the lock clacked into place. Footsteps receded.

Samuel closed his eyes. Now what?

She had sounded angry. But not cold or indifferent. Hurt.

What had he expected? And was he actually relieved to hear the pain in her tone? Did it make him feel good to know she cared, even though he had no intention of recanting? He was such a douche.

Her footsteps returned. The lock turned. The door opened, again only a crack. "There," she said. It shut again.

Samuel looked down. The cordless phone lay next to his right foot. In the pale glow of the porch light he could see the blood on his left knee had spread down, staining most of the lower front of his pants.

He chewed his lip. He'd read recently that researchers had proven exhaustion was mostly mental; when you thought you couldn't possibly go another step, your muscles had fifty percent more output in reserve.

Carefully he propped his left crutch against the doorjamb. Reached for the doorknob. Then a chill gripped him and he collapsed, clutching the knob as he went down. It softened the impact slightly. At least now he had the phone.

He picked it up, turned it on, and had to flex his trembling hand twice before he could dial information. Hopefully Healdsburg had a cab service.

The phone beeped at him. He toggled the power switch and tried again. No dial tone. It beeped again, and this time he saw the red light flash at the top of the unit. He squinted at the text. *Range,* it said. "Shit."

He rubbed his forehead and contemplated chucking the unit, and then himself, into the bushes on the side of the porch. He didn't. Somewhere between Moore's car and the porch, his emotions had clicked off, and he had gone into survival mode. Handy.

He knocked again.

Silence.

"Greta." He rapped louder, scuffing his knuckles slightly. "Greta, I—"

The door cracked. "I hate you."

"Welcome to the club." He held up the handset. "I'm out of range."

The crack widened. Greta's hand shot out, snatching the receiver before slamming the door again.

"Jesus, Greta—Greta, wait!" He used the heel of his hand to pound. "Look, if I stay out here much longer, you may have to call an ambulance instead of a cab."

Silence.

The door swung open. "Don't talk to me," she snapped.

Samuel watched Greta's backside as she strode down the hall and rounded the corner into the kitchen. Guessing she wasn't going to help him up, he turned around and dragged himself butt-first over the threshold.

Inside the front door to the left, there was a bench with a few pairs of shoes tucked underneath. Using his crutches like ski poles, Samuel managed to haul himself onto it.

"Yes," he heard Greta say in the kitchen. "Off Sunnyvale. How long—" She paused. "You don't have anyone closer than— Okay, fine. Yes. Fine. Come." The receiver hit the base with a thick plastic *clunk.*

This was going to be awkward. Maybe she'd stay in the kitchen.

Samuel glanced down the hall and then into the living room, which he was facing. Greta's purse sat on the coffee table, next to a bottle of red wine and a half-empty glass. There was also a paper of some sort, but the easy chair opposite the couch cut off his view.

Greta appeared on the other side of the living room, having come around through the kitchen. Samuel dropped his gaze.

"Fifteen minutes," she pronounced, as if it might as well have been a hundred years.

He nodded at his shoes. The floorboards were slightly scuffed, as if someone had once dragged a heavy bookcase down the hall.

Greta retrieved her purse from the coffee table, sweeping the paper into it and pulling the leather straps over her shoulder in one motion.

"Thought you didn't drink," he mumbled.

She froze, turned half away from him. "I didn't."

"You, uh, didn't start because I—"

"Don't flatter yourself."

"Right." He cleared his throat. "Sorry. Um . . . sorry about everything, actually. Especially what I said earlier. I didn't—"

"Shut up." She started back into the kitchen.

"No, please." He risked a furtive glance. "I didn't mean it like it came out. I never thought of you as my only option. I mean— okay, sort of, but only because I had such a low opinion of everyone else's intelligence. Not because you were anything less than perfect. You—you're pretty much the best thing that's ever happened to me, so really, this isn't even about you." He paused, biting his lip.

Greta stopped, figure framed in the archway. "Save your bullshit. I've heard it before."

He lifted his head. "Before? What are you— Oh." Shit. "Greta, I'm sorry. But for one thing, I didn't get you pregnant. We were just dating. Dating is how you figure out whether someone is right for you, right?"

"Just dating." Her voice was tight with cold fury. "That's all this was to you?"

And then they were shouting. She deserved better, he insisted, whether she knew it or not. She'd deserved better then, and she deserved better than Samuel now. Had she not seen him crawl over her fucking doorstep? Without her help, that was his life. No sane woman would choose that if she truly understood where it went. Hint: it didn't get better. He'd be damned if he'd let her spend her life playing babysitter.

Greta flung her purse to the ground. Did she look like she needed hand-holding? She could take care of herself. She had been doing it long enough. The decision to accept responsibility for someone else was hers, not his. He'd said it himself: it didn't get better. It was a bitter pill to swallow, but she wasn't the one avoiding the inevitable. *Someone* would have to take care of him; foolishly, she'd imagined he preferred someone who cared. All assuming, of course, that he could predict the future. He could get hit by a bus and die tomorrow. She could get breast cancer and spend her last months in the hospital. Granted, his future might be slightly more predictable, but at least she knew what she was in for.

"Oh, do you? Really?"

Two angry strides brought Greta closer than either one of them wanted to be. "Get up." She grabbed his arm, too tight, and dragged him to his feet.

Samuel struggled to maintain his balance as she hauled him to the back of the L-shaped house. The first door hung open on a large guest bathroom; she took him past a second and stopped in front of the third.

"Don't let go," he gasped, feeling her hand relax.

Greta gave an exasperated sigh, but she didn't let him fall. With her free hand, she opened the door and flicked on the light.

It was a small bedroom, filled with picture frames, feminine knickknacks, and a bank of dead machinery. Next to a hospital bed. "This," she said, "is where my mother spent the last three years of her life."

Samuel remembered her saying she'd returned to Healdsburg to care for her mother. He had assumed it was old age. "What did she die of?"

"ALS. Slowly."

Lou Gehrig's. Not a pretty way to go. "How come I didn't know that?"

"You never asked."

"Oh." The unspoken implication was clear: he'd been too fixated on himself to care. He repositioned his crutches, freeing himself from her support. "You've already done this once. Why would you want to go through it again?"

"Doing something I'm good at seemed like a small price to pay for love."

"Oh." He swallowed. "Greta, it's not just about that."

The phone trilled in the kitchen, and Greta consulted her watch. "That's the cab."

Samuel sighed. "Okay." He tried to turn, stumbled, and caught himself on Greta's arm. "Sorry." Then he looked down. "Oh, God, no. Greta, I'm sorry. I'm sorry, I'm so sorry."

She followed his eyes to the spreading radius of dampness. "Bathroom," she snapped.

"God, your carpet, I'm sorry—"

"It's okay."

"Pretty sure it's not." It had been hours since he'd emptied the bag. He left a broad trail all the way to the bathroom. And was still leaking when Greta dropped him on the toilet.

"What can I—"

"Nothing." He was already bent over, removing his shoes. "Just get out. Please."

She closed the door.

It was pointless, but he rushed, writhing out of his pants and underwear in time to stop the last drops from joining the puddle on the floor. He tore at the straps that held the bag to his thigh, intending to detach it and fold the tube over until he could get home. As he lifted the bag off his leg, the tubing slid out completely.

Samuel stared at the end of the catheter, dangling into the toilet bowl between his legs. The numbness that had overtaken him on the front porch began to give way to panic.

Now he was really stuck. It wasn't just that his bladder leaked, but that it was completely unpredictable. The muscle controlling the release of urine might clamp down for days, which would seriously damage his kidneys if he didn't do anything about it. Alternately it might let go, say, in the middle of the taxi ride home. Constant use of the catheter, rather than piping himself several times a day like he was supposed to, had shrunk his bladder to the size of a pea, making the latter option much more likely.

The obvious solution was to have Greta run to his house and grab the kit he kept in his car. That would mean sending the cab away and getting a ride home from her. The last thing he wanted to do right now was inconvenience her further—or, to be perfectly honest, spend any more time with her than necessary. He just wanted to get home, and the cab waiting outside was the fastest route available.

This was Moore's fault. If he'd taken Samuel home like he wanted, if he'd left him the hell alone, he wouldn't be sitting here—

Okay, focus.

There was a bar holding two green towels on the wall facing him. He grabbed one and tossed it onto the tile floor, soaking up most of the puddle but not the acrid smell.

Greta knocked. "Taxi's waiting."

Shit, shit, *shit!* He dumped the bag and the tube in the wastebasket. "Just—tell him to hold on. Start the meter or whatever."

He heard Greta move away. A few moments later her footsteps sounded as she crossed from carpet to wood flooring.

His pants, crumpled on the floor in front of him, were not too— well, yes, they were pretty wet. He could rinse them out in the tub, and that would probably suffice to get him home. It would only take a few minutes to get there. It would be fine. It would. He could tell the taxi driver he'd . . . uh . . .

Oh, God.

Abruptly the stench was overwhelming. Samuel slid off the toilet and wrenched himself around in time to vomit into the bowl.

Greta knocked again.

He coughed and spat. "Just a minute!"

"I sent him away. I'll take you home. Do you need anything?"

Goddammit. "No!" Risking the taxi was one thing, but he was *not* going to soak Greta's car like some feral dog.

"I'm coming in."

"Wait! Jesus Christ, I'm—"

"Use a towel!"

Samuel shoved himself backward and dragged the second towel off the bar just as she barged in.

Greta, hands on hips, looked him over like a cop surveying the scene of a motor vehicle accident. White male, mid-thirties, minor injuries, stranded on bathroom floor. Flight risk: extremely low.

Samuel yanked his knees up, covering them with the towel, which was thankfully oversized. "Well?"

"Give me your keys. I'll get what you need." She lunged forward.

Samuel recoiled. "Don't touch—!" And then he realized she was only reaching over him, one hand on the toilet tank, to turn on the tub. "Oh."

Greta tested the water with a hand and then straightened, flushing the toilet as she did. "Take a bath. I'll—" She looked at him. Carefully. "What was that?"

"Me being freaked out and jumpy?" Why did she even care? He'd ended their relationship. Badly. All she should want at this point was exactly the same thing he did—to get him out.

"You did it at the parade, too."

"Case in point."

Her eyes narrowed. "You thought I was going to hit you."

"You *did* hit me."

"That was different."

"Pardon me if I'm unfamiliar with the nuances of corporal punishment." This was absurd. She was standing on top of a towel soaked with his urine and had apparently decided now was a good time to get personal. Or was this some sort of payback?

Greta rested a hip against the sink and crossed her arms. "You're lying."

"Oh, so now you can read my mind."

She put the toilet lid down and sat on it. "You told me your father stopped hitting you."

His retort died on his lips. "What?" A cold, wiry hand wrapped itself around his heart. How could she possibly—

"When was the last time?" She turned off the tub faucet. Water dripped from the spout, meting out the silence.

He looked at his feet, feeling her eyes on his head. "It's not important."

"When?"

The icy hand slid upward, constricting his throat. "Why do you care?"

"Answer the question, Mr. Cooke."

No. Samuel didn't want her, didn't want anybody, to know that. Didn't want to know it himself. "He . . . he never actually *hurt* me, not after . . ." He shut his eyes.

Greta was quiet. Then she shifted, and her hand came down on his back.

Samuel choked, coughing up phlegm and, suddenly, tears. He folded his arms over his head and sobbed into his knees for a horribly long time.

29

WHEN HE CALMED DOWN—OR, more correctly, ran out of fluids—Greta's hand moved to his head, briefly, and then away. "This was never about your health," she said. "Or me taking care of you, or taking your mother's place. You're afraid I'm too much like your father."

Samuel didn't lift his head. "Please leave me alone."

The toilet lid groaned as Greta leaned forward and got up. "Take a bath. I'll find something for you to wear." She put a hand on one knee and bent to retrieve his pants.

"No, wait—" He grabbed for them, but it was too late. One pocket disgorged his keys; the other, his grandmother's ring.

It bounced on the tile floor, giving off a silvery tinnitus until it rattled and came to rest.

For a moment that stretched to eternity, they both stared at the gold band sitting between them on the floor.

"Oh, God," whispered Samuel. This was, without question, the worst day of his life. Which was saying something.

Greta hadn't moved.

Samuel glanced at her. "Could you pretend you didn't—"

"Yes," she said.

Then she met his eyes, and he realized she wasn't answering his unfinished question.

"*No,*" Samuel said.

Her gaze didn't waver. "Yes."

He shook his head. "No. I can't, I—I don't deserve this. You."

"Maybe that's the point."

"Of what?"

"Love."

Samuel blinked, several times, but he was completely unable to process her words. It seemed important he do so. "Could we possibly discuss this at some point when I'm not curled up on your bathroom floor?"

EVENTUALLY SAMUEL CONVINCED Greta he could get into the tub by himself, thanks. She took his clothes, his keys, his pocketknife, and finally the razor sitting on the edge of the tub, which was when he realized she was removing all sharp objects from his reach. He told her he wasn't that stupid anymore, but she took the razor anyway. Which was smart, because he was lying.

She asked him what he needed, put the wedding ring in her pocket, and left.

Getting into the tub was not as easy as he'd promised, but he managed. He was already bruised anyway. Though the water took on a rosy tinge as he massaged his knee, the bleeding seemed to have stopped. He concentrated on the soap, the water, anything to occupy his thoughts—mainly because he did not trust himself to interpret Greta's words. It was clear that he did not understand her nearly as much as he'd imagined.

After a while he slid under the water and let his breath out, but he wasn't quite exhausted enough to let himself drown.

He remembered only when Greta knocked on the bathroom door that he hadn't replaced the pants in his emergency kit after the chocolate incident. He pulled the shower curtain almost shut, told her to come in, and explained through the crack. She sighed.

"Sorry."

"I put your clothes in the wash, but it's going to be a while. Wait here." She left the bag with his catheter equipment on the sink and returned a few minutes later with a small pair of pink flannel pajamas on a hanger.

"Those are not yours," he said.

"Occasionally the counselor has a student who feels she can't go home for the night. I keep some things on hand. These make them feel . . ."

"Infantile?"

"Something like that."

"They'll do until I get home. Thanks."

She hooked the pajamas on the end of the towel bar. "You're staying here."

God, how did she know? It was like she had a radar detector for desperation. Not that you needed to be Sherlock Holmes to figure that he might be a tad suicidal. "Look, I swear I'm not going to do anything stupid, okay? I just—I'm okay. Okay?"

"I don't want you to be alone tonight."

He held a hand up. "Fine. Just warning you, though, I'm going to flip out if I have to sleep in your mom's bed."

GRETA'S GUEST ROOM was filled with off-season sports equipment, which left only her bedroom. It was the largest in the house, but she still slept in a twin bed. She changed her pillowcase but not the sheets, which was nice because the bed smelled like her. Samuel felt clean and warm under the hand-stitched quilt.

After getting him settled, Greta left and returned with a mug of steaming tea and her first aid kit, which Samuel had used in the bathroom to patch his knee.

She set the tea on the nightstand and motioned for him to pull the blankets back.

"But I just—"

"Let me see."

Samuel rolled his eyes and tugged up the leg on the ridiculous pink pajamas.

Greta made a disapproving "tsk" with her tongue. "Obviously you've never taken first aid." She left the kit beside his foot and went to open the closet. "Drink your tea."

He took an obligatory sip and watched as she reached for a spare pillow. "What's it matter what it looks like? It does the job."

"So does duct tape."

"Which I've used on occasion."

She sat on the end of the bed, making the mattress bounce a little, and slid the pillow under his leg. Pushing the pajamas farther up, she took a moment to examine his brace before unbuckling the clasps. Carefully she peeled back the white medical tape he'd used to affix the gauze to his knee. She fingered the edges of the wound. "Seems clean. Did you disinfect it?"

"Sloppy, yes. Stupid, no."

She pushed the bottle of antiseptic wash to one side and picked out the roll of tape and some more gauze. Measuring out a square the size of his kneecap, she started to place it, then hesitated before it touched his serrated skin. She used her little finger to indicate the faded scar running along the side of his calf. "What's this?"

"Hm? Oh. Suicide attempt number one." He leaned forward

slightly. "No, sorry, that was number two." Number one was on the other calf. It turned out that bleeding yourself out from the leg was pretty hard, but he'd never been brave enough to gouge himself anywhere with functioning nerves.

She nodded as if she'd already guessed the answer and pressed the gauze into place. "Tell me about your father."

Samuel looked at a framed cross-stitch on the opposite wall. It was a lamb with a Bible verse underneath. "Do you sew?"

"My sister." Holding the gauze with one hand, she used her teeth to tear a strip of tape and applied it to his knee. "If you don't tell me, I can't avoid bad associations."

Which assumed they would be spending more time together. Which he was not really sure about. Samuel held his breath until his chest began to burn and then let it out slowly. "You first."

"Hm?"

"Tell me about your mother."

She reached for an ACE bandage. "What do you want to know?" She slid a hand under his knee, lifted his leg, and wrapped it in four quick passes.

"I dunno. Whatever seems important." Whatever he should have asked and never did.

"I embarrassed her." She sat back and put the first aid kit in order.

"In general, or when you got pregnant?"

"She never knew what to do with me. She was very . . . feminine. The pregnancy crushed her. She volunteered a lot at church."

"The *same* church?"

Greta nodded. She closed the kit and slid farther up onto the bed, resting her back against the wall. She crossed one foot over the other.

"So everyone there knows what happened, too."

"Not everyone. But close."

Samuel started to pull the pajama pants down, but Greta put out a hand to stop him. He shrugged and let it be. "Do you ever feel like you'll always be the girl who got pregnant in high school?"

"Sometimes. Then I remember I'm also the person who took the team to the state championships five times. Once as a player, four times as a coach."

"And now you're the woman who saved little Ashley at the fair."

"Ashley." A smile ghosted across her face. "Was that her name?"

"Her mother only screamed it five hundred times."

The smile returned briefly. "I was distracted." She leaned forward and poked a couple of his toes, then waved the okay for him to cover his knee.

"You know I can't feel that, right?"

"Making sure I didn't wrap it too tightly." She picked up the brace. "Do you have to wear this at night?"

"No." He tugged the pajamas down and pulled the blankets up to his middle.

Greta tossed the brace on the floor next to his crutches. "Your turn."

Samuel didn't want it to be his turn. Something else. Anything else. "Wait. What about the wine? You were drinking it, right?"

With a heavy *you are seriously trying my patience* sigh, Greta slid off the end of the bed and left the room. She came back with her purse, sat, and pulled out a familiar photo. "Here."

As he accepted it, Samuel realized it was the paper he had seen on the coffee table. It was unchanged—a young Greta holding the gray-faced infant. On the back, the faded red ink was still there: *Greta and Amelia, b. Feb. 14.* Now, in a fresh blue pen, there was a dash and the inscription *d. Feb. 20.*

He looked at Greta, not sure what to make of it.

"What happened tonight," she said. "With the girl. I realized it was time to let go."

Understanding sank in, slow and heavy. Samuel closed his eyes.

He had utterly failed to realize how saving a child's life might affect Greta. This was big for her—a wound far older and deeper than anything he might have inflicted tonight. Which was why, in spite of what he'd done, she had poured herself a glass of wine. Alone.

In one swift stroke, she had vanquished her personal demons, and then he'd gone and pissed all over it. Literally.

"You must hate me," he said.

"Not everything is about you."

Jesus. Again. "I'm sorry. I'll just keep my mouth shut."

She shook her head. "It's your turn."

"I don't want it to be."

"It's okay."

"No. It's not." Samuel took a quick, deep breath. His father. Right. He didn't know where to start. Maybe if he picked something, the right words would rush out. "He's strong. Like you. Always the guy everyone goes to when they need help. He even carries this huge cable . . ." Samuel made a circle with his thumb and forefinger to illustrate its circumference. "In the back of his truck. So he can tow people when they break down. He's not a talker, but you always know what he means. Or I did, anyway." Which wasn't at all what he wanted to say. "Everyone loves the guy." Neither was that. He swallowed. "I hate him."

He glanced at Greta. She nodded slightly.

"I hate him," he said again. "I hate—" Okay, okay. He forced himself to breathe. God, how was he supposed to explain this? "I don't think he meant it badly, at first. After I got home from the hospital, a few weeks later, Mom went out. He came in to . . . to . . . I don't know. Maybe he wanted to apologize but didn't know how. So he tried to treat me like nothing had happened." Samuel breathed. "He punched my shoulder, not hard, just . . ." He made a fist and jabbed the air. "I freaked out. And instead of backing off, he kept going, like I'd snap out of it. Only I didn't."

He fiddled with a loose thread on the quilt. "After that, it was . . . whenever he'd had a couple of beers, if nobody was around. He'd come in, rough me up, act like it was a game. Like he was going to toughen me up, shake it out of me. And—and I did sort of, you know, learn not to react, but then . . ." He closed his eyes. "I think then it was kind of a challenge, to go until I got hysterical. He'd never, um . . . He never left any marks. Bruises, yeah, but I banged myself up just getting around back then. So it was nothing I could point to. That wasn't so bad, actually. What—what gets to me is, he likes to get me in a corner, or somewhere I'm trapped, and—" Samuel had to stop because he was gulping for air. Even if he wanted to, he doubted he could give Greta any more detail. Just thinking about it made him panic.

"So, um, so then after Mom died, he got really drunk. He would have hurt me that time if Chris hadn't come home. So I went to college." He glanced up. Greta was staring at him, her mouth slightly open. "That's, um, about it."

She blinked. "And that was the last time?"

Samuel pressed his lips together. "No."

She waited.

He looked at his hands. "Fourth of July," he mumbled. "Chris realized they were out of ketchup and ran to the store. I had to, um, use the bathroom to . . ." Greta nodded and he let out a breath. "The lock was broken, but it couldn't wait, and Dad was already halfway through a six-pack, and he—" Samuel squeezed his eyes shut. "I—" He could feel himself locking up inside, as surely as if the old man's unshaven face were shoved in his, breath reeking of stale beer.

"Just tell me what he said." Greta's firm tone brought him back to the present.

He couldn't look at her. "He just . . . he just kept asking why I always came back. He—he said it was because I didn't have anybody else, never would, never could. I—I could tell myself I had my job, my condo, but as long as I kept coming back, he and I both knew I was nothing. Nobody. He—"

"That's enough."

"I . . . I had to leave. I had to try. Or else . . ." Or else he would have done something desperate, and his mother wouldn't have been there to stop him. Samuel's face was wet. He wiped his eyes. "I'm sorry. I should have told you. I just . . . I've never told anyone. Not Mom, not Chris, not anyone." He looked up far enough to see her hand come to rest on his foot. "I'm just . . . so stupid, so weak, I couldn't even face myself—"

"You think this happened because you were weak?"

"He was right, Greta. I went *back*. Over and over. Thanksgiving, Christmas, Easter, God, for ten years. Every single time, I told myself I wouldn't do it again. Being trapped in the house is one thing, but going back? Who does that? One seriously fucked-up person, that's who."

"Sometimes being hurt seems better than being alone."

He ground his fist into the mattress. "The worst thing is I loved him, Greta. I worshipped him. Even now, I wonder, does he love me? Did he ever? And if he did or didn't, how the hell am I supposed to figure out what love is?"

"Well, it's not earned by letting someone hurt you."

He looked up, startled by the certainty in her voice. "Do you really believe that?"

"Yes." She paused. "Sometimes."

He pulled at the loose thread again, and it came out. "You know, I thought you were as screwed up as I was, underneath. But you seem like you've got everything pretty much figured out."

"Not so much as you think. And it's taken a good thirty years."

"I'll probably be dead by then."

She laughed and gave his foot an affectionate pat.

"Wish I could feel that."

Greta leaned toward him, running her hand up the quilt to his thigh.

Jesus Christ. At this moment—at any moment—that was the last thing he'd expected her to do. Samuel felt himself flush, and his body responded. Thank God for the quilt. "I want to have sex with you so badly." Right, well, that helped absolutely nothing.

"All right."

He froze. "Sorry, what?"

Greta met his eyes without a trace of humor. "I have a ring. I think I can trust you to follow through." She gave his thigh a firm squeeze.

"That's—I—um." Oh, fuck. "I think you called my bluff."

She straightened, removing her hand. "Suit yourself."

"You're going to make me wait now, aren't you." Assuming they were sort of engaged. Which he wasn't sure about. She seemed to be. Maybe? He would think about this tomorrow.

"My moment of weakness has passed." She nodded at the nightstand. "Drink your tea."

He picked up the mug and took a sip. It was cool. He set it down.

"All of it."

"If I do that, I'll have to make a trip to the bathroom at four in the morning."

Greta let out a labored sigh and pushed herself forward. She went into her bathroom, came out with a tin wastebasket, and plunked it down on the floor next to the nightstand.

"Seriously?"

She shrugged. Then stood there and watched while he downed the cold chamomile.

He handed her the empty mug.

Greta didn't move.

Samuel looked around her at the open bedroom door. "Good night?"

"Sorry for hitting you," she said. "Earlier."

"No, no. You were right, it's different."

She frowned. "How?"

"For one thing, I deserved it."

She gave him a humorless smile. "Yes, you did. Good night, Mr. Cooke."

He was going to let her walk out the room, leave everything complicated until tomorrow or next week or never. Then she reached for the light switch by the door, and he said, "Greta."

She turned, eyebrows raised in a silent question.

"This is what you do, isn't it. Take in stray cats."

She held up the mug, which had Snoopy painted on the side. "I'm a dog person."

"Cats, dogs, whatever." He paused. "Is that what I am?"

"Maybe. But more."

"How so? What am I to you? What do I *do* for you?"

"You make me feel . . ." She looked around the room, searching for the right word. Finally her eyes returned to him or, rather, his pajamas. "Pink."

"Pink," he repeated stupidly.

"Yes." She flicked off the light.

SAMUEL SENSED IMMEDIATELY that he had slept in late. He was on his side, facing the wall, which glowed with sunlight streaming through the glass doors on the opposite side of the room.

He lay unmoving, bunching the quilt around his face and breathing Greta's scent as his thoughts coalesced. It was fresh soap with undertones of other things. Sports equipment and motorcycle grease, he imagined. His nose wasn't that discerning, but whatever it was smelled like *her*.

Carefully, he probed backward in his mind to the night before, shutting his eyes against the light as he tried to skim over some of the more painful memories he'd managed to add to his collection. The trouble was they were tangled up with the good things, impossible to sift out for future reflection. If he wanted any of it, he had to take it all.

He set the problem aside and pulled back the blankets to survey the situation below. His injured leg had fallen off the pillow, no big surprise, and his knee was swollen, also no big surprise. But it looked okay. Ish. Someday he wasn't going to be so lucky.

The real question of the moment was whether his leg was too swollen to get his brace on. Even if he could manage it, he shouldn't. He checked the bag on his thigh. It was the smaller size he used during the day, and he hadn't gotten up to empty it during the night. Which meant he needed to do so, like, now.

Samuel sighed. He knew he should call Greta and ask her to help him to the bathroom. Or he could be an idiot and go for it himself. Honestly, that sounded more like him. He would just try the brace, if Greta hadn't tossed it too far out of reach.

He sat up and started to drag his legs over when his peripheral vision registered a change. He twisted around, and there it was, right next to the bed. His wheelchair from home, with a set of neatly folded clothing on the seat.

Samuel choked back the lump that surged into his throat. Greta had—what, gone to his house late last night? Early this morning? Loaded his chair into her Suburban and brought it here, along with his clothes. Then sneaked in without waking him, which was pretty hard to do. After all the crazy he'd put her through last night, she'd gone out and done this.

He really, *really* didn't deserve her. Really.

Maybe that's the point of love, she'd said. Samuel didn't know if that was true, but then, as he'd so amply demonstrated last night, he didn't have a clue what love was, either.

He'd obviously hurt her, and yet here she was. Was she crazy? Was *he* crazy?

As much as he wanted to sit here and puzzle it out (not really), he needed to get to the bathroom. He set aside the clean clothes and slid into the chair, being extra cautious with what he was now thinking of as his "bad" leg. Like there was a good one.

He emptied the bag into the toilet and waited while it filled partially again, draining the excess that had backed up in his bladder.

When that was done, he took stock in the mirror. Even after last night's bath, he looked like shit. If Greta had any shaving equipment, she'd removed it, so the five o'clock shadow would have to wait. Somehow the cheery pink pajamas (which, upon closer inspection, were dotted with ladybugs) made him seem even more haggard. He splashed his face and combed his hair with wet hands.

By daylight, the bedroom looked even plainer than he'd first thought. The quilt had a red and blue geometric pattern; everything else was minimalist. A wooden nightstand and a simple, functional lamp. A chest of drawers. An old wooden rocking chair by the window, notebook and Bible on the seat. Curtains in sedate blue. Mild curiosity prompted him to shove the wheelchair over the thick carpet for a look at the backyard.

Had Samuel known Greta gardened at all, he would have assumed practicality: tomatoes, corn, squash. But there wasn't a vegetable in sight, just an incredible profusion of flowers. Sunflowers, roses, daisies, pansies . . . he didn't know what else. There was even a tree with huge white flowers providing shade for more delicate flowers below. The colors were radiant in the midmorning light. It was a view in every way the opposite of Greta's bedroom.

He unlocked the glass door and pushed it open, realizing immediately that it was soundproofed. The birdsong outside bordered on deafening. He bumped over the threshold and onto the L-shaped deck, squinting against the sun.

The garden was so crowded with flowers he couldn't tell how Greta managed to weed or water until he spotted a few stepping stones wedged in here and there. In the far corner, shaded by the tree, was a small wrought iron table with two chairs.

Samuel wondered how he could have missed this for so long. It was pure excess. What was the point of flowers? You planted, watered, weeded, and labored in the sun—for what? Color. Birds. That was it.

"Morning." She stood near the bend in the deck, having come out through the dining room.

"It's beautiful," he said.

She nodded an acknowledgment and stepped to the ground, bending to pull weeds out of a terra-cotta pot that was home to . . . geraniums? Something like that.

"Thanks. For the chair." He hesitated. "Does this mean I'm living here now?"

She glanced up. "You wish."

Samuel grinned. "I totally do." He caught a glint of metal on her hand as she tossed the weeds over the end of the porch. "So . . . I guess I'm not going to get that back?"

She raised her eyebrows, then realized what he was talking about and held up her hand. The ring circled the littlest finger on her left hand. "Do you want it?"

Samuel looked at the garden, running his fingers along the rims of his chair. He looked at Greta, and if it was wrong to take her, he no longer cared. "No," he said. "Not really."

"I'll drop it off at the jeweler's later today. It's a little too small."

Of course it was. He pivoted. "I'll get dressed."

"Later; breakfast is ready." She put a hand on the open door to the dining room. "Anyway, you look good in pink."

"Really."

She snorted. "No."

GRETA HAD MADE blueberry pancakes, bacon, hash browns, and eggs. Samuel sat opposite her at the breakfast table, watching his grandmother's ring flash as she ate. For a while he could think nothing at all except to remind himself to take a bite every minute or two. Gradually, however, he allowed himself to formulate the sentence struggling to free itself in the back of his mind.

This woman wants to marry me.

He thought it again and again, obsessively, turning the words over just as his nervous fingers had worried the ring.

Then he said it out loud.

Greta quirked an eyebrow. "You're getting this just now?"

Samuel laughed sheepishly, recognizing the truth in her words. He remembered the carnations he had given her—nothing at all compared to the riches in her garden, but she had saved and dried them nonetheless. And then her certainty, her firm *yes* when she had seen the ring.

She had made this decision a long time ago.

Which made him feel even worse about how it had happened.

"You going to eat that or just look?"

Samuel realized he was staring at his plate. "Sorry." He stuffed some bacon into his mouth. "Greta?" It came out garbled, so he chewed quickly and swallowed. She looked at him expectantly. "I'm sorry about, well, everything, but—"

"I forgive you. Let's move on."

She was so *definite*. "No, I mean . . ." He was embarrassed to say the word. "Proposing. I wanted it to be special." And it wasn't that he had failed to make it special—he'd turned it into the worst day of his life. Not that it had been much of a Kodak moment for her, either.

Greta ate a little more, then said, "So make it up to me with the honeymoon."

"Oh." He hadn't thought of that. This was happening very quickly. "Sure, okay. Where do you want to go?"

She shrugged. "Surprise me."

"Somehow I knew you'd say that." A honeymoon. He'd never gotten that far in his fantasies. Never even got to the ceremony, actually. Speaking of which. "When do you want to do it?" He felt himself color. "Get married, I mean."

Greta swallowed and nodded as if recalling something she'd meant to tell him earlier. "I called Father Hayes."

"Oh?" Already? Samuel reached for his glass of orange juice and took a sip.

"He said next Saturday would work."

His jaw dropped. The juice drained back into the glass. "Um." Oh wow. "I thought, um, I thought these things took some time? To plan?"

Greta frowned. "I want a marriage, not a wedding."

"Well, next week is, uh . . ."

Their eyes met over the table. Greta's laser stare seemed to demand immediate commitment. He probably looked like a rabbit in the headlights.

He cleared his throat and glanced at the wall, breaking her psychic stranglehold. "Are you sure you don't want something traditional? It doesn't have to be big, but, you know, flowers? Candles? A white—" Oh, he was an idiot. Greta would never allow herself to wear a white dress, and nothing he said or did would alter that.

"I'm sure," she said.

"Well, whatever you want is fine," he said. "But I want a new suit. A good one."

She nodded. "There's a shop in Santa Rosa. Assuming your knee's better, we'll go next weekend."

Whew. That bought him some time. What he needed it for, he didn't know, but his brain simply wouldn't accept going from *end of the world* to *holy matrimony, Batman* in seven days. Perhaps he needed the time to practice believing.

Greta was still looking at him, and he realized he had stopped eating again. He collected another pancake and some hash browns. "Are you going to cook like this all the time? Because it could be dangerous for my health."

"Oh, please." She spread jam over a piece of toast with two swift strokes. "I am insulted by how little you eat."

"What? Come on, I only weigh—" He cut himself off. "Never mind." He applied himself to his food.

She put the toast down. "I'll tell if you tell."

He eyed her. "No deal."

"Two hundred," she volunteered. "More or less."

"Yeah. Definitely not telling."

She shrugged. "I already know I can carry you."

"I hate you."

"No, you don't." She sized him up. "Ninety."

"I'm at least a hundred!" Probably. Braces and crutches counted.

She gave him a thin smile, and he knew she had guessed low intentionally. He sulked through two more pancakes and a fried egg before his mind circled back to *She wants to marry me.*

30

GRETA DROPPED SAMUEL OFF at his house later that afternoon. He told her he'd be fine, but she escorted him inside and made him get into bed while she collected an armful of nonperishable foods, a pitcher of water, three books, and his laptop. She left him with a warning—as if he weren't more concerned about his knee than she was—and a perfunctory kiss.

The instant he heard the front door close, Samuel reached for the phone and dialed his brother. "We're getting married." And promptly realized he sounded like a teenage girl.

It didn't matter; Chris was at a sports bar. Between the blaring televisions, background chatter, and bad reception, it took several tries to get the information through.

"Oh my God," Chris said when it finally registered. "Hold on." The earpiece rustled. "Dad! Hey, Dad! Sam's marrying the dyke! Huh? Yeah!" His voice came back. "Dad says go fuck your brains out. Sorry, he's pretty hammered."

"Never would have guessed." Samuel was so used to Chris's crude language that the insult to Greta barely registered, but a wave of anxiety passed over him at his father's relayed words. He closed his eyes and forced himself to breathe. The old man couldn't know what he'd told Greta, and even if he did, there was nothing he could do. Not anymore.

A cheer went up in the background, and Chris's voice joined in briefly. "Dodgers are playing the Giants. They got a double play and— Never mind, you don't care. How'd you pop the question?"

Samuel's words turned to dust in his mouth. He swallowed. "It was sort of a . . . um. It's complicated."

"Dude, it's a ring."

He wouldn't have minded telling Chris the ring had dropped out of his pocket, but whatever he said was going to make its way to his father. Samuel couldn't stand the thought of him laughing. "Private," he added. "Complicated and private."

"Oh, I get it." Chris snickered. "Way to go."

Samuel sighed and let it go at that. "Right. Well, the wedding's probably going to be pretty private too, so you don't need to worry about—"

The phone erupted with cheering again. Chris excused himself from the crowd long enough to deliver a brief rundown of the season so far. He didn't mention Toni, which meant she was gone and he was between girlfriends again. Samuel was usually thrilled when the girls bailed; this time he found himself sorry she hadn't become something more.

"Hey," said Chris, "you guys should come down sometime this summer. Show Greta around, come watch me play."

"I, um." Had Greta been serious about never seeing his father again? "I think Dad and Greta might not get along so well."

Chris laughed. "You're right; she'd probably kick his ass."

Samuel didn't want to talk about that. He took a breath, intending to end the call, but what came out instead was "Hey, Chris?"

"Yo."

"Did Dad ever . . . hurt you? Like . . ." He bit his lip, hard. "Slap you around or anything."

"What?" Chris snorted. "No. I mean, shit, he whacked me a few times for talking back, but it's been so long I can't even remember. Before the first time you were in the hospital, even. What the hell is this about?"

Samuel let the breath out. "Nothing. Just a stupid question. I'll talk to you later."

He listened to the dead line until it clicked and the dial tone began to buzz.

So the old man hadn't touched Chris since . . . everything. Had he held back because he didn't want to ruin a second player? Or was it, in some convoluted way, a sign of remorse? Samuel was glad for Chris, he guessed, or maybe it was jealousy. Did some part of him wish he were in Chris's place?

No; if he was going to entertain what-ifs, he had to be honest. As a kid, he'd had an almost preternatural aim. Twenty-five years later, he was out of practice, but he didn't have to think twice if he wanted to, say, hit the clock in his classroom with a dry-erase pen. Or pitch Greta an unwieldy handful of keys. So, no, he wouldn't have been sitting in some dumpy sports bar, downing his fourth beer and watching a major-league game with Dad. He'd have been the one on satellite TV.

Would he trade Greta for that?

No. But he was honest enough to admit the only reason he valued Greta more was because that path had been closed to him. Was he supposed to be thankful for all the shit that had happened to bring him to her? And if he wasn't, did that make him unworthy?

God, it was confusing. He'd thought a good night's sleep would straighten things out, but it hadn't. Not at all.

He'd planned to call Rashid next. (Not Moore, whom he was never speaking to again.) But when he remembered Chris asking how he'd "popped the question," his finger hesitated. Ironic, to think that eight months ago his biggest worry had been whether he could hack teaching. He cut short the internal debate with a grunt of disgust and tossed the phone to the end of the bed. Then he opened his laptop and Googled "incredible honeymoons" instead.

GRETA CALLED EARLY Monday morning and offered him a ride, which was her not so subtle way of suggesting he take his chair to school. He declined. "You should take your chair to school," she said.

"Greta." Samuel looked at his bare legs, dangling over the side of the bed, and then at the full-leg brace propped up next to him. He sighed. She was probably right. "If we're going to live together, you're going to have to let me do some things my way. Even if it seems crazy."

"Why?"

Good question. "It's hard to explain. I just . . . I need to."

She was silent. Then she made a noise that sounded like a shrug. "Suit yourself."

Greta hung up, and he sat there staring at his feet, wondering why he wasn't happy. His knee was healing. They were getting *married*. He should be drifting around in a rose-colored haze.

Samuel wrestled his left leg into the brace, dressed, and hobbled to the car, feeling like a prisoner trapped in some medieval torture device.

Not until break did he discover he was missing the CD he'd made for third period. He dug through his backpack twice, but it wasn't there. "Dammit." Half his weekend for nothing. No; technically the whole weekend for nothing, since he'd spent the remainder failing to come up with a good idea for a honeymoon.

"Are you okay?"

Samuel sat up, surprised to find Sadie standing in front of his desk. "I forgot the program I was going to use today." Belatedly he realized she had meant the question in a broader sense. She deserved some explanation for his absurd behavior on Thursday night, but he decided to leave it at that. He still couldn't believe he had tried to give her the ring. "I'll make do. Need something?"

She looked at her hands. "Oh, uh, yeah. I mean, if you have time. I was wondering if you could write me a letter of recommendation."

"Isn't it a little late?" There were only four weeks until graduation, and he'd written letters for Lemos and Nick months ago. And Marcus. Marcus had asked him for one, too. What a prick.

"For the fall, yeah. I was planning on just going to the JC, but Mrs. Velasquez, over in the guidance office? She says you can send out applications for the spring semester. She said it's easier, even, to get in."

Samuel couldn't help but smile. "Sadie, you won't have any problem getting in to college. Trust me."

"Mainly it's scholarships and loans and stuff. Mrs. Velasquez is helping me."

"Ah. Good. What major? Or can you still get away with not choosing immediately?"

Sadie blushed pink and then, conscious of her own reaction, bright red. "Computer science."

Samuel had never understood all the fuss about teaching. Right then, he got it. This young person whom he scarcely knew was about to make a life-altering decision based on . . . he wasn't sure what, but her blush said he had clearly done something she admired. He had no idea how to respond, so he took out a scrap of paper and jotted himself a reminder to buy time. All he came up with was "Oh."

The door opened and Greta stepped in. Sadie looked like she might faint.

"I'll have it by Friday," he told her. She thanked him and rushed out; Samuel blinked and looked at Greta. He pointed at the door. "She's going into computer science."

She slid a thigh up on the edge of the desk. "They do that some-times."

"But why?" He crumpled the paper (as if he'd forget) and pitched it into the trash, wincing as his muscles protested. Four days and he was still sore. "What did I even do?"

"You paid attention to her." She shrugged. "Sometimes that's all it takes."

"I feel so responsible." He flexed his arm, kneaded his biceps, and shook it out. His leg was one thing; he expected more from his upper body. He felt old. "What are you here for?"

"Do I have to have a reason?"

"No, but you always do." Truthfully, he was happy to see her. Relieved, even.

She snorted and stood. "Just making sure you arrived. Thought I'd get some practice babysitting before it's official."

"You are *so* mean." And yet it felt good, the way she took his darkest fears and tossed them into the open. It made them seem smaller. Greta scratched her elbow, and he saw she was wearing the ring, snug on the third finger of her left hand. "You got it back."

She held up her hand, an oddly feminine gesture. "They did it while I waited."

"Has anyone noticed?" He wasn't sure whether he hoped they had or not. Another wave of gossip and public scrutiny might be more than he could handle right now.

"Nobody's said if they have." She folded her arms over her chest, tucking the hand with the ring into the crook of her elbow. "Are you okay?"

Why was everyone asking that? "I might be freaking out." Probably that was why.

Greta shut the door. Then she placed herself between him and the window, leaned forward, and pressed her lips to his.

Her mouth opened slightly, just enough that Samuel wondered if it was an invitation. Indecision paralyzed him, and then it was too late. The sharp, bittersweet twinge of regret he felt as she pulled away told him exactly why he wasn't as happy as he ought to be. Even after everything—even with his ring on Greta's finger—he still didn't believe this was going to last.

"Are you as sick of me as I am?" he asked. "Because I am incredibly sick of myself."

She let out a short, surprised laugh. "No. I'm nervous, too."

Right. She looked cool as a cucumber. "Then why do you look at me like you think I'm funny?"

Greta studied the code on the whiteboard. "Because you worry so much about how you feel." Her eyes dropped to him. "It's natural to be anxious. It's a big decision."

Except he wasn't just going to "feel anxious" until the wedding rolled around. He was going to turn himself inside out with disbelief and worry and a truly phenomenal amount of insecurity. "Screw it," he decided. "Let's get married. This weekend."

She frowned.

"Greta, if we don't do this soon, I'm going to drive myself insane."

NOT UNTIL HE drove home that afternoon did Samuel realize their hasty marriage plans had one very unfortunate downside. He pulled into the drive and sat with the key in the ignition, staring at Maria's beat-up Civic. How was he going to tell her? She'd know immediately she was out of a job; Greta wasn't the kind of woman who would voluntarily relinquish her housekeeping duties.

He could tell Greta he'd changed his mind again, but sacrificing his sanity for his maid didn't seem particularly sane.

Best to get it over with. He shoved the car door open and grabbed the top of the frame, hauling himself out. The full-leg brace was a pain in the ass to walk with, but the knee joint locked when he got up, so at least he didn't have to worry about collapsing. He pivoted and bent to get his crutches out of the car, then dragged himself to the front door.

It burst open in his face. "Mr. Cooke!" Maria was grinning ear to ear. "Mr. Cooke, I made it!" Seeing the utter lack of comprehension on his face, she elaborated: "My number one school! They accepted me!"

Samuel had never seen her so excited. He didn't think he had ever seen *anyone* so excited. She bounced up and down on her toes, vibrating with energy she didn't seem to know how to discharge.

"Congratulations." He shifted, putting out a hand, and she threw her arms around him. The unexpected intimacy caught him off guard, but in a good way.

"Thank you, Mr. Cooke, thank you so, so much for helping me apply!"

"Me?" Oh, right. That one. "Well . . . ah. I." It was hard to formulate complete sentences with her small, firm breasts pressed against his chest.

"Here." Her grip loosened, and she helped him into his wheelchair, waiting by the door. It took him a moment to work the catch on the knee joint; then he sat and handed off his crutches. She propped them against his armchair on her way to the kitchen. "Anyway, I *promise* I will find someone good to take over, so don't worry, okay?"

Samuel hardly could have asked for a better resolution. Thank goodness. "You don't need to." He followed her around the corner, stopping short of bashing her Achilles as she came to a sudden halt.

Maria turned, her eyes searching his. "What do you mean?"

"Well—" The doorbell cut him off. Which was a bit of a relief, because he hadn't quite figured out how to break the news. He couldn't lie to her, and even the abbreviated version of their engagement story wasn't pretty. "I think that's UPS."

"I'll get it." Maria skirted around him and stopped as the door swung in. "Oh!"

Greta turned sideways to step over the threshold, accommodating the large cardboard box in her arms.

"Hey." Samuel backed up, allowing Maria room to escape. "Didn't know you were coming over." The women had never run into one another at his house; months ago, he'd mentioned Maria was shy, which Greta doubtless understood to mean "terrified of you" and had thus far refrained from showing up during work hours. "What's in the box?"

Greta stepped around Maria without so much as acknowledging her presence and disappeared into the kitchen. "I brought some things."

Samuel gave Maria an apologetic wince and mouthed "Sorry" before following Greta.

She had pushed aside Maria's cooking to make room. The box, Samuel saw as she began to unload, contained some of her favorite implements. She opened the drawer where he kept tongs, spatulas, et cetera, and added her potato ricer.

Realization dawned. "Hold on. Who said we were living *here*?"

Behind him, Maria let out a small, quickly stifled exclamation.

"Where else?" Greta opened his upper cabinets, which were full of old manuals and computer hardware, and made room for her rice cooker. "My place won't work."

She was right, of course. There were the steps out front and in back, and the carpet, and the bathroom in the master bedroom only had a shower. Still, the idea of Greta moving in with him, here, felt too much like replacing Maria with a full-time maid.

Greta picked up the box, now half empty, and headed for the back of the house, brushing past Maria a second time.

"Sorry," Samuel apologized again. He had a feeling he'd be doing that frequently from now on.

"You're moving in together?" Maria whispered. Somehow she managed to look excited and frightened at the same time.

"Getting married."

She grabbed his biceps and squeezed, letting out a muted squeal. "Oh my God, Mr. Cooke! What happened? What did you—"

"Later, okay?" He used his eyes to indicate the hallway. "Go ahead and finish dinner. I promise I won't let her eat you."

Maria stuck out her tongue and slipped into the kitchen.

Samuel drew a deep breath and propelled himself after Greta. She was kneeling on the floor in his bedroom, dumping the contents of the box into the empty nightstand on the far side of his bed. "You're claiming that side?"

She glanced up. "Either one will do. If you'd rather—"

"No, no, it's fine." Wow. She had completely missed his humor. He slid through the door and shut it behind him. "Look, can we talk about this?"

Greta straightened, put a hand on the freshly made bed, and lifted herself to sit on the edge. She looked at him expectantly, as if to say, *What's to discuss?*

He rolled to the end of the bed. "Okay, so, I feel weird about you leaving your house to move in here. For one, it's a lot smaller."

"There're just two of us."

And zero chance of kids. "Granted. But what about all your stuff? Your furniture?"

"I have a chest of drawers that can go there." She pointed to the empty wall.

"Okay, but what about everything else?"

"I'll sell it. The house, too."

"Greta, you grew up there! I can't let you Craigslist your entire life." Jesus. Nobody could ever accuse her of doing things halfway. He rubbed his thigh through his pants, working a finger under the brace where it chafed. He assumed this was some bizarre attempt at self-sacrifice, but maybe not. Maybe getting married gave her an excuse to do something she'd been thinking about for a long time. Her mother's presence in the house was stifling, but surely Greta didn't want to chuck *everything*. "What about your garden?"

"You have a backyard."

Barren wasteland was more accurate. "It's a lot smaller."

"Size doesn't matter."

He laughed. "I'm glad you think so."

"It will be nice to have a new space to work with."

Again, totally missed the joke. "How about this. We put your stuff in storage. We keep your place or rent it out if you want. In a year or two, we talk about it again. If my place is too small, we can always remodel yours."

Greta looked at him like he'd lost his mind. "Don't be ridiculous."

"What? What's so—" And then he got it. She was used to living on a teacher's salary, which, if it was anything close to his pay as a substitute, was more like a token of gratitude than a livelihood. The house had come down from her parents, so she was probably paying property tax and pouring whatever was left into retirement.

He'd told her what he'd done before coming to Healdsburg, but unless you knew the industry, his job title was pretty meaningless. Had he even mentioned that he owned part of the company? Probably not. She had no reason to think he'd bought his house outright, either. Then there was his ten-year-old Buick, which he drove not because he couldn't afford better but because his travel chair fit in the trunk. Samuel grinned. He must look practically destitute. And Greta had never said a thing. Jesus, when she'd said she would take care of him, she'd meant it in more ways than one. Thank God it wasn't necessary.

"Greta, I think I might have given you the wrong . . ." Oh. *Oh*. He had an idea. Not a honeymoon idea, not quite, but something that, until then, might suffice. "Never mind. Look, we're not married yet; we don't know how living together is going to work. Let's keep everything as is for a month or two, then reevaluate. Okay?"

She pressed her lips together, then nodded and stood, picking up the empty box.

Whew. He hated to think what other important issues they might have overlooked. There was something to be said for premarital counseling. "Are you staying for dinner?"

She stopped at the door, her hand on the knob. "I have more to pack at home."

"On your way out, could you say something nice to Maria? Or, you know, anything at all? If I were a kid, she'd be on the phone with CPS right about now."

Greta snorted. "I'll see what I can do."

"Also? We need to come up with a better engagement story."

31

GRETA WORE HEELS.

Square, black leather, and not very high. Her skirt was a charcoal gray that nearly matched his tux, cut just above her calves. A blouse, silk, blackish red. And lipstick. Very light but definitely there. Her shoes clunked when she stepped from her living room carpet to the hardwood front hall.

Samuel, standing in the open doorway, didn't tell her she looked beautiful. He wasn't sure she did. He wasn't even sure he knew this person—this awkward, frightened girl in a woman's heavy form. But he did love her, and he told her that.

"Okay," she said.

He checked his watch to cover his smile. "Shall we go?"

Greta cast a glance over one shoulder. Wondering, perhaps, whether she ought to turn around and change into her regular self. Then she faced him, nodded, and led the way.

She reached the middle of the driveway before she detected the change. "Where's your car?"

Samuel finished easing himself down the first porch step before nodding to the Mustang GT. "Right there."

She frowned at the car and then at him. "You rented it," she said, as if that were the only logical possibility.

He laughed. "No, it's ours. I can trade it if you want a different color, though." His first impulse had been cherry red, but then he'd remembered her motorcycle and opted for gunmetal blue.

Greta looked from him to the car and back, clearly torn between ripping him to shreds for his ridiculous impulse buy and the need to be nice because it was, after all, their wedding day. "This is too expensive," she managed finally.

Good thing he hadn't gone for the Corvette. "Greta, it's okay." He started to lower himself to the second step, then aborted the attempt. He'd worn the full-leg brace to ensure against total disaster if his knee failed again—or, you know, in case Greta left him at the altar and he wound up thumbing a ride. Anyway, it had given him enough stability to make it up the front steps without destroying his cheap-ass Men's Warehouse tux, but getting down was something else. "I have some savings."

"Enough for *this*?"

He grinned. "I own my house outright, and above that I've got two million plus ten percent of the company I used to work for. Well, slightly less than two million after the car."

Greta's face went blank. Samuel could only imagine the hasty reordering going on in her mind as the possibilities she had projected onto their future expanded tenfold. She shook her head. "Why?"

"You seemed fairly well off, independent. It didn't occur to me until last week that I don't come off as . . ." He shrugged.

Greta rolled her eyes skyward. "You were *substitute teaching*."

"I know. Sorry."

"You don't even own a cell phone!"

"I know, I know." He cleared his throat. "Look, could you give me a hand here?"

Looking outraged, Greta came to the porch and helped him down, then stayed with him all the way to the car. And, to his shock, waited for him to open her door. She got in, tucked her skirt around her thighs, and folded her hands over her pocketbook. Her nails were trimmed and painted—not red, but clear with white tips. Whatever that was called.

Samuel hurried around to the driver's seat. The engine rumbled like a big cat when he pulled away from the curb; he should have trashed the Buick years ago. "It was a pretty good surprise, though, right?" He glanced at her as he rolled around the end of the block.

She pressed her lips together. "I suppose so."

"And you like the car?"

"Yes." She ran her fingers over the leather seat. "I like the car."

SAMUEL SPOTTED MOORE'S yellow tin can from two blocks away. He pulled over, levered the brake, and looked at Greta. "What the hell is he doing here?"

"We need a witness."

"And he was the best option? What about your sister?"

"It seemed rude to ask her to make the drive just to sign a piece of paper."

Yeah, *just* their marriage contract. *Just* their wedding. "But Greg? Do you know what he did to me?" Samuel didn't care that the outcome, ultimately, had been positive. He cared that Moore had left him on Greta's doorstep without the slightest idea whether she was even home. He cared that his bag had broken on her carpet. He couldn't believe she was pulling this on their wedding day.

Greta paused. Then: "He's your friend."

"So?"

She sighed the way she did whenever he forced her to say something obvious and unpleasant. "You don't have many."

Ouch. "And you do?"

"I don't *need* them."

Samuel put his forehead on the steering wheel. He loved everything about Greta, but every once in a while he wished she weren't compelled to tell the truth, the whole truth, and nothing but the truth. "Just this once," he said. "And not for him. For you."

Moore was sitting on the hood of his Karmann Ghia, cleaning his nails with a key. When Samuel pulled up next to him, he performed a perfect double take and slid quickly to the ground. He hesitated in front of the GT, starting first to the left and then to the right. Samuel looked at Greta. "He doesn't know who to open the door for."

Greta shoved her door open and got out.

Moore's eyes went wide. "Whoa," he breathed. "You . . . um. You look nice."

Her "Thanks" was heavy with sarcasm.

"You, too," he added, hurrying to offer Samuel a hand. "Great suit."

"I'm still pissed," Samuel informed him.

"Oh." Moore backed away. "Because I tried to break in?"

"What?" Samuel hauled himself up and looked over the roof at Greta, who rolled her eyes. "No, I'm pissed because you— Okay, what? You broke into my house?"

"Well, no, Cass showed up. I just . . . I came to see if you were all right the next morning, and you didn't answer, so . . ."

So naturally he'd assumed Samuel had done something to himself. (Did his life seem so unbearable, or was he *that* transparent?) Moore had tried to break in, but then Greta had shown up to get the clothes and chair. Samuel looked at her. "Thanks for telling me."

"It didn't seem . . ." She spread her hands. "Constructive."

"I'm gonna go make sure everything's, um, ready." Moore spun on one heel and hurried into the church.

Greta sighed. "Done tormenting him?"

"No." Samuel stuck the keys in his pocket and joined her on the sidewalk.

This was the point when Samuel had expected absolute terror to strike. The moment when he wondered what the hell he had been thinking and had the sudden urge to turn and run, if only he could.

There was nothing. Every last part of him wanted to do this.

When Greta stopped in the entryway and glared at the ground, he thought she was waiting for him to open one of the giant double doors. He was about to apologize and confess that the task was beyond him, but she turned and said in a low voice, "Do I look all right?"

The question caught him by surprise, mainly because it was so incredibly feminine. But Greta wasn't fishing for a compliment. She really didn't know. "Greg wasn't kidding," he said. "You look really nice. I'm sorry I didn't say so earlier. I'm just not used to seeing you dressed up."

She nodded, eyes on her shoes. "Thank you."

"Hey." He slid his fingers into hers and squeezed. "Let's do this."

She nodded again and started for the door.

"Whoa—gonna need my hand back."

"Sorry."

Inside, the sanctuary was vacant and dim. Moore, waiting with his hands stuffed in his pockets, ushered them into the back offices, past the empty secretary's desk to Father Hayes's room. The pastor rose with a grandfatherly smile and shook each of their hands, covering the gesture with the warm, smooth palm of his left hand. He saved Greta for last, encircling her with an affectionate hug.

The ceremony was brief. They sat before Hayes's expansive pedestal desk and repeated the vows he read from a small leather volume. Samuel got through his half without, thank God, butchering any of the words. Then Hayes turned to Greta and asked if she would take Samuel "so long as you both shall live."

She didn't answer.

Samuel's heart thudded to a halt. He shut his eyes, tight, waiting for the inevitable. Of course. Of course this was how it happened. Why had he even—?

"Greta?" Father Hayes asked quietly.

"Look at me." She was speaking to Samuel.

He didn't want to look. Now—now he wanted to run. Oh God oh God oh God.

Her hand closed around his, so tight it hurt. "*Look* at me."

He looked, and her eyes would not let him go.

"I do," she said.

He swallowed. Good thing he couldn't run. He kind of felt like throwing up, though.

The awkward silence was broken by a small cough from Father Hayes. "The rings?"

The rings? Oh shit, the ring. Did Greta have it? His eyes went to her hand, and no, it was not there. Had she given it back to him? He couldn't remember. Shit. No, he wasn't supposed to be thinking shit, this was a church, so . . . *shit*.

"Cooke." Moore bumped his elbow, and Samuel turned to find him holding the object in question.

"Oh." When had Greta given it to Moore? It didn't matter. Samuel took Greta's hand, sliding the ring on as he repeated the words after Hayes. Could everyone see his hands shaking?

He was surprised when Greta, in turn, produced a thin gold band for him. It was ever so slightly too big.

They completed the paperwork, his signature little more than a shaky scribble, and Hayes murmured a quiet permission to kiss. Greta leaned toward Samuel and they brushed lips.

"Congratulations, you guys." Moore snapped a photo with his phone.

And that was all.

"I'm driving," Greta said in the parking lot.

Samuel handed her the keys.

THEY STOPPED AT Greta's first, and he waited in the car while she retrieved a bag of clothes. She reappeared in her usual shirt and shorts, and he admired her as he liked her best: comfortable and relaxed. Samuel expected the next time she wore that skirt would be at his funeral.

And then they were home. It was five o'clock in the afternoon, not even close to dark. Did she expect them to proceed directly to the bedroom, or would she want to wait? He felt he ought to know and didn't want to ruin anything by asking.

Greta dropped her bag next to the couch. "Hungry?"

They made cautious chitchat over dinner. Afterward, Samuel tried to help clear the table, but they kept bumping into each other. Somehow he managed to knock a glass off the counter, and it shattered on the floor.

"Jesus. Sorry, I—"

Greta cut him off with a growl of exasperation. "Come on."

He followed her into his bedroom. She stopped beside the bed, turned, and looked at him. He swallowed thickly. They had never discussed this part in detail, or, actually, at all, and now he wished they had. He had imagined having sex with her, sure, but fantasies tended to be unrealistic by definition. His, in particular, tended to ignore physics. "I—I need to use the bathroom."

She gestured. "Go."

Samuel locked the door and let himself drop onto the toilet. He wormed out of his pants and detached the urine bag. And there was the catheter. His throat went dry.

Technically all he had to do was fold the tube over and tape it to his thigh, and sex would proceed as normal. So said the medical literature he'd consulted ages ago. Was that what he wanted on his wedding night? Was that what *Greta* wanted? They had the rest of their lives for pragmatism, convenience. Tonight should be special. Clean. But what if he accidentally . . .

He was overthinking this. Like everything else. Greta knew. She had already experienced the worst of what he had to offer. And she was still here.

He took a deep breath, clenched his jaw, and removed the tube.

Okay. There. He'd never had sex; she had. A long time ago, yes, and it hadn't exactly been pleasant, but she had to know *something*. All he had to do was let her lead. Simple.

Right.

Samuel removed the rest of his clothing, braces and boxers excepted. He pulled his jacket, shirt, and tie over the towel bar because now and for the rest of his life, dropping them on the floor meant Greta would be picking them up. She would likely be the one to retrieve them from the towel bar, too, but it seemed more polite.

A shiver ran down his spine, lifting the hair on his arms. He heard himself starting to breathe faster.

No. He was *not* going to sit here and make himself sick. Samuel picked himself up and opened the bathroom door.

Greta had turned out the lights. It was a few minutes to eight, so the sun had not set, but the blinds blocked most of the orange glow. Light from the bathroom spilled across the floor, illuminating his wheelchair next to the bed. Samuel hit the switch and waited for his eyes to adjust.

Greta lay in bed, sheets pulled up to her bare shoulders. He could barely make out white bra straps against her skin. She was looking at him, but it was too dark to read her expression.

He felt naked.

Probably because he was. Mostly.

He didn't know what to say, if anything. Greta didn't speak. He went to the bed and sank down on the edge, his back to her as he set his crutches aside and fumbled for the buckle on the leg brace.

He had done well with the car. He would figure out the honeymoon.

This, though. This he had to get right.

Seriously, what did he say? He'd seen two romantic comedies in the last decade, by accident, and neither one had gone into detail about sex. If he'd been smart, he'd have spent the last week reading Harlequin romances. Then again, Greta didn't go for romantic fluff, so even if he could come up with a couple of cheesy lines, they weren't going to impress her. Greta wasn't much for words, so maybe silence was best.

He would take off his braces, slip under the covers, find her hand, and hope to God she took it from there.

"Is your knee still bothering you?" Greta asked.

The breach of silence made him jump. "No, I . . ." He looked at the leg brace. Was he really going to start his married life with a lie? "It's not one hundred percent." And the thought he had been trying to avoid: "I'm kind of afraid it might never be."

"Give it time before you start worrying."

"I'm trying to." Although the line between not worrying and denial had always been unclear to Samuel.

And now they were sitting here mostly naked on their wedding night talking about his damn knee. He pried the brace off and let it drop to the floor, then bent and removed the smaller one from his right leg. He leaned back on his hands and slid up next to Greta, lifting the blankets to cover himself.

The side of his thigh brushed hers.

Oh Jesus. Oh Jesus Christ.

This whole thing would be so much easier if he could just have a practice run. To touch her, learn the ins and outs of her form without an audience. Impossible, obviously, since his audience was Greta. No, not his audience—his partner. And somehow they had to score a perfect ten on this performance without any prior rehearsal.

He'd settle for an eight, really. Or a five, if it came down to it. Especially since currently his body didn't seem interested in performing. At all. God.

They'd touched before, yes. But making out? Strictly PG groping? The things that set Greta off had no rhyme or reason; there were no repeats in their relationship. Bodily contact always happened in an unpremeditated, split-second moment of impulsive passion.

This, right here, was about as far from spontaneous as it got.

"Well?" Greta said.

He choked and managed to turn the noise into a hopefully inconspicuous cough. "So. How do you want to do this?"

"I think it will be easiest with you on top."

Inside his head, Samuel started screaming.

She lifted the sheet. "Here. Put your leg over mine."

He saw the rest of her bra. Her bare stomach. And yeah, suddenly he was ready. "Okay—let me, um, get my boxers off."

Greta waited, unmoving, while he twisted out of his underwear. Which meant hers were already gone.

And then they touched. So to speak. He tugged one leg over hers, as she had instructed, and tried to turn over without planting himself face-first between her breasts. He saw then immediately that he ought to have put both legs over first, but Greta lifted her knee, helping the second into place. Which left him on his hands and knees, one arm on either side of her body. The whole thing was awkward, uncomfortable. He started to sweat.

Now he was supposed to just, like, *enter* her? He had imagined some sort of foreplay was necessary. Probably should have thought of that before he got into position.

"You're not going to crush me," Greta said.

What did that mean? It was okay to lie on her? Nice to know, but he had to get *in* there first. He was generally acquainted with female anatomy, but the real deal was different. Also? He couldn't see a damn thing.

He thrust his pelvis forward, hoping for the best.

It turned out sex was not like in the movies, where it sort of magically slid in. Or, who knew, maybe this worked fine for other people. As for Samuel, he totally missed the mark, and his knees slid out from under him. Face-planting between Greta's breasts wouldn't have been altogether bad, but his nose ended up around her navel.

"Sorry!" He struggled frantically to get his knees under him, arms shaking.

"Here." Greta grabbed him under the armpits and dragged him forward, which helped with the knees. "There. Go in. No." Her voice was severe. "Right there."

Right *where*? "Maybe we could turn on a light or something."

She let out an exasperated breath. "This is not rocket science, Mr. Cooke."

With that, his body decided the erection was over. Finis. "Oh, God." He clawed at the sheets, pulling himself off of her. "I'm sorry. This is not—I—" Forget it. Just fucking forget it. He tumbled into the wheelchair, shoved himself to the bathroom, and slammed the door.

It was pitch black, but he didn't turn the light on because he didn't want to see himself, not any part. His chair bumped the counter and the soap dish rattled. He seized it and hurled it into the dark.

Greta knocked.

"Go away." He had warned her. She had known it would be like this. And she had insisted. Well, this was what she got. *Hope you're happy.*

The door opened anyway. The light snapped on, illuminating jagged pieces of the soap dish in the bottom of the tub.

Samuel folded his arms over his knees and rested his forehead on top. "Did we just make a huge mistake?"

"Most people don't do it the first night," she said.

"What?" He could see her feet at the edge of his vision, and with a little surprise, he realized it was for the first time. She had always worn socks. Why, he didn't know. Her feet were nice—not all pinched, like some women's, from stuffing their toes into uncomfortable shoes.

"It's from sex ed. Fifty-two percent of newlyweds are too exhausted from the wedding."

He lifted his head. She stood framed in the doorway, nude except for her underwear and bra, both plain white. Illuminated by the fluorescent bathroom lights, her skin seemed loose, flecked with moles and little red spots. This was not how he had wanted to see her for the first time.

He looked down at himself, lifting his arm slightly to confirm what he already knew: he was not going to be performing tonight. "Well, chalk another one up to statistics."

32

SAMUEL WOKE TO FIND himself nestled in the curve of Greta's body, the small knobs of his spine firm against her stomach. Her arm was draped over his shoulder. Samuel felt warm and . . . ugh. Really horny.

He would have entertained the idea of giving it another shot—or so he told himself—but it was Monday morning, and he needed to bathe before class. The clock read 7:28, two minutes before the alarm went off. Might as well see if he could extricate himself before Greta woke and saw his giant erection. Reminding himself of last night's epic fail helped.

He tried to move her arm, but it was heavy. Plan B was ducking under. Then Greta mumbled something unintelligible and rolled away. Samuel sat up, pulling the sheets around his groin. "Good morning."

She yawned, rubbed her eyes, and sat upright, throwing back the blankets. "I should have been at school fifteen minutes ago." She crossed the room in her underwear, grabbing her bag on the way out.

"But it's only—" It dawned on him. "You have zero period!"

She paused in the hall, her hand on the guest room door. "Put something on. You'll have to drive me and come back. I'll use the other bathroom."

Samuel scrambled for his braces. What a perfect start to married life. Shit, shit, shit.

THE HEADS OF thirty teenagers swiveled in unison as Samuel pulled up outside the gym. Which was certainly one way to break the news.

"I'm not going to kiss you," Greta said.

"Yeah, no problem. Hey, uh . . ." He licked his lips and attempted a smile. "I'll do better tonight, okay?"

At home, he showered, shaved, and spent his remaining minutes desperately combing the Internet for a way to make good on his promise. Mostly what he found was porn. Even if he could have managed half the positions he saw, he suspected Greta wouldn't be thrilled.

How did guys *learn* this stuff?

Finally he erased his browser history and drove to school. It was a relief to know all he had to worry about for the next six hours was what to say in front of a bunch of kids. Then he stepped into the hall and saw his classroom door hanging open. Panic surged into his throat.

A quick check confirmed he had both keys, right next to each other on the ring in his pocket. Unless—God, he was an idiot—Marcus had made a copy before giving it back. Three weeks from graduation, the little prick could do practically anything without fear of reprisal.

Samuel approached cautiously, steeling himself for whatever horrific shock awaited. When he edged into the room, nothing seemed amiss. Half of his students were seated, while the others loitered in loose groups at the front.

"Who opened this door?" he demanded.

There was a general rush for seats. "Mr. Moore let us in," Sadie explained. "I told him maybe it wasn't a good idea, but—"

"Is it true?" This came from a girl named Lilah, over on the right.

He followed their eyes to his computer and saw that his screen saver—undulating amoebas—had been replaced with a basic side-scrolling text in seventy-two-point neon-pink Helvetica. He watched as the message inched across the screen.

Congratulations, Mr. and Mrs. Cooke!

A jiggle of the mouse and a couple of clicks confirmed the screen savers for the entire classroom had been likewise altered.

"Well?" someone asked.

"I heard Cass told everyone in her zero period to call her Mrs. Cooke."

"That's so weird."

He cleared his throat. "Um, yeah. I guess it is true." On paper.

"Way to go, man," said Fernando, in the back. Murmurs of congratulations came from around the room.

Samuel felt pleasantly embarrassed. He also felt like a complete fraud. They'd said the words and signed their names, but did it count if they hadn't consummated? He was a little surprised, too, to hear she was taking his name. It would make leaving him that much more awkward.

"I nearly had a heart attack when I saw my door open," Samuel said when Moore showed up during break. "What would you have told Greta?" He pulled Sadie's letter of recommendation out of his bag; he had forgotten to give it to her during second period.

"Oh, you liked it. I can tell." Moore quirked an eyebrow. "So? How did it go?"

Samuel set the envelope on the edge of his desk. "Greg, even assuming you're back in my good graces, it was my wedding night."

"Yeah?"

"That sort of thing is usually considered *kind of personal.*"

"Aw, you're no fun."

"You have no idea."

AND THEN SCHOOL was over and Samuel was back where he had begun, twenty-four hours previous.

"I'd like to do some reading," Greta said on their way to the bedroom.

"Oh?" This was news to Samuel. He had no idea she liked to read. Her choice would surely be enlightening. Biography, he guessed.

"The board is proposing some curriculum updates for next year. I'm on the committee." She went to the pile where she was keeping her clothing until her dresser got moved (Samuel wondered who would do the moving) and produced a spiral-bound sheaf of papers.

"Oh." Damn. "Sure. Let's read in bed for a while."

Greta shut herself in the bathroom to do whatever it was women did at night. Samuel stripped to his boxers and got into bed, retrieving his paperback from the nightstand. It had been a few days, so he flipped back a page or two to refresh his memory, then lay there staring blindly at the words.

Did this mean they weren't having sex? He wished Greta would tell him what she wanted, like she did with everything else.

She came out of the bathroom in a baggy cotton nightshirt that reached her knees. Samuel watched over the top of his book as she circled the bed. She wasn't wearing a bra.

She got into bed quickly, pulling the comforter up to her armpits before grabbing the papers off the nightstand. She turned half away from him to get the best light.

The blankets were taut between them, leaving a gap of cool,

empty space beneath the sheets. Samuel wanted to occupy that emptiness, to leave no room for anything between. But he did not quite know how to cross the gap.

He pretended to read for five minutes, watching the seconds tick away on the clock. Then he took a breath. Licked his lips. And touched her arm.

He felt her stiffen, but she did not pull away. He let his hand drift up to her shoulder. It was awkward, yes, but knowing they weren't going to have sex immediately—not until he took his turn in the bathroom—took some of the pressure off. So did the fact that she wasn't looking at him. They could lie together. Relax. Okay, not really relax. Not with his hindbrain demanding he mount her like an animal.

He moved closer and was conscious of Greta's leg sliding over his to pull them near. And then he was not just next to her but *next* to her, separated only by the thin cotton of her shirt. There was no way Greta could be oblivious to his erection pressing against the small of her back, but she kept reading, or pretending to read. After another minute she slid down and rested her head in the crook of her elbow. Samuel touched her hair. Then her shoulder. Then her waist. He slid his arm under hers and let his hand rest on her stomach.

"Don't—" Greta began, and let the word end in a breath.

"It's okay," he told her quietly. "We're married." He waited.

She nodded.

He slid his hand up, letting his fingers cup her breast lightly. She wasn't large, in that sense. He didn't mind. He let his hand explore, slowly, slowly, feeling her body tense at every move. Slow.

Her nipple was small and hard and round. He felt as though the room had been emptied of air.

"I, um—" He didn't know what he wanted to say.

She moved, shifting to face him. They kissed. Moved. Kissed again. Deeply.

Samuel took a breath. It didn't do any good. His head felt lighter than air. "Do you want to— I can—" He gestured toward the bathroom.

"Do you have to?" Greta asked.

"No, but I thought you—"

"I don't."

"Oh."

He climbed on top of her. She helped. She opened her legs, and the nightstand light was enough to illuminate the way. Her hair down there was thick and dark. He wanted to touch it, to run his fingers through it, but there would be time for that later. He had something else to do right now.

"Okay?" he asked.

She nodded.

He entered her. It took a couple of pushes to get in completely, and then—wow. Oh. Wow. His hands closed around her arms and his mind went white. He was here, he was here, he—

Spent himself immediately.

He knew he was supposed to make it last, but he was so overwhelmed that it was over before he realized what had happened.

"I'm sorry," he gasped, trying not to collapse on top of her. "Greta, I—"

"It takes practice." She disentangled her legs from his as he dragged himself off.

He'd thought the goal was intercourse. Now that it was over, he realized what he really wanted was to pleasure her. "I'm sorry," he said again. "I wanted to make it good for you."

Greta shifted onto her side, facing him. "I thought I was hard on myself until I met you."

Funny. He'd never experienced such depths of self-loathing before Greta. "It's difficult to go easy when I fail so spectacularly." He slid a hand under the sheets and checked himself. "At least, um, was it okay with the . . . ?" Everything seemed intact, although the tube was slick with his—ew. He grabbed the sheet and wiped, wondering if he needed to go sterilize himself. "It didn't hurt or anything?"

"It was . . . different."

Different good or different bad? "Let's do it without next time." Even if conception wasn't the goal, it seemed like the active ingredient should end up in her. And, okay, he was paranoid about the thought of it backing up and . . . well, who knew what might happen. This was something he should ask a doctor about, except he wasn't going to.

Greta sat up, reaching for her underwear. "I'm going to shower."

"Oh." He watched her walk around the end of the bed. "Are you a night-shower person?"

"Sometimes." She went into the bathroom.

"Greta?"

She leaned out, doorknob in hand, just far enough to see him.

"It wasn't *too* bad, was it?"

Greta sighed. "Give yourself a break. It was just the first time." She shut the door, and a moment later the water came on.

Samuel stared at the bathroom door for a while. Then he picked up his book, read half a sentence, and put it down again.

Just the first time, she said.

She was right. Here was where all the fantasies ended: romantic feelings confessed, true love sealed with the ultimate act of intimacy. But whether you liked it or not, marriage was just the beginning. For them, that meant having every night after this one to practice. For the rest of their lives.

It would get better.

It would.

33

B Y THE FOLLOWING MONDAY they had performed sexual intercourse—Samuel couldn't seriously call it making love—seven times exactly, in exactly the same way. He was pretty sure sex was supposed to be mutually satisfying, but Greta behaved largely as if it were just another duty to be discharged, not unlike grocery shopping or cleaning the bathroom. Make dinner, fold laundry, satisfy husband's carnal urge.

He tried to initiate a little foreplay once, hoping it would help get her in the mood. When he reached between her legs, she froze.

"What are you doing?" she demanded.

"Um, nothing." Apparently.

Further Internet trawling unearthed a startling statistic: over half the female population was unable to achieve orgasm via penetration. Though it took him a couple of days, he finally worked up the nerve to ask if she wanted anything, like, um, maybe, uh, a vibrator? She reacted as if he'd suggested they watch a porno. Which wasn't a bad idea, either.

Tuesday night, Greta picked up her pillow, informed him she was getting sick, and disappeared into the guest room.

Samuel spent about thirty seconds staring at the bedroom door. Then he slid into his wheelchair, grabbed his pillow, and pushed himself after her. Greta lifted her head. "What are you doing?"

Samuel pulled the blankets back and got into bed. "I spent thirty-five years alone. Now I have your ring on my finger. That means I have the right to sleep with you every night for the rest of my life."

"You're going to get sick," she said.

Wednesday and Thursday nights were, due to Greta's NyQuil-induced haze, consequently sex-free.

Friday morning, she pronounced herself "over it."

Friday afternoon, Samuel came home to find Greta's sister sitting on their doorstep.

HAZEL GOT UP when he pulled into the driveway, smoothing her knee-length skirt and dusting off the back with one hand. She made a small ladylike dip to retrieve her purse.

Samuel pushed the car door open. "Uh, hello."

Hazel gave him a puzzled look, likely very similar to the one he wore. "Hi?"

"Not to be rude, but—what are you doing here?"

She gave a nervous laugh. "I'm not sure. I was on the way to my sister's house. She called and told me to come here instead."

That didn't at all explain her presence here, in Healdsburg. "She must have forgotten about her curriculum meeting. But—"

"Oh, are you having it here?"

"What? No, she . . ." His sentence drifted off into confusion. The only possible way to interpret Hazel's words was that she didn't know he and Greta were living together. Which meant she had no idea they were married. And yet Greta had given Hazel this address?

When she knew perfectly well he was going to show up first? Either Greta had lost her mind, or she was giving Samuel a gift she knew only he would relish. "You don't know." His laugh turned into a cough, because of course he was getting sick. He shoved his feet to the ground and pulled out his crutches. He wanted a clear view of her reaction to the news.

"Oh," she said as he stood, "it's you! Greta must be bringing you dinner. Sorry, what was your name again?"

Samuel felt his jaw drop.

Greta hadn't even told her they were *dating*.

SAMUEL TOOK COVER in the bedroom with a bag of lozenges while Greta and Hazel went at it in the kitchen. Or, more precisely, while Hazel shouted and Greta replied occasionally in low, inaudible tones. Hazel was pissed Greta hadn't told her about Samuel. Pissed she hadn't known about the engagement. Pissed she hadn't been invited to the wedding. Really, really pissed.

For his part, once he got over the initial shock, Samuel hadn't been fundamentally surprised. He'd encouraged Greta to wait until she felt comfortable telling her sister, and . . . well, apparently that moment had never come. Greta was always straightforward—unless she wasn't, in which case she ignored the problem completely.

The real question was why she had invited Hazel at all.

Samuel stayed out of the way until dinnertime, then ventured into the living room and suggested they start thinking about food. Both women turned and glared; he excused himself before he became the target of their combined wrath.

A couple of minutes later he heard a pot clang and the water come on.

At seven, Greta knocked and opened the bedroom door.

"Is it safe?" He grabbed his crutches.

Greta frowned. "Safe?" Her eyes flickered to the lozenges.

"Yeah, like, you're all done throwing things and— Oh, never mind." Greta's sense of humor simply switched off whenever she was in a foul mood.

He spent most of the meal pretending not to notice Hazel staring at him like he was some revolting insect she planned to squash the moment Greta left the room. Greta, as usual, seemed to have no problem with the long, uncomfortable silences between the half-hearted chitchat they managed to make.

"All right," Hazel said finally. "Tell me how you met."

It wasn't so much a request as a challenge. Samuel looked at Greta, who shrugged and said, "At a basketball game."

"She gave me a ride home." Wrong answer: Hazel's expression told him that he'd confirmed he was as worthless as he looked.

Hazel directed the next question at him: "First date?"

"What is this, a test?"

Hazel glared. She had Greta's laser stare. He glared back.

"Mr. Cooke," Greta said.

"Me? She's the one asking—" Greta had opened her mouth to cut him off, but he beat her to it by choking on his own words. He sputtered, coughed, and then just kept coughing.

Greta got up and handed him his glass of water; he managed to gain control of his respiration long enough to gulp an ounce or two. Then it started again. He pushed back from the table and bent over, elbows on his knees, water streaming out of the corners of his eyes. "I'm okay," he croaked unconvincingly.

"I'll find the Robitussin." Greta strode down the hall to the guest bedroom. Samuel would have told her the bottle had ended up in their bathroom, but he was too busy hacking up a lung.

Finally he managed a few deep breaths and a longer drink of water. He wiped his eyes with his napkin and found Hazel staring at him as if she suspected him of carrying some horribly contagious plague. "It's a cold," he informed her sourly. "Greta had it earlier this week." Whereas he would undoubtedly have it this week, next week, and the week after. Just the way he wanted to finish out the school year.

"You know what this is, right?" Hazel said.

"A cold?"

"Penance."

It was Samuel's turn to stare. Dimly he was aware of Greta coming out of the guest bedroom and going into theirs. "Seriously? You don't think she could possibly just . . . love me."

Hazel tossed her napkin on the table. "Oh, no doubt she's convinced herself she does. And you, too." She made a throwaway gesture in his direction. "You've spent enough time with her to know her head's as hard as a rock. She'll slam her head against this brick wall until she passes out, and when she wakes up, she'll come crawling back home, begging for forgiveness. Trust me, we've been there before."

"I know what happened before. It sounds like you don't know what's happened since."

"Look, I'm not trying to be cruel."

"Right. Thanks so much for your kindness." He intended to thank her more explicitly, but he had to pause for a cough, and then Greta returned with the cough medicine.

SAMUEL WANTED TO give Greta a chance to explain herself, but by the time they were in bed, lights out, she still hadn't said a thing.

"So." He felt another cough coming on and fumbled for a lozenge. "What's the deal with—"

"Let's discuss this after she leaves."

The lozenge didn't help. He shoved his face into his pillow and waited for the spasm to pass. "Which will be when?"

"I don't know. A few days."

"Um . . . okay." The idea of Hazel hanging around for more than one evening wasn't thrilling, but presumably Greta had some reason for wanting her here. They were married now; the least he could do was trust his own wife, even if her decisions seemed weird.

Samuel found her hand under the sheets and ran his fingers up her arm.

"Not tonight." Greta shifted onto her side, her back to him. "The walls are thin."

And suddenly Samuel knew exactly why Hazel was there.

34

HAZEL STAYED FIVE DAYS. Five tense, awkward, molar-grinding days during which she rearranged furniture, bought household wares without consultation, and oh-so-politely left the receipts on the counter. That wasn't even counting the constant stream of passive-aggressive insults.

Under ordinary circumstances, Samuel would have dug in and gone toe to toe, but he was too miserable and exhausted and drugged up to do anything except languish in bed, attempting to stockpile the energy necessary for school.

He tried to pin Greta down for a serious talk, but she went out to eat with Hazel. Every day. Obviously they were discussing him, Hazel no doubt attempting to talk Greta out of her hasty marriage. And Greta . . . well, Greta apparently needed another female with whom to discuss his horrific performance in bed.

When he got home on Wednesday and found the house empty, Samuel wanted to dance a jig and shout hallelujah. Instead he dragged himself down the hall toward the bedroom, every breath rasping in his chest. His stomach sank when he heard the front door open, but it wasn't Hazel. "It's over?" His voice was an unintelligible croak. He cleared his throat and tried again.

Greta nodded. She dropped her canvas teaching bag on the couch and went into the kitchen.

Nothing. Again. No apology or explanation for her sister's visit. Samuel knew he should go to bed, but he was sick of being treated like an idiot. He followed Greta as far as the dining table and watched as she pulled the pitcher of water out of the fridge and poured. "So. Decide to lie back and think of England?"

Greta paused, the glass just touching her bottom lip. "Excuse me?"

Though he'd said it lightly, her pretended confusion tapped the bitterness underneath. "I'm sick, Greta, not brain-dead." Yeah. It didn't matter how exhausted he was. This shit had to end. Immediately. "I get that sex is hard to talk about. For me, too. But you know what's worse than telling me I suck? Using your obnoxious, over-bearing, self-absorbed sister as an excuse."

Greta's fingers tightened around the water glass. "You. Are sick." She said it slowly, deliberately, as if trying to remind herself. "Go to bed. I'll bring you dinner later."

"Did you seriously think you were sparing my feelings? Or was that your way of rubbing it in?" He might as well have been talking to a brick wall: she turned her back to him, opening a cupboard with her free hand. He reached for her arm. "Dammit, look at me!"

Greta did more than that. She hurled the glass at his face.

It was fortunate she didn't have his aim. The cup flew past his ear and hit the dining table. Shards of glass and water drops rained to the floor.

Samuel was speechless. Almost. "What the *hell*?"

"Get out of my way." Greta tried to push past him. "Move!"

"Not until you talk to me." He braced himself between the oven and the breakfast counter. If she wanted out, she would have to knock him down.

She did.

His exclamation of surprise turned into a wordless gasp as he hit the ground; all he could manage was to grab her leg as she stepped over him.

Greta tried to jerk free, but Samuel held on. She fumbled for the counter, trying to find the leverage to pull herself away. Her hands seized the big wooden pepper mill instead.

Samuel let go.

Greta didn't club his brains out, thank God. With a grunt of fury, she hurled the mill after the broken glass. Then she reached for the fruit bowl. And the cookie jar.

By the time she got to the ceramic spaghetti cylinder, Samuel had his back against the refrigerator and his arms over his head. "Are you fucking insane?" His voiceless rasp was barely audible over the din of breaking glass. "*Greta!*"

She turned on him, and instantly Samuel understood that her destruction of the kitchen was the only thing between her fists and his face. He held his hands up in surrender. "I'm sorry! Whatever this is, can we just—" He recoiled as she lunged forward. "Oh, God, please don't—"

"You are the most—" She whipped the cupboard open over his head, grabbed a crystal wine goblet, and flung it against the wall. "The most self-centered, self-absorbed, self-involved—"

"Okay! Yes! Selfish! I get it!" He totally didn't get it. His crutches lay in the middle of the kitchen floor; he reached for the nearest one, just to have something to protect himself. Greta kicked it away.

Now he was scared. Sick and scared and, yeah, really scared. "Greta?" His voice came out a shaky whisper. "Greta, could we—"

"Shut *up*!" She grabbed another goblet, and then another, chucking them against the wall to punctuate the end of each sentence. "I *thought*. You would under*stand*. But you *don't*."

Samuel hugged his knees to his chest, trying to make himself as small as possible amid the flying debris. So far nothing had scored a direct hit, though that was hardly reassuring. "Understand what?"

She glared at him, eyes blazing. "Ask me, Mr. Cooke. Ask me how many boys I screwed."

"You know I don't care—"

"*Ask!*"

"Um. How—"

"Eleven. Eleven, Mr. Cooke. And you—" She went for another goblet, but they were all gone. She ripped out the silverware drawer and slammed it topside down into the sink. "*You* are as far as it's possible to get from any of them and still be a man—and still—*still*, when you are on top of me, it's all I can do not to hit you in the face."

He swallowed. "I—I didn't know—"

"Of course you didn't. You're too worried about your stupid, stupid tube and bag and legs, and I *don't care*! Do you have any idea how ridiculous and petty your five hundred insecurities are? You're so obsessed with yourself, with performing, with getting me to—to—" She slammed a plate against the counter. "As if it has the *slightest* thing to do with you. I thought you didn't care about my past, but the truth is, you're too concerned with yourself to even *notice*."

"Greta, I'm sorry, whatever you need, I—"

"You know what I needed? Time. My sister is pregnant and thinking about leaving her husband and didn't call to say she was coming until she was halfway here. When she met you, she was so embarrassed she begged me not to tell. I thought it might give us a chance to—" She shrugged. "Relax. But every night you're there like some wounded puppy, wallowing in your own narcissistic misery, begging for affirmation. I'm sick of it, Mr. Cooke. Nobody cares. Least of all me."

"I'm sorry. I'll try harder. I can give you time—"

"No. I don't need anything from you." She stepped over him, the soles of her tennis shoes crunching through a carpet of broken glass. "Good-bye."

35

"HI, MARIA? IT'S SAMUEL."

"Mr. Cooke! How are you? You sound sick."

Her voice was warm and affectionate. Samuel missed hearing that. "I'm not feeling great. I'm on my way to school, but I was wondering if you'd be available today."

"Sure! My classes ended on Friday, so I'm free. What do you need?"

"If you could come by and . . ." He cleared his throat, but it didn't help. The cold had moved up into his sinuses and down into his chest. His entire respiratory system was raw. The weekend in bed hadn't helped; he still felt like he was swimming through murky water. "Clean up. I'll leave the door unlocked and a blank check on my armchair."

"Mrs. Cooke is okay with that?"

"Yeah." In the sense of not caring, since she wasn't there. "The place is pretty . . . well, it's a mess. Just throw out anything that's not salvageable, okay?"

* * *

SAMUEL FELT LIKE death with a hangover, but he went to school anyway. His programming class had been working on the final project presentations for weeks, and he wasn't about to crap out in the ninth inning, especially not with Marcus up to bat. Samuel was going to make the little prick work for his 4.0.

He had second thoughts when he stopped in the hall to cough and his handkerchief came away flecked with blood. Not good. Really not good. But there was only this week, three days next week, and graduation on Thursday. He needed to see it to the end. To prove he could.

So he dragged himself into class and fell into his chair and told everyone to stay far, far away.

Sadie approached his desk after second period.

"You're violating quarantine." He dug a tissue out of the box on his desk and blew his nose. "Do you want to spend grad night in bed?"

She gave a shy smile. "It looks like I'll be able to get some loans. I'm still waiting on the scholarships." Her eyes dropped to her feet and she shuffled. "Also? I was walking home from the store this weekend? And I kind of live near Mrs. Cassamajor's house. Her motorcycle is pretty loud, so . . ."

Samuel winced. Was this what parents felt like when their children caught them fighting? He tossed the wadded tissue into the garbage. "Sadie, thank you for caring, but this really doesn't have anything to do with you."

She bit her lip and shrugged. "I know. But you both helped me a lot, and I thought it would be sad if . . . if you didn't go after her."

It would have been tempting to do just that—if only everything Greta had said weren't true. Trying to win her back wasn't heroic; it was an attempt to lure her into the fiction that he could be better. He gave Sadie as much of a smile as he could manage. "I'm no knight in shining armor."

She looked at his crutches. "Then what are you?"

MARCUS WAS LATE. When he hustled through the door five minutes after the bell, Samuel tried to offer a pithy jibe, but his brain was running dangerously low on bandwidth. Instead he decided to sit in Marcus's seat and cough all over his backpack during his presentation.

"Stay away from me, man," Marcus warned when Samuel shuffled down the row. He bent over to dig in his bag. "I'm leaving for Cabo next week. I can't be sick."

"You're such a jerk," Sadie snapped. "I don't know why you care whether it's booze or the flu—you're going to spend your vacation puking your guts out either way."

Samuel's laughter turned into a coughing jag, but it felt good. He was glad he hadn't stayed home. "Forget something?" he asked. Marcus was still digging.

"Fuck this!" Marcus flung the bag away and turned, revealing bloodshot eyes ringed with circles dark as bruises. "And fuck you!" Samuel was blocking the aisle, so Marcus climbed over the desk and stalked down the next row. He slammed the door on the way out.

Sadie and the three remaining boys looked at Samuel, eyes wide.

A phone rang. Samuel waited for someone to pull out a cell, then realized it was the classroom phone by the door. "Can someone get that?"

Sadie hopped up and answered. "It's Mrs. Ortega?"

"Who—" Oh. Right. The full-inclusion lady. Slowly, breath grating through his windpipe, he hobbled to the door. He started to shift his weight to take the phone, but Sadie held it to his ear. He didn't object. "Hello?"

"Sorry to interrupt, Mr. Cooke. I wanted to let you know that Charlotte passed."

"Who?" He didn't remember having a student by that name.

"Charlotte. I had Marcus paired with her? She passed away yesterday evening. There were some unexpected complications. I wanted to let you know in case Marcus seemed upset."

"Oh," he said stupidly. He couldn't quite wrap his mind around the idea that the punishment he'd cooked up had worked. Just . . . not at all in the way he had imagined. "I understand. Thanks." He nodded and Sadie returned the phone to the hook.

Now what? Call campus security? No; let him go. They could reschedule the presentation. He'd come up with something else to fill the period. First things first, though: he needed to sit.

"Mr. Cooke? Are you okay?" Sadie was at his elbow.

"Fine." He started toward his chair.

"Are you sure? You look—"

The desk rushed up to meet his face.

36

H IS HEAD HURT. HE smelled flowers. What the hell? Samuel blinked against blinding light. Flowers everywhere. That was bad. Something bad had happened. At school. Was he dead? Was this his funeral?

"Oh, shit." Moore's face loomed over him. "Greta's gonna be *so* pissed she wasn't here when you woke up."

Not dead, then. But something was wrong. He swallowed. It hurt. Everything hurt. "Greta." Why was Moore using her first name?

"Yeah, I finally convinced her to get some sleep. Seriously, like five minutes ago. She's down in the car. Wouldn't go home. Wait, you're awake again. I should get the doctor, shouldn't I."

Samuel fumbled for Moore's arm and ended up with the bed rail. "Wait. Tell me. What happened." His voice was a croak, and his chest felt like it was on fire. He started to cough, but it hurt so bad that he choked the reflex down. His eyes watered. "Please."

Moore sighed. "Sadie said you just passed out. Whacked your head right on the corner of the desk. You have matching black eyes."

He laughed apologetically. "You've got perfect aim even when you're unconscious."

A woman in purple scrubs bustled in with a bag of clear fluid. "Oh! You're awake. I'll get the doctor."

Wonderful. "How long? Has it been?"

Moore glanced at his watch. "Well, you passed out Monday morning. It's Tuesday afternoon now, almost five."

Over twenty-four hours. Definitely time to leave. He was naked under the hospital gown. No braces. When he looked for them, all he could see was a confusing array of color. His vision felt . . . scattered. Or maybe it was his brain. "Why are there so many flowers?"

"Generally that's what people send when you're in the hospital."

Samuel was having a hard time putting the pieces together. "How does everyone know?"

Moore snorted. "You didn't make this easy. Greta wouldn't let them touch you until she had your medical records, but she couldn't find anything at your place, and your brother wasn't answering his cell. So then she calls me—she left me here with you—totally freaking out, and I say maybe Maria knows. She doesn't, but she tells us where to find your brother's home number. So we call him, and he thinks your old boss might have your doctor's info. Which is right, because he's had to cart you to the ER half a dozen times? You should wear one of those emergency bracelets, dude."

Samuel tried to lift his right hand, but there was a needle in it. He rubbed his forehead with the left instead. There was a throbbing knot of pain behind his eyes. "You need to have something wrong with you for one of those."

Moore lifted an eyebrow.

"Other than being terminally stupid." Samuel couldn't believe he'd let this happen. Again. "Do you know where my braces are?" He groped over one shoulder and then the other, finally located the bed remote, and motored himself into a full sitting position. "I have to get out of here."

"What about Greta?"

Samuel wanted to grab Moore by his ridiculous knit vest and shake. "She won't care. I'll discharge myself and you can drive me home. Braces?"

Moore pointed to the end of the hospital bed. "Cooke, they've got you peeing in a *bag*."

Samuel followed the finger to the bag of orange-brown liquid. He started to laugh. It was an awful, grating, death rattle of a sound.

"Wow. You are so high." Moore went to the beat-up dresser in the corner and started opening drawers. "Let me find a mirror so I can show you how much you *look like shit*. You're shaking like a wet lap dog."

Samuel held out his hand. Moore was right. Screw it. "All the more reason I should get out of here. I'll feel much better at home." He tugged the tape off his right hand and removed the IV. His lack of fine motor coordination resulted in a rather larger gash than he'd anticipated.

Moore gave up on the dresser and returned to the bed. He winced as Samuel used the corner of his gown to stanch the blood welling out of the wound. "Doesn't that hurt?"

Samuel's chest spasmed again, but he held the cough down through sheer force of will. Swallowed. Hard. Breathed. "Doesn't even register on my scale." His chest and head, though, were running about a six. Bearable. Now the catheter and he'd be free. "Turn your back for a second." He waited for Moore to look away, then lifted the sheet to see how they had him rigged.

A cheery rap sounded on the door, and the doctor strode in. It was what's-his-name. Mihalik. The guy from the fair. Because life was just that generous.

Samuel let the sheet fall. "Well, this is embarrassing."

"Oh, you think *you're* embarrassed?" Mihalik tossed his clipboard on the end of the bed and went around to the hanging bag of fluid, now dripping on the floor. Gingerly he picked the needle up by the base and crimped the flow. "Wonderful."

"You guys know each other?" Moore asked, surprised.

Mihalik glanced over his shoulder. "He let me hit on his wife."

"We weren't married then."

"Yes, that makes it much better." The doctor grabbed the bed remote and pressed the intercom. "Jenna, can I get another IV in here? He ripped it out again."

Again? Samuel looked at the back of his left hand. Somehow he'd failed to notice that it was bandaged. "Don't bother. I'm leaving. And if you think I don't know my rights, you can't—"

Mihalik let out a weary sigh. "Mr. Cooke, everyone here is quite familiar with what you want to do, with what you think of doctors and nurses, and your opinions on hospitals in general." He stepped to one side, holding up the used needle as the nurse in purple scrubs took his place.

"What are you talking about? I've never been here before." Samuel leaned to one side to see around the nurse and found himself unable to stop his slide toward the bed rail.

Moore put a hand on his shoulder and pushed him back up. "Do you seriously not remember? That's so weird."

"Remember what?" This was like one of those nutty dreams in which he couldn't control his body and nobody made any sense.

Mihalik moved to the end of the bed, giving the nurse more room as she hung a new IV bag. "You've suffered a fairly serious concussion, Mr. Cooke."

Moore stuffed a pillow between Samuel and the rail. "They've been waking you up every hour."

Oh, God. He looked at the doctor. "What did I say?"

"Far more than anyone wanted to hear."

"I think Greta was the only person you didn't cuss out," Moore added.

Mihalik pressed his lips together as if weighing the ethics of patient confidentiality. "Doesn't 'I'm so effing sorry' count?"

"Oh, right. You said that a lot. Except you actually said—"

"Yeah, I got it. If you guys think this is so funny—" The nurse grabbed Samuel's arm. "Don't you *dare* touch me!" He tried to pull away. "Did you wash your hands before you came in here? You didn't, did you? You stupid, incompetent—"

"*Sorry!*" Moore shouted. Everyone looked at him. He shrugged and made an apologetic gesture toward the nurse. "He's just scared."

"You're an idiot, too, you—"

"Cooke, if you don't shut your hole right now, one of these nurses is going to kill you."

"Jenna." Mihalik pinched the bridge of his nose. "Why don't you give us a minute."

When she was gone, he retrieved the clipboard from the end of the bed, smoothed the sheets, and sat. Samuel's feet didn't come close to reaching the end, so there was plenty of room. "Assuming you're going to discharge yourself at the earliest possible opportunity, humor me with a little chat first."

Samuel glared. "Not if you're going to be this patronizing."

Mihalik's stern expression broke into a reluctant smile. "I suppose I could let up a little." He flipped through the chart. It was thick enough to be unwieldy, which meant they had already subjected Samuel to a battery of invasive tests. "Given that your medical history is longer than *The Gulag Archipelago,* I'm sure you know how this goes. You gave yourself quite the concussion. We didn't see evidence of a bleed on the MRI, but you've been in an altered state of consciousness for over twenty-four hours. At the very least, you need to be watched carefully for the next few days. You've also got a severe bladder infection."

"Dammit."

"Mr. Cooke, someone who has been living with an indwelling catheter for as long—"

Samuel waved him into silence; too late. He sighed.

"Uh . . ." Moore glanced at the door. "Should I wait in the hall?"

"Forget it." Samuel nodded at the doctor. "Finish your lecture. I'm riveted."

Mihalik flushed. "You should have known better."

"I usually do. Unfortunately fatigue and low-grade fever are also symptoms of extreme stress, which is what I've been under for a couple of weeks now." Or the last nine months, depending on how you counted. "Not to mention getting the flu."

"Pneumonia."

"Oh. Brilliant." No wonder he felt a little out-of-body.

"If you were unsure about your symptoms, you should have seen a doctor."

"Funny how you guys always say that, and then I wind up with some brand-new malady. Last time I came in with a UTI, I ended up with a staph infection. I almost died. So far I've had better luck on my own." He couldn't hold back the coughing then; it hit him so hard, his body tried to contract into a fetal position.

Mihalik helped him roll onto his side, where he coughed until he retched and spat blood. "Looks like your luck is holding out wonderfully," the doctor observed.

Bastard.

"Now, I think we're clear on how you feel about IVs, but the one I had you on was delivering an aggressive course of antibiotics. Given your history, it's important to hit this hard and fast. I don't have to tell you what happens if you stop taking the antibiotic before the infection's gone."

"Fine," mumbled Samuel, "put it back in. But I want the rest of it in pills."

"We'll see what we can do." Mihalik hit the call button, and Jenna the nurse returned.

"Did you wash your hands?" Samuel demanded.

Mihalik took out a pen and jotted some notes. "I'd also be happy to add something for the pain. Figured I'd wait until you regained consciousness in case you had any objections."

"Thanks," Samuel said grudgingly. "Nothing mind-bending."

Mihalik ordered up some meds and Samuel lay staring at the bedside lamp, unsuccessfully pretending to be elsewhere while the nurse tied off his biceps, splinted his elbow, and put the line in.

"Good," Mihalik said, "that's taken care of. There are a couple of other items I'd like to discuss. Shall we do it now or wait until your wife returns?"

When Samuel got out of the hospital, he was going to find this guy's house and set it on fire.

"First." Mihalik bent, reached under the bed, and hefted the leather-and-aluminum brace crossways over the end of the mattress. "I'm honestly curious. Exactly how old is this thing? I'd guess early fifteenth century."

Samuel looked at Moore. "There's no way you didn't know that was under there."

Mihalik made another note. "I know a guy who's a genius with molds. I'll set up an appointment. Second, let's discuss your bladder management, or perhaps I should say lack thereof."

"I'm going to go get a soda," Moore announced.

Samuel rolled his eyes at the doctor. "I already know what you're going to say. You want me to let you cut a hole in my side and install a spigot."

"A Mitrofanoff procedure, yes."

"Right. So I have a hole in my side, *and* I'm stuck in a diaper, because who knows when I'm going to lose control."

Mihalik thumped the clipboard with his pen. "And now I know

you haven't had a consult in about a decade. You do realize medical technology improves over time?"

"Yeah, well. There's the issue of having a hole in my side." And letting them fuck with his body. Again. They always thought they knew exactly what they were doing. Samuel had awakened to the phrase "unanticipated complications" too many times to share their optimism. Still, Mihalik seemed decent. For a doctor. Who wanted his wife. Wait. "Why are you trying to help me?"

Mihalik stood, slipping his pen into the pocket of his lab coat. He fingered a rose petal from one of the bouquets sitting on the dresser. When he spoke, his voice was low. "Because she's too good for a jackass like you."

Samuel snorted. "I know."

"But you're the one she wants. So you have to suck it up and think about what's best for her. And getting cancer three years from now because you've got a catheter jammed in there twenty-four/seven is not it."

There was no arguing with that. Samuel had already been playing the odds for far too long. But . . . "I doubt she'll be here in three years." Or tomorrow. "She's already realized she can't stand me."

Mihalik sighed. "Don't I wish that were true."

As if he knew anything. Then Samuel heard what Mihalik already had—footsteps in the hall. Seconds later, Greta barged through the door.

"Get out," she said. "Now."

"I'll make a couple of phone calls," Mihalik said, and got.

She turned her gaze on Samuel. Her hands became fists. "How dare you." She was shaking. "How *dare* you do this to me."

He withered. "I didn't—"

And then tears were spilling down her cheeks.

Samuel blinked. "Greta?" He'd never seen her cry. He hadn't imagined she did. It was a singularly unsettling experience. He fumbled for the rail with his untethered hand and, after a couple of failed attempts, managed to ratchet it down. "Greta, come here."

He opened his arms and she stumbled into them, pinning him to the bed. She was very heavy. "Don't you dare leave me," she sobbed into his shoulder. "Don't you dare leave."

He rubbed her back. "Hey, I'm not going anywhere."

"I can't lose you."

"You won't. Honest. You won't." Another cough seized him. Greta pulled back, holding his shoulders as he spasmed. He coughed until he gagged, but fortunately nothing much came up. "Sorry."

Greta used the sheet to wipe his mouth. "Greg said you were trying to leave."

"Well, I . . ." He was gasping like a fish, but he managed a pathetic chuckle. "I don't think I would have gotten very far." He couldn't even draw his fingers into a fist.

She brushed the tear tracks off her face, erasing all evidence of her lapse in composure. "You're not alone anymore. You have a responsibility to take care of yourself." There was a pitcher of water on the table next to the bed; she poured him a glass.

Samuel hadn't realized he was parched until that moment. He clutched the plastic cup and drained it. "Greta, about that. Being alone. I . . . look, everything you said is true. I can try all I want, but at the end of the day, I'm still me. I don't want you to make a decision you'll regret just because I ended up here." Translation: he didn't want to think everything was okay and have her walk out a month from now.

She folded her hands together and studied them. "No. I decided when I married you."

"People make mistakes." He couldn't believe he was trying to argue. But he wanted her to be sure. *He* needed to know she was sure. "Even about marriage."

"It wasn't a mistake. I shouldn't have left." She paused for what seemed like a very long time, fingering her wedding band. "I promise I won't do it again."

"Are you sure? Like, really sure?"

She nodded. "Everyone has faults. I can live with yours. I know I'm not easy to live with, either."

"Greta, I'm pretty sure you're perfect."

"Mr. Cooke, I—" She looked away, embarrassed. "I destroyed your kitchen. I can't imagine how terrified you—"

"I wasn't scared." He held up a hand to preempt her objection. "Yes, I was scared. But not like *scared* scared. Not the way . . . well, you know." After she left, he'd used a crutch to work a kitchen towel off the oven door and clear a path out. As opposed to sitting in shock for hours. "I've never seen anyone as angry as you were. And if I made you that mad, and you didn't hit me, you're not going to."

"I was close," Greta said quietly. "I wanted to."

"But you didn't."

She looked away. "It might have been about sex. Partly."

"I don't care." Although it did feel slightly validating to hear her admit it. "I think it'll be a while before I'm up to another attempt, so let's just call it quits for now."

She nodded.

Mihalik's cheery rap sounded at the door. Moore followed on his heels, carrying a packaged sandwich and a half-eaten cookie. When he saw Greta, he stopped short. "Sorry," he said before she could give him a tongue-lashing. "Cooke said—he made me—"

Greta dismissed him with a hand.

Mihalik cleared his throat. Everyone looked at him and he nodded at Samuel. "You have an appointment with the orthotist next month. He operates out of the offices across the parking lot."

"Great," said Samuel.

"I also had your charts faxed over to a urologist at Berkeley. He'll get back to me when he's had a chance to review your history in detail."

"Sounds good."

"So—" Mihalik cut himself off with a frown. He looked at Greta, at Moore, and finally at Samuel. "Once you get out of here, you're not coming back. Are you."

Moore answered for him cheerily: "Not a chance in hell."

Mihalik sighed. He studied Samuel's chart as if his own scrawled notes could provide him with inspiration. "Okay. I have you for a week. I'll see what I can do." He left.

Greta shoved a hand in her pocket and pulled out her keys. "Greg." She tossed them at Moore. "There's a bag with some of Mr. Cooke's clothes in the car."

"You didn't sleep?"

"Okay, hold on," Samuel interrupted. "Since when are you two on a first-name basis?"

"Since you decided to knock your brains out, dude." Moore hefted the keys and exited the room.

Greta dragged a chair over to the bed. "He's not too bad." She sat and propped her legs up on the mattress, sighing at the release of pressure. "Tolerable. Occasionally."

"They want to cut a hole in my side," Samuel informed her.

She slid down until her head hit the back of the chair and closed her eyes. "I know."

As if the idea weren't utterly horrifying. "Are you going to make me do it?"

"I'm not going to make you do anything."

"But you think I should." Which was nearly the same thing. Privately Samuel knew she was right. He bit his lip. "Greta, can I tell you something?"

She nodded.

"I am really, *really* scared."

37

THESE ARE BEAUTIFUL, MR. Cooke." Maria drifted around the bedroom, smelling flowers and reading get-well cards. There were more cards than flowers now, since half the bouquets delivered to the hospital had since wilted and gone into the garbage. She stopped at a large vase of sunflowers from Rashid. "Mm, these especially."

Samuel watched her from the bed. "I can't believe she hired you to babysit me."

Maria turned, her eyes wide, and grinned. "Mrs. Cooke isn't paying me. I'm just here to keep you company."

"Seriously? You're getting ripped off." He was pretty surprised Greta had contacted Maria at all, knowing she'd cleaned up the kitchen. "Shoot, I'd pay you just for not being Moore." He and Greta had been taking turns checking in on Samuel at lunch. "If there's one person I don't want to deal with while I'm sick, it's Greg Moore." He shifted and coughed. "They think I'm made of tissue paper. I could've gone today. I'd just be sitting in the stands."

Maria lifted an eyebrow. "It's a hundred and five out there, so if you're suggesting I help you sneak out, you're barking up the wrong babysitter."

It had been worth a shot. He sat up on one elbow, wincing as the incision below his navel stretched. Carefully, he tugged up his undershirt and detached the tube running to the bag at the end of the bed. At some point he had stopped caring who knew. "Here. Help me up."

"Absolutely not. Mrs. Cooke said—"

"Maria." He gave her a knowing look. "As a nurse-to-be, you should know how important it is for the patient to get up and around as soon as possible. I've been in bed for a week. Feel free to tell me if I'm wrong." He waved at the door. "Greta hid my crutches in the hall closet."

Maria rolled her eyes and went to get them. Samuel used the opportunity for a deep cough, trying to clear his respiratory system from the lungs up.

"I heard that." She set the crutches against the bed and took a seat in his wheelchair, watching as he retrieved his braces and fitted them on. "Wouldn't the other ones be a little safer?"

Samuel eyed her. She had cleaned his house for nine months. Of course she'd found his full-leg orthotics. "No." And he wasn't going to the stupid orthotist, either. "So if you could—"

The phone rang. He looked to the bedside table, but the hand unit was gone.

"It's in the kitchen." Maria hopped out of his chair and returned half a minute later, bearing the phone and a puzzled expression. "It's Mrs. Cooke's sister? She wants to talk to you."

Samuel made a face. "Hello?"

"Can I call you Samuel?"

"Uh—sure." He waved Maria out of the room. "You know Greta's gone for the day, right?"

"I apologize," Hazel announced.

"Uh. What?"

"Greta called me when they admitted you to the hospital. She was—well, I've never heard her that upset. And you know how she is. When I found out she had gotten married, I thought you . . . I don't know what I thought. I didn't . . ." Her voice gentled. "I didn't realize how much Greta cared for you."

Samuel cleared his throat. "To be honest, neither did I."

"It's just . . . I need to hear this. Do you love her?"

"I would do anything she asked." He put a hand to the aching hole in his abdomen.

"But do you—"

"More than the entire universe."

Hazel sighed. "Thank you."

There was an awkward pause. Now what? He probably wasn't supposed to know about the pregnancy, so that was off limits. Hey, how's that marriage holding up?

Then inspiration struck. "Oh. Jesus. While I've got you on the phone. We still haven't figured out the honeymoon."

"You mean *you* haven't figured it out."

"Right. Is there anywhere Greta, like, always wanted to go?"

"Hm. She always loved the idea of the European grand tour, like the English gentry used to send their kids on, you know?"

No, Samuel didn't know. He wrinkled his nose. "Like all of Europe?"

"Mostly Italy, I think. All those old churches and stuff."

"*Italy?*" Damn.

"You asked, 'Mr. Cooke.'"

Samuel heard the air quotes in her voice. "You *know*." He gripped the phone with both hands, wishing he could wring it out of her over the line. He was going to *make* her tell him, whatever he had to do. "What is it? Why won't she use my name?"

She laughed. "Look under the bed."

He blinked. "What? It's just a box of winter clothes and—"

"Under the mattress, dumbass. If you know Greta, you'll understand. Otherwise, good luck."

Samuel stared at the dead phone for a second or two before tossing it onto the bedside table. Under the bed? Really? What on earth could she be hiding? He'd started to pull his legs up onto the bed when Maria knocked.

She poked her head in. "Sorry, but there's a girl here. Sadie? She said she's one of your students."

He let his leg drop. What the hell was she doing here? "Okay. Sure."

Maria let the door swing in. "I'll be in the kitchen, Mr. Cooke."

Sadie shuffled in, stopping inside the bedroom door. She wore her graduation gown, open in front to reveal a skirt and patterned blouse. Her eyes darted briefly around the bedroom, then came to rest on Samuel. He watched as the words she had come prepared to say deserted her.

"I look bad," he guessed. No shit; he was sitting in his boxer shorts and undershirt. For a split second he had the urge to cover himself with a sheet, but then he remembered he no longer had a bag of piss to hide.

Nope, the bag of piss was hanging right there on the end of his bed. Fucktastic.

"Are . . . are you okay?"

"I'm not as sick as I look." A totally subjective statement that could not definitively be proven false. "Shouldn't you be graduating?"

"It's just practice right now. It's taking forever because of the whole thing with Irving, and anyways, I don't have to do all the walking and stuff because I'm sitting up in front." She held up a folded piece of paper. "For the salutatorian speech."

Samuel frowned. "Irving?"

"Oh. You didn't know?" She shrugged. "What I heard was some-one in the office is, like, suing him? For sexual harassment. They've been investigating him for a while, but they decided to wait until the end of the year or something. Now the vice principal has to do the graduation."

Samuel stared at her openmouthed. Then he laughed. "Seri-ously? Was it Joyce? Joyce is getting him on harassment?" It had to be. "For my own personal reasons, I have to say that's the best news I've heard all year."

Sadie looked confused.

"You didn't come here to tell me that. What's up?"

She flushed. "I wanted to give you a copy of my speech. Since you, um, aren't going to be there." She made a hesitant motion with the paper in her hand.

Samuel motioned her over. "I won't bite." He tugged the paper from her outstretched fingers and unfolded it.

"No!" She bit her lip. "I mean, could you read it later?"

Which meant at least part of her speech was about him. That was . . . awkward? Flattering? Whatever she had to say, it probably wasn't true. Sadie wasn't very confident, and people like her tended to write off their own efforts, projecting their successes onto others. He folded the paper and set it on the nightstand. "Thanks. I wanted to come, but Greta—" He shrugged. "Let's just be honest: I do what-ever she says."

That got a smile out of her.

"Your project was great, by the way." The librarian had set the sub up with a video camera so Samuel could grade both the presen-tations and submitted material. At some point during the year—he didn't remember when—he had fixed the thing. "I wish I could give you something higher than an A."

She turned bright red. "Um. Thanks." She gestured over one shoulder. "I should go. I got Travis to give me a ride over, so . . ."

He nodded. "Thanks for stopping by. And thanks for helping me get through the year." Even if he hadn't quite made it all the way.

"Me?"

He laughed at her incredulity. "Yes, you." She had been witness to more than one of his many meltdowns over the past nine months, and she still questioned her worth? "Sadie, if I hadn't known someone was listening, I would have quit a long time ago."

She thought about that. "Me, too."

Maria came back to announce lunch as soon as Sadie left, giving him no time to investigate the bed. Something told him he didn't want to solicit help from any outside parties. "Good," he said, grabbing his crutches. "We can eat at the table. Help me up."

Maria frowned. "Okay, here's the deal. I'll help you into your chair. We'll have lunch on the couch. If you feel okay after that, I will help you up. Got it?"

"Do I have a choice?"

"No."

SAMUEL WAS FLOATING. "What the—" He grabbed the first thing he found, which was Greta's neck.

"Shh," she said. "Go back to sleep."

Sleep? He blinked the goo out of his eyes and realized it was dark. He remembered lunch with Maria, and her handing him a book while she cleaned up, and then—and then Greta was carrying him to bed.

"She let me sleep." He felt moderately betrayed.

"Maria left an hour ago." Greta turned sideways to pass through the bedroom door.

"I'm awake now. You don't have to carry—"

Greta set him down and turned on the lamp. "Then you can do

this yourself." She handed him the tube running from the end of the bed.

"Shit!" He had detached it that morning, and now it was dark. His bladder wasn't conditioned to hold more than an ounce or two, let alone eight hours' worth of fluid. He patted his stomach for the spigot—and found it attached to a small drainage bag, clumsily Velcroed over his boxers. Maria. Jesus. Why hadn't she woken him up? He looked at Greta. "Did you tell her to do this?"

"She called."

He muttered a curse. "Can we agree that bodily functions will be left to the one doing the functioning?"

Greta sat on the edge of the bed and watched as he swapped out the bag. "I don't think you understand how much you need to rest. Your body is trying to recuperate. Let it."

"Yeah, and in the meantime, I'm losing all my muscle tone. Another day or two in bed and I'll be stuck in that damn chair for a month."

She glanced at his wheelchair and frowned. "Is that what you're worried about?"

Fuck it, "*Yes!*"

Greta got up and left the room. Samuel heard her go into the spare bedroom and open the closet. When she returned, she dropped two weights next to him. "Use those. I've got some paperwork I need to sort out before tomorrow."

"You think if you leave me here, I'll go to sleep."

She allowed a faint smile. "Maybe."

"I won't."

She shrugged and left.

Samuel scowled at the door. He reached for one of the weights. The number fifteen was printed on the end, and his arm shook as he lifted it over his head. He did it ten times, first with one arm and then the other. He felt like gelatin.

Then he remembered Hazel's call. He dropped the weight and slid over to Greta's side of the bed, careful to leave enough slack on the tube. He shoved his hand between the mattress and the box springs.

Nothing.

He felt around a little more, and then—

His fingers hit something hard. A corner. He shifted, removing as much of his weight from the edge of the mattress as he could, and shoved his hand in farther.

What he pulled out was a book. A very worn, dog-eared copy of . . . He turned it over. *Romancing Mr. Bridgerton.*

What the hell?

He left the book on the bed and stuck his hand under again. Clawed another one out. *Regency Buck. What Happens in London. Pride and Prejudice.*

Samuel pulled his feet into a vaguely cross-legged position and lined the books up on the bed. He studied the modest but inescapably sentimental covers, then picked up *Pride and Prejudice,* a book he dimly remembered having read for a general-ed English class. He flipped through the pages, and it came back to him.

Slender, graceful young women in dresses and bonnets, flirting shamelessly and living in anticipation of the next party or shocking romantic revelation. People driving around in carriages, referring to each other by surnames, pairing off neatly to live Happily Ever After™.

Surnames.

Mr. Cooke.

Greta liked these books. She liked the *men* in these books. Guys who wore suits and white gloves, stuffed handkerchiefs up their sleeves, and carried slender black canes. Who went riding and sat around in book-filled studies making dry, acerbic observations about their fellows. The men in these pages were sharp, delicate, and witty. In short, gentlemen. In shorter? Samuel.

He stared at the covers. This was something he could do. No, it was who he already *was*. This was it. On a very carnal level, this was what made him attractive to Greta.

So . . . wow. This was something he wished he had known, say, eight months ago. Or, hell, two weeks. But Greta had hidden it, like everything else, because it made her vulnerable.

The books told him she dreamed of being like these elegant, effete women. And in every possible way, she was not.

Samuel hated that. He *hated* it. He wanted to tear the pages out, build a bonfire, and burn them all. More than that, he wanted to tear the fantasy out of her mind, even if it meant the loss of her desire for him. Who had made her believe she needed to be like this? Her sister? Mother? A teacher? The boys who had raped her? He despised them. He hoped they all caught pneumonia and died.

And him . . . Was his own presence a constant reminder of what she lacked?

He stacked the four paperbacks and tilted the pile so the spines faced up.

Probably no more than her presence made him wish he had a body like Chris's. Which was to say, yeah, sometimes, but he tried not to obsess. So he was a gentleman. So she was Wonder Woman of the Amazons. Who cared?

He slid to the edge of the bed and reached for his wheelchair.

No.

"Greta!" He wheezed and coughed. "Mrs. Cooke!"

She burst into the bedroom. "Are you—"

"I'm fine." He held out a hand. "Come here."

She started forward—and froze when she saw her books spread out on the comforter. The color drained out of her face, and she turned to flee.

Samuel didn't even try to catch her arm. "You promised you wouldn't leave me. That includes this room."

She stopped in the doorway, her back to him, hands clenched at her sides.

"My dearest Mrs. Cooke," he said quietly, gently. "I simply demand you sit beside me this very instant." That sounded awkward. He'd have to practice his diction. Maybe read a couple of her books.

"Don't mock me," she growled.

He couldn't keep the grin off his face. "Greta, I'm not mocking you. I'm playing along. Because I love you. And you love me. We're in love. Aren't we? Come here. Please. Mrs. Cooke. I beg of you."

"It's *stupid.*" She spat the word like an invective.

"It's totally not." He sighed. "Now will you please come here?"

After a moment's hesitation, she approached stiffly and sat. She glared at her knees.

"Mrs. Cooke." He took her hand. "Greta. You have seen every last inch of me, inside and out; good, bad, and absolutely horrible. I'm not going to sit here and compare scars with you—we both have them. But there's nothing to hide. You have all of me. And you love me. Believe it or not, I love you just as much. Nothing will ever change that. I think your 'stupid' romances are wonderful, and I can't imagine they're any sillier than my sci-fi pulps, which are, if you hadn't noticed, scattered all over the living room."

Greta's fingers curled around his.

Samuel took a breath. "I want you to know, Greta, because I don't think you do, that you're beautiful. No; don't argue." He picked up one of the books. "You're not this kind of beautiful. That's fine, because I'm not interested in that. The first time we met, I knew you didn't take crap from anyone and you didn't care about being polite, and I loved it. You see through everyone's bullshit, including mine. You are strong and confident and bold and complex and intelligent and secretly warm, and I never want you to be ashamed of that, not in front of me."

He watched her face in profile. Had she heard? Did she understand? It was so hard to articulate these things.

"Look, if being who you are means running out on me now and then, I can live with that. As long as it's not forever. I will wait as long as it takes, I will go anywhere you want, and I will do anything you tell me to, because you are the only person in the universe who makes me *want* to be me. Do you understand? You make me want to be this stupid, insecure little nitwit with the crutches and—"

Greta seized his shirt, pulled it up, and detached the drainage tube.

"Hey! I thought we agreed—"

"I didn't agree to anything." She planted a hand in the middle of his chest and shoved. "Clothes off."

Samuel didn't have to be told twice. He wriggled out of his shirt. Greta grabbed his boxers and yanked them down to his ankles. She stepped out of her pants and climbed on top of him. And stopped. "Will this hurt you?"

"What? No." Actually, he had no idea. But another hospital visit was a risk he was willing to take.

If he was lacking in physical enthusiasm, Greta more than made up for it. She exhausted him—not that such a feat was difficult in his current state. Or ever. At last all he could do was lie panting, pinned half under her, his sweaty cheek against her breast.

She rolled off of him and rose up on one elbow.

"Greta," he begged, "I don't think I can go another—" Then he stopped, because that wasn't what she wanted.

She looked down at him, into his face, with frank, open eyes.

Samuel felt like an explorer stumbling into the path of a tiger, petrified as it gazed through his soul with an unbending mix of feral curiosity and predatory desire. This was Greta behind the veil.

"I love you," he said to this shy, wild person.

"Samuel," she said.

He put his hand on the back of her neck, pulling her toward him until they settled together, cheek to cheek.

Her voice was low and quiet in his ear. "I'm not good with words."

He laughed silently, letting her feel it in his body. "Don't worry. I already know how great I am."

She rose up a little. "No. You don't."

He tended to think she was imagining things, but maybe not. Greta was smart, but she was so blind to her own loveliness that it made him crazy. Did she also see something in him, something hidden and deep, of which he was completely unaware? Perhaps it was impossible to know himself fully until he had seen himself through her tiger eyes. He would have to try.

He pulled her down, pressing his body against hers. Together they breathed.

"No hurry." He turned his head, kissed the side of her face. "We've got the rest of our lives for you to tell me who I really am."

Epilogue

THE MAN BEHIND THE desk handed over the room key and pointed.

Samuel turned, following the finger to a massive marble staircase. "Oh my God, you have *got* to be kidding." He seriously contemplated slamming his forehead against the counter. Sixteen hours in the goddamn airplane, twice that in security lines, the most expensive pizza he'd ever eaten, a taxi driver who neglected to mention he didn't have a clue where Via de' Bonizzi was, and now this. "I specifically—*specifically*—asked for the first floor."

The clerk smiled and nodded. "Yes, signore, that is the first floor."

"Then what are we standing on?"

The man spoke slowly, as if beginning to suspect Samuel might be retarded. "Signore, this is *pianterreno*—the ground floor."

Greta came up from behind with the luggage. "What's the problem?"

Samuel sighed. "There's no elevator?"

"Sorry, signore, no."

"No, of course not. Of course there isn't."

Greta shrugged. "We could find something else."

"It's six o'clock at night. You think anywhere else is going to be better?" He hated this god-awful country, with its stupid cobbled streets and irregular curbs and stairs everywhere and insane traffic and hordes of tourists and *everything*. He'd never admit it in a million years, but if Greta hadn't made him go to the fitting with the orthotist, he would have been down for the count hours ago. The new braces were so light he barely noticed them, and they offered enough support that he could stand without crutches as long as he had something to hang on to.

Greta dropped the bags and bent forward. "Come on, then."

They had done this twice already, for smaller obstacles. Samuel clambered onto her back. "Just so you know, if you feel the need to point out—again—that I'm lighter than my suitcase, I will be on a plane back to California *tomorrow*."

Greta laughed. Which pretty much made the whole miserable thing worthwhile.

Acknowledgments

FALL OF 2002 FOUND me standing in the tiny fourth-floor garret of 17 Gough Square, London. This was the room wherein my literary hero, Dr. Samuel Johnson, compiled his seminal *Dictionary of the English Language*. A small dais in the corner held a battered chair. It bore a sign: DO NOT SIT.

Temptation seized me. This was Johnson's *chair*. The good doctor's literary throne, as it were. I looked about, knowing full well I was the museum's only visitor and that the curator was on the ground floor. I hesitated. Then I picked up the sign—and sat.

Only then did I remember there were such things as security cameras.

Shortly thereafter, over a three-day weekend in Samuel Johnson's hometown of Litchfield, I wrote the first draft of the book you hold in your hands. Though it has taken a decade to arrive at publication, I have finally claimed my small place in the great pantheon of English literature.

My path was a long one, which necessarily means I owe thanks to a great many folks along the way. First in line is author and professor

Susann Cokal, who dared to suggest my writing might be less than perfect. Thank you, Susann, for enduring my ego while I was young and proud. Two other great teachers, Gordon R. Langford and Robert Inchausti, also deserve mention for their guidance and inspiration.

Courting Greta suffered many rewrites and revisions; during the last complete overhaul I received fellowship, encouragement, and invaluable criticism from Phillip Brown, Lynne Moore, and Shubha Venugopal. I also owe thanks to authors Lisa Brackmann and Gary Presley, both of whom I admired from afar and am now privileged to call friends. Gary's work provided the right inspiration at the right time, and Lisa was kind enough to hold my hand through one final round of revisions.

Which brings me to Jim McCarthy. Three hundred and fifty agents rejected *Courting Greta*; you did not. For this and much more, I am forever in your debt.

Many thanks are also due to my editor, Micki Nuding, and the kind folks at Gallery Books.

My parents, John and Linda Biggers, have never faltered in bestowing unconditional love and support. Thank you also to the members of my amazing extended family, who were, likewise, ever on my side.

Finally . . . Kelson, love of my life. What can I say? I loved you when I married you, but only later did I come to understand the depth of your generosity and affection. We could have had a nicer car, a better apartment, or even just a dishwasher. Instead you let me write. When success didn't come instantly, or even after a while, you refused to let me surrender. I am beyond blessed to have you as my most steadfast encourager, my lover, and my best friend.

—Ramsey, 2013

P.S. Just out of curiosity, I emailed the museum curator. They moved the chair downstairs.

Courting Greta

Ramsey Hootman

Introduction

Samuel Cooke is a prickly computer genius who's just left his high-paying job to teach programming to high schoolers. He doesn't believe in asking for help; he doesn't think much of his fellow man; and he definitely doesn't believe in love. Greta Cassamajor is the tough, take-no-prisoners gym coach no kid dares to mock—at least within hearing range. She's got her own issues with her fellow man.

An unlikely hero, Samuel only asks Greta out to prove he's got the guts—and when she accepts, he's out of his depth. Pretending he's got his class under control? Easy. Being vulnerable enough to admit why he ditched his programming career for teaching? Well . . . that would require honesty. And if there's one thing Samuel can't exist without, it's the lies he tells himself.

Topics and Questions
for Discussion

1. In *Courting Greta*, Samuel leaves his predictable life in Los Angeles to try teaching high school in a small town. Have you ever done something completely outside of your comfort zone? What obstacles did you encounter, and what did you take away from your experience?

2. In the opening scene, Samuel's brother Chris asks, "Are you okay?" Discuss why this question comes up numerous times over the course of the novel. What is the answer?

3. When Samuel moves to Healdsburg, he meets a number of new people: Irving, Greg, Greta, and Maria. What assumptions does Samuel make about his new acquaintances? Specifically, how does Samuel think other people see him? Do the words and actions of these characters affirm or challenge his assumptions?

4. Physical challenges aside, what is the biggest obstacle in Samuel's life?

5. Samuel decides Greg Moore is a good candidate for a friend because he won't "go away, no matter how often he was brushed off or turned down." In what other ways is Moore a good friend?

6. Both Samuel and Greta try to protect themselves. What mechanisms do they employ to keep themselves safe, and what is it that they are protecting?

7. Samuel uses the word "retard" on several occasions. Did this surprise you? Why might he choose to use a word with so many negative connotations, rather than a more politically correct term such as "mentally challenged"?

8. In what ways do expectations about traditional gender roles influence how Samuel and Greta view themselves? How does their relationship reverse or redefine those roles?

9. When Samuel learns Marcus is responsible for the pranks, he talks to him "man to man," rather than punishing him according to standard school policy. Do you think Samuel handled the situation correctly? What else could or should he have done?

10. When Samuel asks Greta what he "does" for her, she tells him he makes her feel "pink." What does she mean? Discuss what role Samuel fills for Greta. What does he "do" for the other female characters in the book?

11. Did you notice any recurring colors, objects, or images? What are they, and what do they represent?

12. When Samuel goes to the fair with Greta, a local doctor fails to realize they are dating. Many people with disabilities complain of being treated as asexual or non-sexual, often viewed as safe confidants rather than potential partners or rivals. Which characters do this to Samuel? How does he react? Is the situation a negative or positive experience?

13. When Greta agrees to get married, Samuel realizes her mind has been made up for some time. In your opinion, at what point in the story did Greta decide to marry Samuel?

14. Have Samuel's problems with his father been resolved? How do you think he will handle his relationship with his father and brother in the future?

15. What challenges will Samuel and Greta face in their marriage? Will their relationship last?